"[Terry C. Johnston] does stick to the known facts with a fierce dedication . . . and that does make for good reading."
—John M. Carroll, author of *The Two Battles of the Little Big Horn*

All my writing life I have been a quiet but un-shakable proponent of the idea that if you dare to write "historical" fiction you may not tinker with provable history but must remain true to it. Terry Johnston is that kind of writer and it is one of the reasons I admire him and his work. He is the genuine article when it comes to storytelling, but you can also depend on his having done his historical homework. His Custer trilogy is proving this significant point, just as his Indian wars and mountain man books prove it.

I admire his power and invention as a writer, but I admire his love and faith in history just as much.
—Will Henry, author of
From Where the Sun Now Stands

"[Johnston] has so immersed himself in the history of the Plains Indians and in Custer's history that, were novels not his forte, he could very well write a book on Custer and his final battle to match that of fiction writer Evan Connell."
—Dale L. Walker, syndicated columnist

Sitting Bull, Hunkpapa chief—1881
(photo courtesy of Custer National Battlefield)

SON OF THE PLAINS-VOLUME 3

WHISPER OF THE WOLF

TERRY C. JOHNSTON

DOMAIN™

BANTAM BOOKS
NEW YORK • TORONTO • LONDON • SYDNEY • AUCKLAND

WHISPER OF THE WOLF

A Bantam Domain Book / September 1991

*DOMAIN and the portrayal of a boxed "d" are trademarks of Bantam
Books, a division of Bantam Doubleday Dell
Publishing Group, Inc.*

ISBN 0-553-29179-3

Published simultaneously in the United States and Canada

*Bantam Books are published by Bantam Books, a division of Bantam
Doubleday Dell Publishing Group, Inc. Its trademark, consisting of the
words "Bantam Books" and the portrayal of a rooster, is Registered in
U.S. Patent and Trademark Office and in other countries. Marca Regis-
trada. Bantam Books, 1540 Broadway, New York, New York 10036.*

PRINTED IN THE UNITED STATES OF AMERICA

OPM   0 9 8 7 6 5 4

Dedicated to
Greg Tobin
more than an editor who told me how,
he is a friend who showed me why.

The soldiers let loose with everything they had. Unarmed, we didn't have a chance. Men, women, even babies were shot down. Soldiers galloped after those who ran and cut them down with sabers. Then they opened up on us with cannons and pounded everything flat—tepees, people, even horses and dogs. I was struck by bullets in my arm, chest, and leg, but I ran limping down a gully and got away.

Hiding in a cutbank, I looked back at the camp. My wife and child were lying there motionless. A few paces away were my old mother and father, my sister, and, beyond them, my two young brothers. All of them were dead. I waited there in the snow beside the cutbank and prayed for death.

—DEWEY BEARD, Wounded Knee Survivor
Interview, Ricker Collection

The Sioux thus suffered two conquests (at Wounded Knee): a military conquest and a psychological conquest. It was the latter that destroyed them as a nation and left emotional scars that persist today. But the road that ended in the second conquest began before the first. It began in the old life.

—ROBERT M. UTLEY,
The Last Days of the Sioux

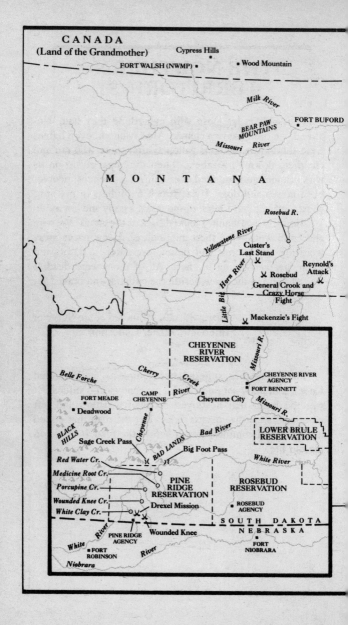

THE NORTHERN
TERRITORIES

0   100   200
Miles

N O R T H   D A K O T A

• FORT ABRAHAM LINCOLN

FORT YATES ■   STANDING ROCK
                              AGENCY

Grand   *River*   • SITTING BULL'S ENCAMPMENT

⚔ Slim Buttes Battle

CHEYENNE RIVER AGENCY ■

S O U T H   D A K O T A

Missouri

BLACK
HILLS

Cheyenne River   BAD LANDS

White   *River*   *River*

                    ROSEBUD AGENCY
                              •   FORT RANDALL
PINE RIDGE   ⚔ Wounded Knee   ■
AGENCY ■

Niobrara   *River*   *Missouri River*

• FORT ROBINSON

•
FORT LARAMIE   *INSET AREA*

N E B R A S K A

Platte   *River*

N

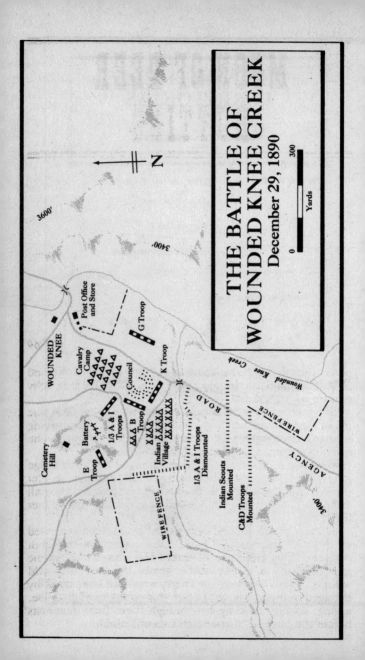

MOON OF DEER RUTTING

I CY snowflakes flung themselves against the stiffened buffalo hides of the old lodge that rattled like nearby gunfire with each new blast of wind.

She grunted with the rising swell of pain exploding at the pit of her. Afraid when it reached its peak. The young woman's dry tongue lolled at the side of her mouth as the rumbling agony washed from her loins.

Gasping, the Cheyenne mother drank at the air in huge gulps. Her sweating hands cramped all the way to her shoulders. Reluctantly she loosened her grip on the two tall stakes hammered into the ground near the fire ring in her tiny lodge.

Ancient, much-rubbed designs had long ago been carved in the old cherry-wood bark, then colored with earth pigment. This same pair of stakes had known the frantic grip of many a mother-to-be across the last fifty-odd winters. That's how long the cherry wood had been used by the aged midwife who sat before this young mother-to-be, urging, cooing, scolding her through these final moments before the birth of Monaseetah's second child.

"It hurts!"

The old one smiled, many of her teeth gone the way of winters past. "Of course it does, Young Grass. This will be no ordinary newborn. You are giving birth to Yellow Hair's child."

Monaseetah threw her head back, sensing the rising swell, fearing the coming of the next pain. The sweat oozed from her pores, making her hot with the work inside the cold, frosty lodge. She shuddered from her great exertion, or perhaps from the numbing cold. Completely naked beside the tiny, struggling fire. Naked, for there was no other way for a mother to give birth among the Shahiyena.

She licked her parched lips. To her tongue they felt like the thorny back of a horned toad she often found here in the southern part of this prairie land the white man called Indian Territory. The wrinkled old woman was there with the gourd cup as pain washed from Monaseetah's trembling limbs. Cool water poured against the young one's gasping lips.

She gagged, the water lurching in her stomach, reminding her of the time she watched the white soldiers spread her dying mother's legs. One after another the soldiers desecrated the bloody, lifeless body in the snow while the young daughter of thirteen summers watched, terrified and transfixed from the bushes along Little Dried River. Sand Creek, the soldiers had called that place.

"My child?" She panted, recognizing her firstborn's angry cry from a nearby lodge.

"He is in the care of another now," the old woman explained again. "Soon enough he will have a sister . . . perhaps a little brother."

"Hiestzi will have a son," Monaseetah gasped with certainty, licking the last salty drops of moisture from her lips as another swell of pain rumbled up within her swollen belly.

"You have talked with your unborn child . . . your son?"

She nodded, biting her lower lip to keep from calling out. The birth of her first child, last winter in the Moon of Seven Cold Nights while she rode with Hiestzi on his trail stalking Medicine Arrow's band of Cheyenne—that birth had been nowhere near this hard for her. Barely eighteen summers old now, Monaseetah realized this second child was making it hard for her. Perhaps like the pony gone sideways in the mare's womb.

She grew more afraid that Yellow Hair's son was too big within her, perhaps reluctant in coming forth to meet his mother.

"It is good you talked with him as he grew in your belly, little one," the old woman said. "He will know the sound of his mother's voice when he comes to meet you very soon."

"His brother does not like this one coming," Monaseetah explained.

"Sees Red? He is but a baby himself. Less than one summer. How do you know he does not like this—"

"I know," she grunted, the pain and pushing returning with a ferocity. "He knows . . . the way his little eyes glare at my belly."

The old woman clucked. "A baby himself, Monaseetah. Perhaps he does not want to share your teats with a little brother."

Quickly she nodded, flinging droplets of sweat on the pounded earth floor before her. "I have two breasts. . . ." she panted, tongue sagging.

"True. You can suckle both at your teats. But perhaps Sees Red realizes you have only one heart. A man-child is still a man. And a man always fears sharing a woman's heart with another."

"I can love both." Monaseetah gritted the words between clenched teeth, burying her chin in her chest, grunting. With all her might praying to push the pain from between her legs.

"It may prove a hard thing for you in the winters yet to come. Sees Red will grow tall each season, learning early that you do not love his father."

"His father was . . . was . . ."

"In the soul of men, such things do not matter to a son," the old woman replied quietly. "No matter what he did to you, that man was the father of Sees Red."

"*Aiyeee!*" Monaseetah shrieked. "He comes?"

"Yes," whispered the ancient one, inching between the young mother's quivering thighs. She held a gnarled hand below that opening to the gateway of life, pressing hard with her fingers beneath the portal where the dark crown of the greasy head appeared briefly, then retracted with Monaseetah's next shudder. "A little more work—you will look into your son's eyes."

"Arggghhhghgh!"

"Keep pushing now," she ordered, with both elbows pressing, struggling to keep Monaseetah's thighs apart.

"I . . . I . . . I!"

"His head is here, Monaseetah. His head—"

"Help him breathe, old one. Help him—*aiyeee!*"

"He is come to see you, little one!" sang out the old, toothless one. She grappled with the slippery body, eventually cradling it against her withered dugs. "It is as you said—a man-child. And he is bigger than even I imagined he would be!"

"I rest now," Monaseetah panted, releasing her sweaty grip on the two stakes, sinking back from her haunches, snagging a red blanket from the soft bed of wool and buffalo robes. Shivering, she pulled it over her breasts and arms, watching all the time as the old woman pulled a finger from the newborn's mouth, flinging some of the bloody phlegm onto the fire-pit coals. Then she rubbed the small of the infant's back, vigorously, stimulating the breathing.

Suddenly animated, the child whimpered, arms flailing for but a moment, then cooed.

"He does not cry," Monaseetah remarked in wonder.

She looked at the new mother, moisture glistening her old, yellowed eyes. "A brave one, this man-child of Hiestzi. Not to cry with his first breath coming."

"I . . . I want to hold Yellow Hair's child." She put out her arms.

The old one laid the infant in the cradle of his mother's hands, stuffing a length of soft otter fur round the wriggling body. "Clean him now, Monaseetah. While he suckles at your full breast. Because Sees Red drinks your milk, this little one will not have to wait for his first meal. Feed him of your body."

While Monaseetah bundled the little one inside her blanket, bringing his smacking lips to her breast, the old woman plied her craft between the young mother's legs.

Gently she pulled inch after purple inch of the thick, engorged cord from the pathway of life. At last she felt the resistance fade. And with the end of the cord's slithering struggle came the afterbirth that filled both old hands. With it placed in the brass kettle, the old one finally milked the thick cord toward the newborn, delivering the last of the nutrients of the womb.

When that was done to her liking, she tore loose a thin strip of sinew with the brown stubs of what she had left for teeth. With aching, gnarled fingers, the old one wrapped the narrow strip round and round the umbilicus, slowly tying it off in a series of knots. With her skinning knife she cut the cord below the sinew clamp.

"The turtle," Monaseetah reminded.

Without reply the old woman took up the slippery cord, sliced off several inches of it, and laid the purple flesh on a stone beside the fire pit. Monaseetah would sew that short piece of this cord of life inside a beaded pouch shaped like a turtle, to be carried by Monaseetah's new son for all the days of his life.

A turtle lived a long, long time.

Monaseetah prayed her new son would live the life of a turtle, despite the coming of the white man, who drove away all those buffalo he did not kill. Despite the soldiers who came again and again hunting the young warriors who raided the white man's settlements. Soldiers whose angry guns made life short for the women and children and old ones left behind in those winter villages they attacked.

She squeezed her eyes shut, trying to drive away the misty memories of the two dawn battles that filled her nightmares . . . blue-coated soldiers and sabers . . . blood on the white snow. The Little Dried River and the Washita—

"His eyes are open?"

Monaseetah nodded, welcoming the interruption from the terror inside her. She watched the old one inch close. Together they peered down into the little one's face.

"His skin . . . it is not dark, Monaseetah."

"No," she whispered. "His father had skin much like the paunch of a buffalo cow."

"Yes, I see this little one's skin is much like the father's and yours, both." She rubbed the otter fur against the side of the infant's head. "His hair, it too is not like his mother's."

"No," and Monaseetah wagged her head again. "The color of my new son's hair is not like the raven's wing in flight beneath the winter sun."

The young mother rubbed more of the waxy coating from the newborn's head, then held the short strands up to the fire's glow. Rusty gold highlights shimmered in the dancing light.

"Different from the other Cheyenne boys," the old woman commented quietly, turning back to the fire to warm a kettle of bone soup.

"My son is not full-blood. But he is still Shahiyena."

"Will he always be?" She looked over her shoulder at the young mother. "Pray he learns to defend himself, Monaseetah."

"Why, old one?"

She gazed back to the fire. "Soon all will know you had this son of a white father."

"He is my son too."

She sighed, stirring the warming soup. "He is your son—yes, Monaseetah. Yet nonetheless the little one is son to the most feared, most hated pony-soldier chief among the white men."

The young mother gazed down at the light hair glimmering in the fire's glow, studying the intense eyes staring back at her from beneath the wrinkled lids and furrowed brow.

"Then I ask that you too sing your prayers for this new life, old one."

She turned about slowly, a creak in her old bones, staring at the young mother's tear-tracked face.

"I will," the ancient woman answered in a whisper. "I will pray as I never have—for the son of Yellow Hair."

BOOK I

BOYHOOD
1874–1877

CHAPTER 1

1874

"Your brother likes to eat dust, Sees Red!"

At the edge of the camp circle, Yellow Bird dragged his face out of the dirt, the warm wetness oozing from his nose. His older brother stood among the other young boys, laughing, pointing, jeering.

His pride hurt more than his smashed nose. In all these months since his mother had brought her two sons out of the territories to live here with their Cheyenne cousins of the north, Yellow Bird had been struggling to fit in with the boys, who had immediately accepted Sees Red. Not one of the youngsters had yet to befriend the younger of the brothers.

He felt the sting of tears at his eyes. Not for the hurt nose. Nor the hurt pride. Yellow Bird ached for a friend. His despair tasted more bitter than the alkali dirt he spit from his bloody lips.

"Little brother," said Sees Red, hurrying up. "Let me help you. Your face is a mess."

"Why do you help him, Sees Red? He is only half your brother."

The boy, barely ten moons older than Yellow Bird, self-consciously backed from his young brother. He looked at Yellow Bird, then his playmates sheepishly before he shrugged and trotted away to join his laughing friends. He looked back over his shoulder.

"Go play near our mother's lodge, Yellow Bird."

"I want to play with you!" he shouted in defiance, the blood still running from his nose.

"You are not big enough yet."

"I am as big as you already!"

Sees Red stopped as the others hurried on through the confusion of hide lodges. "You are different, little brother. Give them time."

"Come play with me then, Sees Red. Please."

He shook his head. "Another time. I like playing the games of older boys."

Yellow Bird watched his brother run off to catch the others, all screaming and scurrying through the lodges, dogs and puppies nipping at their heels, old women cursing them for tipping over fire tripods and old men laughing in remembrance of years forever gone. The dust in their swirling, maddened dance of play finally settled, slowly drifting down through the shafts of sunlight like flecks of spun gold against the gentle blue of a summer sky.

Turning away before the sting of their childish taunts hurt him more, Yellow Bird kicked at the powdery dust with his bare toes, yearning for the red earth of the Cheyenne reservation far to the south in the territories. True that it was hotter there than this northern land—but winters were not so long. And the horned toads were fun to catch. Turtles too.

Yet what he remembered best were his friends. The Southern Cheyenne boys who had been infants with him. Learned to walk, talk, and were weaned from their mother's breasts all at the same time. Boys who knew Yellow Bird's hair, skin, and eyes were lighter than theirs—but for them it did not matter. He was one of them.

But here Yellow Bird was not only a Southern Cheyenne— he was an oddity. Not accepted as they had taken to Sees Red.

He heard high laughter and looked toward the stream

the village had camped beside many days before when the
antelope herds were located. A large group of girls and some
boys younger than Yellow Bird splashed about in the
frothing water of the stream. Chattering, laughing, yelling,
encouraging one another as a line of older girls stretching
from bank to bank advanced downstream on the group. He
knew the line was driving the fish toward the expectant
youngsters.

For a moment the old thrill was there in his belly,
tickling him.

Yellow Bird was down the damp bank and into the
shocking cold water before he knew it. Among the others,
splashing and laughing, watching the surface churn as the
fish trapped between the two groups broke water, leaping
in a vain effort at escape. The little ones were on them,
grabbing, flinging the fish onto the banks where a few
mothers and some of the older girls waited with their
baskets and kettles.

Behind the noisy, playful children now, a half dozen of
the older girls plunged into the water, stretching a woven
net across the width of the stream, firmly trapping the fish
between the line of herders and the net.

The shrieks grew louder, every child soaked as he
plunged after the slippery bodies of the little swimmers.
Those waiting on shore laughing just as hard at the noisy
fun of the fishermen in the roiling, foamy water.

When there seemed no fish left for them to hurl onto the
grassy banks, Yellow Bird crawled beneath the shade of an
overhanging cottonwood, gasping. Water dribbled down his
nose, hanging pendant like a drop of sunshine. It felt good
to laugh, he decided, even if it was among the company of
girls. More of them splashed out of the water, plopping
onto the banks of the stream, chattering excitedly about
their great feat and the huge catch of so many of the little
swimmers.

"Why are you not with your brother?"

He looked up into his mother's eyes as Monaseetah
settled beside him. At her knee she set a kettle filled with
squirming tails.

Yellow Bird stared at his toes, not daring to look at her.
His eyes would betray him once more. They always had in

these past four summers of his life. He could keep little from her. Nothing in the way of secrets. Surely nothing in things of the heart.

"My brother's friends do not want to play with me," he whispered.

Monaseetah smiled at a group of young girls hurrying by, calling out their greetings to Yellow Bird. When they had passed out of hearing, she spoke. "It is hard being different from the rest."

"Mother," he said, finally daring to look into her dark eyes. "I do not want to be different. I want to play like the rest. If the boys do not want me to play their games of war with them, then I am forced to be a husband for the girls who want me to play their games of marriage."

She chuckled softly. "Soon, Yellow Bird—you will learn that girls and marriage are very serious. But time enough." She gazed at the rippling water rolling past their feet across the pebbled creek bed.

He watched as his mother's eyes once again focused on something distant, something he was not old enough yet to understand. It was what Yellow Bird knew had brought her here from the south country.

His mother had always been the one and only person who could calm the fear within him.

Except when that look came over her face as it had here beside the stream they called the Rosebud. And her eyes could no longer mask the hurt she carried inside.

"Sit, nephew," said the veteran Cheyenne warrior called Scabby. He patted the ground next to him.

Yellow Bird obeyed, plopping onto a patch of dried grass where the morning sun had warmed the earth and burned away the early frost of autumn. "My mother said you wanted to see me," he responded nervously.

"Woman—" Scabby flung his voice over his shoulder at the lodge behind him.

Immediately the warrior's wife appeared with two steaming bowls of meat chunks and bonemeal, boiled soft with huge slices of tipsina. Cooked properly, the potatolike root was Yellow Bird's favorite.

"Thank you," he said, accepting his bowl. He watched

the woman disappear, crouching into her lodge once more, pulling the elk hide over the entrance. For a moment the youngster watched as Scabby gingerly pulled steamy pieces of meat and tipsina from the bowl, blew on them, then plopped them into his mouth. His breath made a filmy gauze about his face in the cold air.

Yellow Bird's hands grew warm holding the wood bowl.

"Eat, nephew."

Scabby smiled at him, licking his fingers hungrily, then ran his tongue over his lips. Yellow Bird dipped his hands into the stew and brought forth a piece of elk.

"No, nephew. Try the tipsina." The man sucked on a finger drenched with the thick bonemeal juices. "The woman picked them especially for you. I know how you like them."

The boy brought forth a slice of the soft root. He bit into it and smiled. "It is good, uncle. *Very* good."

They ate in silence for some time. Both the rising sun and Scabby's stew did much to drive the anxious chill from Yellow Bird's chest.

"When you grow older, nephew, we will smoke together after we eat," Scabby explained as he set aside the bowl he had licked clean with a pink tongue that reminded Yellow Bird of a small grass snake. "But for now I will smoke alone. For what I do is very important, and we want the spirits happy when they join us here."

He almost choked on that tiny bit of elk meat. "Spirits, uncle?"

He chuckled easily at Yellow Bird's discomfort and waved to a friend walking by with his war pony in tow, headed for an early-morning watering at the creek.

"This is no matter of war or love, little one. But it remains an important matter still the same."

Yellow Bird watched the man drag a long coyote-skin bag onto his lap. Until now it had lain hidden under a flap of Scabby's blanket capote.

"It is not every day that a man gets the opportunity to present his adopted nephew with his first bow."

"A . . . a bow?" Yellow Bird felt the wings of excitement take flight within his belly. Long had he been waiting for this moment, growing impatient as other boys his age in camp received their first bows.

After the warrior had smoked his short bowl of tobacco, blowing his smoke to the four winds, above to the Greatest of All and below to the Earth Mother both, Scabby set aside the pipe and finally pulled the coyote-hide flap aside so that he could draw out the short weapon he had crafted for the child. Sewn to the coyote-skin tube that would carry the bow was a long quiver, holding two dozen newly crafted arrows. Scabby lifted one of the iron-tipped shafts into the new day's light, then laid both gifts into the youth's waiting hands.

"Not that many moons ago, I chose to bring my lodge north to join our cousins," Scabby explained as he looked off at the ridge, growing a rich red hue with the rising of the sun. "Like your mother and a few others, I had grown weary of that land in the South where the white man and his soldiers told us we must stay. It grows too hot. There is not near enough snow come wintertime. And the waters are all too warm for a man to drink."

He looked down at Yellow Bird and found the youth caressing the length of the bow, his tiny fingers running the length of the wrapped-rawhide bowstring.

Scabby smiled when the boy gazed up into his face. "Like your mother I wanted to come north once more, where the water flows so cold it can make a man's teeth ache. Your mother is here to continue her search for a man. I am afraid of her search."

"She is looking for a man, uncle?"

He looked away. "For your father, Yellow Bird."

"My . . . my father?" He tried out the words on his tongue. He knew that his mother had sent away her first husband, Sees Red's father, because of his cruelty to her. But he had never known much of his own father, nor had he ever thought to ask.

Scabby pulled a second shaft from the quiver. He ran a finger tip over the iron point. "This is a special day for me too, Yellow Bird. Every year fewer boys are given their first bows. More and more men are hunting with guns. More and more the bow maker's craft is fading."

He pulled on Yellow Bird's blanket, turning the youth to face him.

"But you—it will be more important than all the rest of the Cheyenne boys for you to learn the bow."

"You do not want me to learn to shoot a gun, uncle?" He felt the first stirs of confusion, some fear smothering the wings of excitement in his tiny belly.

"Yes," he sighed. "You must learn to shoot a gun. But you must learn the bow as well. And learn to shoot it with accuracy. For in you, as in no other Cheyenne boy, will there be a need to keep the old ways."

"This talk of the old ways . . . and what you say about my mother coming north to look for my father—this scares me. Is this why the other boys do not want to play their games with me?"

Scabby patted the youth on the shoulder, then pulled the boy into the crook of his shoulder. Yellow Bird felt the man shudder before he spoke once more.

"Nephew, you are different. It is because of your father and the blood he gave you that makes you different from all Cheyenne."

"My mother is looking for my father here among the Northern Cheyenne? He is Shahiyena?"

Scabby shook his head. "No, your father is not among the Cheyenne."

"He is Lakota?"

"No, he is not Sioux, little nephew."

"Tell me of my father." Yellow Bird recognized the rising of his own voice.

Again the man wagged his head, clenching his eyes shut. When he opened them, Yellow Bird saw the mist of tears wetting them.

"After you were born, your mother asked for my help in raising you. I knew you were without relatives. Your grandmother gone many seasons before your birth. Your mother's father killed by soldiers the winter before you were born. And your own father abandoning your mother the summer before you came to her."

"Uncle, who is my father?" Yellow Bird's voice was strangely raspy, like the draw of an old iron file across granite. "Why did he leave my mother?"

"I cannot tell you these things, for long ago I promised your mother that while I would help as I could in raising you, I would let her be the one to tell you of your father—the man he is and what his blood leaves you."

Yellow Bird started to rise. Scabby pulled him back down beside him while the village throbbed to life around them.

"Let me go, uncle!"

"I cannot, until you understand that you are not to ask your mother."

"Why can't I?"

He sighed, bringing the boy's face close to his. "A man cannot ask such things unless his mother speaks first of it."

"And if she never wants to tell me?"

"She must."

"Why must she, uncle?"

"Monaseetah has promised me to tell you by the end of your sixth summer."

He moaned, sinking inside. "Two more summers to wait, uncle."

"She promised me, because we now know for certain that your father is in this north country."

"My father roams this great hunting ground?"

Scabby looked away, seeing the sun tear itself red and bloody from the ridge top in a blaze of orange light. "Yes, nephew. It will not be long until you know of your father. For, you see, like the Shahiyena and the Lakota bands, your father roams this great hunting ground in search of his prey."

CHAPTER 2

THE first true snow of winter was warming beneath the new buffalo-hide moccasins his mother made him last week in anticipation of the cold weather. The great expanse of white and shadow reluctantly gave way beneath his feet as he felt his way into the stand of trees not far from the village.

Yellow Bird stopped and looked back. Over the ridge he saw the clearly defined rising ghosts of fire smoke signaling the awaking of the Cheyenne camp for the day. He had already been up and gone enough time to climb and descend that ridge into the drainage of a nearby creek, leaving his mother and Sees Red wrapped warmly in their sleeping robes.

Out where the sun danced across the new snow, the air itself sparkled with frost. Back here in the shadows of the aspen and alder, the air seemed much colder. He blew into the cuff of one blanket mitten, momentarily warming his fingers. Then switching the bow, he warmed the other hand. And he itched the quiver more snugly over his shoulder, determined not to let the cold deter him from his hunt for game this early morning.

It had been almost two moons since his adopted uncle had given him this first bow. Every day he practiced with it and Scabby's iron-tipped arrows, and every day his mother would send him to his practice with the same admonition.

"Be careful, Yellow Bird. Do not aim your arrow at a person. Harm no one's horse or dog."

Hour after hour he had strengthened his arms so that soon he discovered he could shoot farther than the last day of practice. Still, it took longer for him to gain control of his aim, learning to repeatedly drop each arrow near a mark. He never failed to pass by Scabby's lodge, to thank him at the end of each day's practice for the gift of the bow.

In Yellow Bird's gratitude there were still things left unsaid: how thankful a young boy was to have something to occupy his time when the other boys would not play with him; how thankful he was no longer to have to play the role of baby for the young girls at their woman's play. Yellow Bird drank deep of the cold air, filling his lungs and swelling his little chest.

Enough of the games played by boys and girls. What he was about was the work of a man, of a Cheyenne warrior.

It was time he would seek out game bigger than sparrows and wrens. This morning he would bring home something for his mother's stew kettle. Time would come when Scabby and Rolls Down could no longer provide for Mona-seetah's lodge. Time would come when Sees Red and Yellow Bird would be the hunters.

"Although you enjoy your hunting, nephew," Scabby had explained one frosty autumn morning as they sat together in the sun, waiting for the slick of ice to melt from the water kettle, "a Cheyenne boy does not hunt only because he likes it. It is to be undertaken as serious work."

"Work, uncle?"

"Yes. Always try hard to be a good hunter. Provide for your family first and those who cannot provide for themselves."

With a few blunt-headed arrows, he had hunted for those sparrows and wrens darting among the branches of the trees overhead. Knocking a small bird off a limb, he had rushed forward to claim his wriggling prey, snapping its neck in his tiny hands. Then he stuffed the head up beneath the strap that held his breechclout round his waist. Today, however, he had promised himself some four-legged quarry.

A few times he had secretly followed Sees Red and some of the older boys as they went hunting the hares that scampered before them, always staying just out of range of their small bows. While the group had chased after their game, Yellow Bird had followed behind, hugging the shadows of tree and bush so the older ones would not know they were followed by the spindly-legged, light-eyed one.

Many times he had to clamp a hand over his mouth so that the boys would not hear his laughter when a jackrabbit surprised them all, bolting away right from the very midst of their little hunting party, scurrying this way, then that, before it disappeared among the sage and bunchgrass and scrub oak. But the boys had doggedly pursued, watching where the rabbit would stop in the distance, panting, its ears pinned back, making itself small beneath some scruff of bullberry while the hunters closed in.

Slowly the crescent of young hunters would draw in on the spot where their quarry lay, hoping to get close enough to make a killing shot when the rabbit elected to bolt from cover again.

One day soon he would be tracking antelope, or riding at the edge of a herd of buffalo with his bowstring pulled taut above the huge, shaggy beasts. His dreams of making meat for his mother and brother, of bringing home to his lodge huge, dripping quarters of flesh that would be the envy of all the sneering boys in camp—

A faint scrape of movement across the softening snow caught his attention, training his eyes and straining his ears into the stripe of shadow and light and shadow that lay before him in the ever-increasing darkness of the black timber. From the corner of his eye, Yellow Bird spotted the twitching of the long ears of the snowshoe hare, all but lost against the old snow and ash-hued light save for the heaving of its rib cage beneath the nervous flick of its laid-back ears.

He smiled to himself, slowly bringing the bow up as he shuffled his right foot back, all the while drawing the string tight, the arrow nock to his cheek beneath the light eye. He brought the iron point down over his target, held, and released—just as the hare bolted off.

"I have been robbed again, grandfather!" he whispered in exasperation, trying to keep an eye on the path taken by the rabbit, while at the same time watching the path his arrow had taken.

Knowing he shouldn't, the boy stomped on the snow in anger, realizing it would alarm other game in the area. Yet the venting relieved him of much of the nervous wings that had troubled his belly since leaving camp that morning.

Now he could get down to the work at hand. As his adopted uncle had instructed him, hunting was serious business.

Later he found himself leaning against the rough bark of a sheltering tree, feeling more of the cold as he ventured farther into the timber. From the position of the sun behind him, Yellow Bird figured it had moved the distance of three lodgepoles since he had entered the thick stand of old growth. Soon it would be time to eat—he would stop to finish off the hunk of elk he had wrapped in a piece of smoked hide and stuffed inside his shirt. A handful of snow would wash it down when he had finished.

But as he was thinking of cold elk, the sound of quarry returned to his ears. Not so faint this time. Perhaps something bigger, he thought, as he checked his arrow and moved off to close on the sound. Perhaps a badger. Something truly worthy of a lonely hunter.

Yet it was another snowshoe. Bigger than he had ever seen. So big that he found himself staring at it, staring back at him, instead of releasing the bow. As he brought the string back to his cheekbone, a hiss from behind him made the hair stand on the back of Yellow Bird's neck. At the same moment the snowshoe bolted off. The boy wheeled on the sound at his back, staring down the shaft, into the yellow eyes of a huge gray wolf.

His hands began to tremble, mouth sucked dry as if by the cold wind that suddenly gusted through the timber, rattling the branches free of snow and the arrows in the quiver at his back.

Those huge yellow eyes held the young hunter transfixed, mesmerized in their depths.

Yellow Bird had heard many tales of such animals round the fires. Yet at this moment he sensed that no other soul could have ever seen a wolf as big as the one before him. He tried to draw in a breath, realizing he was still holding it in his quivering chest.

The wolf took two steps out of the shadows, closing on Yellow Bird.

Gasping involuntarily, he once more brought the bow-string back, his little hands shaking all the harder, determined that he would kill the wolf when it drew closer. One carefully aimed iron point, driven deep into the chest of the leaping wolf could do it, he decided. The wolf took several slow, considered steps toward the boy.

And the youth was no longer sure he had the strength to let fly the arrow, much less any strength left in his tiny legs that would allow him to turn and outrun the beast.

You have no need to fear me, Yellow Bird.

He wagged his head once. The voice came from inside his head, but outside as well. Almost as if it had been the voice of the wolf.

I am speaking to your heart, little one. That is why you hear me inside.

"You are talking to me, wolf one?" He gulped.

Put down your bow and iron-tipped shaft, Yellow Bird.

"How do you know my name?" He was more scared than before, realizing that either the wolf was talking to him . . . or that he was being driven mad with the power of those yellow eyes glaring into him across the shadow-crusted snow.

My spirit was there the night Scabby first used those words over your little body in the naming ceremony.

"Years ago," he stammered, lowering the bow slightly. "When I was but a few days old."

Far to the south, Yellow Bird. Where you were born in the cold five winters ago. I have stayed close. I will always be close.

The hair at the back of his neck prickled with heat, and he suddenly felt like losing his stomach he was so scared. No words came forth.

I understand. It is good that you are afraid of me. Good that you will always be afraid of me. For we have much to accomplish together.

"Together," his voice quivered.

You see the yellow of my eyes, little one?

"I . . . I see—"

Have you not once looked at the color of your own reflection in a quiet pond? Have you not wondered more times than you will admit why your eyes are so different from the other boys . . . why your hair is not black like theirs?

"How do you know this?"

Heammawihio sent me to watch over you, little one.

"The Great Everywhere sent you to be my spirit helper?"

But instead of answering the great wolf slowly turned from the small clearing and nosed into the thick tangle of dark timber.

"Wait, wolf brother!" Yellow Bird called out.

The beast stopped, baring its teeth. *Do not follow me. Where I go, you cannot. I come back to you when you are ready.*

He watched the animal disappear as if in a winter fog. There one moment, gone with the next blink of his disbelieving eyes.

Yellow Bird stood shuddering, shaken to his core. A child once more, knowing he stood in the presence of something that caused even old men to tremble.

"This did not happen," he consoled himself. "The wolf did not speak."

Inside he felt himself growing cold with more than winter's cloak. A gnawing uncertainty, a momentary brush with the great mystery of life leaving the man-child with none of his questions answered, filling him with more than dread. Leaving Yellow Bird with all the more requiring answers.

"I am frightened," he whispered to himself, finally lowering the trembling bow. "I saw the wolf on my path. His eyes frightened me into believing this nightmare—that he talked to me. It simply cannot be so."

Yellow Bird turned in the skiffs of snow and darted toward the nearest, biggest patch of sunlight he could locate through the maze of timber. The softening snow clung to his legs like the tangle of creepers matted along the creek banks in that land of his birth far to the south. He fell, face pitching into the shocking cold of the vast ash gray of the shadowy snow. The bow and single arrow tumbled from his little hand as he shrieked in surprise and terror.

Frantic, he pulled himself up, gasping, spitting the cold from his mouth, grunting in fear and feeling for the first time the warmth between his legs as his loins chilled beneath his blanket capote. Realizing now that he had wet himself there before the great wolf.

Ashamed, frightened to the center of his being, the boy clawed at the snow to retrieve his bow, with no thought of the forgotten arrow he was leaving behind.

CHAPTER 3

1876

"SLEEP now, my little one," Monaseetah murmured to Yellow Bird.

She cradled her youngest across her lap, shivering at the great cold of this predawn darkness seeping like a blood-ooze from an old wound. At last she recognized the calming regularity of his gentle puff of breath smoke. Still she rocked him gently back and forth, cooing away his fears and the terrifying nightmare that had thrust the child awake, screaming.

It had taken but a moment for Sees Red to roll over and fall back to sleep, pulling the robes over his head. Much longer for Monaseetah to calm Yellow Bird enough so that he would curl himself within her blanketed arms beside the lifeless fire pit. Shivering now with the damp freeze that for the last nine suns had not released its grip on this land, the Cheyenne mother raised her tired eyes to the smoke hole. From the darkness leaking into a smudgy gray, she could see that dawn would not be long in coming.

March, the white man called it—midway through the

Sore-Eye Moon, when the late winter cold and sun battled through each lengthening day to render a paralyzing brightness to the snow that blinded a person. Years ago Monaseetah had learned to smear the flesh below her eyes with a mixture of charcoal and bear grease if she had to venture out of the lodge for wood or water. Too many times she had suffered the terrifying torment of the prickly blindness that came without warning, bringing with it the insufferable sting of hot, rolling sand beneath the eyelids, when clamping them fiercely brought no relief.

She welcomed this cold darkness in the lodge here beneath the sliver of Sore-Eye Moon, her eyes long adjusted now to the lack of light, watching as the stars wheeled overhead through the tunnel of her smoke hole. Watching the sky drain its charcoal, slowly turning the color of dead ash in her fire pit.

A pony snorted close by, answering the faint whicker of one farther away. Soon enough this entire village camped on the west bank of the upper Powder River would awaken for the coming day. The entire village had moved here just above the mouth of the Little Powder only two days before when scouts had spotted a long soldier column. But the soldiers had gone over the hills to the headwaters of Hanging Woman Creek, following it down to the Tongue River.

Everyone felt much safer then. Old Bear's band would stay out of the way of the soldiers who were marching about this cold winter.

A hundred lodges of various bands gathered for winter hunting round Cheyenne chief Two Moon's forty lodges. Among these hundred were forty lodges of visiting Oglalla Sioux under Crazy Horse's friend He Dog, come here to join the Cheyenne in the hunt for the game believed to be in the surrounding country. In addition the village boasted some twenty lodges of Miniconjou Sioux stranded here by the severe cold, unable to continue their desperate migration back to the agency to secure the government's handouts, resigned to begging after some of the white man's food to eat. This winter had been colder than normal. More snow. Ice thicker on the creeks and rivers. Because of it the nights had seemed longer. But Monaseetah knew morning would come soon.

She gazed down into the child's face. Were it not for the high crook to the nose and the gentle swell of his cheekbones, Yellow Bird might remind any white man of the youth's father, Monaseetah mused. The buffalo-blood tints to Yellow Bird's rust brown hair, his light eyes not quite the color of the summer sky when a thunderstorm brews itself to a boil, not quite the greasy yellow color of old marrow, but more the liquid ooze of a dog's seepy eye, all of that she had long ago accepted would betray the child's mixed blood. So different in coloring were his mother and father, skin and hair and eyes. At times she almost believed she discerned the faint hint of the reddish brown spots that had dotted Yellow Hair's fair skin.

"Hiestzi," she whispered, watching her young son stir in her arms. "Your son one day demands to know you."

Gently she laid Yellow Bird back among her robes and blankets, tugging the soft, curly warmth beneath his chin as he slept on, more peacefully now. Almost every night, it seemed, the terrible nightmare came to awaken them all to Yellow Bird's screeching howls of terror.

Monaseetah remembered the terrors of her own nightmares. A mother butchered and stripped, her body defiled by soldiers. The agony of belonging to a cruel, vengeful Cheyenne husband who beat and sodomized his young wife. And finally the recurring vision of her father's bloody body lapping against the icy bank of the Washita, a winter long ago gone now.

She too knew of the private battle brought of the nightmares when one is young.

"Do not fear, Yellow Bird. Your mother will do what she can to protect you from all harm. Never will I allow anyone to—"

At the crack of a rifle, she wheeled about. Knowing.

"The soldiers are charging!" an old man's voice called out from the bluff above Monaseetah's lodge. "The soldiers are here!"

A second shot, then a rattle of gunfire. The low booms of soldier guns. Fired in volley. Monaseetah knew. She remembered. If anyone knew in their soul the sound of soldier guns, it was Yellow Bird's mother.

"Mother?"

She wheeled again. Sees Red crawled from his robes. Her youngest was lunging for the safety of her arms once more.

"Soldiers!" she shouted, now that the village beyond them was awake, people shouting, ponies neighing or screaming humanlike with bullet wounds. Beyond at the edge of the camp, the gunfire had grown constant. Between shots she believed she recognized the shouts of men. White men.

"Soldiers, mother?"

"Come . . . now!"

She yanked Yellow Bird up with her, scooping as best she could the buffalo robe with him. "No, Sees Red!" She ordered, watching him stop, shaking with cold. "Bring your robe, your blanket—something!"

When she swept aside the stiffened antelope-hide door flap, Monaseetah found the world outside a swirl of smoke and darting, flitting forms.

Sand Creek; The Washita . . . and now the Powder.

Whirling, the woman bumped against her two sons, sending Yellow Bird sprawling over Sees Red. They clawed to their knees in the darkness of the lodge, following their mother over the fire pit more by feel than by sight. Yanking her belt from the dewcloth rope strung between lodgepoles, Monaseetah quickly lashed the ends at her waist around a blanket she would wear for warmth. Then she pulled the long butcher knife from its bare sheath at her hip. She jabbed the point through the frost-stiffened lodge skins and with both hands struggled to work the blade down through the resistant buffalo hides.

Pulling aside one flap of the dew-cloth, Monaseetah motioned frantically to her sons.

"Come!"

She grabbed Sees Red first, shoving him out the slit in the back of their lodge.

"Yellow Bird! Fly to safety with your brother!"

She hurled the youngest through the stiff opening, then crouched through herself. She found Sees Red and Yellow

Bird sprawled on the ground as a half-dozen young warriors darted past, brandishing bows, not rifles. Monaseetah waited for them to pass, then a wild-eyed pony, charging by with a long tether tied to its lower jaw, a picket pin slapping the hard, crusty snow as it tore by.

"There! Go now!" she ordered, pointing, pulling at the boys both struggling with the bulk and weight of their robes.

"Do not leave your robe, Yellow Bird! You will pray for it soon!"

His eyes were all that answered.

Obediently Sees Red scooped up a loose end of his sleeping robe and dived into the madness. She grabbed her youngest's arm, shoving him forward into the swirling panic.

A wild pony careened round a nearby lodge, crashing into the trio, sending all three sprawling into the trampled snow. On the pony's back clung a young half-naked warrior, slumped against his animal's neck.

Monaseetah recognized the stench as she clambered to her feet, watching the pony bolt off with its bloody rider. The obedient animal pulling more and more of the steamy, greasy gut-coil from its bullet-riven belly with each painful, prancing step.

From the direction of the rifle fire, she knew the soldiers had already reached that flat meadow between the village and the combined pony herds. Sees Red tripped. She caught him.

He whirled on her. "They're killing—"

"Run, Sees Red!" she interrupted her eldest.

"This way, mother!" Yellow Bird shouted, pulling from her.

"No," she said, and was uncertain just as quickly. Something in her son's eyes as he gazed up at her, the rattle of gunfire working itself closer and closer from the far side of the camp. Young children and infants were crying out for help.

"Not the river, mother," Sees Red protested. "I'll follow you."

She watched her oldest pull on her arm, trying to head in

the direction she had originally led them. But something tugged at the gut of her as well.

"No, Sees Red—we follow Yellow Bird." She allowed her youngest to lead off, toward the snowy willow along the Powder as the shouts of wounded soldiers and the curses of cold infantry loomed louder.

"But, mother—"

"They ride white horses—the soldiers are already in the center of the village, Sees Red! Now follow your brother to the river!"

As Sees Red turned on his heel, he glowered at his mother, but followed his younger brother nonetheless into the nearby willow and alder, away from the infuriating buzz of bullets, that slap of soldier lead against tree and lodgepole.

All round them arose the babble of Cheyenne mixed with Lakota and an occasional white man's curse. Brass horns blaring and ponies crying out in pain or fear. Now a second company of soldiers riding bays burst into the heart of the pandemonium.

"They have the herd!" shouted old man Rolls Down as he lumbered up out of the fog roiling up from the Powder River.

"The soldiers?"

"Yes, Monaseetah," he answered breathlessly. "We have no other choice now but to head downriver."

"Away from the attack?" Sees Red demanded. "Won't our warriors fight these soldiers?"

Rolls Down said to the youngster, "We wait for another day, nephew."

"Then I will have to fight alone!"

Rolls Down and Monaseetah both snatched the impetuous youth before he could dart from the willows. Many more frightened women, children, and old ones scurried by, out of the fog, then beyond to disappear into the gray light of predawn.

"You will go with your mother, nephew. Now!"

He struggled, but Rolls Down's grip tightened until Sees Red winced in pain.

"You are hurting me—"

"Better an old man's hand than the soldiers' rifles, my son," Monaseetah admonished.

"We best go now," the warrior whispered. "You are heading downriver?"

"Yes," she answered. "Yellow Bird was leading us."

He looked down at the skinny youth, shivering in the knee-deep skiff of old snow heaped about his legs. Yellow Bird struggled to keep the old cow robe clutched around his shoulders as he shook uncontrollably.

"We will go with the others, staying together with Two Moon and Old Bear," he explained, pointing for them to lead off down the Powder, away from the village and the direction of the army's attack.

"Our people have suffered much before, my sons," Monaseetah said softly, and the frosty, stinging fog enveloped them.

"Sand Creek," Rolls Down said. "The death of Black Kettle at the Washita . . . and now they follow us to the Powder."

"When will we turn and fight?" Sees Red demanded, flinging his anger over his shoulder at the adults.

"Soon, little one," the old man answered. "Very soon the Shahiyena will turn and sting the soldiers who poke their sticks into our nests!"

Throughout that gloomy, cold day, stragglers from that camp along the Powder gathered in the surrounding hills. They came in singly, or in pairs, helping one another through the snowdrifts. Still more, small groups mostly, limped in to the gathering points, bringing the old and the sick on their backs and in their arms. As the morning wore on, it amazed Monaseetah that so few bore any wounds caused of soldier bullets. Instead, most complained of frostbitten toes and fingers.

For the winter army under the soldier chief called Red Beard Crook, the mercury continued to hover well below zero for this, their tenth day in a row. But as far as the dispossessed of that village along the Powder knew, it was another unbearably cold day, like the nine gone before it.

Below in the valley the Cheyenne watched the dark antlike soldiers in their bulky coats lumbering through what had once been their village. The soldiers raided the lodges for their rich stores—robes, blankets, saddles, and dried meat. All of it, in addition to the ammunition and powder, was heaped into growing piles. Then the white men put the wealth of the Northern Cheyenne to the torch.

As the flames grew, lighting the low-bellied clouds with the red fires of destruction, the people watched in frustration and despair. With each thump thundering from their tribal medicine drum, now in the hands of the army's Shoshone scouts, the warriors grew more angry. Groans of despair and cries of frustration echoed all about Monaseetah.

"Not only have they captured our pony herd, but the soldiers have made us poor again!" Two Moon complained.

"Do you remember when I brought my band of Fox warriors to join your village before the last moon grew full?" asked Last Bull.

"What is it we should remember?" demanded Rolls Down.

Last Bull wheeled on the old man. "I brought news that the soldiers were coming to fight you."

Two Moon stared at the ground, listening to the angry muttering of Last Bull's warriors who gathered close, every last man of them shivering in the cold beneath a leaden dawn sky. Below, the valley fires climbed, their rose glow cast on the underbelly of the clouds, oily smoke rising like unanswered prayers from the decimated village.

"I remember," Two Moon admitted, finally raising his eyes from the scene of destruction to gaze at Last Bull. "You did not know what fort these soldiers would leave to hunt for us—but you said they were marching after all Cheyenne and Lakota who were off their reservations."

"No!" Long Dog protested. "The treaties allow us to hunt where we want, as long as we stay away from the white man!"

"But the white chiefs back east want us to stay on the reservations, don't you see?" Scabby said, shoving through the tightening knot of warriors and bystanders. "They want us near them so they can sell us their whiskey, rotten meat, and the flour so full of beetles."

"This is true," Two Moon said. "The only way we can

keep our young men from drinking the white man's whiskey is to keep our camp far from the white man!"

"We did not listen to Last Bull," Long Dog repeated.

"Nor did you pay heed to Spotted Wolf and Twin when they brought their bands in," Medicine Wolf spoke softly, the red glimmer of the fires below evident in the moistness of his eyes.

"Do any of you know who is missing?" Two Moon asked.

"I saw one Cheyenne fall," answered Wooden Leg. "I know of two more wounded."

"I cannot find my grandmother," a young woman complained.

"She is blind?" Two Moon asked.

"Yes," the woman answered. "I got my children out of the lodge, then returned for her. She was already gone."

At that moment there erupted several loud explosions in the valley below. They could no longer hear the Shoshone pounding on their sacred drum. Its sound was buried under the booms like the coming of summer thunder, rattling the trees and rumbling along the ground beneath their feet. Lodgepoles were sent careening into the air, tumbling down in smoky ruin like tiny bits of kindling.

"Our powder supplies!" Scabby groaned as the murmuring of the crowd increased.

"When will we get a chance to kill these soldiers who steal our horses and burn everything we own?" demanded Sees Red at the old warrior's side.

"Soon enough, young one," Scabby answered, "the Everywhere Spirit will deliver the soldiers to us."

CHAPTER 4

1876

As morning wore into afternoon, a buttermilk-pale sun spilled through cracks in the overcast sky. At the base of every clump of alder and squawbush, a handful of the survivors huddled, wrapped in what blankets and robes they had dragged from their lodges at the moment of attack. Beside them lay the bundles of their most prized possessions the women would not leave behind when the soldiers slashed their way into the sleeping village.

A handful of the Cheyenne and Oglalla warriors had escaped atop war ponies kept tethered beside their lodges. This brave band served as a rear guard when Two Moon and He Dog gave the command to cross the Powder and push into the snow-covered hills beyond, heading north by east. A few of those horsemen rode in among those on foot from time to time, each man giving his blanket over to the old ones, or to a group of children who walked huddled together.

These horsemen no longer needed their blankets, for now they wore long blue wool coats designed for the frontier army, but perfect for a warrior on horseback covering the retreat of his people.

Inexplicably the soldiers did not follow up the escaping bands. Instead, they contented themselves with the destruction of the village. As the Cheyenne and Lakota put each successive hill behind them, the pink glow tinting the cloud underbellies and the black smudge staining the horizon grew more faint.

With the retreat of the soldiers that night, horsemen warily returned to salvage what they could from the torched village. The white men had left one lodge standing.

"The old blind woman?" Monaseetah asked Scabby as he kneeled beside her and the boys in the muddy slush softening the ground the next morning.

"Yes." He handed her a small handful of dried meat. "Divide this among yourselves. It is all I was given. I divide it among my family and yours. There was so little left, and so many mouths to feed."

"Have you eaten, uncle?" Yellow Bird asked, more than his belly feeling the pangs of emptiness.

Rising, Scabby peered down at his adopted nephew. "No. But I am not hungry. I must go select a horse for you among those we stole back from the soldiers last night."

"Our herd no longer belongs to the white men?" Monaseetah asked, her voice rising in excitement.

"Not all," Scabby apologized. "The soldiers were not watchful, so a few of us crept in and ran off what we could. I will select a strong one. The three of you will have to ride together."

"We do not mind," Sees Red answered. "Perhaps we can chase after the soldiers now."

The old warrior shook his head and cupped the youth's chin in his smoke-blackened hand, tender and raw from digging in the smoldering piles once their lodges. "We cannot. The chiefs have decided to wait here until the thaw comes behind the storm."

"Then?" Yellow Bird inquired.

"When the thaw comes, we are to march behind He Dog."

"He Dog, the Oglalla?" Monaseetah asked.

"He will take us to the camp of Crazy Horse."

Without another word of explanation, Scabby was gone to fetch a horse.

After waiting near the smoking ruins of their village across the next three days, picking from the ruins what they could like a band of scavengers, the survivors were finally told they would move across the Little Powder. For four more days the survivors limped cross-country, through a soggy landscape laced with melting snow and rising creeks. Each night after the sun sank behind the Big Horns, they made camp, bedded down their ponies, and built their tiny fires. What had been mud and slush by day took no time freezing hard come star time.

What little game the hunters shot during the day was quickly eaten, most of it given to the old and the very young. Those able to gather wood kept busy throughout the long hours waiting for dawn. They kept their minds off gnawing bellies, trying to forget the cold, making sure the fires warming the rest did not go out.

The last two days were the hardest. A wolfish wind keened over the prairie, knifing down the coulees where the people tried huddling from its icy blast. Yet it was there that the snows drifted deepest.

No longer is the winter our protector, Monaseetah brooded as the two little ones shivered beside her. *Yellow Hair has seen to that, coming to attack the Washita camp of Black Kettle. No longer is the winter a time when the soldiers are too cold to march*.

Down the coulee she heard the shrill cry of a pony being slaughtered, recognizing that sound as almost human, knowing the young warriors were killing another of their most prized possessions so that the people could eat of its raw, warm flesh. So that the old women and men could warm their frozen feet in the steamy bowels when the carcass lay butchered.

Truly the old times had passed. No longer was winter a time when aging warriors huddled about the warmth of lodge fires to tell again their stories of battles and pony raids and fights with the white men to the little ones. Winter no longer meant a time of peace for the people of these high plains.

As short as each period of daylight was, able to travel

only as fast as the slowest person left on foot, the bands hobbled more than forty miles to the East Fork of the Little Powder. From a muddy ridge top late one afternoon, they spotted the movement of some faraway horsemen.

Soon a handful of He Dog's Oglallas returned excited, laughing and slapping one another in glee. Word traveled along the length of the miserable caravan that they had reached the end of their march. Tonight they would sleep among the Oglalla of Crazy Horse.

Yellow Bird was old enough to understand that it had been a hard winter for all the bands, including the thirty lodges under the great Oglalla war chief. Yet the Lakota and a nearby band of ten Cheyenne lodges came forth to offer what they could to the survivors of the Sore-Eye Moon battle. At the center of camp, each woman came forward to announce how many of those made poor she could accept in her lodge.

"Cheyennes, I can sleep five of you. Come, share what we have to eat tonight."

It touched Yellow Bird's heart to see the mist cloud his mother's eyes as she watched the old and little ones limp off behind their hosts. Tears coursed down Monaseetah's cheeks, and with each one her youngest son came to know the strength that lay in staying together as a people. The white man wanted to divide the bands—the only way the soldiers would ever defeat the tribes. Yellow Bird vowed he would not let the angry look of rage etched on his brother's face deter the swelling of his heart as they made their way to an Oglalla lodge.

Though of few summers the boy realized that each family was now crowded together, food and blankets stretched to their limits. Despite the winter winds howling outside the noisy lodges, guests and family stayed warm in the togetherness.

That night the head men from each band held their first council, devoted solely to the telling of the soldier attack on the Cheyenne village. Scabby stopped by Monaseetah's lodge before going to bed down with his wife and daughters hosted by a nearby Oglalla family.

"We think the soldiers are hunting Cheyenne only," he whispered, kneeling at the fire pit, a circle of Sioux and

Cheyenne faces all intent on his every word and movement of his hands in sign. "They roamed the countryside north of our camp. They could have attacked the Oglallas of Crazy Horse. Or hunted down the Hunkpapas of Sitting Bull. Instead they circled back and attacked a village of Cheyenne."

"Then the Cheyenne must go to war with the white man!" Sees Red cheered.

Scabby waited for the muttering in the crowded lodge to quiet. "I believe the Cheyenne leaders will decide on staying with the Oglalla for some time now, little one. We have few ponies and only a few old weapons. We are not ready for war—not yet."

"But soon, uncle?"

He turned to his adopted nephew. "Yes, Yellow Bird. In my mind I think the chiefs will decide to stay with Crazy Horse until we are ready to stand on our own once more. Perhaps we will hunt together come the short-grass time while our ponies grow strong. We can send our men with robes and furs to the agencies for more weapons and bullets. So while we gain our strength once more, we will travel with the Lakota."

"The soldiers are not looking for the Sioux?" Monaseetah asked.

He shook his head. "The soldiers attacked the Cheyenne."

"Does any man know who led these soldiers against the Cheyenne camp?"

Scabby held Monaseetah's eyes for a long moment. To Yellow Bird it appeared as if the old warrior understood the reason for the young mother's question. As if she might know of some pony-soldier chief.

Finally he wagged his head. "Many suns ago some of our scouts believed the soldiers were led by Red Beard Crook. But that was so long ago, and those soldiers marched away. The white men who burned our village might be Red Beard's soldiers. Perhaps not."

Monaseetah's voice implored him, hoping for some bit of hopeful information. "Did any man recognize the marks on the soldiers' tiny war flags?"

Again he shook his head, looked at the fire pit. "I wish I had good news for you, Monaseetah. The sad thing that must rest on your heart is that if the army wants to have a big war with the Cheyenne, soon with the coming of the short-grass, all the soldier chiefs will be chasing us."

Yellow Bird looked from Scabby to his mother's face, sagging with resignation.

She nodded. "Yes. It weighs heavy on my heart. Wanting something so badly, fearing it every bit as much."

Scabby rose on creaking knees to leave the warmth of the lodge and return to his family. Yet Monaseetah's voice halted him at the doorway.

"With the soldiers chasing us now that the short-grass is about to raise its head, then his returning to the warpath will surely mean more Cheyenne have to die."

As Scabby had predicted, the combined bands could draw no other conclusion from the attack on Two Moon's camp than that the soldiers had declared war on the Cheyennes. Each man knew the Lakota bands were peacefully hunting on territory ceded to them by the white man's treaty. Yet at the same time every man understood that by hunting here in the Powder River country, the Cheyenne tribes were on land not permitted to them.

After deliberating on the matter for four more days, Crazy Horse and the other Lakotas determined that they would accompany Two Moon's people on their journey to visit the powerful Hunkpapas. There they would allow their medicine chief, Sitting Bull, to determine what course of action to take concerning this declaration of war against the Northern Cheyenne.

The bands marched north for three days, down the Powder, where the Hunkpapas were reported to winter. Enough ponies in the camps now so that no one had to walk. Suffering heavy, wet snows that hampered their march for two days, however, Crazy Horse finally led his combined forces to the country of the Blue Earth Hills. There below Charcoal Butte, after a long journey of seven sleeps, they found the great encampment of Sitting Bull and Gall.

There were more lodges there below that butte than had been in Two Moon's, He Dog's, and Crazy Horse's village combined. Outposts and sentries spread the word quickly at the approach of the weary column. Pots were already aboil by the time the travelers reached the outskirts of the camp.

"The Bull has ordered two huge lodges to be erected in the center of his camp," Monaseetah explained to her sons.

"Sitting Bull? The medicine man of the Hunkpapas?" Sees Red asks, excitement on his words as he tore at a strip of dried venison handed him by one of the young girls carrying parfleches of food throughout the camps.

"He is the same," the young mother answered, beaming. "No one will be crowded in their lodges now. I wish my father could have seen this."

Then her eyes shot to her youngest, seeing there again the question, the answer for which she was not yet ready to tell him. Instead she pulled Yellow Bird close and bent over him, wrapping the boy in her arms.

"Your grandfather would have been proud to stand here beside you at this moment, little one."

"I pray for someone else, mother."

Before she could reply, a Hunkpapa herald rode past, calling out his announcements.

"Our friends the Cheyenne are very poor now. Every man, woman, and child who has a robe, a blanket, or a lodge to share with our guests, bring it to the center of camp."

A renewed bustling of activity overtook the busy village as the sun sank far to the west and the air grew chilled. Slowly the Cheyenne herded toward the center of the great encampment, eventually joined by many Hunkpapa women and girls bearing gifts in their arms. Instead of sadness now, the Lakotas were replacing cold hearts with happy celebration. Monaseetah watched a Sioux warrior lay a medicine pipe at the feet of Wooden Leg's father to replace one lost in the soldier attack. At her own feet a young Hunkpapa girl laid a buffalo robe.

The Sioux women called out, ready to donate a needed item.

"I have a blanket. Who needs it?"

The Cheyenne answered.

"Here! My family needs it, and a robe."

Blankets, parfleches filled with dried meat, clothing,

and even spare lodges, all were passed among the weary travelers. Even ponies from the great Hunkpapa herd.

"We must never forget this day, my sons," Monaseetah whispered, her voice cracking, eyes moistening as she looked over the excitement of the bustling camp.

"Never forget that the soldiers drove us into the snow!" Sees Red hissed, his fist slamming into the palm of the other hand.

"No. We must never forget the generosity of Sitting Bull's people."

"If we had it to give, we would help them—wouldn't we, mother?" the youngest asked.

"Yes, Yellow Bird. Some day, perhaps, we will have the chance to return what they have done for us."

"And some day soon, as Scabby has vowed," said Sees Red as he plopped atop of the folded buffalo robe before them, "we will return what the white man has done for us."

Directed by the Bull's camp police, the visitors moved off to an assigned flat of smooth ground, where they erected their camp. Every family had a lodge now. Although most were small, they were shelter against the great cold and the capricious snows that always visited this high land just before the coming of the short-grass time.

The young Southern Cheyenne mother stood outside, appraising her lodge, faint smoke climbing from the spiral of poles. "This will do until I get some hides for making us a larger home."

"I will hunt for you, mother."

"Thank you, Sees Red. Some day you and Yellow Bird both will hunt buffalo for me . . . the way my father hunted the great beasts. For now I will have to find some gifts to give the men we will ask to hunt cows for us."

"Give me the chance!"

She laughed easily, pulling Sees Red into her arms. "Soon enough you will have a chance at all things, my son."

Then Monaseetah gazed over her shoulder at Yellow Bird. And some of the bright smile left her beautiful face. "Soon enough you both will grow up and have to do all those things a man does."

CHAPTER 5

For six sleeps Sitting Bull, Gall, and Crazy Horse held council with Two Moon and the head men of the Northern Cheyenne bands. During those days of argument and agreement, posturing and wrangling, Lame Deer's large band of Miniconjou came in, fleeing their agency but wanting no trouble with the white man.

All agreed with Sitting Bull that the best approach to take was to stay out of the soldiers' path.

For years the Hunkpapa chief had refused to live on the agency or to have contact with the white man. He had no need of government traders. Everything necessary for the old life of his people was to be found on the plains, in their nomadic existence following the herds: hides for lodges, all the food needed by the bands, and complete, unfettered freedom. Slowly and sadly most of the tribal leaders had come to understand the wisdom of the Bull's philosophy.

Their great council determined the bands should move northward, farther still from the soldiers who had marched out of the south. That morning after their sixth sleep among the Hunkpapas, the Cheyennes pulled out, leading the great procession toward the next stream they would find flowing into the Powder from the east. Because it was the Shahiyena the soldiers were looking for, all had agreed the Shahiyena should be first in the line of march. Wary young riders roamed far ahead and on both flanks of the procession.

Since the Oglalla of Crazy Horse had been the closest of friends with the Cheyenne, their band marched directly behind Two Moon's people. Then came the Miniconjous. Bringing up the tail were the Hunkpapas of Sitting Bull. His warriors acted as a rear guard, constantly on the watch for any soldier columns following the trail of their march. The growing procession now numbered almost 250 lodges.

Due to the poor condition of their winter-gaunt ponies, they moved slowly from camp to camp each day. At their three-sleep camp on a tributary of the Powder, the Sans Arcs added their lodge circle to the great village. Each day a handful of Hunkpapa, Oglalla, or Miniconjou families abandoning the reservations would join up.

By the time the Cheyennes pointed the march west by northwest, the entire procession numbered more than four hundred lodges. The next sleep brought them to another creek feeding the Powder River. It was here that the new grass was seen poking its head through the skiffs of old snow and muddy earth. Now near the end of the Moon of Ducks Coming Back, the people rejoiced. Winter was behind them, and the time when their ponies would grow strong had come at last.

The young herder boys busied themselves during the longer hours of sunlight, moving the swelling herds several times each day, working hard to prevent the hungry ponies from ranging too far from the six lodge circles. Six, for it was here that the Blackfeet Sioux joined the march. Here too a few lodges of the Santee added their count to the swelling encampment. Poor in the way of horses, the Santee employed big dogs to drag their property over the prairie to join up with Sitting Bull's people.

At an encampment on the Powder, Lame White Man brought in his large band of Southern Cheyenne to join Two Moon's circle. It was a time of rejoicing for Monaseetah, Scabby, and Rolls Down, seeing old friends from long-ago times in the southlands, here together again in the country where the water ran cold and sweet. Here where they could roam free once more. Free, were it not for the persistent reports from the newcomers that soldiers were moving in force. Almost every day word was brought by the new arrivals that the army was on the march—from the west, the east, and the south.

"Where are we to go, mother?" Yellow Bird asked one evening as twilight brought a purple glow to the bluffs overlooking their camp beside the Powder. Fires dotted the long necklace of camp circles hugging the creek bank, lodges lit like smudged, yellowed lanterns.

For a moment she looked up at the ridges above Mitzpah Creek before answering, stirring the antelope and bone-meal stew in her battered kettle. "We can only go north—if the white man drives us there."

"North?" Sees Red asked, wiping his mouth free of grease with the back of his hand. He had been sucking on a long sliver of antelope back fat. "There is nothing up there except the Grandmother's Land."

"Grandmother's?"

"Yes, Yellow Bird," she answered, reluctantly. "Sees Red is right. It is a country where the Grandmother across the big water rules her red-coated soldiers."

"Instead of the white Grandfather who rules his blue-coated pony soldiers in our land," Sees Red added.

"You have seen this place, mother?"

"No I haven't," Monaseetah replied.

"But some of my friends have told me the Indians roam free and live in peace there," Sees Red said.

She sighed. "Perhaps."

"Perhaps we should go there, mother. Hunt the buffalo as my grandfather did!"

Monaseetah smiled at Yellow Bird's enthusiasm, then rubbed both their heads. "It is not an easy thing leaving the land where you were born, going far from all that you know."

Nearing the country surrounding the great Elk River—what the white man called the Yellowstone River—the Chey-

enne turned the point of their march almost due west in
that first week of the Moon of First Eggs. Hunting parties
were out nearly every day of the march, bringing into each
evening's camp the pack animals burdened with the fresh
meat the thousands of hungry mouths required. As the sun
sank and kettles stewed, the social life of the great encampment was set in motion. Young men courted the shy girls by
waiting along the path leading to water or by playing love
songs on their ash flutes. Families hosted dinners for guests
from other camp circles. There were contests and games of
chance and councils, horse trading and horse giving.

No one could remember ever seeing an encampment so
large. It was a time to remember, all of them living life in
the old way. Roaming free, hunting the great and small
animals. Loving and fighting, courting and mating according to the dictates of the centuries gone before in time. A
time now back in their hands to hold.

Most rejoiced. A few despaired, wondering when the
idyll would end. Knowing it must, one day come that
summer.

At the camp where the Four Horn River flows into the
Tongue, another large band of Cheyenne joined Two
Moon's circle. Dirty Moccasins had led his people west
from their reservation, up the Powder and over the divide
down to Otter Creek, where they found sign of the great
encampment. There was cause for celebration as the
newcomers distributed gifts of tobacco, powder, sugar, and
coffee from the reservation.

And every day more and more young men rode in from
the agencies, bringing word of the concentrations and
movement of troops. Most of these bachelors had no family
with them, nor a lodge. Instead the young ones spread
blankets and hides over the willow thickets, forming small
shelters for themselves beside the creek. With the rising of
each sun, warriors departed the great village, their pack
animals laden with dressed buffalo furs not needed for
replacing old lodges, heading back to the agencies and the
white traders where they would buy guns and bullets.

Everyone was busy—man, woman, and child. If the
village was not on the march, then all were at work or at

play. Enjoying the warming of the season, the lengthening of the days, awaiting the evenings of rest and of fun.

White Cow Bull was older than many of the other Oglalla bachelors who had been camped with the Cheyennes when the soldiers attacked Two Moon's camp in the Sore-Eye Moon. He had been a faithful follower of He Dog for some years now, one of the most decorated of Crazy Horse's warriors. While he hungered to even the score with the soldiers for their bloody robbery over the past winters, White Cow Bull hungered ever as much for a companion.

It was time, he decided, to find a wife. Time to begin a family of his own.

Trouble was, the woman his thoughts persistently returned to was not Oglalla. A sensuous, liquid-eyed beauty he had first talked with when he arrived at Two Moon's camp of Cheyennes. She herself had journeyed north with a handful of southern emigrants.

The fact that she already had two young sons by two different fathers was nothing to deter the older White Cow Bull. He told her he would not mind calling her sons his own when he had wed the Cheyenne wildcat.

Trouble was, she had spurned White Cow Bull's every advance. His words of affection, his waiting for her by the creek. His offering to supply meat for her lodge or to take the boys hunting. She had even paid no attention when he played his flute outside her lodge each evening while shadows deepened and lovers coupled throughout the great encampment.

Time and again Monaseetah had told him she was waiting on the return of her second husband, the father of her second child. He had promised to come back for her, she told White Cow Bull. She would wait for him.

Disturbing as her declaration was, more so was the rumor whispered among the Northern Cheyenne camp that Monaseetah's second husband, Yellow Bird's father, was not only a soldier—he was a pony-soldier chief.

Still, there was something about the woman that refused every one of White Cow Bull's efforts to shake the thought of her from his mind. She stayed with him even after the drums quieted and all that he heard was the buzz of the mosquitoes and the murmur of the creek beside his blanket-covered wickiup. As if she had been burned onto his mind, disturbing not only his waking hours, but making his sleep tormented and fitful.

Dreams of making love to her, hot and damp mating, interrupted by the nightmarish blare of bugles and the shouts of white pony soldiers charging into camp. In each dream White Cow Bull found himself left to suffer the agony, the indignity, of Monaseetah leaping from their bed, running half-naked into the midst of those white horsemen, screaming out, calling for her Yellow Hair.

White Cow Bull bolted upright on his blanket bed, swiping the damp moisture from his eyes, shivering with a cool breeze moving its gentle breath along the creek bank. Another night troubled.

Again he dragged the Winchester repeater into his lap and found nearby the oiled cloth he kept handy. Working the oil over and around and in and out of the action. Again and again . . .

White Cow Bull promised himself he would be ready.

"A few young Oglalla have reported spotting some Sparrowhawk scouts," said Scabby as he dropped the rear quarter of elk at Monaseetah's fire.

Her eyes narrowed on him. "Sparrowhawk scouts. Which means?"

"They are scouting for the soldiers." His eyes followed the two boys as they sauntered up to the evening fire to hear the warrior's news. "Seen up on Elk River a week ago. Must be a large army of them to hire so many Sparrowhawks to be their eyes and ears."

She slowly stirred the blood broth she was brewing in the battered kettle. "They have been watching us since Ash Creek?"

"Yes," he answered, kneeling to accept her proffered taste of the broth from her horn spoon. "This is good, Monaseetah." He licked his lips. "Your father and mother would be proud of you."

"Tell us more of the soldiers, Scabby." Sees Red pushed forward. "And their Sparrowhawk spies!"

He laughed in a gush of sound, like the wind rattling through dried cottonwood. "Many of the young men,

Lakota and Cheyenne both, hunger to go after the Sparrowhawks. To teach them a lesson."

"They should not be the eyes and ears of the pony soldiers!"

Scabby jabbed a finger at Sees Red, chuckling again. "Yes! But Sitting Bull has his police constantly moving in and around this great camp"—and he swung the arm and horn spoon in a wide arc—"to be sure no one leaves to fight the Sparrowhawks until it is time."

"Will it be time soon?"

He studied Yellow Bird's face. "I am afraid so." But a smile crossed his face. "One of these days real soon, these soldiers and their scouts are going to poke a stick into a hornet's nest."

"And we will sting them sure!" Sees Red cheered, spreading his arms and flapping them like a maddened insect in flight. He and Yellow Bird both danced off, spinning about and buzzing loudly as they scurried into the cottonwoods bordering their camping spot here on the east bank of the Rosebud, some eight miles above its mouth in the Elk River.

Scabby watched them go and sighed before his eyes found Monaseetah staring into the bubbling scum on the top of the blood broth she slowly stirred.

"Why does the Bull not want the young ones to go fight the Sparrowhawks?" she finally asked.

The smile drained from his face. "He says the energy of our men should be put to hunting, to feed our families. The size of our villages are for defense against the army only. To be sure, no soldier-chief is foolish enough to attack us."

"We are where we should be?"

"The white man's own treaty says it, Monaseetah. This is Indian land—when he took the Paha Sapa from us all. This is the last of the great hunting grounds where we and the Lakota can find all that we need."

She looked at him finally. "The last?"

"That is why I chose to bring my family north with the others two winters ago—when you came looking for the one you seek. Because none of us can live the old way in the south. There are no more buffalo there. The great herds we once hunted with the Kiowa are gone. White hide hunters have worked many summers, so now the beasts' bones bleach in the sun on the great southern plains. Only here can we find the buffalo and elk, the deer and the curious, funny goats with their white tails flagging us in farewell when we miss our shots!"

She stirred for a long time, so long that Scabby grew restless and rose to his feet, itching to return to his own lodge.

"Wait, my friend," she asked. "Tell me more."

He knelt again, whispering. "What is it you want to know, little one?"

"Tell me of Charcoal Bear. Is it true he has brought the Medicine Hat?"

Scabby could not hide that smile of his, gapped as it was with rotten teeth he had pulled in the past two winters. "Yes, Charcoal Bear is a great medicine talker of the Northern Cheyenne. He is keeper of the Hat. And he brought ten lodges with him, besides the sacred medicine lodge where the Fox soldiers guard the Hat, night and day."

"This Hat, I have heard tell, is as sacred to these Northern Cheyenne as our Arrows are to our people in the south."

"It is so, little one. Therefore, there is much reason for celebrating and good feelings now in camp," he explained, arms swinging expansively. "The Lakota have their great medicine man, The Bull, guiding them. And now we have the Buffalo Hat to watch over us."

"No harm will come to this great camp now, will it?"

"No."

Her eyes gazed at his a long time before she finally asked. "But that does not stop the soldiers from trying, Scabby. Our strength never stopped them from trying."

CHAPTER 6

FROM their first camp on Rosebud Creek, the great village moved upstream to camp below a low, pink-tinged peak known to them as Teat Butte. It was here at this campground ten summers before that a Cheyenne woman had walked away from her lodge and her newborn child three days after giving birth and hanged herself in the hills. Talk rumbled among the Shahiyena again of that powerful act of suicide among one of their own people.

For days on end at this camp, the men and women crossed the stream to hunt the sizable herds of buffalo found on the west bank. It was here too that almost every day an old herald rode through the lodge circles with new reports of Sparrowhawk scouts spying on their great village. A band of Northern Cheyenne warriors, the Crazy Dogs, strutted and crowed, bragging that they would go after the Sparrowhawks, no matter that Sitting Bull's police would attempt stopping them.

After building a huge bonfire and painting their naked bodies, the Crazy Dogs began their war dances, barefoot among the prickly-pear cactus and scrub sage. Just as the dancing grew feverish before a large crowd of hundreds drawn to the hypnotic call of the old-men drummers, the herald returned to the camp circle, announcing that his report had been in error. A rumor only. No new information on the Sparrowhawks.

Dejected and disappointed, their feathers preened and their weapons oiled, the Crazy Dogs had no choice but to allow their bonfire to go out. And with it the sudden flare of war fever among the Cheyenne.

From the Teat they marched up the Rosebud to Green Leaf Creek, congratulating themselves in the fact that the herds of antelope and buffalo had not been disturbed by the movement of the army through the countryside. Everyone believed it was a good omen—one that meant the soldiers must surely be headed away from the area. If not that, then surely the animal spirits would have become unsettled. Instead the beasts had waited for the people of the earth to come to them in the great hunts.

After using the murky, yellowed waters of the Rosebud for many days, the clear, cold water of the Green Leaf was welcomed by all. As was the water flowing down Lame Deer Creek, where the next camp was established.

Early one morning, as he sat sullen and lonely on the bank of the Rosebud, Yellow Bird had been dragged away by some young Hunkpapa boys to play shinny-ball with them. He did not have to think long on it: stay on the bank watching the others, who ignored him, fish for the pink-and-white fish in the river; or go with the Hunkpapa boys for a rough-and-tumble game of skill and speed brought to the Cheyenne years ago by the Lakota.

A thin Sioux boy named Wind, not much taller than Yellow Bird, loaned his Cheyenne guest a short, curved stick he would use in the game the Hunkpapas called "knocking the ball." Before he knew it, Yellow Bird was chosen to be on the thin boy's team and was in a matter of moments in the midst of the madness that was the game.

Both teams fought for possession of a flattened ball made of deer hide and stuffed with buffalo hair, striking the ball and their opponents with the curved sticks. Yelling and grunting and sweating and rolling in the yellow dust—it was all part of the chase by both teams to drive the ball down the two-hundred-yard-long space of ground they had chosen for their playing field.

His lungs heaving with the high, dry air of these northern plains, Yellow Bird finally approached the end of the field marked by two mounds of dirt in which the players had driven tall stakes with streamers of trade cloth attached. It was between these two mounds that Wind's team was attempting to drive the ball. Closer and closer the flags loomed toward Yellow Bird as the opposing team seemed to swarm, growing in numbers as both sides neared the goal.

Then suddenly Wind was hollering, his mouth a small oval in his bony face. "Yellow Bird! Run on!"

Yellow Bird had no warning, no chance to prepare for what happened next as Wind drove the ball toward the Cheyenne youth just as half a dozen of the opposing team swarmed on top of Wind, burying him in a swirl of dust and sage, bloody cuts and bruises.

The ball sped toward Yellow Bird.

He looked from it for an instant, watching the entire field of play suddenly swerve in his direction, following the ball. It seemed the entire world was bearing down on him as he tore his eyes from the others and turned the ball with his stick.

Into the soft yellow dirt he dug his bare toes, gritting his teeth against his stinging lungs, and tore off, scuffing the ball before him as far as he dared, drawing closer and closer to the right-hand flag. With every step it seemed the other, bigger boys came closer to him as well, eating ground on him with every one of their long strides. The way things looked to Yellow Bird, none of them were the least bit intent on the ball. They appeared to be concentrating on him.

Smaller, perhaps a bit quicker, he dodged the first two and skirted the third, finding himself less than thirty feet from the flag. His ears filled with the mad cheers of his teammates and the curses of his opponents, Yellow Bird brought his stick back, ready to drive the first goal past the stake. He flung the ball forward.

Yellow Bird felt the breath driven out of him as if by the huge hand of a grizzly, pummeling him forward through the air several feet, landing on his belly and nose. As he crawled to his hands and knees, shaking the cobwebs from his mind, spitting dirt from his mouth and sensing the warmth and wetness dribbling down the back of his neck, he became conscious of the shrieking of the boys behind him.

Warily he turned at the commotion, his head ringing, then collapsed a moment in the dust. As he cleared his eyes, he noticed several of the older boys scuffling, kicking, and gouging. At the center of it all was Wind. All round the combatants swirled more of the boys, cheering their heroes and jeering the hoped-for losers.

As Yellow Bird clambered to his feet and lumbered into the moving crowd, it became apparent to him that Wind and another boy from Wind's team were outnumbered and badly taking the short end of the scuffle.

"Wait up there," said a husky Sioux boy as he snagged Yellow Bird's arm, keeping the small Cheyenne from joining the fray.

"I must go help. They are fighting over me."

The older boy smiled quickly with a neat row of teeth. "They likely are, little Cheyenne. But with that knock you took on the back of your head, you are in no shape to go asking to lose some more blood."

"It is my fight, not theirs!" he yelled, ripping his arm from the Sioux.

"You have fire, little Cheyenne," he said with admiration, then laughed. "Here, together we will both even the odds!"

Together they dived into the skirmish, punching and jabbing, pulling the bigger youths off Wind and his friend until there were none left who wished to continue the scuffle. In a matter of moments, the big Sioux boy had soundly bounced heads together so that all the attackers sat on the ground, holding their wounds and spitting dirt from their lips.

"It's not fair!" one of the biggest and bloodiest of Wind's attackers shouted. Many of the others on his team agreed. "You are not even Hunkpapa, are you?"

"I am Miniconjou. Black Horse's band."

"You cannot play!"

The Miniconjou youth laughed. Yellow Bird liked the

way he threw his head back and showed his tonsils. As if he really enjoyed laughing as easily as it came to him.

"I was not playing, little foolish one. I was trying to end the fight so you would go back to playing shinny."

"It was none of your affair!" another youth groaned.

"You keep shoving against me, it will become my affair all over again," the Miniconjou warned.

"Perhaps we will make it your affair now!" a brave Hunkpapa hissed.

"You!" Wind pushed up against the Hunkpapa boy, wiping the blood that dribbled down his chin with a dusty hand and licking the split lip with the tip of his tongue. "You were the one who hit the little Cheyenne on the back of the head. That is why I jumped you. And that is why I will stand beside the little Cheyenne and this big Miniconjou horse."

Wind smiled at both the big youth and Yellow Bird.

"We should go back to playing shinny," grumped one of the opposing players. "If the little Cheyenne wants to play with us, he must expect that we play hard."

"But we have vowed never to hit with our sticks above the shoulders," Wind reminded. "Is your word not worth a Hunkpapa's vow?"

Some of the others hung their heads, grumbling. Finally one of them glanced at the offender who had bloodied Yellow Bird. He spoke up.

"It was not right. This is a game we play. A hard game," he said, then turned to Yellow Bird. "But we do not mean to hurt anyone in our play."

"There!" Wind cheered. And he grabbed Yellow Bird's arm, raising it to the sky as a half-dozen horsemen loped onto their playing field. "And the little Cheyenne's goal counts as well!"

"G-goal?" Yellow Bird stammered, still blinking the dust from his eyes.

"Looks that way to me too," said the Miniconjou boy. More of Wind's team cheered, jumping and shouting as the horsemen reined up in their midst, scattering dust over them all.

"You boys must end your play now," declared one of the

horsemen, from the red band on his left arm, clearly one of Sitting Bull's camp police, the *akicita*.

"And who are you to stop our play?" Wind demanded, puffing out his ribby chest.

The horseman laughed with the others. "Little brother, I am today's chief of the camp guard. Besides, I am your big brother—the one who will whip your ears to your chin if you do not heed my orders."

"But why do you stop us?" asked the big Miniconjou, cocking his head.

The horseman regarded him a moment. "The medicine dance of the Hunkpapas begins now." He pointed to the sun rising full off the bluffs to the east. "The dancers are coming forth from the sweat lodge now. It will not be long until they hang themselves from the great tree of life."

"We must go see this!" Wind said, excitement cracking the sweaty dust on his face.

"I hear Sitting Bull himself will dance!" cheered another of the boys as the horsemen reined away toward the creek bank.

"We must see this great medicine man hang himself from the spirit tree, making his prayers to Wakan Tanka," Wind said, pulling Yellow Bird and the Miniconjou with him, hurrying toward camp.

"Who is this Wakan Tanka you speak of?"

"It is the Great Mystery, Yellow Bird," the Miniconjou answered. "You call him the Great Everywhere Spirit. He is ours too."

"And who would you be?" Wind asked, turning on the Miniconjou boy.

"Me?" he asked, then laughed that roar of his again, slapping his muscular chest. "I am Ghost. Son of High Pipe, in Black Horse's band."

"The old Miniconjou chief?"

He nodded as they hurried, joining the growing, swelling crowds moving south, upstream along the bank of the Rosebud toward the sun-dance arbor not far from the carved rocks, where the ancient ones had painted their long-ago symbols.

"He may be an old man, Wind. But Black Horse took many scalps that glorious day of the Battle of the Hundred in the Hand. His stories of killing every last soldier sent against our people will make the hair stand on the back of your neck!"

"Eeeyiii!" Wind replied, slapping Ghost on the shoulder. "I want to hear these stories, my new friend. In their telling you best include Yellow Bird of the Southern Cheyenne. It is always good to hear these things, the sort of talk that will make our hearts swell in pride!"

Yellow Bird had never seen such a gathering for the medicine dance, in the south or in his two summers now in the north country. No one could recall ever seeing such a powerful sacrifice. Nor would they ever again. This day would not only touch the lives of those who witnessed its great mystery, but it was to live on in the hearts of all the plains tribes, spoken on the tongues of the people with great reverence across the generations to come.

A Hunkpapa virgin had selected the Prayer Tree, swatting it four times before young men cut it down and carried it back to the Rosebud camp on poles as if it were truly the body of a respected warrior. After an elaborate dedication and painting ceremony, the tree was planted in a hole in the ground, then a bed of white sage laid at its base. On a nearby altar a buffalo skull rested, its empty eye sockets looking to the east. A long-stemmed medicine pipe stood before the earthen altar.

This great summer the Prayer to the Sun was conducted by Black Moon, hand picked by Sitting Bull as the great Hunkpapa mystic was himself going to be chief of the dancers, having vowed to make his sacrifice at this critical time in the life of his people. As were all such sacrifices, this year would be a profound religious experience not only for the dancers, but for the spectators as well. The vision experienced by Sitting Bull would be cause for celebration, inspiring the hopes for the people, bringing them great resolve to resist the white man and his ways.

"The bravest and the purest among our people sacrifice themselves on the Prayer Tree," Wind explained in a whisper to Yellow Bird.

"It is a renewal of our faith, a unifying force among our many peoples," Ghost added in the Cheyenne's other ear.

"This is surely like what my people call the New Life

Lodge, where the dancers tie themselves to the pole," replied Yellow Bird in awe, watching the first of the Hunkpapa warriors rise from the base of the pole, the rawhide tethers lashed to skewers poked beneath the muscles of his bloody chest.

"Sitting Bull is there," Wind said, pointing out the great chief seated on the ground at the base of the monstrous pole, at the center of the greatest of all dance arbors. "He had danced to the Sun many times. If ever you see the man close, you will recognize the scars on both his chest and back."

"He has hung himself many times?" Ghost asked.

"Yes. Many times has he prayed and made a vow. Then offered himself to the Sun," Wind whispered in reply. "But just before last winter, Sitting Bull made a powerful promise—that if we Hunkpapas were allowed to live for another year in peace, far from the white man, he vowed he would offer up his very own flesh to the Sun."

"H'gun!" Ghost exclaimed, using the Lakota expression for admiration.

Already one of the Bull's arms hung bloodied, having sacrificed fifty small bits of flesh to the Great Mystery. Now the medicine man Jumping Bull worked on the second arm with a sharp awl and a small stone knife. One hundred bits of skins lay at the foot of the Sun's pole. Flesh given over in prayer and sacrifice, in thanksgiving. Beginning at the wrist and working all the way to the shoulder, Jumping Bull used the awl to puncture the skin, lifting it free of the flesh below. With the knife he would then slice off that small section of flesh.

Fifty times up each arm the long, agonizing process was repeated, while Sitting Bull sat before the Prayer Tree, never flinching nor crying out. Once both arms had been sacrificed and the blood flowed freely, it was time to dance.

Slowly he rose, to stand with the others lashed in prayer to the pole, each man staring at the sun in quest of a vision. For the rest of that day and through the night, Sitting Bull danced. Past the second sunrise and into the climbing of the new sun to its zenith.

It was then that Sitting Bull appeared to grow faint. His eyes half closed, the whites rolled back while his knees buckled and he collapsed in the smooth, pounded dirt at the base of the Prayer Tree.

"Sitting Bull is visiting the Other Side now," Wind whispered, nudging Ghost on one side of him, Yellow Bird on the other. All three were napping in a patch of shade near the dance arbor, keeping a vigil with the rest who stayed day and night to watch the prayer givers.

"I don't understand," Yellow Bird said, rubbing the grit at his eyes.

"Sitting Bull is gone from this life now," Ghost explained, scooping up four handfuls of dirt and tossing them into the air as he spoke. "For a while his eyes will be blinded to this world, so that he may see into the next."

"See into the world of the dead?" Yellow Bird found himself more than a little frightened.

Ghost nodded, his face ashen as he witnessed the rare occurrence. "Sitting Bull is visiting the Great Mystery and all those gone before—to talk of the future."

CHAPTER 7

"B LACK Moon walked to the center of the ring, right to the base of the great pole after Sitting Bull had whispered his vision in Black Moon's ear," gushed Yellow Bird, excited, watching the widening eyes of those who listened to his story.

"What was his vision, nephew?" Scabby inquired.

"Yes! Tell us!" Sees Red agreed.

"While he journeyed away from the land of the living, a voice from the Great Above called out to Sitting Bull."

For a moment Yellow Bird stopped, his eyes slowly going to his mother's face. Instead of sheer excitement he found written in her eyes a magical wonder, awe. And for that moment the boy was certain she alone understood what had happened to Sitting Bull when he talked to the Great Mystery.

"Tell us, my son," she said in a low voice. "Tell us what the voice told the Hunkpapa chief."

He swallowed, licking his lips that had been dry from the moment he first heard the announcement, during his mad dash through all five intervening camp circles to reach the Cheyenne village, there to search out his family and friends, burning to give word of this wondrous thing he had witnessed with his own eyes!

"The voice told him, *I give you these because they have no ears.*'"

Sees Red drew back, disbelief on his face. "That's all?"

Yellow Bird shook his head. "Then Sitting Bull looked up, to where the voice had come from—and saw against the pale sky hundreds of falling soldiers and Indians on horseback—"

"Cavalry!" Scabby shouted. "*Aiyeee!* It is a good omen—I know it!"

"The soldiers and Indians were falling like grasshoppers into our camps!" Yellow Bird got it all out in a rush as if he had been holding his breath for days. "Heads down—that was important, Black Moon told the crowd."

"Yes! Heads down means they are defeated by us, Yellow Bird," Scabby said.

"Cavalry?" Monaseetah asked, almost absently, only half listening now.

"Yes, mother! Offered to us and to the Lakota."

"Our prayers have been answered!" Scabby shouted, leaping to his feet by the fire pit outside his lodge. While his two wives and three daughters clapped, the old warrior danced round and round in a swirl of dust and joy.

"Too long we have waited," said Talks Last, the oldest wife. "Through the killing at Sand Creek."

"And the killing along the Washita," Sees Red added, joining Scabby in an exuberant, shuffling dance of joy.

"Not only . . . but Summit Springs as well," Talks Last replied. "It is our people who will finally win."

"Cavalry coming," Monaseetah repeated, her eyes climbing beyond the tips of the lodgepoles aswirl above them. "Coming to our camps, my sons."

"Yes, mother!" Sees Red screamed it, grabbing Monaseetah's hands, pulling her up to dance with him, spinning her in a wild circle. "Soon!"

"My prayers have been answered!" she raised her face to the sky.

"You have prayed for us to kill the soldiers?" Talks Last asked.

"No," she shook her head, coming to a stop. "I have prayed for the return of one soldier. It is the Moon of Fat Horses. It is the time for his coming."

Scabby pulled away from the others suddenly, kneeling beside Yellow Bird, raising as he did a small cloud of dust that hot midday in the shade of his old lodge beside the cool flow of the Rosebud.

"Tell me, nephew. Did Sitting Bull say anything else?"

The boy nodded. "Later, after he had taken water on his tongue, he warned the others."

Sees Red stopped his humming, stopped pounding on his belly with a drumbeat and hurried to his brother's shoulder. "A warning? For the soldiers?"

"No, a warning from the Hunkpapa's Great Mystery. He said, *These dead soldiers who are coming are the gifts of God. Kill them, but do not take their guns or horses. Do not touch these spoils. If you set your hearts upon the goods of the white man, it will prove a curse to this nation.*'"

He tore his eyes from Sees Red's face, looked at Scabby, then his mother. Monaseetah slowly closed her eyes as the tears welled within them.

It was the old warrior who spoke first. "Truly this is the most powerful medicine I have heard of in my time, to the time of my father's grandfather. We are given this victory—to keep our way of life pure for all our assigned days. Not to take anything of the white man from the battlefield—for it will pollute our hearts, the very soul of our nations."

"Not even his guns, old man?"

"No, Sees Red—no one should take the soldiers' clothing, his boots, not even his horses and guns."

"But his guns will allow us to kill more soldiers who come after—there will always be soldiers coming."

Scabby shook his head violently. "No, you are not understanding, for perhaps you are still a child inside." He tapped his chest with a finger still bloody from skinning an antelope. "If we do as we are told by the Everywhere Spirit, we will never have to fight the soldiers again. This is his final offering to us—for all the years of suffering by our people. The soldiers, offered up in sacrifice—as Sitting Bull has offered his flesh in sacrifice to the power of the Sun."

"You believe this is what is asked of us, Scabby?" Monaseetah finally spoke.

"Yes." He scooped up some dust into his palm, slowly letting it trickle out. "To survive—so that we will not dry up as a people and blow away with the dust, we must stay away from the white man and all things of the white man." He blew the last of the dust from his palm.

"Why do you keep coming here when my mother does not want you to court her?" Sees Red demanded of the warrior who had settled himself in the shade near Monaseetah's lodge.

"I still wish to talk with her," White Cow Bull answered, pulling up a stalk of grass. "If she does not want me for a husband, that does not stop me from wanting her for a wife, little Cheyenne."

"Aren't there any pretty Oglalla women?"

The warrior looked over at the young face of Yellow Bird. "There are many pretty women among my people. But, alas," he sighed, "none so beautiful as your mother. She has captured my heart."

"I think the closeness between our two peoples has made your mind soft," Sees Red grumbled. "Thinking about women, when you should be thinking of war against the soldiers."

He laughed easily. Yellow Bird liked that about the warrior. The way he liked Wind and Ghost, and their easy laughter.

"Time enough for fighting, little Cheyenne warrior." He jabbed a finger at Sees Red, who sprang back. "Never enough time for love in a man's life. Other men will always bring war to your camp, don't you see? It is up to you and you only to bring love into your life."

"Why is it that you want my mother?"

"I have told you she is the most beautiful flower I have ever seen—in the mountains or on the prairie."

"No, White Cow Bull. Why do you want a woman who does not want you—want a woman you cannot have?"

He smiled, sadly. "I am cursed, you know. Ever since I was a boy like you, I have wanted what I could not have. That is why I still have not taken a wife, why I have still not fathered any children." He gazed longingly at the shady door of Monaseetah's lodge. "But if I wanted any less a woman, I would probably love her less as well."

The oldest boy placed his small, balled fists on his hips, daringly. "My mother has told you she is waiting for Yellow Bird's father to return for her?"

For a long moment he regarded Sees Red, then gazed at the younger brother. "Yes. But I have promised myself that I will wait until she finally realizes that the soldier chief is not going to return to her."

"He will!" shouted the smallest Cheyenne, leaping to his feet, furious. "I know he will!"

Yellow Bird swung a tiny fist at the Oglalla. It was caught in the warrior's grasp, held while the little Cheyenne kicked wildly, flaying away at the man's shins.

"All right . . . all right, little warrior. I will wait with you and your mother—"

All three turned at the shouts coming from the north end of the Cheyenne camp, farthest up the Rosebud, in the direction of their march. The Shahiyena were the first circle in the great and growing procession crawling across the northern plains that early summer. In the next moment a half-dozen young Cheyenne warriors burst into the lodge circle, howling like wolves.

"They have spotted soldiers!" White Cow Bull exclaimed, releasing Yellow Bird's tiny hand, hurrying toward the commotion.

An old man, the camp herald, was clambering atop his old horse, urging it into the midst of the young warriors so that he could hear their news before spreading the report to this and the other camps.

"Soldiers have been seen!" His high, reedy voice raised itself above the hubbub of women trilling their tongues, men shouting their war songs, children screaming in excitement, and dogs yapping at the heels of all.

"Soldiers are coming in our direction. Indians are with them. The soldiers have Crow eyes and are coming down-river!"

White Cow Bull turned and lunged back at the boys, grabbing a shoulder of each in his hands. He bent to speak to their faces. "Tell your mother I was here."

"She knows," Sees Red said.

He released the boys. "Tell her I said it will not be long now that she will have to wait."

Yellow Bird called out to the warrior as White Cow Bull darted away. "Wait for what?"

The Oglalla shouted over his shoulder. "Wait for your father to return."

He plunged on through the excitement of the Cheyenne camp to snatch up the rawhide rein of his pony. In a fluid motion he was atop the animal, pulling it hard around and jabbing his heels into his ribs. It snorted, wild-eyed, leaping away at a gallop, heading for the Oglalla circle, next camp down the Rosebud.

He wanted to share this momentous news that came with all the charge of a summer thunderbolt with He Dog and Crazy Horse.

In the time it took the summer sun to travel the distance of one lodgepole to another, the excitement overtook the Oglalla camp. Like a prairie fire news of the coming soldier columns spread through the Miniconjou, Sans Arc, Blackfoot, and on to the Hunkpapa circles. Almost as quickly Sitting Bull and his head men dispatched their camp police to carry their instructions back upstream.

"Young men—leave the soldiers alone unless they attack us. These are the words of Sitting Bull."

These *akicita* rode through each camp, giving the order in the midst of the great excitement caused by news of soldiers. Here and there women had begun tearing down their lodges. Children scurried about searching for their mothers, dogs barked, and old ones called out for help. Older boys were intent on bringing ponies in from the herds. Older girls prepared travois for the move of that great encampment.

That afternoon White Cow Bull learned that the Cheyenne Little Hawk, who had led the scouting party that first spotted the soldiers, had gone out again in search of the white man. His group bumped into the soldier column and were turned away in a shower of bullets from Shoshone and Crow scouts with the army.

Above the valley of the Rosebud, the summer sky could wait no longer. After days of threatening, the swollen bellies of the gray clouds ruptured and poured rain on the countryside before Little Hawk and his warriors returned. The sky drizzled off and on for the next three days.

During the rain the village had moved another dozen miles south, up the Rosebud. Then from their camp at the mouth of a creek flowing out of the Wolf Mountains, the Cheyenne steered the great procession due west. The chiefs had decided they would hunt buffalo along the Greasy Grass of the Sioux, called the Goat River by the Cheyenne—marching slowly north along that steam, toward the Elk River, where the great antelope herds were said to be.

Still a third time Little Hawk did not heed Sitting Bull's admonishment against provoking the soldiers or their scouts. Instead the Cheyenne warriors kept a daily watch on the army columns moving north, without themselves being seen now.

The soldiers were coming, drawing ever closer. And unlike those cold days of the Sore-Eye Moon, this time the Cheyenne promised themselves they would be loaded for bear.

CHAPTER 8

LITTLE by little the camps had swelled with new arrivals from the agencies.

Not only the usual summer visitors who abandoned the reservations as soon as the grass grew tall enough, to spend the warm days living the old nomadic life. These were the bands who returned to the agencies when the first snow blew south out of the Grandmother's land. Better to eat the white man's sour meat and camp near his trading post than starve on the great plains like the winter roamers.

Even sons and fathers and uncles that spring left their families behind at the agencies to ride out alone or in groups, heading west to the Powder River country, to the Rosebud and on to the Greasy Grass. From Standing Rock and Spotted Tail, from Red Cloud's Pine Ridge and north on the Cheyenne River as well, they came this summer, lured not only by the camaraderie of a summer hunt in the old way, but this year spurred on by the rage they each shared with the white man's robbery of the sacred Black Hills. Many still bristled each time they talked of the government's sending its soldiers to attack the Cheyenne in the Sore-Eye Moon.

Because of that smoldering rage, the numbers of those leaving the agencies loaded down with guns and bullets swelled to record numbers. Not only were there more of them, but in this short-grass time there burned in each breast a fire requiring the cooling quench come only of revenge. There was a blood debt owed the people.

Besides the Cheyenne, Oglalla, and Hunkpapa, the encampment had swelled to overflowing with Santee, Blackfoot, and Sans Arc Sioux. In addition, many of the Brule bands had eventually wandered west to locate Sitting Bull. Even some bands of Arapaho had joined up in the recent weeks.

So when the young men dressed and painted and tied up the tails of their ponies for war, there were more warriors who rode out against General George "Red Beard" Crook than any of his soldiers had ever seen. It was a fine, sunny day there in the middle of that Moon of Fat Horses, a day when time stood captive above the Army of the West. Those warriors believed they could see no greater victory.

"They drove the soldiers and scattered all their Indian friends from the battlefield!" Sees Red shouted as he ran through the Cheyenne lodges, camped high up on the creek on the backbone of the Wolf Mountains that separated the Rosebud from the valley of the Greasy Grass.

Other boys were announcing the same thing as the victorious warriors were seen returning in the distance, waving their rifles, fresh scalps tied to some of the weapons.

Monaseetah heard the familiar voice of her oldest rise out of the mad clamor. She stood, wiping the fat and blood from her hands where she had been at butchering what was left of the deer carcass. No men had been hunting for days. At least hunting for game. The camps were badly in need of meat now. Now at least the men have returned, she thought.

And now there would be celebration. Making for even more need of meat.

She stopped herself, her hands wrapped round her braids, where she usually rubbed the fat to make her hair shine. She realized what she had been doing—consciously forcing out of her mind the thought of the soldiers and the fight and the dead left behind in every clash. Thinking only of food and celebration—when she should have been thinking instead of the soldier chief and—

"Yellow Bird!" she shouted above the noisy clamor.

He burst from the trees and willow along the creek. "Coming, mother! I heard, I heard. Isn't it wonderful news!"

She watched him come, kicking at the dogs nipping at the heels of the children spreading through camp with the excitement. Behind him were the two Sioux boys who had in these past four suns become constant companions to her youngest.

How different from them he is, she thought. How much better than the Cheyenne these Lakota treated her Yellow Bird.

She smiled. "Your friends can stay. We will have something to eat soon." Monaseetah turned to slice some more meat to broil on green limbs over the low flames of her fire.

"We want to go to Sitting Bull's camp, mother!" Yellow Bird announced, the two bigger boys at the young Cheyenne's shoulder.

She studied their faces, then Yellow Bird's, unable to deny him. "I suppose that is where there will be the most excitement, won't it?"

"Yes!" Wind answered. "Word was that a great dance will be held there tonight."

"There will be dances in all the camps," Ghost chided. "Yet you must remember, my little friends—our warriors have not yet won the battle Sitting Bull saw in his powerful vision."

"But we have won this battle!" shouted Sees Red as he swirled up in a dust cloud. "The soldiers have been defeated, and there are scalps to dance over!"

"Little Cheyenne," Ghost began, grabbing Sees Red's shoulder, "Sitting Bull said the soldiers would fall into our camp. This battle was won far from our camps."

"We will dance over the scalps anyway!" Sees Red tore away, hollering for some of his friends to wait up for him.

"Your brother—he refuses to believe," Wind said to Yellow Bird.

"No, he believes what he wants to believe. Sees Red wants a victory over the soldiers so badly that he will believe this is Sitting Bull's vision-victory."

"It is not," Monaseetah said quietly. She watched the three boys look back at her. "The biggest fight is yet to come."

She watched Ghost, the oldest, regarding her carefully. He spoke first. "A fight even bigger than this, with a victory for our peoples?"

"You must believe in Sitting Bull's visit to the land of the dead," she whispered, feeling her eyes growing hot and moist. "What he has promised will come to pass."

Among the Cheyenne there would always remain a special place of mystical reverence for the hermaphrodite—half man, half woman—among their people. *Hemaneh.*

As the victorious warriors neared the villages, the Cheyenne dropped off to the side where a half-dozen *hemaneh* stood waiting as was long the custom among their people.

From every bow and rifle, from belt and war pony's chin, now came the fresh scalps, handed down in obedience to the waiting *hemaneh*, who tied each scalp at the ends of long poles. Turning about, with the warriors in procession behind them, the parade of the scalps began. As the parade reached the outskirts of the Cheyenne camp, all came running. Old men and women, the lame and feeble as well as spry youngsters. Mothers and sisters and sweethearts too. All hurrying to see these young warriors with faces painted black for victory.

And on a drag behind his pony, Scabby lay wrapped in his blanket, his wounds tightly bound, eyes glazed in pain.

Monaseetah followed the quietly weeping Talks Last, not daring to step in to touch the old warrior, not daring to insult the kind man's two wives in their time of grief. Though for some time now she had considered herself part of Scabby's family, this was nonetheless a time of privacy for the warrior who seven winters before had taken Monaseetah and her first son under his wing once the soldiers had released the Cheyenne captives, returning them to their reservation.

She put on the best of smiles, watching the men carry

Scabby's blanket into the lodge, his wives and daughters fluttering about him like wrens on a huckleberry bush. Not needing Monaseetah. Perhaps even wishing her gone now.

Sniffling, dragging a bare arm under her nose, Monaseetah turned from the lodge. Her eyes filled, stinging.

To see the pain etched across that man's face the way wind scoured ice ridges on old snow was more than Monaseetah felt she could bear just then. Too much the excitement of the past days. The promise of soldiers coming to fulfill Sitting Bull's vision—then the actual report of an army's approach. And now the great victory, at the same time knowing still another group of soldiers was destined to fall into their combined camps.

The dance that evening found Monaseetah joining the others milling about, moving through the crowds, the two boys at her side. The air filled with the high-pitched trills of the women while the men yelped or boomed their deep voices. And behind everything was the insistent, nonstop beat of the drums. More than half a hundred of them. Old men drummers and the young ones learning to become proficient with the ancient songs. Chanting and beating and exclaiming the victory that was surely the beginning of what would be their most splendid hour.

She was careful to keep her eyes averted from the young bachelor warriors. To have come to this dance was a brave thing, she knew: not looking for a partner for herself—yet just her being here might be mistaken as a bold pronouncement to the village that at last she was receptive to courting.

With some misgivings Monaseetah had decided she would take this chance, willing to accept the wondering stares and the whispering behind her shoulder just so that in the many winters they would count in their lives, her boys could relive this grand celebration again and again. There might never be again so joyous a time, so wondrous a freedom as that which throbbed about them at this very moment.

After taking the scalp poles to the center of the village, where they were planted for all to see as the victorious warriors returned from battling the soldiers, the *hemaneh* had gone to each lodge, asking that wood be brought for the communal fire for the night's dancing. Twilight deepened as the fire leapt and crackled, shooting and hissing, occasionally exploding with a spurt of sparkling fireflies into the purple of dusk beneath the Wolf Mountains. Tomorrow the Cheyenne would lead the huge procession over the divide, starting down toward the beckoning green valley of the Greasy Grass.

Soon enough for that. Tonight was a time for celebration.

Most of those who had come to the dance, man, woman, and child, had painted their faces. Red for war. Black for victory. Some of the old drummers had even painted much of their sweating bodies. They wore no shirts, as did some of the women, who had blackened themselves from the waist up in provocative jubilation.

She gazed down at her two sons, proud that she had allowed them to decorate themselves with their own earth pigment mixed with back fat.

Dancers swirled and cavorted about the drummers gathered at the center of the camp circle until the drums stopped and the old camp herald announced it was time for a courting dance.

"You must do this, mother," Yellow Bird suggested quietly.

She shook her head, smiling. "I cannot, little one."

"Please, mother," Sees Red pleaded. "We have never seen you dance."

"This dance is for those who are happy."

"Aren't you happy, mother?"

She gazed at her youngest, looking at his face, and for a moment remembering the pale face of his father. "Yes, I suppose I should be happy. I have you both with me. You are my world now. And our people have won a great victory—"

"Then join the dance, mother!" squealed Yellow Bird.

"Go! Now!" Sees Red prodded, helping his brother push her toward the throbbing, pulsing center of it all.

"I cannot—"

"Dance!"

She giggled self-consciously as she stepped shyly across the pounded earth toward the long row of young women. Most were younger than she, now in her twenty-fifth summer. Still, there were but a handful who could compare with Monaseetah's beauty.

The young, hot-blooded bachelors, fresh from their fight, stood in a row facing north. Several yards away the women stood in a row as well, facing the men, looking to the south where the great victory had taken place. Now a *hemaneh* gave the order, and the old women and men shuffled forward, filling in the square on east and west with their garbled shouts of excitement and remembrance of their own youthful summers.

At the command of the *hemaneh*, the drummers started a slow beat, cue for the young men to begin, urged on by the shouts and cheers of the old ones, who clapped and yelped in joy. The bachelors shuffled forward, jostling, moving, swinging this way and that as they jockeyed in position coming ever closer to the line of women. Once there the young men inched behind the women's line, taking places behind a chosen sweetheart.

Feeling the press of someone behind her, Monaseetah turned, finding two young Cheyenne warriors shoving one another about, scrambling to be the one to dance with her. She looked away, embarrassed to find others staring. For a moment she bit her lower lip, considering leaving the dance, deciding to grab the boys and hurry back to her lodge.

But before she could free her rooted feet, Monaseetah heard two loud grunts behind her. She wheeled about, frightened.

Both young men lay sprawled on the ground. Some old women picked them from the dust, laughing and cackling at their misfortune. For an older Oglalla warrior stood now in their place, wiping his hands off on his leggings, moving toward Monaseetah with the widest of smiles.

"I have waited long for you to dance, pretty one," White Cow Bull whispered in the tongue of her people.

"I cannot dance with you," she stammered in reply. "I am waiting—"

"Dance with me while you wait then," he whispered in her ear as the drums picked up their beat, throbbing more insistently.

The lines of partners pounded the earth, sending shudders through the camp like wavelets on the big rivers lapping against the grassy banks. Hypnotic was the drumbeat. And the falling light. Along with the dusting of stars overhead. And his breath hot against her ear.

Monaseetah pulled away from his insistent lips, peering up into his dark eyes. "I will dance with you if you do not touch me."

White Cow Bull obediently dropped his hands from her shoulders.

"You must realize that I am waiting for one to return to me as he promised."

"In the Moon of Fat Horses," White Cow Bull reminded. "You have told me he was always going to come back to you in the Moon of Fat Horses."

She nodded, the hot tears of fierce pride stinging her big eyes. Monaseetah blinked them away and swallowed down the hot ball of shame.

"He will come," Monaseetah whispered, her body swaying in company with the other dancers. Moving forward and back, undulating, forward and back from the Oglalla warrior. "He promised."

CHAPTER 9

1876

THE Cheyenne led the grand procession down the gradual slopes of the Wolf Mountains, along Medicine Dance Creek, as the camps continued to swell with the addition of more summer roamers and young warriors. The young men always came, looking for girls. Hoping for coups and scalps, honors and ponies. Always the young men came for the laziness of the summer days, and the coolness of the prairie evenings.

At their first camp across the divide, the Burnt-Thigh or Brule Lakota left behind a burial lodge. Inside lay the fully dressed body of a warrior who had eventually died of massive wounds suffered in the recent fight with the soldiers up the Rosebud. Other bands had buried their dead in caves or back in the rocks of the Wolf Mountains.

By now all in that great gathering had come to call their great victory the "Battle When the Girl Saved Her Brother" for the courageous rescue of a fallen warrior.

At their first camp along the Greasy Grass, the village stayed nestled for six sleeps in the undulating curves of the gentle stream. The celebrations continued, coupled with feasts and dances held each sundown as the earth cooled. On those magnificent benchlands west of the encampment, the great herds luxuriated among the tall grasses. At sunrise hunters came and went while women labored over fresh buffalo hides. Scouts moved in and out of camp, daily following the retreat of that army that had marched against them. In each circle the happiness grew when word came that the soldiers were moving quickly to the south once more. Away from the hunting grounds. Away from the great gathering filled with so much powerful medicine.

The Northern Cheyenne camp had swelled, the horns of the great crescent of browned lodges no longer in sight of one another. By any man's count there were ten-times-ten-times-ten, and more than half again that many, in the Shahiyena circle alone. All but a handful of the tribe had come to wander together this great summer. Most of the nation's forty chiefs had brought their bands. Absent were but two chiefs, perhaps holding out on the reservation. One band under Little Wolf. The other led by Dull Knife.

Two Moon and the other Cheyenne leaders had originally determined to continue due west, cross-country to the Bighorn River. But when word came on the sixth day that large herds of antelope had been spotted to the north, the chiefs decided to lead the villages down the Little Bighorn, all the way to its mouth. Upon reaching that point, it was decided, the hunters could ford the Bighorn River in pursuit of the antelope, taking much meat and those skins so highly prized by the Cheyenne.

So the bands set off again, marching slowly downstream toward the mouth of the Little Bighorn. After a short, lazy march, the Cheyenne went into camp near the mouth of a small creek flowing from the southwest into the wider Greasy Grass. Across the river and a few yards upstream, a broad coulee ran eastward into the wrinkled, rumpled blanket of grassy, sage-covered landscape.

Six great circles and two minor ones now lay beneath that retreating summer sun, celebrating the arrival of newcomers and the reunion of old friends again that twilight, as the ground cooled and the fireflies came out and the frogs croaked along the stream banks.

On that balmy evening a crippled, leathery old Sans Arc village crier hobbled among the poor lodges of his tiny camp circle. The herald's high, reedy voice sang out the unthinkable news.

"Soldiers are coming, people! Heed my words! The Dream says it is so! Soldiers come with tomorrow's sun!"

Neither his people, nor the other camp circles paid the old man any visible heed, though in the past few days scouts had learned of the presence of another army roaming the country. Lakota and Cheyenne eyes had for themselves seen the Fireboat-That-Walks-on-Water, plying the Elk River to the north. It had been anchored now for several suns at the mouth of the Rosebud.

Some scouts had even noticed the dust of a large complement of soldiers marching up the Rosebud, then climbing high near the divide of the Wolf Mountains, evidently heading south to the spot where Crazy Horse had scattered Red Beard Crook's forces a handful of suns ago. Other scouts had come across deep, furrowed trails marking the passing of many iron-shod hoofs.

But despite the warnings, there was yet no anxiety. For some it was unthinkable that any soldier-chief would attack a gathering so large as theirs nestled along the Greasy Grass. For a few the news was reassuring—they who remembered the details of Sitting Bull's prophetic vision.

The soldiers will fall into camp. Almost as if committing suicide, the white men will fall into our camp.

By sundown that evening The Bull had ordered his camp police to patrol the perimeter of the village circles, to assure that no small band of hotbloods in search of personal glory took it upon themselves to attack the soldiers coming— thereby ruining his powerful vision. All honor and glory must come when the soldiers came to attack the camp itself.

While the drummers took their places near the center of the Cheyenne circle at the northern end of the great encampment, four young warriors intent upon their own personal glory announced they would sacrifice themselves during the coming battle with the pony soldiers. Little Whirlwind, Close Hand, Cut Belly, and Noisy Walking enjoyed the adulation swirling round them this, their last night on earth. Tomorrow they would give their lives in battle.

As the sun sank like a red-earth ache behind the distant Big Horn Mountains, a solitary figure slogged out of the river called the Pa-zees-la-wak-pa by his Hunkpapa Sioux. Up from the fragrant thickets of crabapple and plum and wild rose along the Little Bighorn he climbed, into the tall grass and mats of wild buffalo peas strewn over the rumpled hillsides. A lone chief come here to sing his thunder songs and pray for guidance now that time stood on the precipice, ready to grant his great vision.

With a purple sky deepening to black out of the east, this short, squat man left behind little offerings of tobacco and red willow bark, each skin bag tied to a short, peeled willow shaft he had jammed into the ground near the crest of that hill at the northern end of the swayback ridge. His powerful thunder medicine had told him that here on this most hallowed ground, the last and most desperate fight would take place.

Here on this knoll the powerful Sitting Bull prayed his final blessing for those *wasichu* soldier souls soon to be sacrificed, given over to the fury of the Great Mystery.

Down below in the long, threaded thong of camp circles clustered in the undulating curve of the river, the celebration and revel of life continued that summer evening, into the dark of night, through to the coming of a new sun. Drums and songs and dancing. Joy and laughter and courting as the music throbbed on in its sensual, earthy rhythm until the sky lightened in the east.

Babies born crying out while weary couples grunted and murmured, copulating beneath the last far-flung stars, slowly going out with the coming of a new red sun.

A sleepy summer dawn hazed over the valley of the Greasy Grass, and with its first pale light seeping over the brown, hoary caps of the Wolf Mountains, a shrieking death wail erupted in the Hunkpapa camp.

Four Horns, the wife of Sitting Bull's uncle, had died of illness as this new day was itself born.

Filled not only with a great grief, but with a renewed awe at the mysterious workings of the Great Powers Above,

The Bull realized this woman's death presaged the great victory of his Sun Dance Dream. A victory to be born beneath this day's sun.

Far back into the memory of any of the old Hunkpapas, tradition had been passed down that with the death of the wife of an important man would come a momentous event.

Sitting Bull closed his eyes and quickly prayed again as he had on the hillside above the sleepy river. When he had gone to that very knoll where he knew the soldiers would at last look down upon this great encampment spread before them, while the fury of the nations swept them all from the earth, like breath smoke gone before a hard winter wind.

Farther north in the Oglalla camp, White Cow Bull sat at a smoky dawn fire, refusing to lay his head down to sleep. Unlike most of the warriors who had gone to their robes just before dawn after a long night of dancing and girls, the weary one sat staring into the yellow flame licking its way along the dry cottonwood limbs, sensing the portent of something great.

Perhaps last night's dancing with Monaseetah would be the key to things now. She had been reluctant that first dance they had shared nights before. But last night she had actually smiled when they had joined the others. Still, she steadfastly refused to heed his words of love, not allowing him to walk with her back to her lodge—earlier than most, so that she could put her sons to bed. Earlier than the rest of the young couples courting beneath the swirling dust of stars.

But he would do as he had promised her—wait while the soldier chief came for her. Monaseetah seemed to put much value in a promise. Perhaps she would soon see the value in White Cow Bull's promise as well.

He looked up from the flames struggling this cool gray morning, the feel of hairs standing at the back of his neck. His friend, his war chief, Crazy Horse, was behaving very strangely.

Before most battles The Horse was normally a man composed and reserved. But not as this sun rose reborn behind the Wolf Mountains.

Crazy Horse stomped in and out of his lodge many

times, back and forth to his war pony, checking and rechecking his weapons, repeatedly inspecting his personal war medicine he carried in a small pouch tied behind an ear.

With grease and purple vermilion pigment, the war chief mixed his personal paints, smearing the war pony with magic symbols. That done, he paced back and forth again, in and out of his lodge, captive of some strange power that refused to release its grip from the spirit of Crazy Horse.

Some magic, the spirit helpers told White Cow Bull, that would make this a day like no other gone before it . . . or ever again.

In the pit of him, White Cow Bull knew their most important fight was at hand.

The Miniconjou youth liked the chill feel to the waters here in the Greasy Grass. The cool grass at the bank beckoned him. He climbed out and lay back, naked before the coming of the new sun.

"My oldest has had enough of a bath this morning," said High Pipe, the boy's father.

Ghost moved up on one elbow. "I have. The grass feels good, and the sun warms me. You swim, father. I will doze here before we go back to camp for breakfast."

"If your sisters have it prepared for us," he said, laughing gently as he scooped up handfuls of the lazy water.

High Pipe emerged from the water minutes later, turning to face the sun as it first poked over the Wolf Mountains. Spreading his arms out, he prayed for its blessing on him and his family. As the warrior opened his eyes, he found his eldest son praying beside him, arms outstretched as well.

"It is good that we pray together, Ghost."

He smiled at his father. "We have been blessed."

After pulling on breechclouts and moccasins, the two strode back to their camp circle, where High Pipe found his old uncle anxiously awaiting his return.

"You must collect your horses, High Pipe," the wrinkled one solemnly advised, dark eyes darting suspiciously now to that bony ridge east of the river.

"Why, uncle?"

"Something is going to happen this day," Hump asserted. "Tell the boy to bring your horses into camp so that your wives can pack them when trouble begins."

"Uncle, there are plans to move the camp circle today," High Pipe soothed, a hand on the old one's shoulder. "The chiefs have decided we will move north some, toward the country of the antelope. The Shahiyena lead the way. No need for alarm."

"You know some Cheyenne boys?" The old man looked at Ghost.

"I know one. Yellow Bird. He is my friend."

The old eyes were back on High Pipe, squinting as if grimacing in pain. "Something bad will happen to us for staying so near the Shahiyena!" he whined.

"What, uncle?" asked High Pipe. "Tell me what you see."

"Many dead. Much blood. More blood and death than any one man among these camps has ever seen! And I hear our peoples crying out in joy and sadness—both." Hump wagged his gray head and stared at that ridge across the Greasy Grass.

Then he tore his eyes from the blood red ridge lit with a new sun and looked into the face of Ghost before he spoke.

"Nephew, this will be a day for celebrating—yet a day we will long remember with a stone of sadness upon our hearts."

CHAPTER 10

Yellow Bird felt sorry for the old man. Box Elder deserved better than to suffer the cruel ridicule of the bold, young warriors who mocked and laughed at him. Poking at him with sticks as if to count coup on an enemy.

After a fitful night Box Elder had arisen from his lonely lodge, convinced he must tell the entire camp of the nightmare vision: watching an advancing horde of pony soldiers descending from those ridges to the east of their camp . . . hundreds of soldier horses marching down the coulee to the wide ford of the Goat River . . . headed straight for the Cheyenne village.

Again and again he tried to explain now to anyone who would listen, he had tried to close his eyes and sleep. But still the same vision troubled him.

At dawn he hobbled from lodge to lodge among the great circle of Northern Cheyenne, warning them of what he had seen in his disturbing dream. Most kept their mouths shut while others cackled behind his back when he tottered off to spread the tale.

Yet Yellow Bird had listened in rapt attention beside Monaseetah that morning, then studied his mother's face when the old man finished his tale. Try as she might, Monaseetah was unable to hide the confusing mix of apprehension, outright fear, and unbridled anticipation on her face. Yellow Bird had no idea why she would be so fearful of the frightening vision, while at the same time also be expectant, excited at its coming.

Box Elder had tottered off to continue his rounds, when he was accosted by some of the young "Crazy Dog" warriors who hurried over to make sport of the old man. They laughed and jeered at first while he tried to shoo them away, waving his old carved stick at them. Then the youngsters openly and loudly howled like rabid wolves at the dreamer—the supreme insult that showed they believed the old man had finally gone mad, telling all they believed it best if Box Elder were dragged into the surrounding hills and left for wolf bait, as crazy as he was.

The old man's dream had troubled her since early that morning when he had interrupted her cooking of breakfast at the fire outside the lodge.

So much recently. The Hunkpapa mystic's great vision. Then defeat of the soldiers to the south. And recently word in one camp after another of strange occurrences foretelling the approach of a great event. All of it rode heavy on her shoulders, like a bundle of winter firewood gathered at great expense of her strength.

Then too—Monaseetah thought, if the others truly believed they would be attacked by soldiers, perhaps more of them would have torn lodges down, packed up, and tromped off without delay during the morning hours. Yet from what she saw of her own camp circle and the Oglallas nearby, the only lodges coming down were those belonging to families who wanted to get an early start on the day's journey farther down the valley, another five or eight miles toward the Elk River.

True enough, no more than a handful of women in each circle busied themselves pulling lodge skins from the poles now as she drove the bone awl through the smoked hide, stuffing the end of a strip of sinew through the hole, again and again, sewing up a new pair of moccasins for Yellow Bird. She looked at him now, sitting sullen in the grass nearby, beneath a shady cottonwood. He had refused to go find playmates today. Not the Hunkpapa boy, Wind. Not even his tall Miniconjou friend, Ghost.

"I will stay close to you today, mother," he told her that morning, with no further explanation.

Those eyes of his, watching her as she went about her duties of fire building, scraping hides, boiling breakfast, fetching water, going out to the immense pastures to find their ponies and bring them to the stream to drink . . . as if he did not himself know why he was staying at her side—but driven to stay there nonetheless.

It was that way now as she went to comb the creek banks for more firewood with Yellow Bird at her side. He was on his knees, scooping up small limbs and handing them to her, when the warrior's voice found them in the shade of the cottonwoods.

"Let me help you with that."

Frightened at White Cow Bull's silent approach, she nearly dropped the deadfall she had been dragging.

"I can manage," she said, the brave, pretty smile brightening her face. "I have learned to do on my own."

"You do not have to manage on your own." He stepped closer, smiling at Yellow Bird. "Hello, little Cheyenne warrior."

"Hello, White Cow Bull." Yellow Bird was glad to have the company. "You can help me look for wood."

"Good," the Oglalla replied, glancing for a moment over at the young mother. "Together we can both make short work of this, can't we?"

For some time he and Yellow Bird worked through the tall grass, locating the limbs with their toes. Eventually White Cow Bull appeared ready once more to strike up a conversation with Monaseetah.

"After leaving you I did not sleep well last night."

"Perhaps you should have returned to the dance."

She watched him look away to Yellow Bird and shrug his shoulders. "Yes, Monaseetah—I could have gone and courted many a girl. But I promised I would wait with you. Remember that promise?"

He drew in a long sigh and stuck a shaft of grass between his lips. He sucked on it for a few moments, walking beside the young mother while Yellow Bird continued looking for deadfall.

"This morning I rode about with Crazy Horse—he was nervous as an old woman this morning at dawn—ready for battle, that one is."

She turned to him. "Crazy Horse knows too?"

Her question caught him short. Then he slowly sensed some understanding. "Yes, I believe he does."

Monaseetah let out a long sigh. "Let us go back to camp now, Yellow Bird. You both must bring your wood with you."

They started back, silent until the Oglalla filled the void. "I had a nap—"

"I am glad you got your rest."

He pursed his lips a moment, as if exasperated by the flare of the woman's every response to all that he had to say to her. "When I arose, I left my wickiup and went to a fire tended by an old woman whom I have been providing with meat. She is without family, much like yourself."

She glanced at him. "I am young. Just give me a chance to provide for myself, and I will do it."

He held up a hand in apology. "I know you can, Monaseetah. The old one cannot. So I bring her meat, and she makes some of my meals whenever I ask."

"She fed you, like a beggar?"

He chuckled. She could not help joining him. The young Oglalla's laugh made her feel good inside.

"Yes, but it was not her food that made me lose my appetite this morning. It was what she had to tell me."

She noticed that Yellow Bird had stopped too and turned about, staring at the two of them, inches from one another. Only then did she realize she was holding her breath.

"What did the old woman tell you?"

"This day the soldiers attack our village."

"How did she know that?" Yellow Bird asked.

"She told me she knew nothing more but what she saw behind her eyes. Then she was gone, not wanting to say more."

"And you are scared of what she said," Monaseetah declared.

He stammered a moment, narrowing his eyes at her. "What if I was a little frightened of what she had to say? I do not like an old woman trying her best to scare me."

She smiled at him, perhaps for the first time that day. His admission only made it harder for her not to like him.

"Why do you laugh at me?" he demanded.

"I'm not laughing at you," she said.

"Yes you do!" he snapped. "Every time I come to court, you laugh at me. Thinking I am the fool. Well, I think you are the fool, Monaseetah. That soldier-husband of yours will never return for you. It has been far too long for him to come back already. Seven years should be long enough for anyone to wait."

He looked down at Yellow Bird, who had come to his mother's side. On the Oglalla's face she recognized the instant remorse at having spat out those words so thoughtlessly.

White Cow Bull's face softened as he knelt by the boy. "I am sorry, Yellow Bird. But I spoke the words that were in my heart about your father. I mean you no shame. Seven years is long enough for your mother to wait for any man—especially a lying *wasichu* soldier who does not know how to speak the truth!"

"We can manage without you, Oglalla!" Monaseetah snapped.

"Mother!"

"You want me to leave?" the warrior asked.

"Yes! I want you to take your hateful words and go back to your camp—or wherever you want to go!"

White Cow Bull started to stomp off.

"Mother! Do not send him away like this!"

The Oglalla turned and flung his words over his shoulder. "Perhaps your mother deserves no better treatment than this, Yellow Bird. To be forgotten and abandoned by a lying pony-soldier chief! I am sorry for you, little Cheyenne warrior. You have a soldier father and an empty-headed crazy woman for a mother!"

Yellow Bird watched after him until the warrior disappeared in the play of sunlight and shadow. He whirled on her.

Monaseetah could see by the look on her son's face that he was numbed, shocked, and anxious at what had just been said.

"*Soldier-chief*, mother?"

She nodded, unable to say more. Feeling the sting of tears at her eyes, watching the first welling of tears at his own. She knew if she opened her mouth to say more, all might betray her before her youngest. Try as she might, while she still loved Sees Red, many times she felt sorry for her youngest son.

"Is this what Scabby wanted you to tell me?" he asked, pulling at her skirt violently, then flaying away at her with his tiny fists. "What you made him promise not to tell me?"

She choked on it. "Yes."

"He is dead now!" Yellow Bird shrieked at her. "Killed by another soldier's bullet. One of only two men who have ever been good to me, mother. One of them killed by a soldier bullet—the other you have driven away!"

He swung again and lost his balance. Tripping over her pile of deadfall, he stumbled, crashing to the ground. She bent to him. He pushed her away.

"I am your mother," she said softly, tears creasing the dust on her face as she knelt beside him, wrenching him into her arms, cradling him.

Monaseetah held him there for a long time in the shadow of the cottonwoods, until far, far away she thought she heard gunshots. But put it out of her mind as summer thunder this morning along the Goat River. Nothing more than summer thunder.

The sun continued its climb out of the east, straining for midsky when the shouts aroused her. She realized Yellow Bird had gone to sleep in her arms, cradled against her breasts, sobbing until sleep overtook him.

She pushed some of the long strands of light hair from his face, looking at him cradled in her lap in peace. Remembering his father's face, innocent, asleep like this.

"Pony soldiers!"

The shouts drew closer. Accented by the approach of pony hoofs. Joined by running feet. The shrieks of women and the cries of the small ones. Wailing of the old and infirm. A pony snorted in fear nearby.

"The pony soldiers are on the hills above us!"

She had Yellow Bird up and by her side without thinking.

"Run for your horses!"

He did not question her now, at her side as they burst from the shady timber bordering the river.

"They are charging into camp!"

She glanced over her shoulder, refusing to slow long enough so that Yellow Bird could do the same.

What she saw sent a cold splash of water down her spine.

Soldiers in blue loping down the long, wide coulee toward the shallow ford at the river, near the bottom horn of the Cheyenne camp crescent.

Monaseetah turned from the war flags the soldiers carried and hurried on. Faster now than she had ever run before.

"They will ride over our camp!"

A person's face shot by as she ran, not knowing them.

All that was important was that she recognized the flags these soldiers were flying in their gallop down the coulee, coming to cross the Goat River, headed to attack the Cheyenne camp.

More than the little red striped flags, she remembered that larger banner . . . remembered the Washita of that long winter gone. Now she was more frightened than she had ever been in her life.

Down the coulee thundered Hiestzi's pony soldiers.

CHAPTER 11

1876

I N the air hung a pall of dust. Thick, choking, yellow
dust. Huge particles suspended in a swirling dance on
the sunlight's slanting rays.

"Look at these pony soldiers!" shrieked an old woman
nearby. "They are only boys! They should have brought
more Sparrowhawk and Shoshone warriors along to do their
fighting for them, but here they lie—wasting into the earth
now, their blood stilled!"

As his mother had dragged him up this long, sage-
covered slope, Yellow Bird watched the travois carry the
wounded Lakotas and Shahiyena down to the villages. But
now there were no longer any wounded left on the bloody
hill. Only the screaming, shrieking women and old men.
And the soldier dead.

So quickly the young, fighting men have abandoned the
slope, riding south to press their attack on another group of
soldiers. Yellow Bird heard one of the women explain that
the first band of soldiers had attacked the Hunkpapa
village, but that Gall's warriors had turned the charge back

on itself, forcing the soldiers to hole up like a badger unable to move from its winter hole.

"Look, mother!" Sees Red shouted, running up to them, his feet kicking up tiny sprays of the fine dust as he came skidding to a stop.

"What did you find?" Yellow Bird inquired, taking the small tin bottle from his brother.

"Smell it."

Yellow Bird worried the cork from the neck and sniffed at the bottle. The odor made his nose want to sneeze while his eyes tried to water. He yanked it from his face. Monaseetah took the bottle from him.

"It is the white man's whiskey. You found it on a soldier's body?"

Sees Red swept his arm the length of the ridge. "The bottles are in almost every pocket. Every boy is getting one of his own. I got this for myself."

"You drink that and your stomach will throw itself on the ground," Monaseetah scolded. "It is fire in your belly."

"This whiskey is powerful medicine?"

"Yes."

"I will keep it then, mother. I want you to look at this. There are many, many of these found on the soldier bodies too."

"What is that?" Yellow Bird asked, studying the small, flat leather packet.

"Mad Wolf's woman gave it to me. She told me it was tied around one of the soldier's arms."

Yellow Bird took it, looked inside at the green paper.

"Throw it away," Monaseetah whispered harshly, continuing to sit beside the pale, freckled body growing red beneath the sun.

"It is evil?"

"Yes, Sees Red. Evil medicine."

Yellow Bird watched his brother's eyes fall to the soldier's body. "This dead one you watch over . . . he is—is he Yellow Bird's father?"

She nodded.

For a long time Sees Red stood studying the body. He finally looked at his mother, his eyes flicking over the wounds she had made in grief on her arms and legs and hands. Anger began to draw the boy's eyes together in the hooded look of rage, like a snake about ready to strike. "You have cut yourself in grief for one who has died. One of our warriors, mother?"

"No," she answered in a whisper, staring at the ground. "For Yellow Bird's father."

"You abandoned our people to go with this white man when you would not stay with my father?"

"It is not so simple to explain to you, my son."

"You threw my father away for this soldier?"

"I was a long time back in my father's lodge when you were born, Sees Red. Your father and I were apart. This soldier-chief came to the Washita long after I had returned to my father."

"What I see is that you wanted a soldier for your husband, not my father—a Cheyenne warrior?"

"Someday you will understand. I will help you—"

"I see plain enough!" Sees Red whirled on Yellow Bird, his face swollen in anger. As red as a hot knot of pain made by the bite of a wasp. "Your father is a thief! He is a killer of women and children, Yellow Bird! I spit on you!"

Sees Red hurled his phlegm into his young brother's face. Not once, but twice. A grave insult among the Cheyenne.

Still the boy stood there, unable to say exactly what he felt, looking into Sees Red's face, sensing the hot moisture run down his cheeks. Angry at the white man for being his father. Angry at his mother for taking up with the soldier-chief. But he was most angry with himself. Looking down at the body, Yellow Bird grew sickened to think he carried the soldier's blood in his body. Revulsion welled, knowing in his own hair and eyes he would carry constant reminders of the soldier-chief.

"You have done a bad thing to your brother," Monaseetah said to her eldest.

"I have done nothing to be ashamed of, mother. Yet you—you should be ashamed of making yourself the wife of this soldier-chief!"

"Don't talk to our mother like that!" Yellow Bird shrieked, his anger boiling over now. He lunged for his brother. "I won't let you—"

Sees Red stepped aside, thrusting the younger boy into the dust, where he fell against the three dead soldiers. "She is not my mother. Not anymore, Yellow Bird." His dark Cheyenne eyes glared at Monaseetah. "From this day I have no mother. You are to be pitied, woman. You are nothing better than a woman who lies with soldier dogs!"

"Sees Red!" she called after him as he tore off, headed downriver along the crest of the ridge.

"I will go after him," Yellow Bird said as he scrambled to his feet, feeling more frightened than ever now that Sees Red had spoken those words of hate.

She put out an arm to stop him. "No. Let him go. He will run out of anger soon."

"Will he understand, mother?"

She took a long time at it but finally shook her head. "Sees Red will never understand. He will always be my son, whether he wants to be or not. But he will never understand what happened with his father—what I felt for your father."

Yellow Bird tore his eyes from his mother's face, to stare down at the sunburned, freckled, and whiskered face of the soldier. He looked a long, long time, until he finally recognized the hot sting of tears coursing down his cheeks.

He could not be angry at a dead man. Nor could he bring himself to be angry with his mother. No, Yellow Bird felt cursed. Destined to carry his anger at himself deep inside where it would not show. Anger that he must hide his father's blood.

"No! I had nothing to do with the soldiers coming. I am Cheyenne!"

Monaseetah turned at the sound of the loud voices rising above the clamor at the edge of camp. Spiteful cries for vengeance rose among the Sioux women who swarmed toward the commotion.

"Kill them! Kill every one of them!" some shouted.

At the edge of the camp circle close to the Oglalla village, a large crowd had formed, surrounding a small band of warriors and women, their ponies dragging travois behind them.

"No, do not kill them. Let us be sure!" others cried.

"I told you I was Cheyenne. I am Dull Knife. Bring me someone who knows who I am," the deep voice demanded. But he could not make the crowd understand his tongue.

Monaseetah shoved into the angry mob, bursting to the center to address the newcomers.

"You are Dull Knife, chief of the Northern Cheyenne?"

She watched a wry smile cross the warrior's face. "I am Dull Knife. You are Oglalla who speaks my tongue?"

"I am Cheyenne."

"Still I do not know you, woman."

"I am from the south. My father was Little Rock, of Black Kettle's band."

Dull Knife drew close now, examining her face while around him the Oglallas muttered.

"He was killed on the Washita," Dull Knife said. "His daughter was captured by Hiestzi, the Yellow Hair soldier-chief."

"I am Little Rock's daughter."

She watched him gasp a bit with the repeat of her claim.

"Then I have heard of you. Monaseetah is your name. You were married to the Yellow Hair by Black Kettle's sister, Mahwissa?"

"Yes," she replied as a Cheyenne warrior pushed his way into the circle.

"If you are Dull Knife, why did you wait so long to leave the reservation?" demanded the warrior. "Better that you were here before the great fight. Perhaps instead you were all the time with the soldiers, leading them to our camps."

Dull Knife took two great steps, which put him almost on the young warrior's toes.

"You foolish child," he chided. "Do all these people think that I am a crazy man? Riding with the soldiers—then coming down to the villages of my people after I have led those soldiers to this camp?"

"Yes," argued another haughty warrior. "You and your friends came here when you saw the battle going badly."

Dull Knife snorted at the newcomer. "Look here at these women and children. Is this the way a man scouts for the army? With his women and children along? Ha! I am not a white man. I never helped the white man. And any of you who now says that Dull Knife is a traitor must be willing to fight me."

"Where have you been so long?"

He whirled on a new questioner. "We were on the Rosebud last night. There we saw a large camp of these soldiers. When the sun rose this morning, we watched the soldiers cross the divide. We did not make a camp last night for fear their Indian scouts would see our fire or smoke. This morning we followed their trail over the mountains. That's where we found a wood box filled with the white man's crackers. We ate all that we could before we traveled on. When we heard all the guns firing, we steered to the south and saw some of the fighting. My people were afraid to come out of hiding when the firing stopped. We believed the soldiers had wiped out your camps. But when we saw the villages still here, we decided to ride in."

The story was translated in the Sioux tongue, yet still some grumbling continued as the crowd broke up.

"You should have been here before the fight," a warrior muttered as he reluctantly left.

"Stayed too long on the reservation."

"They made a mistake. Not bad enough to kill them."

Monaseetah hung back as the great crowd went in a hundred different directions.

Dull Knife touched her arm, turning her to face him. "You were brave to talk for me like that."

She said, "There has been enough killing this day, Dull Knife."

"Yes. I am glad you were here to prevent these angry ones from killing my people. How can I repay you?"

Her eyes were drawn to the hillside, abandoned now except for the white bodies of the soldiers and the dark carcasses of the horses.

"There is nothing you can do for me. Nothing anyone can do for me now."

He looked into her eyes. "There will come a day. And with the coming of that day, you tell me how I can repay you for your kindness, Monaseetah."

Many of those families who had returned from the hillsides were in the Cheyenne village, preparing their dead for burial. After a ritual washing and painting, the bodies were dressed in their finest, then laid on a robe with their favorite weapons and pipe and articles of medicine. The women ultimately wrapped the buffalo hide around the body and tied it securely with long rawhide thongs to prevent predators from getting to the bodies of the departed ones.

With the bodies placed on a travois, the woman led the ponies into the nearby hills where the dead were left inside small rock caves, sometimes crevices. The entrances were sealed with boulders dragged up by the women, who could then begin mourning.

Cutting their hair off in chunks. Gashing their arms and legs and hands. Perhaps chopping off a finger in their grief. Through it all the firing continued up the river where the soldiers were said to be holing up like a cornered badger fighting off a grizzly bear.

According to custom every lodge mourning the loss of a warrior in the battle was now put to the knife, cut apart and made unserviceable by the other women in camp. Everything belonging to the warrior that had not been given away by his wife was put to the torch. Those left behind in this life would have to suffer without a lodge or property of their own during this period of mourning.

During it all most of the women in the villages were preparing to move their camps in accordance with tribal custom, which dictated that move whenever a death occurred in a camp, either from battle or from other serious cause. With the falling of the sun, the Shahiyena camp circle moved north a short distance that day. The Cheyenne determined how far the move would be for the rest of the camp circles by stopping once they got out of sight of their old campsite that had been across the river from the battle hillside.

But here the women did not raise the lodgepoles and stretch over them the buffalo hides. Instead the women went about their duties as they would when fleeing from an approaching column of soldiers. They, along with young girls, went along the creek banks to cut stout willow limbs for use in making the small dome shelters on which they would throw buffalo robes or blankets. These would serve them for only one night as they migrated from the scene of Sitting Bull's great vision-battle.

As the sun sank blood red upon the peaks of the Big Horn Mountains, most of the Lakota and Cheyenne warriors returned to their camps from the fight with the soldiers upstream, leaving a portion of their number to watch the circle of white men who had been surrounded during the entire falling of the sun. Groups of young men came and went, scouring the countryside for sign of more soldiers. Another army perhaps, word had it.

In each village the camp heralds moved to and fro among the temporary shelters. Announcing bits of news, rumors, stories from the momentous day of battle.

Yet there was no celebration, no dancing, and certainly no joy at this great victory over the white man. Too many of their own had died. Many more were seriously wounded, attended by the shamans and medicine men of each camp. More still keened in mourning for any man among them to feel like strutting the steps of the scalp dance.

Time enough to celebrate this greatest of all victories. Now it was time to mourn those who had crossed over to the other life. Now it was time to think on the portent of this great happening.

CHAPTER 12

B y first light the next day, the young warriors were already gone from camp, moving south in great numbers, crossing the stream and into the rugged bluffs to continue their sniping at the soldiers hunkered down behind the dead bodies of their horses and small mounds of dirt they had scooped up through the short summer night.

Six families mourned among the Shahiyena village. Two more warriors were seriously wounded and not expected to live long, especially if the village was given the order to move on soon. Many whispers spread this day, rumors of soldiers coming from the north, looking for the soldiers who had blundered into the great encampment.

Once some young Cheyenne warriors had looked upon the bodies of three dead Indians scouting for the army, the villages soon learned they had not been attacked by the same soldiers they had fought a handful of suns ago—the Rosebud battle army. Instead these dead scouts were Arikaras, Corn Indians. Not the Crow and Shoshone who rode as the eyes for the soldier-chief Red Beard they had whipped up the Rosebud Creek.

Up that bloody hillside lay an altogether different army.

That second day as the sun rose, Monaseetah still sat her vigil beside the body. Young boys, along with the old men and women, had returned with the coming of the new sun. It was great sport to count coup on the naked white men, stabbing them with knife or willow-limb lance. Poking eyes out, shooting the lifeless bodies with arrows or hacking off hands and feet with a camp ax.

Female relatives of the dead and wounded warriors now returned to exact a hideous revenge on the soldiers left naked on the slope. A fury left unspent until the rising of a new sun.

A lone dog wandered among the dead scattered the entire length of the ridge top. At times it would stop and raise its muzzle to the sky, howling pitifully before it would move on, sniffing at the ground, searching about among the blood and the bloating bodies, looking for that which it would never find.

White Cow Bull had himself come searching for Monaseetah but found her unwilling even to look at him. Instead she sat and rocked by the fire kept burning by her sons. Her eyes seemed to stare at nothing at all, if not some great distance.

The Oglalla warrior turned from her, kneeling instead near her boys. Pulling a small round object from his belt pouch, he held out his palm. It was made of a shiny metal on one side, while on the other beneath a clear glass were some strange markings.

"Put it to your ear," the warrior suggested.

Sees Red put the object to his ear and immediately dropped it. "It's alive!"

White Cow Bull laughed, scooping the object from the grass. "Perhaps, little Cheyenne. But it will not hurt you. Here, Yellow Bird."

The younger brother held it to his ear, listening to the tick—tick—tick—tick—

"What does the white man use this for?"

The Oglalla said, "I don't know, little Cheyenne. Maybe to scare your big brother!"

"It is not funny to scare me with the white man's medicine, Oglalla!"

"I did not mean to scare you. Only to show you this special thing. Look at the pretty marks here on the shiny side, like the leaves of the bullberry . . . and in the center this drawing of the elk."

"It is a fine thing, White Cow Bull."

He looked at the youngest boy. "You really do like it, Yellow Bird?"

"Oh, yes. It is a magical thing to have."

"Then you will have it, my little warrior." He opened Yellow Bird's palm and laid the pocket watch in it. "Let it's magic be yours."

"Thank you!" he exclaimed, beaming as he put the watch to his ear and turned away. "I must show the others my new white-man magic, the gift of White Cow Bull!"

By midafternoon camp heralds moved through the camp circles, spreading word just brought in by the far-roaming scouts. More soldiers were on their way. Coming from the north, down from Elk River. The chiefs had held their council. It was decided that Sitting Bull's battle was enough for now.

The young men stomped and complained, wanting to set out immediately for the north. To squash another army. Instead it was determined that the villages would continue as they had for many moons, attempting to avoid the white man, and staying out of the way of his armies.

Orders were given for the camps to make ready in haste.

Late in the afternoon young men were directed to leap atop their ponies, carrying torches ignited in the women's cook fires. Better than a hundred of these riders swept along the west bank of the Greasy Grass, setting fire to the undergrowth to hide the retreat of the entire encampment. Everyone was moving now, leaving the scene, marching up the river valley. All except a few scouts who would wait behind until complete darkness, keeping an eye out on the soldiers still hunkered on the bluff. Straining their eyes and ears north for some sign of the new soldiers coming their way.

As Monaseetah passed by the old campsites and climbed with the rest atop the western benchland in a wide procession, all that was visible were a few lodges left behind by the Sioux for burial of their dead, along with the hundreds of abandoned wickiups used by the young bachelor warriors back in the willow and cottonwood bordering the stream. Both Sees Red and Yellow Bird sat in silence atop their ponies. Monaseetah's animal pulled their single travois.

Her eldest had not come looking for her until that first night had passed and the sun had climbed high in the heavens, bringing another day of great heat. Monaseetah had been helping Scabby's widows and daughters prepare a midday meal when Sees Red wandered up. A look of defiance still etched on his young face, he would not tell his mother where he had gone, nor how he had spent the night.

Monaseetah thought it enough that he had returned. For the time being it was enough that she had both boys at her side. Yet from that moment on the hillside beneath yesterday's hot sun, she would be able to mark a widening gulf between her two sons.

That night the procession marched until complete darkness overtook them. Then the women broke out kettles, fetched wood and water, and made a hurried supper before everyone fell atop their blankets for a short sleep. At dawn the caravan was well on its way, moving along the high benchland toward the beckoning snowcaps of the Big Horn Mountains.

At that night's campsite, permission was granted for the camps to celebrate their victory. Besides the ceremonial unwrapping of the great Buffalo Hat, the victorious warriors brought out the many soldier scalps, and thousands of coups were counted. Some of the men even put on soldier clothing and began dancing to the beat of the old drummers. One warrior society decked itself out in soldier tunics, donned the white man's hats, then rode upon captured gray horses as they strutted through camp in an orderly column behind one of the captured battle flags. At the head of the procession rode a Cheyenne warrior who had learned to blow on the bugle good enough to force a wheezing, shrill sound from it.

Enough to remind Monaseetah of the eerie cry of eagle wing-bone whistles beneath a hot sun.

It was during the next day's march that the Cheyennes turned the procession east, skirting the southern end of the Wolf Mountains to return once more to Rosebud Creek.

After one more sleep the camps turned downstream, marching past the site of their day-long battle with the soldier-chief Red Beard. Scouts were constantly out, roaming far and wide to learn of the presence of soldiers, as were hunters searching for game to feed the thousands. Orders had been given the hunters against going too far from the line of march for fear of bumping into an army column or their Indian scouts. Many grumbled for several days, while no belly among the thousands was full.

At their camp three sleeps down the Rosebud, the Cheyennes held another dance. One after another the young warriors danced out to the center of the ring and recited his battle coups before the entire village. It was here at last that young Wooden Leg presented his face scalp, the long whiskers taken from a soldier he had killed in the last moments of fighting.

From there they crossed the narrow benchland to Otter Creek, another sleep over to Pumpkin Creek, and finally across the divide to the Powder River country. Back to the country where the bands had first gathered in the Sore-Eye Moon. Sixteen sleeps now from the day of that greatest of all battles when the soldiers had fallen headfirst into their camps.

Yet strangely there was little to cause them to celebrate. Every man, woman, and child was hungry. There was no horse not suffering from want of forage and rest. The march had been long and hard, pushed to the point of exhaustion by the fear of more soldiers dogging their back trail. So it was after four sleeps here in the valley of the Powder that the chiefs held a council, deciding to splinter the groups once again, each band to head in a direction of its own choosing, hoping each group could hunt more effectively for meat and skins now that there appeared to be little reason to fear the coming of soldiers.

"We have whipped them soundly!" shouted some.

"No," others protested, "we have only stirred the hornets' nest. The rest will come."

"Let them come! We will be ready for them!"

"But the army will keep sending more soldiers to find our camps—more soldiers to kill our women and children!"

"That is woman's talk!"

So while the arguments flared, the bands splintered for their individual survival, hoping they could avoid the white man, praying they could stay out of the line of fire when the soldiers marched.

For three more sleeps the bands camped together, reluctant to part once the decision had been reached. First, the Santee Sioux split from the Hunkpapas. Next, Crazy Horse and the Oglalla marched in a different direction. On and on until the Cheyenne were alone to continue their way north, down the Powder River.

On their march downstream some scouts returned to camp one evening with word of finding two bodies. An old man and woman dressed in Sioux garments. Both bodies had been found squatting in some brush. Most believed they had been hiding when they were discovered and murdered by soldiers. Many iron-shod hoofprints marked the area.

"Perhaps they were too old to keep up with their band this past spring," Monaseetah murmured to her two boys as the sun sank over her left shoulder.

"Left behind to die?"

"Yes, Yellow Bird. Many times the old ones choose a death with honor, giving their meat to the wolves and great birds on wing, rather than cripple their people with their needs."

"But the two old ones were not given a chance to die with honor!" Sees Red spat.

Yellow Bird regarded the orange flames licking the fire pit. "No. The two old ones died with more honor than any who choose to starve to death in the wilderness. They died as our warriors died—by soldier bullets."

Monaseetah regarded Yellow Bird carefully for several moments, in awe at his words and the angry spirit in them. She found his eyes climbing to hers.

"What is it you look at, mother?"

She felt her face grow hot, embarrassed at the warmth of the feelings of love she felt for him at this moment. "I . . . I'm just admiring my youngest son—he who appears to be growing up very quickly."

Yellow Bird stared again at the fire while the twilight deepened. "The past moon has brought many changes to my life. I would like, I want the earth to slow down a bit and not move so fast under me."

They ate in silence their dinner that night. Each one of them in his or her own thoughts.

At the mouth of the Powder, the Cheyenne found half-a-hundred bags of corn abandoned by one of the summer armies. Some of the warriors fed the corn to their army horses. Others tried boiling it in their kettles. Most of the women simply poured the kernels on the ground and took the sacks. The sacks were worth something if the corn was not.

Throughout the waning days of that summer, the Cheyenne migrated in search of game, keeping scouts out in search of roving soldiers. One solitary encounter caused some momentary anxiety once more as summer grew old and faded. A single warrior was killed by a chance meeting with a small group of soldiers and their Indian scouts.

When at last the leaves began to turn, so too did the Cheyenne in their march of the seasons. Now they came about and headed up the Powder while the great shaggy herds grew long coats in concert with the shorter days. Each day, above the Shahiyena, flew the great long-necked honkers, migrating south with their own seasonal imperative. So like them were the Cheyenne people, headed for the hunting grounds they had haunted for centuries. Migrating back to the country where pony chief Red Beard had found them back in the cold of the Sore-Eye Moon.

Yet with every step through the ages-old river valleys, the people moved closer to the sunset of their way of life. Only a few would admit that one day soon they would no longer look upon this land and see such unmatched beauty in the white-draped peaks overhead, the golden splash of leaf and rich red of limb among the bright emerald of the evergreens.

Instead, come a day soon, the Shahiyena would face a world as white and forbidding as any left behind by a blizzard.

The snows came early that year.

CHAPTER 13

November 26, 1876

In as many directions as the wind could blow, the Shahiyena and the Lakota bands splintered themselves.

Sitting Bull took his people to the Grand River. Crazy Horse led his Oglallas up the Tongue. Other bands followed where their particular medicine called them as the leaves turned and the high country grew white.

In no way did that mean the warriors and their families were afraid of the soldiers or had become peaceable. On the contrary, the young warriors, fired by their two recent victories, spilled across a large piece of territory, striking the white man when it suited them. Small freighting outfits. Miners' camps in the Black Hills. And always on the look out to butcher any unwary soldier patrols.

With Scabby gone, no longer among Two Moon's band to advise young Monaseetah, she elected to stay among Dull Knife's Cheyenne. With some two hundred lodges, she felt, his camp was large enough to withstand any random attacks by soldiers. But what was more prominent in her thinking was that Dull Knife had only recently left the reservation. Perhaps, she believed, because of that, Dull Knife's band would not be attacked by the soldiers. Her unspoken hope was that with Dull Knife's people, she could find a home where her two sons would grow content. Perhaps Yellow Bird would be safe.

She feared with all that was in her that the soldiers knew of her youngest son. Her nightmares told her the soldiers wanted to capture Yellow Bird more than anything now that his father had been killed. Son of the great Indian fighter. Monaseetah remembered the anxious words of warning Hiestzi had spoken to her that warm, sunny day in the stockade at Fort Hays. The day he learned she carried his child.

Yellow Hair warned of the danger in white men knowing he had a half-breed son. It frightened her again now, with a prickling of cold down her spine, just to think about the fear he had put into her—never to let the white man get his hands on the child.

That much she remembered. As well as the promise she had made to Yellow Hair. Monaseetah had vowed to keep the child far from the white man.

Already the Indian summer had come and gone on the high plains. Now was the time when Hoimaha would blow his icy breath across the land. Winter had come early this year.

It was late in the Moon of Deer Rutting. And for three days wide-roaming scouts had reported sighting army troops. There were those who disbelieved the news, feeling as if they had given the soldiers two sound whippings that would keep the bands safe for some time to come. Others hungered that the soldiers would come for another battle where more white scalps could be taken.

Then a young Cheyenne warrior rode in, coming from the faraway agency near Fort Robinson. He brought news that confirmed the worst of rumors. The army was planning to come after the Lakotas and Shahiyena. With his own eyes he had seen other Indians gathering there at the fort as well—Shoshone, Sparrowhawk, Ute, and Pawnee. They would take the white man's money, to be the eyes and ears for the soldiers.

Once more Box Elder, the dim-eyed old shaman, limped

round the camp circle, crying out his announcement that the bands should stay right where they were, but he advised them all to search out good hiding places to run to when the soldiers came, and there throw up some sturdy breastworks for that time.

"Many . . . many pony soldiers come this way soon. Many other tribes are with them too. These are already on the trail to kill all the Shahiyena. I have been praying that the Everywhere Spirit will protect us."

Many of the people obeyed the warnings of the rheumy old man. He had been right many times before the great battle on Goat River. And he had been right in his prophecy of that day.

Many went to the rimrocks not far west of their camp. Here they planned to go when the soldiers attacked, to find shelter, leaving their lodges behind in the valley.

Crow Split Nose walked through camp late that afternoon, announcing Box Elder's advice. "Go to the rocks tonight. Hide in the trees where we have chosen to stay. The soldiers come at sunrise tomorrow."

"Why are we leaving our lodges standing, mother?" asked her youngest.

"We do that to fool the Indians scouting for the soldiers. With the lodges left standing, they will think we are sleeping in our robes."

"And if they think we are in our sleeping blankets?" Sees Red piped up.

"Then our warriors who are staying behind to hide in the village will be able to catch our enemies in their trap."

Yet late in the afternoon, Last Bull's Fox warrior society threw cold water on the plan, going through camp to shame and bully those who believed in Box Elder's prophecy. Again they howled like wolves and laughed at the old man's words. More important, as camp police the Fox warriors told the people no one was allowed to abandon camp for the rimrocks. Instead they announced they were holding a big dance that night at the center of the village, where they would build a huge fire.

In this way, Last Bull stridently boasted, no one would be asleep in their lodges when the soldiers came.

Many were doubtful of tempting the soldier scouts.

Some remained resolute in following the prophecy, busying themselves in saddling ponies or packing up their belongings.

Seeing so many still preparing to go to the rimrocks, the Fox warriors again burst through camp, warning that all those who attempted to leave would be severely punished, beaten with willow switches and their lodges cut to ribbons, should they not obey Last Bull's orders to stay in camp. To add potency to the warning, the two hot-brands of the Fox Society themselves, Last Bull and Wrapped Hair, stomped through camp with their knives, cutting the cinches of some who were preparing to move out.

"Better to stay and fight the soldiers!" they shouted. "As we did when we wiped out the soldiers who attacked our great camp on the Goat River!"

At the same time the rest of the Fox warriors were dragging deadfall into the center of the camp circle, where they would light their "skunk," a huge bonfire for the night's dancing.

With the coming of twilight, the Fox warriors made the rounds to every lodge, forcing all the families to attend the dance. A few of the more prudent families with daughters in their number even tied the girls together to keep any of the young warriors from grabbing a girl and running off with her during the dance. Mothers watched over the young women like hawks over a nest that cold, frosty night.

When at last the eastern sky was streaked with gray-and-orange light, the people wearily started for their lodges and their sleeping robes. It seemed that for once Box Elder had been wrong.

In her tiny lodge the fire lay long dead with gray ash. Monaseetah bolted upright, the blankets and single robe she barely had time to warm slipping from her shoulders. She felt strangely hot. Sweating.

She had suffered another of the nightmares. Standing over the pale body. Yellow Hair—as he lay sprawled across the two dead soldiers. In her dream she once again cleaned his body, staring into the two lifeless blue eyes, talking quietly to the man who was once her husband as she went through the burial ritual.

Yet each time the recurring nightmare ended in the same manner. In her dream she returned to the bloody hillside before dawn the day after Yellow Hair and the others had been killed. And where she remembered leaving the body, Hiestzi was not to be found.

The rest of the white bodies were there. Only his sunburnt, freckled corpse had disappeared.

At first she had wanted to believe her dream meant he might yet return to her. But then her good sense prodded her that with those two horrid wounds, Yellow Hair could not live to walk away.

So instead Monaseetah was left to wonder in fear each time she dreamed of that hillside cloaked in blood, the keening wails of the squaws ringing in her ears. Awaking in the cold lodge, shivering with the cold sweat of stark terror seeping from her every pore.

As she wiped her hand across her damp cheek, Monaseetah heard the first warning shout. She tore her eyes from the gray-lit smoke hole surrounding the spiral of poles above.

Another shout—a shriek of warning.

Then the first rattle of gunfire.

Sees Red and Yellow Bird burst from their robes like jackrabbits hazed from a den by a hungry coyote.

"Come!" was all Monaseetah said as she poked her head out the doorway, then motioned them to follow her.

Everywhere the scene was one of wild commotion. Men, women, bent backs and short legs, all scurried through the deep snow, into the shocking cold of predawn. Everyone heading for the breastworks they had thrown up in the rimrocks. All of them angry for not being there already. The Fox Society had kept them prisoner in their own village.

The shouts of warriors crashed against her ears as the staccato of gunfire erupted more insistently. The men were giving orders to those who would flee while they remained behind to cover the retreat, as they had done so many times before when the soldiers came to attack a sleeping village.

Some of the first had reached the cliffs, desperately climbing, clawing at the snowy rocks with their hands and feet. Many of the first Pawnee into the village now turned to direct their fire on those nearing the rimrock instead of aiming at the clusters of Cheyenne scattering from the lodge circle itself. In their fear-tinged anger for Last Bull, most of the people forgot to bring along a blanket or robe for warmth.

Across the shallow creek bed, Monaseetah made out fragments of the white man's tongue during momentary lulls in the gunfire. Beneath the heavy hanging cloak of cold fog trapped in the valley, she saw horsemen racing south along the stream. From the north end of camp came the shouted warning that Pawnee were leading the attack, guiding the soldiers in a massed charge.

She stopped, the snow piling above her ankles while her two sons jumbled to a stop against her. It was so hard to see anything. The moon still hung low in the western sky, giving a faint, translucent, and ghostly glow to the hoary fog. Her mind raced, trying to recall the landmarks surrounding the camp. To her left, the east, steep slopes stood, running all the way toward the high mountains.

There remained but one way through that bulwark into this valley. The way Dull Knife had led his people in.

Monaseetah knew that way was not for her. As sure as she stood there with bullets whistling overhead, the soldiers had closed that passage, stationing snipers and sharpshooters to cut down all who tried to escape. Exactly as Yellow Hair had done winters ago on the banks of the frozen Washita.

To the west some of the women and children were scurrying past the fork in the stream, heading toward the high cliffs that rumpled themselves into steep mountainsides. More and more now were taking the chance the soldiers would not follow them into such difficult terrain.

Another smaller group hurried due south searching for an escape route, crossing the forks of the stream and seeking a way out of the valley, racing up the gentle slopes to safety beyond.

The Pawnee scouts tearing through the village, shooting and yelling, spurred Monaseetah into action once more. She would take the boys south, into those hills with the others.

Suddenly she was in motion, dragging her sons along.

Behind her she thought she recognized the Shoshone tongue. Glancing over her shoulder as she broke the ice crossing the shallow creek, Monaseetah watched a large detachment of mounted Indians wearing army coats and feathers in their hair explode from the thick, icy fogbank, galloping to the west, toward the steep benchland overlooking the valley where her people climbed the rocky face hoping to escape.

Her heart throbbed in her throat, sensing now just how close they had come to death at the hands of the white man's scouts. The Pawnee and Shoshone both had become the soldier-chief's eyes and ears this winter after the great victories of the long-ago summer.

Her feet felt the first rise in the frozen land. Monaseetah heard the high-pitched yells of the warriors, followed by the sharp cracks of their carbines erupting in the center of the village. Cheyenne warriors had stayed behind to kill the Pawnee and Shoshone who would forget their red heritage and lead white soldiers like wolves to sleeping Indian camps.

They were fighting back, she knew. As best they could from behind lodges, at the edge of snowy ravines, hunkered down with their guns behind nothing more than the dead body of their favorite war pony.

It did not take long for the evacuation of the village to run its course. With the women, children, and weak ones safely ensconced among the rimrock above the camp, the warriors could at last pull back to the cliffs. There they began to snipe in earnest at the soldiers below as the cold fog began to lift.

The only Indians left in the village were the white man's scouts.

Yet those Pawnees and Shoshone did not tarry long in that Cheyenne circle. Receiving their orders from a white soldier, they bolted on across the stream, reining their ponies for the bluffs in pursuit of the fleeing Cheyenne. Soldier tongues angrily ordered the Pawnee to scale the steep bluffs just west of the village, with the hope of flanking the warriors who were atop the rimrocks and busily sniping at pockets of soldiers.

In the gray light of that winter morning, one Indian looked pretty much the same as another to the cold, frightened, and confused young soldiers. Believing the Pawnee to be Cheyenne warriors, the troops began shooting into their scouts. Forced to seek cover behind what rocks they could, the Pawnee battalion skulked back to the safety of the village.

Away from the edge of the rimrock, some of the young men took time to ignite warming fires for the women and children and the old ones strong enough to make the climb.

After a morning of long-distance sniping back and forth, the Cheyenne watched the Pawnee regroup in what had once been the center of their camp. The army scouts fanned out in all directions, pulling Cheyenne valuables from the lodges, preparing to put the village to the torch. High upon the cliffs the survivors could only gather in knots about their warming fires, watching the Pawnees complete their destruction.

Once more Monaseetah stood shivering, cold up to her calves, her dark eyes glaring down on those soldiers turning to ash everything she owned. Again and again the same nightmare returned to her life. All that was left to her were her two boys, and the single blanket they shared, the same crimson blanket she had clung to with her life since the moment Yellow Hair's soldiers had charged into Black Kettle's Washita camp.

Along with her youngest son, that blanket served as a reminder of the tall, blond pony-soldier chief who had won her heart that long winter gone.

For the rest of that day into the winter twilight, the Pawnee and soldiers kept at their methodical burning of the Cheyenne camp. All the while the warriors in the surrounding hills attempted to pen the soldiers down with their sniping fire or worked to regain their prized pony herd. Neither attempt proved successful.

Yet in the breastworks the women had scrambled to erect around their position, Dull Knife's Cheyenne resolutely sang their strong-heart songs to make their warriors fearless of the challenge.

Their many throats grew raw that winter afternoon.

CHAPTER 14

November 26, 1876

M ONASEETAH turned at the rumble of the old man's chant, watching Still Water, the Arrow Priest, walk forward carrying his bundle of Sacred Arrows. He stopped at the edge of the cliff, the setting sun radiant behind him, the women and warriors fanning out from the priest on both sides.

Still Water slowly opened the coyote-skin bundle, pointing each of the four arrows toward the burning village, toward the captured pony herd on the far side of the valley, more especially toward the soldiers and their Indian allies.

The Arrow Priest sang his powerful song at the top of his lungs, calling for revenge. His eerie voice caused many of the whites and Indian scouts in the village to stop their destruction, simply to stare at the Cheyennes boldly gathered at the face of the rimrock. When the medicine song had finished, Still Water gave a shout. His was answered by hundreds more as the defeated stomped their feet mimicking the thundering sound of buffalo in stampede.

Three more times the priest sang his song, and each time the people cried out, stamping their feet wildly.

Down in the village stood ten Cheyenne who had come here scouting with the soldiers, commanded by the white squaw man William Rowland. They more than any others halted in their tracks, turning to listen to the loud death chant, knowing those medicine arrows were pointed at them. Knowing there was reason to fear the power of the old man's curse.

Some of Rowland's scouts ran away to hide. A few realized they had but one chance now under the curse of the Arrow Priest—to beg forgiveness from their kinsmen for the wrong they had committed. Scattering into those lodges yet to be burned, the Cheyenne scouts scooped up all the cartridges and powder they could find, hurrying into the timber to hide the treasure from the soldiers.

A brave pair of those Cheyenne scouts stood at the base of the rimrocks, asking forgiveness of the Arrow Priest and telling where they had hidden the cache of ammunition.

"It will be there," they hollered up to their kinsmen. "We leave it behind—unharmed—when the soldiers leave your village."

"I think it is a trap," Sees Red whispered to his mother.

Yellow Bird nodded. "My brother is right. These bad Cheyenne want our warriors to come down for those bullets. But the only bullets will be the ones they use to kill our warriors."

When soldier-chief Mackenzie turned his eleven-hundred-man force away from the decimated village, the Indians on the rimrocks decided they had no reason to return to that smoky valley. They would march again to find the Oglallas.

With the setting of that winter sun, Dull Knife's Cheyennes turned their eyes from the oily smudges on the snow that marked the lodge rings, looking back longingly one last time at the blackened ruin of everything they owned, and marched upstream. They left behind a few young warriors to follow the movements of the soldiers and perhaps collect the ammunition left behind in the timber.

In the vanguard of the march rode a few young warriors who were fortunate to still have their ponies. Most of the old men, women, and children had to shuffle on foot through the deepening snow and growing cold of coming night. Those horsemen went ahead some distance in the deepening twilight before they stopped to build a big fire. The others—men, women, and children—then came on toward the beckoning light.

"We would not be so poor and so cold were it not for the foolishness of Last Bull," grumped one of the old women near Monaseetah.

"Yes," groaned another, struggling with a large bundle at her back. "We knew the soldiers were coming—but that Fox chief cowed all the others into staying. Saying they would be called cowards."

"It is not a coward who runs to fight another day," complained a toothless old man.

"So now we have nothing," the first woman added.

"What you old ones are saying, is it true?" asked Monaseetah, stopping in the snowy trail.

"What do you ask?" demanded an old woman.

"Did the village leaders know the soldiers were coming?"

"There is no doubt," the old man said. "More than one group of our scouts crossed wide trails of iron-shod hoofs in the days before the attack."

"A group of four scouts actually found the soldiers in camp. Our men got close enough to hear not only the white man's tongue, but Pawnee, Arapaho, and Shoshone in their camp."

"We should have gone to join Crazy Horse's camp when Hairy Dog said we should leave," said an old woman, shuffling up beneath her burden. "I'll never let Last Bull cow us with his medicine power again."

"But the other chiefs are afraid of him," the old man said. "There is wickedness in Last Bull's power to control people."

When all the walking ones had reached the huge bonfire, circling the flames to warm themselves, the young warriors again plunged into winter's cloak of darkness, riding some distance until they built another fire. Again the people left the warmth of the dying fire, heading for the next bright beacon of a new light, crossing the snow country in the darkness. In this manner they struggled from one fire to the next through the wilderness that would take them to the Tongue River.

Long after the moon rose blue above the distant snow, the survivors climbed the Powder River divide. There among the scrub and sage and cedar, the horsemen built large fires for all to warm themselves while trying for sleep. Those who had robes and blankets shared with those who had none. There was no food, and nothing to cook it in as well. Every stomach suffered from emptiness, but the little ones complained most of their hunger and the great cold.

At first light the ragged procession wound its way toward the backbone of the Big Horn Mountains. By midmorning four young warriors joined up with the line of march, leading some seventy of their ponies they had recaptured from three unfortunate Pawnee who had become separated and lost from the main soldier column. Now more of the survivors could ride. Only the ablest among them said they would walk, allowing the old and little ones the backs of those strong Cheyenne ponies.

That night at their fires in the snow, the chiefs decided to kill and butcher a pony so that hunger would not stalk them the way the soldiers had.

After that camp seven warriors turned back to the battle site, saying they would look for more ponies that had broken free of the soldiers and returned to the burnt-out village. More than fifty were rounded up by the young men and driven out of the valley on the back trail of the survivors.

On and on they marched, eating horse meat, sleeping wrapped up with one another in shared blankets and robes on ground swept clear of snow, following the ridge of the Big Horn Mountains south until the leaders reached the headwaters of Lodgepole Creek. Following it down to the area of a large lake near the Piney Creeks, they skirted the ruins of an army fort built ten winters before when a young Crazy Horse had decoyed ten-times-ten soldiers into an ambush that no white man survived that winter day.

It was near the fort ruins that they ran onto an old buffalo cow floundering in the deep snow. The young warriors shot her, causing all the people to rejoice. Now they sucked on the rich, raw meat, the strengthening juices freezing on their chins. Wolf Tooth was already an old man that winter. While the cow was butchered, he claimed the green hide for himself. Having been lucky to escape with his life when the Pawnee attacked the village, Wolf Tooth had brought along no robe nor blanket.

Now he cut out the belly velvet from the underside of the cow's hide and pulled it over his shoulders like a protective mantle, which reached his knees. Wolf Tooth lashed the flaps together at his neck and once near his waist. Not far down their trail, he was shocked to find out how quickly the green hide had frozen to him in that terrible cold and ended up wearing it for the rest of the journey, unable to thaw it from his clothing.

From the Piney Creeks they limped over the benchland to Crow Standing Creek and followed that on to Tongue River, just above the mouth of Otter Creek. With nothing but water and occasional horsemeat to survive on, Dull Knife's Cheyenne followed the frozen course of the Otter until they crossed over to Box Elder Creek.

There at last the young scouts brought back good news to the shivering, trail-weary pilgrims.

Just ahead in a lazy bend of Otter Creek stood many lodges. They had reached the Oglalla camp of Crazy Horse.

CHAPTER 15

1877

Snow clung in dirty patches about clumps of sage and bunchgrass. The ground lay soggy this early spring, the fires smoky in the Cheyenne camp. For days on end, the sun had not poked its head out of the low pewter-bellied clouds. It made Yellow Bird all the sadder still.

The winter had been hard, even for those peoples who roamed this high plains country. What made it worse was that his people were poor once again. No lodges, no ponies, no robes nor blankets. And little to eat after soldier-chief Mackenzie drove Dull Knife's village into the snow with a vengeance.

While the Oglallas gave over to their friends what they could, sharing lodges, ponies, and robes, Yellow Bird felt it was not the same as owning something of your own labor. He was approaching the seventh summer of his life, and wondering at times now if things were actually all that bad in the southern country, on the reservation his mother had abandoned. More and more he dwelt on it these cold, late winter days. Turning it around in his mind like a

smooth round stone. Thinking it best for his mother to
return to the land the white man had given them in the
territories.

As far back in his young life as he could remember, theirs
had been an existence of waiting and running and fighting.
If they weren't fighting the soldiers, then they were waiting
for the next surprise dawn attack on their village. Which
meant that while the Cheyenne were waiting, they were
always struggling to regain all they had lost when the
soldiers did come marching.

Always, the soldiers came marching.

Crazy Horse had taken the Cheyenne beneath his wing
once more. After only three sleeps, the Oglallas marched
south until they struck the Tongue River near Hanging
Woman Creek. It was there the bands splintered once
more. Some of the Cheyenne stayed with Crazy Horse,
following him up Hanging Woman Creek. The rest chose to
stay with their chiefs, Two Moon and White Bull, who
decided to wander up the Tongue.

"We will stay with our own people," Monaseetah said as
she stirred the antelope stew in the battered, hand-me-
down kettle given her by an Oglalla squaw.

"I say we should stay with Crazy Horse. He is the
bravest, mother. The army will not dare attack his camp!"
Sees Red protested.

She glanced from her eldest to Yellow Bird. He sat in the
smoke of the greasewood fire, intently watching the stew
bubble.

"Where would you go, Yellow Bird?"

He looked up, reluctant to tear his eyes from the savory
stew. "I would go wherever you go, mother."

"That's not fair!" Sees Red shouted. "Yellow Bird does
not want to be a warrior—he knows nothing of fighting the
white man."

She smiled at him. "I suppose you know all about
fighting the soldiers, little warrior?"

Sees Red nodded, pride etched on his copper face.
"White Cow Bull has been teaching me."

"He has, has he?" Monaseetah asked, returning to
chopping the *tipsina* into the boiling kettle. "I think this

Oglalla warrior is trying to get to my heart through my sons."

Yellow Bird liked it when she smiled. Despite the charcoal smudges on her face and the wisps of hair plastered to her damp forehead, she still remained the prettiest woman he had set his eyes on. And he liked the way her eyes took on a special light these past few weeks whenever the subject of White Cow Bull came up.

He smiled back at his mother, recalling her feeble attempts to cover up her true feelings whenever the Oglalla warrior came round. It was only natural for him to do so since White Cow Bull had taken the three of them under his wing the moment the Cheyennes limped into the camp of Crazy Horse in the early days of the Moon of Deer Shedding Horns.

"You need a husband, mother."

She turned to him. "Do I, Sees Red?"

He nodded. "A brave warrior for a husband."

"Do you think White Cow Bull would volunteer?"

The two boys looked at one another and burst out laughing.

"He has been courting you since last robe season, mother!" Yellow Bird exclaimed. "For so long now that even his people are making fun of him for chasing after the woman who wants no man."

She stopped stirring, her smile disappearing. "Is that what they call me now? 'The woman who wants no man'?"

Both boys nodded, sheepishly.

"Perhaps these Oglalla simply do not like me," she said under her breath.

"They are only having fun with you—the way the older boys poke fun at my little brother," Sees Red said.

"A cruel way to have their fun."

"Do you want a man?" Yellow Bird asked innocently.

She looked into his open face, knowing she could not lie to him. "I want a man who will care for the three of us, Yellow Bird. As much as I want a man to care for."

"White Cow Bull!" Sees Red shouted as he leapt up, startling two of their camp dogs. They barked noisily at him.

"I . . . I do not know if it will be White Cow Bull," she

replied quietly. "Perhaps I need some time to think about this."

"How long, mother?" Yellow Bird bent down, peering into her tear-tracked face. "Will you decide by morning?"

"He has brought no ponies," she whimpered, feeling overwhelmed.

It tore at the young boy's heart. "Did my father bring you ponies?"

Her eyes glared into Yellow Bird's, then softened. She swallowed the hard knot at her throat. "No, your father gave no ponies for me."

"I am sure White Cow Bull will make a better father to us than Yellow Bird's father was," Sees Red added. "He is Indian. He would not dare use you in his night robes, then abandon you."

She shook her head. "Yellow Hair was returning for me. I know it."

"Mother, those soldiers were coming to destroy our village. Just as they did when your mother was killed at Little Dried River—"

"No!" She said it, firm.

"And when your father was killed at the Washita!"

She shook her head violently. "*No!* Yellow Hair was returning for me—as he vowed he would."

"They came to attack the villages . . . not look for a silly Cheyenne woman!"

She slapped Yellow Bird high on his cheek. It stunned all three into silence. Monaseetah quickly retrieved the bone ladle and resumed stirring the chunks of antelope and tipsina root.

His cheek stung where her fingers had caught him. But more so, his pride had been blistered, knowing he had driven her to this anger with him. Worse yet, that she could not accept the truth of it. It lay like a cold, flat rock in his little belly—this thought that, despite all the evidence, she still clung to the belief that Yellow Hair had been returning for her when he brought that long column of soldiers down the coulee toward the river crossing.

Again the image of his body swam before his eyes. A nightmare of blood and mayhem and mutilation swirled about that clean, freckled, fish-bellied body of the man she claimed had been his father. He wished now that the Sioux had mutilated that sunburnt body. Wished so hard in that way the Cheyenne and Lakota would have made his father no different from the other soldiers they hacked apart on that bloody hill.

Maybe that would have helped. Maybe now he would not feel so different, so apart from all the rest. If his father had been treated the same as the other soldiers after the battle, perhaps Yellow Bird would be treated no differently now.

But that all lay behind him. There was nothing a young half-breed boy of seven summers could do about anything, he decided. Much less could he do anything about who his father was . . . or how his father's body was cared for atop that hot, bloody hill reeking with the stench of death and retribution.

For a moment Yellow Bird was struck with the thought that his father had died to atone for a great blood debt owed both the Shahiyena and Lakota bands. What troubled him deeper still was the fear that one day he might die to atone for the sins of his father.

"I am sorry, mother," he whispered finally.

She whirled, dropping the horn ladle, and swept him into her arms. The tears burst free as they embraced.

"I am sorry, Yellow Bird. Sorry for waiting so long on the promise of a man who never meant to return for us. Sorry for not seeing it sooner. For wasting so many precious days thinking on Yellow Hair, when he had no thoughts of me."

"Mother—"

She put her smudged fingers against his lips, silencing Yellow Bird. "No," and wagged her head. "Let me say it. I want to forever wash my soul clean of him."

Monaseetah held him at arm's length, sniffling back her tears, the runny nose. "Sees Red, you take Yellow Bird with you and find White Cow Bull. You tell him . . . tell him I will make up my mind on marrying him soon."

"When, mother?"

She raised her eyes to the distant snowy peaks of the Big Horns. "By the time the grass grows tall, I will know in my heart what to do."

Yellow Bird stopped once and looked back as he took off

with his brother. His mother knelt hunched over the smoky fire made of damp wood, stirring their supper. He was angry once more for the way he had hurt her, driving her to strike him. More than anything Yellow Bird felt his heart hurt with cold, icy stabs of pain, thinking on all the years of her life—this beautiful woman with a good heart—all those years wasted on a dream with no chance of fulfillment.

There were times, he thought, as he continued on with his brother to find White Cow Bull, times when Yellow Bird wished he had been the one to pull the trigger of that pistol the older ones say was held against Yellow Hair's head in those final moments of the great battle.

Many were the times he had prayed to be granted the chance to stare into those blue eyes of his father's—then pull the trigger that blew out Hiestzi's brains.

Some of the Cheyenne had gone up Hanging Woman Creek with the Oglallas. Monaseetah had kept her boys with Two Moon and White Bull as they journeyed up the Tongue River. In doing so she had pulled away from the young Oglalla warrior, once more repeating her promise to decide by the time the grass grew tall.

"I will wait," White Cow Bull repeated. "I have waited for you this long, pretty one. I can wait a few more moons."

He touched her cheek with his fingertips, then wheeled suddenly and leapt atop his pony. Fiercely he kicked it into a burst of motion, yelping at the top of his lungs as he tore away, galloping after the stragglers at the end of Crazy Horse's line of march.

Sees Red and Yellow Bird did not ask, nor did they say anything of it, much less gloat. But they knew how their mother would decide. The tears were there on her cheeks for the reading.

By late winter the army was back on the trail of the Cheyenne. This time a soldier-chief called Bear Coat Miles was in charge of hunting down the villages. The soldiers succeeded only in capturing two Cheyenne squaws who were returning to Two Moon's camp from the Oglalla village many miles away. The Cheyenne efforts to rescue the prisoners from Bear Coat's soldiers were to no avail.

But later in the spring as the short-grass poked its head through the muddy ground, Bear Coat sent one of the Cheyenne women back to speak to the people of Two Moon's village. With an interpreter along, bringing tobacco and powder and other presents, Wool Woman told the assembled camp that the soldier-chief was asking them to go to a fort called Keogh and surrender themselves to the army there.

It had been a hard winter of little to eat, constantly watching over their shoulders, wondering each time they closed their eyes if they would be awakened by gunfire and the shouts of soldiers. The little ones cried most from hungry bellies. And the old ones who remembered the glories of last summer remembered as well how short-lived those glories had been.

Perhaps it was better to live in peace on the agencies, where the trader and Indian agent passed out the rations to the obedient Indians. Perhaps then the cries of the hungry children would not haunt the fathers and mothers and old ones. If following the old ways meant hunger, death, and danger, and watching all that you own go up in black smoke—perhaps then agency life would be better. At least it offered a chance of some peace.

Dull Knife decided to take his band into the fort named for one of the soldiers the Cheyenne warriors had killed the previous summer. They would go to this Fort Keogh and surrender.

"You are certain you do not want to come with us?" Talks Last repeated her question.

Monaseetah looked over the tired ponies and ragged travois of those who were straggling past, following Dull Knife up the Tongue, headed for the soldier fort, where they would surrender and be given tents and rations.

She shook her head, certain of her decision once again. "No. I will take my sons with the others who are leaving now to catch up to Crazy Horse."

"Then you have decided to stay with the Oglalla warrior."

"Not yet," she answered in a sigh. "Among the Oglalla I am hoping to find someone who will take me to find Sitting Bull's camp."

Talks Last studied the young mother. "Why the Hunk-papa?"

"He will be the last to surrender."

"You want nothing to do with the white man now?"

"I have learned of the mistakes you make when you listen to your heart, old woman."

Talks Last nodded. "I wish you well in finding the Oglalla . . . and in talking someone into leading your family to the Hunkpapa camp." Her eyes bounced over to the youngest of Monaseetah's boys. "You will keep him safe from harm, this son of the great Yellow Hair?"

She nodded, her eyes misting. Sniffling, she fought back the tears as she stepped beside the old woman's pony. Talks Last bent over so they could embrace.

"He will be safe as long as I keep him far from the white man . . . especially soldiers. Long, long ago Yellow Hair himself told me it was far better for our child to grow up Indian. Among the whites he would always be threatened by men who thought less of Yellow Bird because of his Cheyenne blood. He could never be more than a spirit without a home."

Monaseetah watched after the woman and her daughters while the entire procession disappeared among the hills bordering the Tongue River.

"Are you coming, mother?" Yellow Bird asked. "The others won't wait for us."

His voice startled her. She turned, embarrassed, seeing the small band of Cheyenne, numbering no more than two dozen, disappearing downstream.

"Let us go now," she replied, climbing atop the pony that dragged their pitiful few belongings tied atop the swaying travois.

Yes, let us go, she thought as she followed her two sons into that uncertain country to search for Sitting Bull's Hunkpapas.

Let us go in hopes of finding Yellow Bird's spirit a home.

CHAPTER 16

June, 1877

FOR days now there had been much grumbling from the Hunkpapas who struggled across the barren landscape like a fugitive centipede, nosing north. At the head of the column rode the resolute one who would not be deterred in reaching the medicine line.

"We can find peace in the land of the Grandmother," Sitting Bull reminded them last night, attempting to soothe ill tempers brought on by the cold, and the wet, and the long, endless march.

"We can sleep sound there, our women and children can lie down and feel safe. I do not understand why the redcoats gave us and our country to the Americans. We are the Grandmother's children. And when we go across the medicine line, we shall bury the hatchet. My own grandfather told me that the redcoats were our people and good people, and that I must always trust them as friends."

Yellow Bird crept up among the shadows to listen to the debate as sour tongues wagged.

"Why this grumbling?" asked the Hunkpapa warrior,

Whirlwind Soldier. "For many suns now we have all had a choice. Indeed, for as many as three robe seasons—you have been free to go."

"Free to go?" demanded one of the unhappy ones, Big Mule.

"Certainly. Before, you could go in to the agency where the white man wanted us to stay and die. Now we have but two ways to go. We can turn about and go south to the land of the Spaniards. Or continue north behind The Bull—to the Grandmother's Land."

"We still have a third choice," a new voice entered the discussion.

"Do we, Shave Head?" Whirlwind asked.

"Let us return to our reservations and be fed for the hard times."

Whirlwind Soldier shook his head, his eyes seeing that Sitting Bull had finally turned his full attention on him. "For me, that is no choice. Of the three . . . there remains but one direction for my life now. The Spaniard's land is much too hot and the water too warm. And staying here where the soldiers roam free, destroying our villages, murdering our women and children—that is no choice for me. Tomorrow I will follow Sitting Bull across the medicine line."

Sitting Bull rose at last, the murmuring growing low. For a moment of silence he thought back on the battles and the buffalo chases that had occupied his people ever since the short-grass time of a year gone when he led his people into the valley of the Greasy Grass for their greatest victory.

"Just before the first snow of last winter, you warriors fought the Bear Coat's soldiers. We whipped the Bear Coat good, then got away. I want to stay far away from the soldiers. Here, in this land, we can go nowhere without seeing the head of an American. Whirlwind knows my heart. There is but one place for me now. I am tired of being chased like a rabbit."

"Our scouts have been across the Medicine Line and talked with the Lakotas already gone there," Whirlwind said. "They have thrived this past winter—while we have not been able to fill our bellies. Up there—plenty of wood and many buffalo!"

An instant acclamation rose from the hundreds gathered at the series of fires.

The next sun climbed early, yet not early enough to catch Sitting Bull's people still in their robes. They had been up long before the sun gave its benediction to the broad land, packing and saddling and preparing for this momentous day.

For weeks now their ponies had been growing sleek on the new grass. And today the men decked their favorites in paint and ribbon, tying hawk's feathers in manes and tails. Even the old horses pulling the travois had been brushed in anticipation of the great event.

They had waited to set off in the gray light, until at last two young heralds tore back along the line of march, announcing that Sitting Bull had set off, his nose pointed north. With yelps and cries of joy, the Hunkpapas and their guests spread across the prairie beneath that wide, new-day's canopy as cloudless as it was blue.

It stirred young Yellow Bird's soul to hear the excitement in those hundreds of voices raised in thanksgiving. Now in his seventh summer and the proud possessor of his own pony, he let the frisky animal prance and cavort alongside Monaseetah's two ponies. One she rode, the other pulled the drag with their simple possessions and tiny lodge.

"May I ride to the front of the march, mother?"

She smiled at him. "Why is it you want to ride up there?"

"I want to be one of the first to see this Medicine Line."

"Good morning, little Cheyenne warrior!"

They both turned to see Wind come galloping up on his gray pony.

"You are in a hurry this morning," Yellow Bird cheered.

"Can you come with me?" he asked of the young Cheyenne, then turned to Monaseetah. "To the head of the march?"

She looked about, searching down the wide column. "I do not know where your brother is."

"He is back there," Yellow Bird said, pointing. "With some of his friends."

Monaseetah settled back on her pad saddle, patting the pony's neck. "Yes, you may go."

The words were barely out of her mouth when Yellow Bird was pummeling his pony's ribs.

"You take care of him, Wind!" she shouted after them as they raced one another into the distance.

Tears streamed from the corners of his eyes. How he loved the throbbing of the pony's muscles between his legs, hearing it suck at the wind in hungry gulps, nostrils flaring, its mane lashing the side of his young face.

They neared the head of the march neck and neck, then began to slow together. Wind reined his pony left, and Yellow Bird his to the right. As suddenly two warriors appeared on either side of him, grabbing for the rawhide rein. Yellow Bird sat up, frightened, pulling back on the rein so they could not grab it. He glanced to his left to find Wind struggling with two more warriors.

"You are the little Cheyenne?" a warrior demanded in his ear. The Hunkpapa snagged a fistful of Yellow Bird's rein.

He nodded, swallowing hard.

"You should learn to have better manners," the second Hunkpapa said.

"No one is to cross the Medicine Line ahead of Sitting Bull," the first declared.

"Go with your friend now and find a place in the line of march."

"Are we close?" Wind asked as he was led up by the other Hunkpapa police.

The first warrior nodded. Then he smiled. "We were all your age once, young fellows."

The four laughed with the boys. Then the second Hunkpapa spoke, "We are very close."

Like Yellow Bird, Wind boosted himself as high as he could, both boys straining to peer far to the north. Nothing they could see was distinctive.

"I see no grand line on the prairie," Yellow Bird complained as he settled his rump on the pony's backbone.

The warriors laughed again.

"You will see no line on the ground, little warriors," the first *akicita* advised. "Look for tall piles of stones."

"Like those?" Wind was pointing, excited.

The four strained to see far to the horizon. "Perhaps the little one has the best eyes of all! I see no stone piles."

"Do you see them, Wind?" Yellow Bird asked.

"No, but I do see those four riders racing back here."

"Aiyeee!" shouted the first Hunkpapa policeman. "Sitting Bull's messengers sent out ahead of our columns this morning. They are returning!"

Now all of them could make out the forms bobbing against the blue horizon—five horsemen whipping their ponies into a lather.

"I don't need to see the piles of stones, Wind!" the young Cheyenne roared as the four Hunkpapa police tore off toward the head of the march where they would escort Sitting Bull's party. "In my heart I know those riders are coming back with great news—they have seen the Medicine Line with their own eyes!"

"The earth lives!" Wind shouted, stretching a hand down to the grassy prairie below his pony's belly.

"So lives the sky above!" Yellow Bird raised his arm its full length and spread his fingers, yearning toward the blue.

"All things about us live!" They cried out the words together, watching the riders come closer and closer to the head of the columns.

Behind them the line of march was quickly beginning to widen. Word was being passed down from mouth to mouth, causing great anticipation. Everyone wanted a glimpse of the medicine line, wanting to see the Grandmother's Land. Rather than walk behind others in a gauzy dust, many of the marchers spread onto a wide front. Sitting Bull himself served as the point of that great arrowhead leaving the land of the Grandfather behind for all time.

"We say farewell to the land of death!" Wind cheered, leaning over to slap Yellow Bird's bare thigh.

"Greetings to the land of life!" the young Cheyenne replied. "Come back with me, my friend. I want to ride with my mother when we cross this Medicine Line."

They wrenched their ponies about in a tight circle, tearing back along one arm of the great arrow spreading across the prairie behind Sitting Bull. In the space of a few heartbeats, loud shouts erupted behind them, coupled with cries of joy and the trilling calls of the women—all of it mingled with the snorts of excited ponies and the squeals of the tiny ones strapped to their mothers' backs or safely caged atop the travois packs.

"Mother! Mother!" shouted the little Cheyenne.

"I see, Yellow Bird!" she hollered back at him, pointing and waving the arm as he came racing up. "Look, my son!"

Yellow Bird wheeled his pony in a haunch-sliding circle, kicking up tufts of the green sod beneath its feet. All along the procession throats thundered to the heavens. Dogs barked and hand drums throbbed, some warriors even bringing out their eagle wing-bone whistles that had served as an eerie background to the fierce fighting along the bony ridge beside the Greasy Grass just a month shy of a year now gone.

That joyous cacophony raised the hackles at the back of his neck. Then he grew wide-eyed, sensing the first change in the air. It tugged gently at his light-streaked hair he wore without braids that morning.

"Yes, breathe deep of it, Yellow Bird," Monaseetah called out to him as he and Wind slowed beside her. "This is the smell of freedom!"

He craned his neck like a magpie pecking over carrion, looking in every direction. "I see no difference in the land, mother. It all looks the same to me."

She giggled like a young girl. "It may not look it, but the land there, beyond those big stone piles, is very different."

"No line?"

"No, Wind," she answered.

"Just these stone markers! We have come to the land of the Grandmother!" Yellow Bird exclaimed as they passed between two of the pillars stationed some one hundred yards apart. Down the invisible line they looked in both directions as their animals pranced across the boundary. For as far as they could see, stone markers stood stretched from horizon to horizon, east to west, signifying their portal to freedom.

"Aiyeee!" Wind said, about to slap his pony's flanks with his elk-antler quirt. "We are safe from the bluecoats now."

Monaseetah twisted on her pad saddle, looking back at the stragglers crossing the line, looking farther back still on what once was. "Now the bluecoats can no longer hunt us

down and kill us, Yellow Bird. Here you will be safe from
those who are afraid of Yellow Hair's son."

Wind stayed his quirt, choosing not to spur his horse
away from his Cheyenne friend. "Who is this Yellow Hair?"

"He is my father," Yellow Bird said, still looking into his
mother's eyes. He felt such warmth in the strong smile she
gave him. "I never knew him, but I am told he was a brave
pony-soldier chief."

Yellow Bird watched the young Hunkpapa boy glance for
a moment at Monaseetah.

"Wind, my mother was captured by Yellow Hair's soldiers in the winter snows beside the Washita," Yellow Bird
explained, as if shedding a weight. "I am her child by this
Yellow Hair."

"*Hau! H'gun!,*" the Hunkpapa boy gushed, touching the
fingers of his right hand to his forehead in the Lakota
expression of respect. "This Yellow Hair . . . then, he
must be the one my people know as Long Hair."

"He is the same," Yellow Bird replied.

"*Aiyeee!*" he cried. "This is truly a medicine day for us
all. Word was told around our fires this past winter—news of
it coming from the agency Indians—that it was Long
Hair . . . your father who led his soldiers to the Greasy
Grass."

Yellow Bird watched his mother turn her face from the
Hunkpapa youth, recognizing the moistening of her eyes. It
tugged once more at his heart, pounding with excitement
and fear both in his chest.

"What you say is true, my friend. My father did lead his
soldiers to our great encampment on the Goat River. And
for it he gave his life over to the Everywhere Spirit."

"Wakan Tanka was satisfied that day," Wind said reverently.

The wind tugged at Yellow Bird's loose hair. He so loved
the feel of it, that crisp, clean bite to a wind that danced
right out of the north with nothing to hinder or fetter it.

*You are safe now, little Cheyenne. Safe from those who would
do you harm.*

Yellow Bird twisted round on his saddle blanket, instantly sensing something familiar about the voice. Yet he

found no one near but Wind and Monaseetah who could have spoken.

Something familiar in that distant echo at his ear struck him. Then he remembered. It had been almost three summers now since the whisper had troubled him.

I told you I would be with you always, Yellow Bird. I am with you still.

A drop of winter ice water spilled down his short spine as his pony's ears perked, its nostrils flaring. The animal pranced suddenly, as if it had been spooked by a rattler.

That, or had seen a ghost.

BOOK II

YOUTH
1877–1881

CHAPTER 17

June, 1877

THE heat was oppressive to her here. Funny how
different the weather in Monroe, there on Lake Erie's
Michigan shore.

Here the breezes blowing in off the waters of Lake
Michigan brought her little relief. Soon enough, she figured, she could leave this horrid, closed-in city and get back
to the lakeshore house in Monroe. Despite the fact that
house remained filled with so many ghosts.

Again she lifted the small watch pinned over her right
breast. Its hands seemed to crawl all the more slowly in this
heat. She chided herself for checking the watch so much. It
had moved but two minutes since the last time she looked.

So anxious to get this nasty business over with so she
could get back to Monroe. A sense of urgency growing as
every June day passed, inching closer and closer to that
dreadful anniversary. Numbers fell before her eyes, the
same way the calendar pages fell like game cards in her
dreams come most every night. The twenty-fifth . . .

She turned slowly, her knees feeling like heavy water.

And found the plush high-back chair. Without a thought to spreading her crinoline dress and petticoats, she crumpled into collapse.

The twenty-fifth . . . the first anniversary approaching . . . so soon—

A knock at the door to her hotel suite startled her, a sound, sure rap at the door in the other room. Instead of going Libbie looked toward the window, sensing the rising breeze coming in off the lake as she listened to Maria scuff across the carpet in the main room, heading to answer the door and the caller.

He's late, she thought. *This is the one I've spent two horrid weeks waiting to meet? The last thirteen days of asking discreet questions . . . getting recommendations from constables and private detectives alike. And this is the man they recommend to me? Someone who shows up for an important interview . . . late?*

Libbie strained at the muffled voices, Maria's and his at the door. She distinctly heard her black maid direct the man to the chair by the fireplace, just as her mistress had instructed. In the next moment Maria was at the door to the grand bedroom.

"Miz Custer, your gentleman caller is here. He says he has no card."

She waved a hand at Maria. "That's all right." Libbie rose from the chair, sensing the strength return to her knees as she swiped palms down her bodice and the stiff skirt.

The man claims he's a private detective . . . and he has no card of introduction?

Then she remembered that here she was no longer among Monroe's high society, born and raised as the daughter of an important member of the community: Judge Daniel Stanton Bacon.

And with that remembrance came a short jab of pain to think that for years now she had been out of that society swirl, following her husband here and there, from battle-fields of the Civil War, to the heat and sand of Texas, to the forts of the high plains—Riley, Hays, Rice, and Abraham Lincoln.

She sucked in a long breath of the hot, humid air—and swept through the door, her black fan in hand.

His back was to her. Nonetheless, he evidently heard

her enter the room, for he rose before turning to look at her for the first time.

She stopped at the perfect spot, right in the center of the room near none of the furniture. And waited for him to come to her.

His hat in one hand, he pulled the other up as he approached. She noticed it and presented hers. He swept hers into his without shaking it. Libbie glanced down at his hand, always the mark of a man's character. Nicotine stains on the fingers. The nails cut short. Strong, powerful hands. Clean as well. It was a mark in his favor.

"Mrs. Elizabeth Custer?"

"I am," she replied. "You must be . . . Mr. Fagen."

"Harley Fagen, ma'am." He finally released her damp, gloved hand.

"Please, Mr. Fagen," she said, afraid the damp hand betrayed her nervousness. She swept an arm sweeping back to his chair, "Take your seat."

As he turned from her, the breeze moving past the window curtains brought to her the distinct smell of rye whiskey. While neither she nor Autie had been drinkers, Libbie had come to accept that those who served in the frontier army often fought the boredom and tedium of their duty and fell back on strong drink. She knew the smell of sour-mash bourbon. Autie's brother Tom had developed a particular taste for it while serving at Elizabethtown in Kentucky. Too, Libbie could recognize Scotch whiskey— Billy Cooke's favorite. Both of them hard drinkers and unabashed womanizers.

But unlike many other kinds of liquor, this odor of rye was distinct to her suspicious nose. She made a mental note as she settled herself on the settee across from Fagen's chair that the man had shown up for the interview with rye whiskey on his breath.

One thing in his favor, she noted, spreading the skirt of her black dress delicately, *the man does have good manners . . . waiting for me to be seated before he takes his own.*

He set his hat on the oval end table next to his chair as he settled. Clearing his throat, Fagen was the first to speak. "First off, ma'am—I want to tell you how sorry I was to hear of the circumstances of the general's death."

That declaration caught her off guard completely. Libbie blinked at the sting of moisture, suddenly furious with herself that she had not kept control of the interview. Wanting it strictly business.

She cleared her throat as well, buying a moment, swallowing down the bile.

"I'm sorry, Mrs. Custer," Fagen replied quickly, inching up to the edge of his seat. "I . . . I didn't mean to sadden . . . or embarrass you."

She fluttered the fan before her face a moment longer. Then slowly dropped it. "No—no harm, Mr. Fagen."

"I shouldn't've said what I did, ma'am," he apologized. "Just—that I served in the Mexican campaigns . . . and come through the last war of rebellion with my hide in one piece. I can respect a military man like the general was."

"You served in the cavalry, Mr. Fagen?"

He shook his head. "Just a footslogger, ma'am. No glory in that. What I'd given to ride with your husband, though."

She straightened, feeling a painful pang at the wistful sound of his voice. Autie had always had that way about him. To surround himself with men who were fiercely sentimental about their service to the Republic.

"Maria," she said, turning to her maid, "would you be kind enough to serve the tea."

He looked at the table between them, set with the tea service and a plate of small cakes. Fagen took the hint. "I was told you're looking to hire a private detective, Mrs. Custer."

Libbie took her cup in one hand, balancing the saucer on the other. "Yes. I've been here in Chicago for some time now—asking about as discreetly as I can. Mostly through the help of old friends. Some of the general's old contacts, really. And interviewing."

"Two weeks, ma'am? And you haven't found a private detective yet? This is Chicago, Mrs. Custer. The place is crawling with 'em—"

"I have my reasons for rejecting those I've interviewed."

He regarded her carefully a moment. "If you pardon me—let's just put all our cards on the table. I've done my own checking, ma'am." Fagen took his cup of tea, sipped at it, and set it down on the table where he likely intended it to grow cold. "Yes, and discreetly, like you. In all this time here, you've talked with only two others before me. Only two men halfway interested in your mysterious errand. And I've learned that both of them wanted no part of this."

She too set her cup down, picking up the plate of cakes. "Something to eat with your tea, Mr. Fagen?"

"Am I right, ma'am?"

She set the cakes down, fussed with her lace napkin, then looked him in the eye.

"What you say is the truth, sir. I myself have no idea why the other two refused me help. But I was hoping to find someone here in Chicago. If not . . . I will travel all the way to New York City if I must—"

"Cost you a helluva lot more, pardon me, ma'am," he excused himself, coming once more to the edge of his chair, where he leaned forward, resting his elbows on his knees. "Truth of it is, them other two you was trying to hire was just too young for the job, I'd figure."

She nodded, recalling the other two she had called here for their private interviews. "Yes, perhaps they were. And perhaps you're different because you aren't as young as they?"

"Precisely, ma'am," and he scooted back into the chair, settling comfortably. "I'm going to mark my fifty-first birthday in a few weeks. So I'm a man who's gone and worn the green off, so to speak. I've got me some staying power—to see things through."

She studied him all the more closely. The black wavy hair with a brush of gray at the temples. Any man these days could be wrinkled. It was so hard to tell, with so many young men living outdoors. Remembering her dear Bo. How Autie aged on that godforsaken frontier he loved. The wind and the sun and the cold and that interminable heat come summer to the high plains. Hard to tell . . .

"Fifty-one, you say?"

"Yes'm. Now, suppose you tell me what it is you've got on your mind so I can tell you one way or the other if I want the job." He jabbed a finger inside his damp collar. "I've had me about as much of this starch as a man can take in the heat." Fagen glanced at the window. "Mind if I open that a bit more, Mrs. Custer?"

"By all means," she answered, feeling some relief that he had spoken so forthrightly to her.

Instead of coming immediately back to his chair, he stood, waiting a moment before he spoke. "Would I have the lady's permission to remove my coat?"

"Of course, Mr. Fagen." Libbie smiled, liking the honesty of the man more and more.

He slid the wool coat from his arms, emitting the fragrance of scented snuff as he folded it carefully, then laid it over the back of his chair. He sat.

"Now tell me, Mrs. Custer. What is it you're wanting done so badly that it scared off them two green fellas you tried to hire already for the job Harley Fagen wants?"

She sat back, startled at his directness. "You want this job, Mr. Fagen? Just like that?"

"It has something to do with the general, doesn't it, ma'am?"

She nodded, no longer scared that the meeting had been wrenched from her control. "Why . . . yes. It does. Very much so—"

"Then I want the job, Mrs. Custer."

"But you don't even know the details of what it is that I'm wanting done."

"Suppose you tell me and then give me a chance to say yes . . . or no when I get up to leave you."

"All right, Mr. Fagen. What I have to tell you is in the strictest of confidence—and must not go from this room."

He nodded, impatiently. "I understand, ma'am. Tell me all of it." He glanced at Maria, standing patiently near the door.

Her eyes followed his. Then she understood. "Maria knows everything, Mr. Fagen. She is more than merely household help: She is a trusted friend and confidant."

"All right, so long as I know who to trust with what, Mrs. Custer. Tell me what it is about your husband that's so secret. What about this job or the general that scared off two detectives already."

Harley Fagen stopped at the corner down from the hotel awning. He glanced back at the uniformed doorman, absently watching the activity of guests coming and going, carriages and teams caught in a blur of shimmering summer heat.

He couldn't figure out why she had booked herself into such an expensive hotel. From what he knew, her father had been one of Monroe's elite upper crust, but only by virtue of his profession. There had never been much money in the Bacon family.

And Lord knows the Custer family a'times borrowed a pot to piss in, he thought, smiling to himself.

Fagen pulled back the cap on his tiny silver-plated snuffbox. He swirled a thumb and fingertip in the powdered mixture, then brought them to his nose, drawing deeply into one nostril as he closed off the other.

He blinked repeatedly with the sting, until the burn left his nose and eyes. As long as he had been at it, that mixture never failed to slap his head around each time he got his nose involved.

Swallowing and of a sudden feeling an immense thirst, Fagen stuffed the snuffbox back into a vest pocket and licked at the fingers.

"No, Harley, my boy," he whispered to himself. "No lieutenant colonel in the army makes enough money so his widow can afford those splendid accommodations."

Shaking his head, he stepped back out of the doorway, away from the shadow and into the summer sun, feeling a trickle of cold sweat running down his scalp, from his hatband to his rumpled collar.

He tore at it now, loosening the collar and letting the tie flap round his neck in the hot breeze he stirred up as he strode quickly down the street.

"It can be one of only two things, Harley," he continued, talking to himself, bumping and jostling past the other pedestrians sauntering down the wide boulevard. "Either the lady is putting up as proud a front as she can—poor as she might be . . . or Mrs. Custer might be getting some . . . some help from some quarter."

He nodded, bringing his fingertips up to his nose again and gently closing off one nostril, then another, to be sure he had snorted all the mixture deep into his nose. It would never do to let some of that special pale powder go to waste, doing nothing more than coating the hairs in his nose. It was habit by now, this second sniff. Long a habit now.

Fagen rubbed his nose vigorously, sensing the first lightening sensation behind his eyes. *Good*, he mused, smiling.

"Now, where were you, Harley?" he said to himself as his pace quickened slightly, the mixture acting on him.

"You finally got yourself a job, old boy. Washed out of the Pinkertons the way you was . . . but you got yourself a good job. Working for no less than Mrs.—by God— George Armstrong Custer herself. And at good pay."

He clapped his hands twice, excited, his blood seeming to surge within his veins as he turned the corner, heading crosstown now. He'd need a good horse. No, she'd given him enough money for two and supplies. Plus a draft he could draw on when need be, from a Chicago banking firm.

Your lady thought of everything, General Custer, he said to himself.

A job. Money for expenses. And a chance to get out of this stinking trap of a city to boot.

Hired to snoop around and find out some things for Mrs. Custer. Perhaps even run down some proof.

"And while you're at it, Harley Fagen," he told himself in dodging a huge freight wagon as he crossed the street, "you're gonna find out just who in hell is bankrolling this little jaunt the general's wife wants you to take out to Indian country for her."

CHAPTER 18

June, 1877

No one needed telling that this would be the place of their camp. Two sleeps now inside the Grandmother's Land they had marched. Now among the hills near Pinto Horse Buttes.

Here they would camp beside the bubbling creek, with plenty of wood and water. Tall grass grew beyond on the shelf that seemed to stretch for as far as the eye could see. It was good. And the people could sleep here in peace.

The women circled the ponies, each group stopping at its appointed site in the great circle, leaving room for the council lodge at the center of it all. Excited and happy, the squaws chirped their orders to children. Sending boys after deadfall for the fires, girls going after water from the clear stream. Once the fires were started and the pots set to simmering over the flames, boys led the ponies onto the grassy shelf, leaving the women and girls behind to erect the tripods, lay the rest of the poles in their proper order, then pull the lodge skins over the spiral cones.

Yellow Bird looked back at the growing camp. Almost all

the people had arrived by now. Here and there a lodge already stood against the afternoon sky. And what a sky it was, stretching on forever, just like the great plains back home. . . .

He squeezed that thought out of his mind. This would be his new home. Now and forever. Wherever his mother led him . . . until he was old enough to be a warrior and had to leave Monaseetah's lodge—until he was old enough to take a wife for himself. But for now he believed his mother needed him every bit as he needed her.

Stretched upon his back in the tall, fragrant grass, watching the soft puffs of clouds floating overhead across that endless blue prairie, Yellow Bird sucked on a stalk of green. His hands cupped the back of his head, and he lay there, sensing the slow rising of warmth from the earth itself. Like sitting near the fire on a cold winter's day. No, more like his mother holding him, soothing his nightmares away when darkness sank about their lodge each night.

At the woman's scream he rolled onto one elbow so he could see above the top of the tall, waving grass. A hundred ponies blocked his view.

The shouts of the men and the barking of dogs brought him to his feet. More women shouting now as he tore through the pony herd, here and there dodging the hungry horses.

When he reached the edge of camp, he found women and children busy at their lodges and belongings. But now many of the frantic squaws were tearing the lodge skins from the poles. Older girls and boys were hurrying ponies into camp, a few already lashing drags to the travois horses.

Most frightening were the war songs shouted out in discordant chants by the warriors, old and young. They scurried from their lodges, carrying bows, shields, and rifles, taking no time for paint or medicine smoke.

Brandishing their weapons, the men hurried to the creek bank with their strong-heart songs bursting from every lip.

Some of the women pointed as they jabbered. Many of the men who stood far down the bank pointed as well. He could not see what it was they were looking at, for trees dotted the creek.

Yellow Bird knew not where to go. Should he first go to

his mother's lodge? Perhaps she is afraid for him—wondering where he is. No, he decided. She will be worried about what is going on. If he goes to the creek bank, he could find out, then go tell his mother the news. That was the way of a young man—not a boy.

Here he would grow up among the Hunkpapas, Yellow Bird reminded himself. Here he would one day become a man.

As he came to a stop behind the rest, he could just begin to make out some figures on the far side of the creek. Yellow Bird pushed his way through the crowd of legs and breechclouts and skin dresses, until he burst through to have a clear view of the creek, and the gentle slope on the other side that drove itself into a crazy, gray wrinkle of cutbank.

Atop the cutbank sat two mounted men. Just sitting there, waiting. Impassively the pair stared back at the massing Hunkpapa warriors on the opposite bank.

He could not tell, but it appeared the men were wearing leggings and long coats. The prairie wind tugged at the unbraided hair spilling over their shoulders. Under one man's leg he thought he recognized the bulge of a rifle butt. Both sat slightly slumped, waiting.

Yellow Bird ran a little farther downstream, to get closer as one of the two men turned to the other and appeared to say something. The second sawed his horse about, then pushed it to the top of the cutbank in a series of leaps. From there the second stranger waved—not at the Hunkpapas, but to the prairie beyond the far cutbank.

All about him the warriors grew anxious.

"These two could be scouts for the American army," talk had it.

"They have tracked our village here from the Medicine Line."

"Bringing the soldiers to attack us."

There was a rattle of weapons and more screams from the women when four more men appeared at the top of the cutbank.

"Red Coats!" someone shouted.

Yellow Bird blinked his eyes. It was something so new to

him, seeing the four horsemen in their hip-length red coats, gold braid spilling off shoulders and cuffs. Shiny brass buttons adazzle with the gold braid on the front.

One of the four in red shouted something to the solitary horseman still down near the water.

The horsemen dismounted, dropping his reins to the ground, and stepped to the edge of the water.

A loud rattle of weapons erupted as he came to a stop. Every bow and rifle pointed at the opposite bank.

The man held up his right arm. Then his left. Then his hands began slowly moving in sign.

"He is saying he comes in peace!" announced Four Horns. Sitting Bull's uncle had taken a stand closest to the creek bank, warriors spread like hawk's wings from either side of the old man.

"Tell him to put down his guns!" yelled someone behind Yellow Bird.

"I have no gun on me!" the stranger hollered back in Lakota, holding open the flaps of his long coat.

Those words spoken in their tongue greatly confused the Hunkpapa warriors and squaws. This was a hard thing for any of them to understand. Much less a boy of seven summers.

One of the redcoats nudged his horse into motion. The animal picked its way down the cutbank, making slow, sure steps, as if it too understood that it was best not to hurry things. The redcoat slipped to the ground beside the long-haired one.

Yellow Bird was not sure, but under the longhair's hat, he looked Indian. While under the redcoat's hat was a big nose, and a dark smudge on his upper lip . . . perhaps hair. Like the fishbellied white men he had seen butchered on the hill above their great camp. Yes, it was the same, he decided, as the redcoat pulled off his hat and wiped a hand inside the crown. He said something quietly to the long-haired one.

"The Grandmother sends her greetings to you. Are you Lakota?"

Four Horns turned to look up the bank at Sitting Bull. The Bull nodded.

Four Horns flung his voice across the noisy creek. "We are Hunkpapa."

"Is Sitting Bull with you?"

Again the chief gave his uncle permission to speak for him.

"Sitting Bull is here."

The redcoat appeared animated at that, putting the flatbrimmed hat atop his head once more, gesturing to the interpreter.

"The Grandmother has sent our police to welcome you to her land. May we cross over?"

With those words there arose a great stir of excitement among the Hunkpapas.

"These are the Grandmother's Red Coats we have heard so much about," Sitting Bull spoke softly. "I am told they speak straight. Tell them I will see them." The crowd parted for him as he climbed the gentle slope into the village.

"Sitting Bull will see you," Four Horns announced.

The redcoat and his interpreter leapt atop their big horses and signaled the other four men to follow them into the stream. As they splashed out of the water, onto the grassy bank, moving slowly so as to inspire no fear, Yellow Bird studied each man as he passed in single file through the same rift in the crowd through which Sitting Bull had passed.

Two Indians . . . perhaps half-breeds. *I am a half-breed*, he thought to himself.

And four redcoats.

At the top of the bank, the first redcoat slid from his saddle, rubbing his buttocks. Four Horns and the headmen approached in a crescent. Yellow Bird hurried as the redcoat shook hands with the old men of the Hunkpapas.

"Where is the great Sitting Bull?"

"He is waiting for you. In his lodge," Four Horns explained.

"It is good," the redcoat said. "We will have something to eat perhaps?"

Four Horns nodded. "Yes, that would be good."

"Then we can have a smoke?"

The old Hunkpapa beamed. "Yes. The Red Coat will smoke with us."

"I will smoke with you in peace, Four Horns."

Yellow Bird had seen how the redcoat's eyes constantly glanced about, watching the actions of the stirred-up young warriors who glowered severely at him. Yet the redcoat's face betrayed no fear that he would be cut down in the time it takes a man to draw a breath.

"You have a name, Red Coat?"

"I am Walsh."

"Come then, Walsh. Sitting Bull would like to meet with you. You look tired. Would you like to rest before we talk?"

The white man shook his head. "No, Four Horns. There is time enough to rest tonight after we have talked."

Four Horns stopped and looked closely at Walsh. "You would stay here in our camp tonight?"

There was a lot of murmuring from the crowd. It was not lost on the white man.

"Yes," he replied. "I would stay in Sitting Bull's camp, my men and I, for the night. It would be an honor."

The old man smiled, then pointed the lodge out. "Come, Walsh. I believe my nephew will like you."

The next morning Yellow Bird climbed from his blankets early, expecting to get a start on the day before the rest of the village. Yet he was surprised to find his mother gone from her robes. As he poked his head from the lodge door, he found her at her cook fire, already busy at breakfast. Instead of greeting a sleepy village, he discovered a camp alive with chatter and dogs wrestling, people moving goods and ponies this way and that. Everyone up and ready, expectant of something.

"Good morning, my son!"

"Is Sees Red the lazy one?"

"Seems he is the last in all of camp to rise."

"It is early, mother." He pulled his blanket more snugly about his shoulders. The sun had just peeped over the faraway horizon.

"Yes. Come eat. Everyone is up to hear this redcoat's words early this morning."

"He will talk to the village?"

She nodded. "Last night he spoke with the old men and

counselors until late. They agreed that he could address the whole village, first thing this morning. Everyone is waiting."

"Is everyone here?" the interpreter asked when Walsh stepped into the center of the huge gathering.

"All but a few old ones too sick to leave their beds," Sitting Bull began. "Three warriors with wounds and one a broken leg."

"Then Walsh will begin," announced the interpreter in Lakota.

Walsh stood beside the half-breed Metis. "I am James M. Walsh. Superintendent in this region. I work for the Grandmother across the big ocean." He pointed east.

"You are on her soil now. Land that belongs to the Grandmother."

The crowd murmured in excitement and satisfaction.

"When you live on the Grandmother's land, you must live by the Grandmother's rules."

Rules? thought Yellow Bird. *What are these?*

"If you do not obey the Grandmother's rules, then you will have to go back south of the Medicine Line. Do you understand?"

"Our people understand," Sitting Bull replied.

"I have said the same thing to all the other Lakota who have come across the Medicine Line before you. They have obeyed the redcoats. I hope Sitting Bull's people will obey our laws too."

Walsh dragged a handkerchief across his forehead before continuing.

"You are not to kill. You cannot steal. You are not allowed to injure another person or harm his belongings."

There was some murmuring from the knots of young warriors dotting the crowd.

Walsh went on, paying them no heed. "You Hunkpapa men have a heritage of protecting your women and children and old ones. The Grandmother is happy with that. It is good."

He took the hat from his head and swiped the handkerchief round the sweatband. "Most important, the Grandmother tells you that your warriors cannot ride south across the Medicine Line to steal horses, hunt buffalo, or harm Americans on the other side."

Sitting Bull stepped forward, raising his arm to quiet his people. The young warriors had grown agitated, more than merely muttering now.

"Hear me, my people!" Sitting Bull shouted above the clamor. They quieted. "If we obey the Grandmother's laws, she will protect us from the Americans. We will have no fear of the Blue Coats attacking our villages, killing our women and children."

Now the angry muttering softened even more. Many of them were bobbing their heads.

"Yes, my people. We are tired of being chased and harried everywhere we go. We want only a chance to travel beneath the great sky and hunt buffalo when we need meat or lodge skins. Red Coat Walsh says he will protect us from harm—if we do not break the Grandmother's laws."

"This is good that your people understand," Walsh said. "But there is one more important thing the Hunkpapas must know. The Grandmother has her own Indians here in this land. They are not happy about the Lakota coming up from the south to hunt buffalo and live here. If they hurt a Lakota . . . or take something from a Lakota—I will punish them."

The crowd agreed with that. Walsh put his hand up for silence.

"But if the Lakota harm any of the Grandmother's children or steals anything that belongs to the Grandmother's children—I will be the one to punish the Lakota."

These are brave words for a man who brought along only five friends, Yellow Bird thought. A half dozen surrounded by all these angry, fuming warriors ready to kill the redcoat with such bold words on his lips.

"We are the Grandmother's Indians too," Sitting Bull protested after he had settled his warriors.

Walsh shook his head. "No, Sitting Bull. The Hunkpapas are not the Grandmother's Indians. You belong to the Americans."

Yellow Bird pulled away from his mother's arm, tearing through the crowd. Running, running up the slope, onto the vast prairie. His young mind flared in torment again.

Why were they here—his mother, brother, and he—if not to be safe in the Grandmother's land, if not counted as the Grandmother's Indians?

Why had his mother brought him here—if they still belonged to the hairy-faced bluecoat soldiers who haunted the land south of the Medicine Line?

CHAPTER 19

July, 1877

I T had to be the hottest month of the year. Certainly hotter than anything he had ever suffered. Even down in the southwest, chasing the sun-grinners, riding behind Ol' Zachary T. himself. But up here on the high plains, it was something else—seemed the whole sky radiated heat, and the great, monotonous, endless roll of the earth itself reflected all that heat back again. Broiling a man in his own juices.

Harley Fagen swiped the damp handkerchief across his brow. A lot of good it did. He was sweating there again before he got the damned thing stuffed back in his hip pocket.

Hours ago Fagen had removed his coat and vest, flopping them over his arm, while at the end of the other hung his battered valise. Its two straps and buckles had seen more repair than Fagen could recall.

Yet at last, in this midday heat, he set foot on the station platform at Bismarck, Dakota Territory. He checked around the corner of the building, just to be sure he had landed in the right place. The middle-aged man smiled, deepening the crow's-feet at his eyes. He had made it. For there across the muddy Missouri River stood Fort Abraham Lincoln. Fourteen months ago to the day, George Armstrong Custer had marched his Seventh Cavalry from that sprawl of gray-washed officers' homes and barracks, stables and quartermaster's stores.

It was up to Harley Fagen to get some answers for the general's lady. Discreetly.

"You have business in town?" the clerk at the ramshackle hotel asked, turning around the guest register, ". . . uh, Mr. Fagen?"

"No, at the fort."

The clerk slapped the key on the counter, waving for an Indian dressed in a white man's wool suit to come over.

"Never mind him," Fagen protested. "Don't need any help with this . . . just one bag."

"Don't plan on staying long, Mr. Fagen?"

He stopped, glaring back at the nosy young clerk. "Not so much that, as I like traveling light."

After he had splashed some cool water on his face and torn the rumpled paper collar from his damp shirt, Fagen began to feel a little more human. He changed shirts, then pulled from his bag the three pistols he wore on every assignment.

Not that this was a dangerous task, but Harley had spent most of his adult life tracking after all sorts, and suffering all sorts of surprises. It was just that, well—the pistols made him feel a little bigger, helped him walk a little taller. The smallest .34-caliber derringer went into his boot, the second he stuffed in the waistband of his britches at the small of his back. And the third he caressed for a long time. Spinning the cylinder, working the hammer and trigger, up and down, round and round.

He rose from the edge of the spring bed, dragging the belt holster with him. With it buckled round his hips, he slid home the .45-caliber army model below the gap in his vest. When he pulled on his wool coat, the pistol butt protruded slightly from the gap of the coat.

He turned, staring at the aging man in the cloudy mirror

hung above the dresser. Fagen sighed, unbuckling the holster.

In resignation he tossed the belt and three guns back into his valise, then pulled out the large, handsome silver-plated flask. Harley drank from it thoughtfully. He would have to buy a rifle and hire a guide if he headed into dangerous country from here.

He looked down at his hands, wondering why they didn't shake. A sane man's hands would be shaking, he thought. Just thinking of Indian country, knowing what those bastards did to Custer's men, how they carved them up.

Yet his hands never trembled.

Perhaps he had had enough. Fagen stuffed the cork back in the flask and set it atop the pistols in that battered valise.

At his second-story window, he looked out across the river at the spread of buildings hunkered unprotected beneath the cruel high-plains summer sun. On the rail trip out, he had decided he would seek out Benteen first.

Not that Mrs. Custer had suggested the seventh's senior captain—Harley Fagen figured out on his own that Benteen would know a lot of what he needed to learn. If only because the captain had been one of those who had ridden into Indian Territory behind Custer that cold winter so long ago.

Mrs. Custer had suggested others, like Godfrey, who would be sympathetic to her needs. Hadn't taken long for Fagen to realize the woman would nurse the memory of her dead husband for as many years as it took to get the general out of her system. He wondered, doubtfully, if she would ever get on with her own life.

She had given him a list of names, men to interview. But to find out what he needed to know, Fagen would have to seek out those who did not appear on Libbie Custer's list—men like the mean-spirited Benteen, who either tried too late to come to the general's aid that summer day, or had become so mean-hearted that he never lifted a finger while Libbie's husband died.

Fagen strode to the door, deciding to ferry across the river. He could wait over there until after evening mess if he had to, just to get an audience with Benteen.

Harley smiled as the door clattered closed behind him. Once again he felt alive. On the scent like a hound.

Smelling the scent of danger . . . and death.

He stared at his reflection in wonder, at the face of the boy who stared back at him from the still water left in the shallow depression on the prairie, where he had gone to hunt with his bow. Yellow Bird felt his eyes sting, thinking on Scabby. Realizing he would never see the man again. His body left behind, long ago last summer. Dying a warrior. Fighting the soldiers.

Was it that he cried for himself?

Up here in the Grandmother's Land, the men grumbled that no longer could a man be a warrior. The redcoat Walsh, the one the Hunkpapas had come to call the White Forehead Chief, had forbidden them from raiding other tribes, stealing horses, making war. The only thing left, they complained, was hunting buffalo—and there were too few of them left.

Too few of them, some of the old men had said, like the Sioux. Disappearing from the prairie with their brother, the buffalo.

"Yesterday I was fleeing from the white men," Sitting Bull had said that first meeting with the redcoat soldier named Walsh.

Time and again in the last few weeks, Yellow Bird had turned the chief's words over and over in his mind, the way he would knead riverbank clay into toy ponies beside his tiny willow-limb lodges.

"Fleeing from the white men, cursing them as I went. Today they erect their lodges by the side of mine and defy me. The White Forehead Chief walks to my lodge alone and unarmed. He gives me the hand of peace. Have I fallen? Am I at the end?"

Yellow Bird still did not understand why his mother had cried when Sitting Bull had spoken those words.

The Hunkpapa soldiers, the one hundred *akicita* warriors chosen by Sitting Bull, were everywhere, making certain none would raid south across the Medicine Line. Or steal ponies. The redcoats had made it plain: Sitting Bull would be responsible for the actions of his young men.

The boy lay back, naked except for the breechclout and moccasins, all he wore on these long summer days. Across his shoulders, at the back of his hips, he felt the infusion of the Earth Mother's heat. Giving back to him what it had soaked up from the sun-above. A sprinkling of clouds spun a lazy swirl overhead.

Yellow Bird's thoughts drifted, until he remembered a fragment of instruction from Scabby. The Everywhere Spirit of the Cheyenne. Heammawihio.

It was with his childlike wonder that Yellow Bird felt again at the great circle of all things. Yet a stone of sadness told him he was different. With two bloods was he truly a part of that circle? He ached to know.

When Heammawihio had first created the Shahiyena, he made them to live forever as the spirits live. When a man died, he was to be dead only four nights. Then he would live again. But Scabby had told him that soon enough the Everywhere Spirit had learned this would not do. It had made his children too brave. There had been too much killing—each man able to come back to life after four nights.

Yellow Bird thought on death, sensing the tumble of hurt inside as his mind remembered the soldiers on that hillside. They were dead forever. His father, dead forever.

Not like before. Once people were like the great, soaring eagle. Scabby said a man could go out and kill an eagle, taking home with him the feathers to use. That man could return in four days to the place where he had killed the eagle, to find there near the nest an eagle.

"The eagle lives again, uncle?" he had asked Scabby summers ago.

The old Cheyenne warrior had wagged his head. "It is for me to wonder about, little warrior. Heammawihio gives life still to the eagle after four nights. Perhaps what a man sees is the spirit of the eagle he killed. Perhaps another bird. No matter—because I believe the spirit lives and soars unfettered across the whole of the sky."

He watched a long, long time, waiting for an eagle, a hawk, some bird to wing across the great patch of blue directly above him. One day soon he would go hunting eagles. He had promised himself that much, listening attentively to the lessons given at Scabby's knee.

No matter how hard he tried, still he felt cold in his chest thinking on the dead warrior. Wishing it were so that Scabby could have come back to life, that things could return to the way they had been before the soldiers started chasing them last summer. Before the soldiers got so brave they charged into that great camp. Then the people had to scatter to stay away from the soldiers. Running far, far away. So far they had crossed that medicine line.

Long, long ago on the other side of the big water, all white men lived in a faraway land, Scabby had instructed one winter night two robe seasons ago. But Heammawihio had warned the Shahiyena that one day the white man would cross that big water in his great canoes. It would begin a time when there would be much trouble and many fights. So many of the Shahiyena would be killed by the white man come that trouble and blood.

Scabby had said that time had come upon the Cheyenne when he had been a boy. And every summer the killing and misery had increased.

Yet all was not lost.

Yellow Bird thought back to the last night he had seen the warrior alive. Lying on his bed of pine boughs and soft blankets, cradled in a bear robe. Scabby had instructed his wives and children to prop him up slightly so that he might witness the sights of this great camp one last time. A messenger brought word to Monaseetah that the old warrior wanted to see Yellow Bird before he closed his eyes for all time.

He remembered sitting quietly at the man's side, touching the back of the veined hand, listening to the hard breathing across the hours of that last night. Near their feet Talks Last and the rest kept the fire going into the first gray streaking of dawn along the east.

"After Heammawihio had been with our ancestors a long, long time—teaching them how to live as he wanted," Scabby had whispered to Yellow Bird, "he told them he was ready at last to go up into the sky, where he would be to watch over them. So when a man dies, little warrior, he goes to live with Heammawihio for the rest of time."

Scabby had coughed up much lung tissue then. The talking came harder, and Yellow Bird remembered crying more, squeezing the strong, veiny hand.

"My time of trouble is soon to pass from me. When I go soon, I will go live with the spirits. My time of trouble will be over forever."

Back beneath the blue-everywhere sky, Yellow Bird sensed the soughing of the tall grass as it dried under the summer's sun, rustling all about him like the rubbing of deer antlers, season after season after season.

"Little warrior," Scabby had whispered, "pay heed to all that the spirits tell you—for your time of trouble comes closer with each step you take, each day you live. My trials are almost over. Your travail is yet to come."

He figured he would not have to buy a horse until he got down to Kansas.

Harley Fagen found it almost impossible to sleep tonight. Not certain it was the clatter of the train's great steel wheels on their tracks, or the hot cinders blown back through the car windows. The passengers had two choices: close the windows to escape the cinders, thereby denying themselves any chance at a cooling breeze coming in off the prairie; or open the windows to enjoy some respite from the sweltering heat of that summer night and worry about an occasional hot cinder.

More it was what Benteen himself had told Fagen two days gone now.

There had been a Cheyenne woman involved with Custer. In fact, Benteen had even snatched up his copy of Custer's book and pointed out, then and there, the dead man's references to the one called Monaseetah.

A comely beauty, Fagen remembered Custer's words as he stared off into the inky darkness of the far prairie, the only light provided by the sputtering oil lamps in the car, their wicks turned down so passengers could sleep through the rocking journey south.

You young, randy rake of a bastard, and Fagen smiled.

Benteen had told him of that winter long ago gone when Custer had kept the Cheyenne beauty as his personal concubine. Times were, Custer had to fight off the drunken advances for the woman from his own brother, Thomas Ward Custer.

"Make no mistake about it, Mr. Fagen," Benteen had said, "all officers serving that winter under Custer fully understood there could be no hint of dalliance with Custer's private property. Only the general's brother had the balls to try when he was drunk."

"Could Tom Custer—would Tom Custer be one to bed the Indian woman?"

"First off, she was no woman," Benteen had explained. "Oh, she was in body. A powerful lot of woman too. But a child in years. But . . . yes—Tom Custer would have been one to bed any woman who would spread her legs for him—a rounder, that one. And . . . no—Tom Custer could not bed Monaseetah. She was the general's *special* one. Custer and his young brother had had women before . . . but there was something different about this Cheyenne beauty. The general would let her nowhere near Tom's smooth talk."

"Tell me of the child?" Fagen had asked.

Benteen's eyes had narrowed. "All I know is what I've heard in bits and pieces. Fragments of the truth, you understand. There was this matter of the surgeon's report at Fort Sill—mind you, that's the post Custer and Sheridan established during their winter campaign."

"What of this report?"

"Late that fall—some time after Custer had speedily sent the captives back to their reservation—at the same time hurrying his pregnant concubine far from Hays and Libbie Custer's knowing eyes, I might add—it was documented that a boy-child had been born to one of the young Cheyenne women."

"Monaseetah?"

"Yes. A child fair of hair . . . and light eyes the spitting image of his father's."

Fagen recalled his unintentional gasp of excitement at the prospect of finding the child. Custer's child!

Benteen had pointed him south. To the territories. Cheyenne reservation. With his suggestion to look up the chief of scouts for that winter campaign long ago. The civilian just might know the whereabouts of the woman and her boy-child. A scout who himself was married to a Southern Cheyenne woman.

Harley Fagen let his eyes droop as the drowsy rock of the railcar swayed him to sleep. Sleep came, sure that he was moving closer to the biggest story this nation had heard since Custer himself was defeated last summer. Perhaps even bigger than the defeat of the Seventh Cavalry in Montana Territory.

He was going south to hunt for Ben Clark.

And somewhere down the line, Harley Fagen knew he would have to cough up money for a good photographer. Damn, but wouldn't it be worth it—that picture of the boy and his mother splashed across the front page of every paper in the country? Right beside a purloined photograph of the general himself.

Damn the secrecy Mrs. Custer had sworn him to—hell with her!

CHAPTER 20

Summer, 1877

"WHY would I return?" Sitting Bull demanded of his three very uneasy guests.

The Catholic bishop of Dakota, Martin Marty, had journeyed north to try coaxing the Hunkpapas back across the international border on his own. He had been assisted in his efforts by the chief of scouts for no less than General Nelson A. Miles himself, John Howard, and a half-breed interpreter whose nervous eyes never stopped moving across the assembled crowd.

"Would I return to have my horses taken from me, my weapons stripped from my hands?"

"You must understand that those are just precautions the army is taking—"

Sitting Bull slapped a fist into an open palm, shutting the interpreter up like the closing of a trap's jaws.

"Tell me what have the Americans to give me in return for my people coming back? Once I was rich, but the Americans stole it all when they took the Black Hills from me. No. I came here to remain for all my days with the White Mother's children."

The more the Black-Robe tried to talk Sitting Bull and the elders into returning south, the louder became their protests, and the angrier the young men. On and on the bishop droned, not heeding the warnings of his scout Howard, nor the interpreter's.

"Give these three to us!" shouted one of the warriors.

"Yes! We will send their broken bodies back to the Bear Coat!"

"No!" Sitting Bull shouted above the clamor, watching the young men press in close, eager for blood.

The bishop leapt to his feet, for the first time sensing his imminent danger. John Howard kept pulling at his robes, begging him to sit before matters came to blows.

"You will not have the blood of these three on my hands," Sitting Bull declared. While the young warriors grumbled and reluctantly wandered away from the council, he turned back to Bishop Marty.

"Tell the Black-Robe he keeps his scalp today because of the strength of Sitting Bull among his people. Tell the Black-Robe that we are happy here, at home once more in the land of our Grandmother. And you tell Bear Coat Miles that one day we will meet again—he and I."

"What . . . is to become of us now?" the interpreter asked, his voice tight, as pained as a wagon's ungreased wheel on a dry axle.

Sitting Bull turned his full glare on him. "You live because I want you to live. I will turn you over to the redcoat Walsh. The next time you come across the Medicine Line, your scalp will hang at my door."

The Hunkpapa watched the bishop make the sign of the cross. "What is this you do?" He mimicked the sign.

"The Black-Robe makes the sign of the cross."

"Yes," he answered, remembering. "The son of God's cross. In your great book—I recall the story. The bad people captured the son of God and killed him on the death tree: This cross the Black-Robe makes."

"Sitting Bull remembers the story of Jesus and how he was crucified, Bishop Marty," the interpreter whispered.

"Ask Sitting Bull if he will make the sign with me."

The Hunkpapa chief laughed when the question was posed of him. "It is funny that you ask, Black-Robe. My people have been making the sign of the cross for seasons long before the coming of you white men. See here, how you touch the four directions. See here how each time I smoke, I blow the sacred breath in the four directions. God taught us first."

"I can't believe that God could teach you about his holy son, Jesus Christ, before the Jesuits came among you," Marty said.

Sitting Bull felt the rise of his gall. "History is repeating itself, Black-Robe. Once before, in your magic book—the story is told of the bad ones who nailed Jesus to the death tree. Now the white man—the bad ones—are trying to nail the Indian to the death tree."

"That's totally absurd. For you to think that you Indians—"

"Hold your tongue, Black-Robe!" Sitting Bull shouted, waving in a handful of his camp police to take the three white men from the council lodge.

"Mark my words, Black-Robe . . . and you," he said, whirling on Howard, "take my words to Bear Coat Miles. This time the evil ones will do no killing on the death tree. No more will the white man hunt down my people."

"This cannot be!" Monaseetah exclaimed after Yellow Bird had run up to her, breathless in the chill autumn air that spoke of early snow. "Is it so? White Cow Bull has come to Sitting Bull's camp?"

"Yes, mother. It's true!"

She clambered to her feet, trying desperately to hide the wide smile betraying her face. "Is he coming here to our lodge?"

"For now he is talking with Sitting Bull, Spotted Eagle, and the rest of the leaders."

"He knows we are here with the Hunkpapas, doesn't he?"

"Yes. I hollered out to him," Yellow Bird replied. "He waved and shouted back to me before the men surrounded him and took him to Sitting Bull's lodge—everyone talking at once."

She wiped her hands down her skin dress. "Maybe I

should change into something better." Her face drooped. "I have nothing better to wear."

He took her hand in both of his, tugging her into following. "Come, let's not wait for him. We'll go find him, bring White Cow Bull to our lodge for supper."

"Yes," she gushed. "I have so much—so much to tell him now."

She found it hard to believe as she trotted beside her youngest son, through the milling, gathering crowds, on every lip the words of happy disbelief. Monaseetah felt giddy, like that winter long ago, having accepted now that the soldier-chief she called Hiestzi had not been returning to her at all. Yellow Hair had not come for her. Instead he was leading his pony soldiers down on the great encampment beside the Goat River.

Freed of the waiting. Freed of the yearning for an answer to that broken promise—Monaseetah had decided she would at last take her life into her hands. From the time she had been a girl, others had decided things for her. Taken things from her. Soldiers at Little Dried River and the Washita. Then forced to flee with Sees Red and her unborn child . . . Yellow Hair's child.

Ultimately made to watch the magical power of the Everywhere Spirit hand Yellow Hair and his soldiers over to the fury of the Cheyenne and Sioux people.

And forced to run in fear for Yellow Bird's life, knowing what the white man would do to Yellow Hair's half-breed son if they could ever catch him.

She had made this journey north, hoping that White Cow Bull would not give up. Hoping that he would keep his promise when Yellow Hair had not kept his.

"Crazy Horse had listened to the lies of the white man," White Cow Bull was telling the assembled warriors.

The men sat in a huge circle. Behind the men sat the women and restless children. Hundreds of them. Listening to the tale of treachery brought by the Oglalla warrior weary of the long trail north. He would rest when he had finished his words.

He alone stood, at the center of the great circle, at times pointing as if he were firing a rifle, or carrying a rifle to mimic the soldiers, at other times pointing a pipe stem to the heavens above. The earth below, that which swallows all men come their time of death.

"Red Beard Crook promised Crazy Horse he would have his own reservation, in some good hunting country. The Red Beard promised there would be no more fighting between the soldiers and the Oglallas. The Oglalla children would not cry for empty bellies. Oglalla women would not cry out for their dead husbands.

"Crazy Horse listened to the *wasichu*'s promises . . . listened to the words of the Oglallas who had surrendered already. He was sure some of it would be true. He did what he could for his people."

White Cow Bull looked now at Sitting Bull. The Hunkpapa nodded.

"Yes, Crazy Horse did what he could for his people. He always had. I do not agree with him—this returning to the reservation. But Crazy Horse thought only of his people. He was a brave Lakota." His fingertips touched his forehead in respect.

"H'gun! H'gun!" the ring of warriors shouted their approval with the Sioux word for bravery and respect.

"He had prayed long. He prayed hard for guidance before coming in."

"But they killed him!" Spotted Eagle shouted.

He turned with the angry words, his own voice calm above the frenzy of the crowd. "The soldiers came to our camp for him, but Crazy Horse had word of their coming. We fled to Spotted Tail's Agency, where the soldiers caught up with him."

"How did they kill the medicine man of the Oglallas?"

Monaseetah could see how it affected White Cow Bull to tell the story of it, how his body grew tense. He must be fighting inside now, she thought, fighting to keep control. To keep from crying.

"We followed the soldiers back to Fort Robinson," the Oglalla went on. "By the time I arrived, Crazy Horse was dying."

"Did they shoot him?"

He wagged his head, holding up a hand to silence the great rumblings from angry throats. "No. Crazy Horse was stabbed. They wanted him to give up his own knife. The soldiers said he took it from his belt to fight them, to escape. Those who saw said the soldiers drove a long bayonet into his belly. He was a long time in dying."

"I do not believe Crazy Horse would ever be an agency Indian!" a man shouted.

"He would not give in to the ways of farmers!" another hollered.

"It is your turn to be angry. But my anger is gone like the rains of summer," White Cow Bull replied, his voice calm, soothing the renewed murmurs of the seething crowd. "I too was angry at the treachery of his murderers. But I now realize that like Crazy Horse, I am one against the many. We no longer can come together as in those days gone when we defeated the Red Beard and the Long Hair. Instead I come north to flee the Americans. I can no longer fight them. I must go far, far away to live the old way. To this land of the Grandmother."

She found his eyes touching her at last. As if White Cow Bull had known she was there all the time, knew where she stood among the hundreds, back behind so many others with Yellow Bird at her side. The Oglalla's eyes looked into her. And she answered with her own.

He smiled, there in the center of that great circle of Lakota power. "I am weary, my friends. It has been a long journey bringing this news to you."

"Would you stay for supper with us?" Sitting Bull asked.

"I would on another night perhaps," he replied, touching his forehead with fingertips in respect for the powerful chief. "Tonight I would eat with old friends and rest."

"You will stay your days with us?"

"I will, if you would have me to, Sitting Bull."

The Hunkpapa stood, raising his arms to embrace the tall warrior. "There was a day when you rode at the left hand of Crazy Horse—a day when you and the most powerful of the Oglalla swept the last handful of soldiers from the top of that bloody hill along the Greasy Grass. Now it is a new day. When we no longer talk of fighting other tribes, of killing the white man. It is a time of peace here. Of hunting buffalo and eating *pte*'s meat. A time of making love to our women."

White Cow smiled. "Yes, it is a time at last to make love

to our women. No longer worrying about soldiers bringing death at each dawn."

"You will ride at my left hand, White Cow. As you rode with Crazy Horse."

"Hau, h'gunnn! This is a great honor!"

"Go, eat . . . and sleep. Tomorrow is the beginning of your new life."

White Cow Bull turned as the crowd dispersed, his eyes fixed on the young Cheyenne mother who stood waiting, Yellow Bird clinging to her side.

"Yes. This is the beginning of my new life."

CHAPTER 21

September, 1877

SITTING Bull sat with his chin cradled in a palm, an elbow propped on one knee, pondering the dilemma brought him by White Bird.

All about him the Lakota were gathering, whispering in muted tones, passing on bits and flecks of that dramatic story White Bird and five Nez Perce warriors had carried north across the medicine line. A story destined for the ears of the great Hunkpapa medicine man.

Chief Joseph had fled with his people from their Oregon country when the white man wanted their land and sent the bluecoats to take it from the peaceful Nez Perce. A soldier-chief they called One Arm Howard had grown impatient with the slow process of negotiating with the Indians, so White Bird said the soldier-chief simply hurried matters along by turning his head when the white men stole Indian land and cattle.

Young warriors had fought One Arm's soldiers, then fled to join up with Chief Joseph's band. Every day more and more men, women, and children flocked to the temporary refuge that was Joseph's village. The chiefs of the Nez Perce nation decided it best to avoid any more fighting with the soldiers. They would flee to the east so no more of their people would have to die. Perhaps east of the great spine of mountain peaks, out onto the buffalo prairie, their people could find peace.

Sitting Bull had listened without a word as the Nez Perce messengers told of the beginning of their dramatic journey. He could understand Joseph's desire to stay far from the soldiers who provoked trouble whenever they marched, wherever they went.

The Nez Perce had crossed the Bitterroot Mountains into Montana Territory, camping in a narrow valley called the Big Hole in the last moon of summer just gone. It was there they were attacked by soldier-chief Gibbon's soldiers, who killed and butchered, then set off chasing the survivors southeast.

The Nez Perce warriors protected the fleeing women and children, fighting skirmish after skirmish with soldier outfits that outnumbered the bands of weary warriors. On through the smoking medicine land that the white man called Yellowstone Park they pushed, hopeful that the Crow would help them.

But for too long the Crow had been friends with the white man and the army. Many Sparrowhawks scouted for the soldiers. They turned their backs on the Nez Perce.

"It does not surprise me that the Sparrowhawks would not help you," Sitting Bull grumbled, severely troubled. "They are the eyes and ears of the soldiers. They have Lakota blood on their hands. The Sparrowhawks may have red skin, but they have white hearts."

"Come one day soon," said White Bird, the Nez Perce war chief, "we will show the faithless Sparrowhawks the power of our united peoples."

White Bird knelt, scooping up dirt to symbolize the mountains his people had crossed, scratching in the soil the winding route his people had taken in their flight. At each place the Nez Perce warriors had battled the soldiers, White Bird stabbed his stick into the ground. Again and again and again the stick pierced the earth. Each time it struck, it made the sound of thunder to young Yellow Bird's ears.

White Bird went on to describe the desperate flight of the Nez Perce to the breathless Lakota camp, all the Sioux hanging on every word, no one speaking. Only an occasional cry of a small infant interrupted the great silence of that gathering.

White Bird straightened. In the Nez Perce's eyes, Yellow Bird could see a great weariness, a desperation, a flickering hope.

"All along the way we have left the bodies of our people. Mourning our dead, we have moved on without rest. Our men without time to hunt, our women without time to give birth and suckle their young."

He stepped again to his crude map, drew a long line, then jabbed the end of his stick into the ground. "The Hunkpapas of Sitting Bull are here."

White Bird moved his stick across the line, to a small mound of dirt he had formed with his trembling hands. He rammed the stick into the mound. "Here are the Nez Perce. Across the Medicine Line. In the land of the Americans. We are so close, yet we have little strength to make it the rest of the way after so long a journey. Chased and harassed by the bluecoats."

He raised his stick and brought it crashing across his knee. "If we do not get the help of your people, the Nez Perce will be surrounded and must then surrender to the Bear Coat, who is drawing his soldiers ever closer, closer still, in a loop around our people. Will the Hunkpapas of Sitting Bull help Chief Joseph's Nez Perce? We need your brave warriors!"

After so long a silence, without any expression of any kind, strong emotion erupted, like spring floods bursting through a beaver dam. The warriors shouted, every throat filled with a war song. Women trilled their high, keening wail of death for the bluecoats who had been on their heels ever since the short-grass time a summer long past. Dogs barked with the confusion, old men hammered noisily on their hand drums, children shrieked in joy.

White Bird wore a broad, bright smile on his weary face as Sitting Bull rose to his feet to speak to his people.

"We must go, Sitting Bull!" White Cow Bull shouted,

giving voice to the will of the people. "I will ride with White Bird if no others go."

"I will go!"

"I too!"

"We all will ride!" came the shouts from around the entire circle.

The hairs on Yellow Bird's arms rose in prickly excitement, thrill, and anticipation. Perhaps White Cow Bull would allow him to come along as a shield bearer, to hold ponies during the fight—in some way to be included in this battle with the bluecoats. His mouth went dry at the heart-pounding prospect of the ride.

Just as the young men began moving from the great council circle, as some of the women began stripping the covers from the war shields, Sitting Bull limped to the center of the ring. In but a moment the village fell silent once more, answering the one raised arm of their chief.

"Once more would I see the blood of the Americans on the ground. Once more would I see our people dance with the scalps of the soldiers sent against peaceful villages. Once more would I hunger for a great victory like that along the Greasy Grass!"

The crowd began to raise its collective voice, when silenced again by The Bull.

"But we have given our word," Sitting Bull continued when all had quieted. "Even more, *I* have given *my* word to the Red Coat Walsh."

"What have you said to the Grandmother's soldiers?" White Bird asked as he stood.

The Bull looked at the Nez Perce war chief. "I have promised that my people would not cross the Medicine Line."

"The Red Coats do not have to know we warriors have ridden south!" White Cow Bull stepped closer to the center of the great ring.

Sitting Bull wagged his head. "The Red Coats have their eyes and ears as well as the Americans. If we disobey their laws, if we break our promise to the Red Coat Walsh, then the Grandmother will let the Blue Coat soldiers come to destroy us."

"We will be ready for them!" Spotted Eagle shouted,

jumping to his feet and shaking his Winchester repeater decorated with brass tacks commemorating each white man killed with the weapon.

"No," Sitting Bull replied. "We do not want the Blue Coats to cross the Medicine Line. We came north to the Grandmother's Land so that we would have to run no longer. I am tired of fleeing. I want to chase buffalo instead."

Yellow Bird watched as the Nez Perce war chief's shoulders visibly sagged. The war spirit seeped from the Hunkpapas like the white juice oozed from milkweed split open on the prairie.

White Bird stepped before Sitting Bull. "This is the will of the Hunkpapa?"

After a moment Sitting Bull raised his eyes. "I have given my word. And I will not break my promise to Walsh."

The Nez Perce chief signaled his five warriors to bring up the fresh ponies traded from the Hunkpapas. "We had prayed you would help. More than any other, we had counted on you and your people. Sitting Bull's Hunkpapas were at one time the heart of all resistance to the greedy white man and his murdering soldiers. My heart is cold, and it is on the ground, Sitting Bull. For I see the fight has gone out of you and your people."

Sitting Bull's chest swelled, and his great chin jutted. "Once your people cross the Medicine Line, our warriors will meet you there to hold back the Bear Coat's soldiers. We cannot cross the line, but we will fight there to help your people flee to safety."

Crawling atop the Hunkpapa pony he would ride south to rejoin his people, White Bird gazed down on the might of the Hunkpapa nation, then brought his eyes to rest on the chief.

"Pray that Joseph can bring our people to the Medicine Line, Sitting Bull. Pray that the women and children and old ones who are tired and cold and poor for want of meat—pray that they have the spirit to make it to the Medicine Line—before the Bear Coat's soldiers surround and murder us all."

The five young Nez Perce fell in behind their war chief as White Bird reined his pony about, wedging themselves through the massed Hunkpapas. As the six reached the outskirts of the lodge circle, the stunned, silent people of Sitting Bull heard the faint foreign words of the Nez Perce death song, rising on the chill air that warned of an early winter.

Yellow Bird shivered, but not from anticipation. This time he shivered with the coming cold. A cold he feared would never leave his heart.

Monaseetah was as proud of White Cow Bull as she could be of her sons. Perhaps because she loved the Oglalla.

Ever since he had come north and crossed the Medicine Line, White Cow had been at Sitting Bull's side, if not with Monaseetah. His counsel had proved wise and considerate. All but a few of the Hunkpapas listened to White Cow and paid heed to what the Oglalla had to say.

She was proud of him now, as he and the rest of the band leaders had gathered in the bracing cold of the afternoon outside the Hunkpapa council lodge, round a crackling fire to argue the request of Red Coat Walsh.

The thirty-three-year-old career officer in the mounted police had been handed his toughest assignment: convincing Sitting Bull and his advisers to accompany him to meet with American representatives at the nearby Fort Walsh. The U.S. government had made an official request of the Canadian government, which prompted those eastern bureaucrats to send their arbitrary orders west, oblivious to the difficulty of carrying out their dictates. This would prove to be but the first of many supreme tests of Walsh's powers of diplomacy.

For hours the warriors had harangued and lobbied back and forth, arguing this way, then that, continually passing the pipe and deliberating on the wisdom and necessity of this journey to the Grandmother's fort. At last Sitting Bull himself held the pipe, signifying his readiness to speak.

"My heart does not feel warm at this moment. The first snows of winter are nearly upon us. My bones tell me that. But the Red Coat Walsh has never lied to us. I believe him when he tells me it is necessary for us to sit down with these Americans."

He glanced over at the Canadian, finding Walsh's eyes

on him as the redcoat listened to the whispers of the interpreter at his ear.

"We will go, Walsh. I will take twenty men with me. All but one will be the head men of our camps. Bear That Scatters will come to aid me. But also I am asking the wife of Bear That Scatters to journey with us as well."

Walsh shifted uneasily. Monaseetah saw he was not certain of the reason Sitting Bull had asked a woman to come along on this diplomatic venture.

"The Red Coat wonders why I bring the woman," Sitting Bull spoke the Canadian's mind. "Among my people, indeed among the people of the high plains—it is well understood that a party of travelers who has a woman among their number is not a war party, intent upon making trouble for those who are encountered along the way. That is why."

Sitting Bull turned, his voice fading as the ruckus grew louder on the outskirts of camp. Others turned as well. Two riders were led into camp by the *akicita,* accompanied by barking dogs. Women cried out, pulling at their hair. Somewhere, not far off, one of the old men began beating a war drum. A fast, stirring, unmistakable beat.

The two visitors were led through a crack in the council ring, where they slid wearily from their horses. Monaseetah recognized their hairstyle as Nez Perce. The first landed on shaky feet, regained his composure, then pulled back his blanket. He flung it to the ground at the feet of the Hunkpapa chief. Many gasped in surprise at the bloody appendage that hung from the warrior's right shoulder. What had once been an arm was now no more than shredded flesh.

"What is this?" asked Sitting Bull.

He swallowed deep. "I come from White Bird. His brother in war, Looking Glass, is dead. A white soldier's bullet in the forehead. Here." The weakened warrior tapped a finger to his own brow.

"You need attention, my friend."

The Nez Perce shook his head, waiting until his companion limped up beside him. Around his thigh he wore a bloody bandage, already marked with the brown crusts of dried blood.

"We will rest when we have given you the words spoken to us by White Bird himself."

Wearily the first Nez Perce sank to the ground. Water was brought to them both before his companion continued with their message.

"Joseph brought our people to the Bear Paw Mountains—two days' ride south of the Medicine Line. It was there the Bear Coat surrounded us. Looking Glass and White Bird pleaded with Joseph to fight on to the death. Joseph said he had seen enough of slaughter. Too many women and children. The old ones too. Near dark the soldiers still fired their big guns into the holes we had dug for our families. Looking Glass, that mighty war chief, was killed just before dark."

Bear's Cap, a Hunkpapa veteran, leapt to his feet. "We must go help them! You cannot stop us now, Walsh!"

All round the circle other warriors leapt to their feet, throwing off their blankets. Walsh and his interpreter fell behind a protective ring of camp police as Sitting Bull attempted to regain control.

"Tell us," the chief asked the Nez Perce, "how you escaped."

"White Bird slipped away from Bear Coat's trap when darkness fell on the Bear Paw Mountains."

"How many fled with White Bear?" asked White Cow Bull.

The Nez Perce turned to the questioner. "Ten-times-ten warriors. Perhaps that many women and children followed, refusing to surrender with Joseph."

"Hear me!" Sitting Bull shouted, suddenly animated. "Take my word to all our camps. Prepare beds and fires. Cook meals for the guests who will soon be among us, seeking refuge." He whirled on some of his most trusted warriors.

"Yellow Dog, you and Storm Bear and White Cow Bull—you must lead our warriors south to the Medicine Line. Do not cross, but protect the Nez Perce who are fleeing the Bear Coat. And—if any American soldier dares come close to the Nez Perce, or dares to cross the line—you are to shoot to kill!"

CHAPTER 22

As it turned out, some two hundred battered and bloody Nez Perce limped across the Medicine Line into the Grandmother's land. A hundred warriors, along with another hundred women and children, were met by more than two hundred of Sitting Bull's finest.

Two days it had taken the hungry, wounded survivors to march from the Bear Paws to the international border. In the meantime General Nelson A. Miles had concerned himself with the surrender of Chief Joseph and made it plain to those who surrendered that he could not care any less for the ragged band of escapees fleeing north.

Nearly all carried some bloody reminder of the long march. No more than what White Cow Bull could count on both hands remained untouched by soldier bullets or shrapnel from the army's big guns. Some of those strong enough carried the weaker ones or the little children—little ones, bleeding, with bones poking from their wounds.

The Oglalla's mouth went dry as he watched them pass, unable to speak when a young mother rode by, gripping her pony's mane between her bloody fingers for fear she would fall. The front of her blanket glistened with still-oozing blood where a bullet had entered her right breast, then glanced upward where it shattered her jaw on its way out. Wrapped in the folds of her bloody blanket at her back hung her infant, its eyes blackened with hunger, wide in fear.

Nothing could have stirred more hatred in the breast of the Lakotas than the sight of those broken refugees they made welcome among their lodges. Nothing, until Red Coat Walsh returned with his renewed request to have the Hunkpapas attend the meeting with the American commissioners at the Grandmother's post.

"Who leads these Americans who come north to speak with us?" Sitting Bull asked after the meal was eaten and the pipe smoked.

"I am told he is an army general," Walsh began. His eyes touched each of the warriors gathered inside the warmth of the huge council lodge.

"His name?" White Cow Bull inquired.

Walsh swallowed. "General Alfred Terry."

"One Star?" Iron Dog growled. "He is the soldier-chief responsible for the war made on us last summer. He is the one who sent Long Hair to attack our camps of women and children. This One Star sent Long Hair to his slaughter at the Greasy Grass."

"H'gun! H'gun!" most of the tongues in that lodge shouted, giving voice to the courage word.

"We will not go!" hollered Flying Bird.

"No, we will send a party of warriors to meet this One Star and his party!" yelled Storm Bear, rubbing one hand across the other. "He will join Long Hair in the great beyond!"

Many of the warriors laughed, including White Cow. Yet Sitting Bull did not. Instead his eyes watched the uneasiness of their redcoat guest, then stared unblinking into the flames of the fire at his feet.

"My friends," the Hunkpapa chief eventually silenced those in the lodge, "I have decided. Our plans are not changed. We should go meet with One Star and his friends.

I will take my twenty, and Bear That Scatter's woman as well."

White Cow Bull glanced at the Bear, finding the old man smiling knowingly at Sitting Bull, nodding as if enjoying some private amusement.

Walsh's interpreter busily whispered in his ear. The redcoat's shoulders sagged noticeably with relief.

"We will go with you to the Grandmother's fort tomorrow," Sitting Bull announced to Walsh. "Although it is plain by the choice of One Star to lead the Americans that the Americans intend to demand our military surrender—rather than coming in the spirit of making peace with the Lakotas."

"Hau, h'gun!" the voices rocked the lodge again.

Sitting Bull pointed the stem of his pipe toward the smoke hole above him. "One Star comes to the Grandmother's Land expecting to find us begging him that we might return to the reservation. Instead the Americans will find the Hunkpapas a people who remain as free as the buffalo. Until the buffalo are gone from the prairie, the Lakotas live on in the old way!"

It took two more days, fraught with delays and niggling concerns among the Hunkpapa delegation, but Red Coat Walsh was at last able to lead the twenty-two delegates toward the Canadian post called Fort Walsh erected in the Cypress Hills country. Sitting Bull, twenty trusted warriors and advisers, and the wife of Bear That Scatters.

White Cow Bull could clearly see that the presence of the old woman along on the journey troubled the Canadian and his interpreter. As clear as it was to see that the old Hunkpapa chief had something up his elk-skin sleeve.

At last, on the seventeenth day of October, all things were readied. The Americans had been waiting most of the day for the Hunkpapa delegation to enter the fort grounds and take their seats in the largest council room Fort Walsh boasted. At one end of the room stood a large stone fireplace. Near it sat the American delegation, General Alfred Terry in the center chair.

When Sitting Bull led his warriors into the room, the Hunkpapas made a show of shaking hands with the Canadians present, representatives of the Grandmother's government and her police as well. General Terry stood, with his fellow commissioners, waiting to shake hands with the infamous Sitting Bull.

But when the Hunkpapas neared the Americans, they turned back to their own side of the room, having shaken hands with the only men they wished to honor. Sitting Bull sat down, his back turned on General Terry. Dressed in his finest—a long, blackened elk-skin shirt with white dots—he settled himself comfortably as the American delegation was formally introduced.

Alfred Terry rose to speak, all six and a half feet of his dark, brooding stature. Towering over the shorter Indians who had spread themselves across the floor, he began with a long litany of offenses committed by the Hunkpapa tribe, among other Lakota bands, against citizens of the United States government, offenses against the treaty honored by the U.S., and the final blow being the flight north into Canada to avoid punishment for their crimes.

The room grew warm during the long dissertation. Most of the Sioux delegates allowed their blankets to fall from their shoulders as the soldier-chief droned on. Not one of them paid much attention, until the interpreter provided by the Canadians began listing the Americans' demands.

"The Hunkpapas and all your confederates will be accepted on the same terms allowed the other bands that have surrendered to the United States government. We will be at peace with your people. For their surrender to us, the army and my government offer your warriors a full pardon. You will be given land for raising crops. Your families will receive clothing, and when you cannot hunt buffalo, agency sutlers will distribute food to you."

Terry waited, watching that single pair of black eyes nearly opposite him across the room. Sitting Bull stared at the floor.

"Finally, the Hunkpapas and your confederates will give up your horses and your weapons so that you can live peacefully on your reservation. You will receive staples and cattle to the full value of the guns and horses you surrender over to us. It is our intention that you turn in these weapons and animals prior to leaving this country."

Again there was no immediate agreement, nor loud,

resounding rebuttal from the Hunkpapas as they listened to their interpreter. It was as if the soldier-chief's words had fallen on deaf ears. Only a few raised their eyebrows at Terry's next declaration: All who surrendered would be forced to march to their new reservation—more than a thousand miles away—on foot.

To White Cow Bull's way of thinking, One Star Terry looked immensely disappointed that the Sioux gave no recognition to his offers. This silence, along with the stoic sneers on the delegates' faces—it seemed to unnerve the Americans.

Sitting Bull allowed some of his fellow chiefs to speak before him, as if the council were not important enough to warrant his words. When he rose at last, he gazed across the room at One Star Terry and the general's aides and began his own recitation of offenses by the white man against his people.

"For sixty-four years you have kept me and my people and treated us bad. What has made us to depart from our own country? I will tell you. It is all the people on your side who started us to making trouble. We had no place to go, so we took refuge here. It was on this side of the boundary I first learned to shoot and to be a man. For that reason I have come back. I would like to know why you came here after me.

"I did not give you my country, but you followed me from place to place, and I had to come here. I was born and raised here with the Red River mixed-bloods, and I intend to stay with them."

Boldly he strode across the rough floor toward the Canadians as he continued speaking. "I was raised hand in hand with these people, and that is why I shake their hands. That is the way I was taught."

Sitting Bull dramatically shook hands with Superintendent Walsh and the major's supervisor, Colonel James F. McLeod. This done, he pointed to General Terry with a disdainful wave of his hand.

"My fathers, you know well how the Americans have treated us, and what they have done for us. They take me for their son, but they have come behind me with their guns. When first our nation learned to shoot with the gun to kill meat for our children and women, it was by the English we were taught; but since that time we have been in misery; I tell you the truth. Since I was raised, I have done nothing bad. The Americans tried to get our country from us; our country, the Black Hills country, was filled with gold; they knew that the gold was there. I told them not to go into it. I did not wish to leave my golden country; I had not given them the land any more than you would have given it. The Great Almighty and the queen know that there is no harm in me and that I did nothing wrong."

Many of the American delegates shifted uneasily on their stiff chairs. Sitting Bull used his eagle-wing fan a moment before he continued.

"At the present time in my own country, my people suffer from the Americans. I want to live in this country and be strong and live well and happy. I knew that this was our Great Mother's house when I came here with my people. Now I see plainly that there are no more deer, elk, or buffalo on the other side of the line: All is blood. I don't believe you will do me harm, as long as I behave."

He walked slowly to the great stone fireplace, giving the interpreters time to catch up.

"Today you heard the sweet talk of the Americans. They would give me flour and cattle, and when they got me across the line, they would fight me. I don't want to disturb the ground or the sky. I came to raise my children here. God Almighty always raised me with buffalo meat to live on. We will pay for what we want here. We asked the Americans to give us traders, but instead of this we got fireballs. All of the Americans robbed, cheated, and laughed at us. Now we tell you all that the Americans have done to us, and I want you to tell our Great Mother all. I could never live over there again. They never tell the truth; they told me that they did not want to fight, but they commenced it."

Taking his four last steps, the Hunkpapa chief stood before General Terry, ready for his final words.

"This is the way I came to know the Grandmother's people, and that is the way I propose to live out my days. We did not give you our country. You took it from us. Look now how I stand beside the Grandmother's people," and he pointed to Walsh and McLeod.

"Look at me! You think I am a fool, One Star—but you are a greater fool than I am. This house, the home of the English is a medicine house—a place of truth—and you came here to tell us lies. We do not want to hear them. Now I have said enough. You can go back where you came from. Say no more. Take your lies with you. I will stay with these people. The country we came from belonged to us. You took it from us. These people are good. We will live here. With bullets here we intend to kill meat and hurt nobody. They let me trade here; everything I get I buy from the traders. I steal nothing. The buffalo feed me and my people. Here I will stay."

Turning from the stunned Americans, who still hung on the interpreters' words, Sitting Bull sat, his blanket slurring across the floor as he settled among his warriors. He signaled Little Knife to speak, then Iron Dog, who both reinforced their chief's strong words.

At the end Sitting Bull rose again, calling forth the one woman in the room.

"I present to you the wife of my friend, Bear That Scatters."

Both half-breed interpreters hastily whispered among the American delegation. Hard looks of loathing crossed their white faces as they learned of the gravity of this immense insult—Sitting Bull had given a woman to scold them.

"I am The One That Speaks Last, wife of Bear That Scatters. Hunkpapa," she began, unsteady and hesitant before this great assembly.

"Your soldiers kept our people running all the time." Her fingers raced across the open palm of her other hand. "We had no time to hunt. No time to dance and celebrate life. We had no time to spend with our children."

Made more bold by the muttering agreement of the warriors behind her, the old woman stepped before the seated Americans.

"You never gave my people—you never gave me . . ." The interpreter's voice dropped off, embarrassed.

Terry twisted round in his chair, irritated with the

halfbreed at his shoulder. "Well, dammit! What did she say?"

"She said she will stay in the north—in the Grandmother's Land, because down in the south your army never—"

"Never what?" the general demanded.

He swallowed, dragging the back of his hand across his lips, still searching for a more polite term to use for the more descriptive and earthy Lakota word. "You never gave her time to—"

"Time to what?"

"*Breed.*"

"Breed!" Terry smoldered.

As soon as One Star blanched at that polite term, the twenty warriors roared their approval. The woman sat down among them, smiling and self-satisfied with the effect she had on the Americans. Sitting Bull said nothing, nor did he laugh with the others. He did not have to. The grin on his face said it all.

Across the room sat the great One Star, the soldier-chief who had commanded Long Hair's troops into the field one summer ago. With all of the infantry and cavalry at Terry's disposal, One Star had been unable to keep the Sioux at peace. Yet here in this same conference room stood the Canadians Walsh and McLeod, who, with a handful of determined redcoats, managed a territory filled with many tribes of Indians and far larger than Sioux country south of the medicine line.

His dark, brooding eyes lit with fire, General Terry stood, his great height attempting to intimidate the seated Indians. Trembling to control his rage, his words came out sour and pithy.

"Shall I say to the Grandfather in Washington City that you refuse the offers he has made to you? Am I to understand from the shameful way you have treated me today that you refuse the Grandfather's offers?"

Sitting Bull did not rise. He fanned himself for a moment, enjoying the sight of the fuming soldier towering over him.

"I could tell you more, One Star. But this is all I have to say. If we told you more—why, you would pay no attention to it anyway. This side of the Medicine Line does not belong to your people. You belong on the other side. Go home. I belong here. I am on my land now."

Sitting Bull's insult had been delivered. The Hunkpapas had triumphed over One Star. The Americans could make no mistake in understanding the great chief's words.

Never did Sitting Bull's people intend to return south of the Line.

CHAPTER 23

Winter, 1877–1878

I T was a grim Superintendent Walsh who accompanied
Sitting Bull's delegation back to their villages following
the disastrous attempts of General Terry's commission
cajoling the Hunkpapas into returning to the United States.
The Canadian had unfinished business with the Nez Perce
refugees. His superior, Colonel James F. McLeod, made it
clear that it was up to Walsh to control the growing
population of American Indians with his small force of 115
Mounties, already spread thin across not only the canton-
ment at Fort Walsh, but the subposts guarding Pinto Horse
Buttes, Wood Mountain, Kennedy's Crossing, and the East
End as well.

Even before Sitting Bull's warriors could leave the fort's
gates, General Terry had implored Colonel McLeod to
speak one last time to the Sioux. The Canadian urged
restraint upon the Hunkpapas, repeating two vital points:
the Grandmother did not consider the Sioux her children;
and the only hope for the Sioux remained with the buffalo.

"When the buffalo are gone, what will you do to help
your people then?" McLeod had asked.

"In the land of the bluecoats, the buffalo are dying off, disappearing from the land. Here in the land of the Grandmother, the buffalo will always be strong. The Lakotas will remain strong beside our brother, *pte*. As life blesses the buffalo, so it blesses the Sioux."

Sitting Bull added thoughtfully, "Everything bad for my people began with the Americans. If they liked me, why did they drive me away from them?"

The redcoats shrugged their shoulders, unable to answer.

While the great chief had been away from the village, a white scout and a Nez Perce interpreter had come north, across the line, seeking out the Lakota camps where White Bird's refugees had taken sanctuary. They brought an offer of peace from the Bear Coat.

Had it not been for the discipline exercised by Sitting Bull's camp police, very likely the two messengers would have been torn limb from limb by the vengeful Nez Perce survivors of the long, bloody march—the two hundred who had managed to limp across the medicine line at the same time Chief Joseph surrendered the rest of his band over to General Miles. The *akicitas* escorted the Bear Coat's emissaries to the medicine line, protecting them from Nez Perce warriors who would be long in remembering their bloody trail north to escape the bluecoats.

There in the Hunkpapa camp, as the snow flew that last week of October, Walsh held council with White Bird's refugees. The Nez Perce were instructed in the Grandmother's laws and what would be expected of them now that they had taken sanctuary north of the medicine line.

The days passed and the skies cleared—bringing the sharp smell of the retreat of winter's first real storm to fill the air. Selecting twenty of his best warriors to join him in the cold, Sitting Bull accompanied a small party of Nez Perce warriors in their journey south to the Bear Paw Mountains on a double-edged mission. Nearing the site of Chief Joseph's surrender, scouts came in to report that no soldiers remained in the vicinity of the recent Nez Perce defeat. White Bird's men were now free to dig up the ammunition they had buried before taking leave of Chief Joseph to flee north.

With each week Monaseetah saw a few more of the Lakota bands trickle across the line. As winter tightened its grip on the agencies and reservations south of the boundary, the Oglalla grew more convinced that the murder of their spiritual leader, Crazy Horse, foretold of a time of hardship and want. White Cow Bull welcomed his tribesmen come north to join the growing camps of Sitting Bull in the land of the Grandmother, where the buffalo still waited the warrior's arrow, where the bluecoats dared not stalk the Sioux.

Many times Monaseetah thought back to those days of late autumn, when Red Coat Walsh had stood before the refugee Nez Perce, Oglalla, and Miniconjou warning them all that the stern rebuke Sitting Bull had given to One Star Terry served only to turn the Americans' hearts forever hard against the refugees.

"Why should we worry, White Forehead?" asked White Cow Bull, using the Lakota name given Walsh. "We do not intend to go back—ever."

Walsh peered at the Oglalla warrior, a hardened, needling look etched on his face. "None of you can ever go south of the medicine line expecting to keep your ponies or weapons. Your problem is no longer the Americans—it is obeying the Grandmother's laws now that you say you are here to stay. If Sitting Bull allows any of his warriors to carry their rifles into the land of the bluecoats, then I become their enemy. Any man who goes south to cause trouble, to steal, to kill—he is thereafter and forever an enemy of the Grandmother's police."

"I told you, we do not have to worry," White Cow Bull said, growing visibly irritated with the tall Canadian. "We need nothing south of the Medicine Line. Here the buffalo are plenty."

Walsh wagged his head, staring at the toes of his muddy boots. He sighed, "Perhaps not this winter, perhaps not the next—but there will come a time." He ground one gloved fist into the other palm. "The buffalo do not stay on one side of the line. They will not last."

Lying here before dawn beside White Cow Bull in the coldest time of day, Monaseetah waited for that patch of sky she stared at through the smoke hole to turn gray so she would be forced to crawl from her robes. She hated the thought of it, for here it was warm next to his body. And she was made content listening to the snores of her man, hearing the deep breathing of her two sons in their beds.

White Cow had come to her lodge that first night he reached the Hunkpapa camps, after giving Sitting Bull the news of Crazy Horse's death. While the moon was nibbled away into nothing, then grew again as the days grew colder, the Oglalla warrior·slept curled in his blankets by the door, his rifle in his hand, unable to shake the worry from his heart. For too many years had he lived with the fear of soldiers coming in the night. Time and again he had reminded her how long it would take before he would become accustomed to sleeping with nothing more than the sounds of the prairie to awaken him each morning.

She had allowed him that time to grow easy with their life in this new land, just as she had given him time to get around to asking her. Monaseetah smiled with the remembrance now, scooting her naked body back against the warm strength of his sinewy back.

Early one morning not long after coming north, White Cow Bull had shown up outside her lodge with two ponies. She awoke to the sound of his voice, surprised to find him gone from his blankets by the door. He had called out the names of Sees Red and Yellow Bird, calling them from their mother's lodge.

As they stumbled from the lodge door, shivering and grinding the sleep from their eyes, the Oglalla handed each the rawhide rein to a pony.

"These I bring you, little warriors," White Cow Bull said. "They are for your mother. I bring them here this morning to ask the men of this lodge to approve that the woman of the lodge become my wife in all our days to come."

She remembered hearing Sees Red giggle a bit, then a grunt stopped him short. Yellow Bird must have poked his bony elbow in his brother's ribs.

"You little warriors are the only men of this lodge. It is for you to say—yes or no. Will White Cow Bull have a wife, or will he be lonely?"

"Should we ask our mother?" Yellow Bird whispered.

"It is good that you little warriors ask your mother if she would have me," the warrior explained, plainly anxious in putting it to Monaseetah to decide. "For many winters now she is without a father. I can only come to you, the men of this lodge, to ask for your mother to be my wife."

Yellow Bird bubbled, "She will say yes!"

That got him an elbow in the ribs.

"Let her tell us for herself!" Sees Red growled, his fists balled at his hips. He looked up at the warrior. "Then we will tell you."

White Cow handed Sees Red the rein for one pony, the other to Yellow Bird. He stood nervously before them, his hands seeking something to do in the freezing wind that drove snowflakes along the ground like last autumn's leaves.

Likewise, the boys stood, unaccustomed to having the sleek war ponies near at hand, not sure what they should do as well.

"Tie the horses to the stakes, little warriors," White Cow suggested, clearing his throat, smoothing his hair and the feathers worn there on special occasions.

Having tied the ponies to the lodge, the boys looked at one another, then the warrior.

"You will ask your mother?" he prompted them again.

They looked at one another. "Yes," Sees Red answered for them both.

White Cow Bull waited. "Now?"

"Yes!" Yellow Bird exclaimed, diving toward the door flap.

"You go now," Sees Red ordered the warrior.

"Go?"

"We will come for you with our answer," the eldest announced sternly, suddenly very full of himself.

"Where am I to go? I have no lodge of my own."

"Then wait," Yellow Bird suggested anxiously. "Over there in the sunlight."

He turned and saw the patch of yellow light near the cypress stand. "Yes," and he bobbed his head like a nervous bridegroom. "I will be there, with my blankets and my robe—waiting—for Monaseetah to have me."

She had listened to his feet shuffle off across the frozen

ground while the two boys plunged into the warmth of the lodge before she took her hand from her mouth, stifling her own girlish giggle.

"Mother?"

"Yes, I heard," Monaseetah said, patting the robes on either side of her. "Here, sit. Both of you."

"What shall we tell him?" Sees Red asked in a whisper.

She hugged them both to her fiercely. "We won't tell him anything."

"What?" Yellow Bird drew back from her embrace. "But I know you—"

"Not just yet, my son. Let White Cow Bull suffer a bit longer out there in the cold—he is in the cold?"

"Yes, Mother," Sees Red answered.

"Is he sitting in the snow?"

Yellow Bird's head bobbed up and down. "Yes, Mother! He sits in the snow."

"We should not treat my new husband so badly, my sons. You should learn respect for him," she whispered, drawing them before her again. "But first, you two must go gather the rest of the camp. Bring them here to our lodge—to wait for me to come out. Now, go!" She urged them out the door.

Monaseetah rolled slowly now as the first milky graying of dawn poured from the smoke hole above her. The pale light sparkled with hoarfrost as she snuggled against the warm, naked strength of White Cow Bull. She rubbed her nose against the scent of his flesh drawn tight across his shoulder blades, remembering the look on his face when she had peeked from the door flap, watching the others gather all about him, leaving only a narrow path from his perch at the edge of a snowdrift straight across the trampled snow to her lodge door.

Women sang out and men chanted. Old ones beat their hand drums, and one old woman rubbed some deer antlers together. An ancient calling of the bucks during the rut, when male chose female in the long-ago ballet of mating.

She remembered his face, how it had dropped, his eyes like swelling pools of rain as she had pushed back the door flap at last, one foot at a time coming forth. She had stood before them all, embraced by their cheering, keening calls of joy for the couple. Again she recalled how he tried to stand, stumbling once, gazing at her special beauty—realizing that she had loosened her braids and brushed her hair, smeared vermilion across her cheeks and moistened her lips with back fat.

Even more, Monaseetah remembered how strong he grew when they were alone at last in her lodge that very afternoon. Married by the whole of that great encampment before her two sons were gone to stay with friends for those four days and four nights, the couple enjoyed their time beneath the last sky of autumn.

Strong he had become, as strong as her love for him.

Monaseetah prayed now that her youngest son would live out his life among these generous people, having no contact with the white man. Or woman. Knowing that in a time to come, when he was older and ready for such matters of the heart, his would surely be broken by a white woman—as hers had been broken by a white man.

Her hand reached round his taut belly, gently kneading the manhood of White Cow Bull. He rolled toward her slowly, looked down at Monaseetah with tears in his eyes, and took her.

"I must catch my breath, Wind!" Yellow Bird collapsed into the snow at the bottom of the hill after he had tumbled from the sled they were sharing.

Like other boys and girls from neighboring camps, the two had fashioned their sled runners from a pair of ribs taken from a buffalo bull. Stout cedar limbs were lashed to either end of the two runners. A child sat on the back limb, his winter moccasins locked against the front limb as his friends pushed him off the crest of a long, sloping hillside. The ride down the icy snow was exhilarating, for these sleds often raced faster than a war pony could run.

Skinny Wind clambered out of the snow, dusting off his buffalo-hide mittens, and scooped up the rawhide lariat they had tied to their sled. He started up the hill, shouting over his shoulder. "You sit there too long—little Cheyenne—you'll freeze!"

Down the slope toward him tumbled many others. His eyes smarted with the cold on this first sunny day following

the new snow now deep in the winter moons. More than
ten-times-ten of them, and he stopped counting. Big
children and little—some of the smaller ones plopping on
their bellies on a piece of stiffened rawhide for their race to
the bottom below. Many were the times in the days of
spring and summer mothers gave their children buffalo
hides and sent them to nearby hills for sledding on the
grass. It saved those mothers much backbreaking labor in
scraping the hair from those skins the women hoped to use
for moccasin soles.

A gust of wind knifed along the bottom of the slope,
kicking up some of the powdery snow, slashing across his
cheeks. When his eyes cleared from the sting of the icy
flakes, Yellow Bird felt drawn. Something at the corner of
his eye drew his attention from the sledding hill.

A wolf.

Just then appearing beneath the clear, blue sky of
midwinter on a low rise of land. A grayish animal, not quite
pure white. Almost lost against the pristine horizon, had it
not been for the pale blue of that winter sky.

His fear growing, Yellow Bird recognized that blue—the
same color in the wolf eyes that day long gone in the forest
glen.

More so like the blue of the eyes that stared back at him
whenever he gazed into a pool of rainwater on the prairie,
looking for the water striders or other wriggling larvae.

For the space of three more heartbeats, the wolf stood
motionless on the crest of the far hill, its head cocked
slightly to the side, as if listening to something. Then
raising its muzzle, the creature released a long, mournful
wail before disappearing behind the top of the slope.

"Your turn, Yellow Bird!"

He turned, surprised at Wind's voice. The Hunkpapa
boy dragged the sled up.

"Did you see him?"

"See who?"

"Not who," he replied, testy, turning back to the far
slope. "See what—the wolf. Over there . . . you couldn't
miss him."

Wind shook his head, plopping down into the snow,
breathless again. "No," he apologized quietly.

"You had to!" Yellow Bird leapt to his feet. "He was right there!" He pointed, wagging his arm. "You were looking right at him when you were walking over to me here."

Wind shrugged. "Perhaps the snow has burned your eyes, little Cheyenne."

"The snow has not burned my eyes!" he cried. "I saw it—you had to see . . ."

He let his voice drop off to silence, listening to the laughter and shrieks of excitement from the hundred children behind him on the slope. Staring, staring still at the top of the far hill.

Afraid that he would die an old man, only then accepting that no other living soul had seen the wolf—only he.

CHAPTER 24

THE weather remained mild throughout that winter and into the spring. An occasional snow proved reason to celebrate among the many camps spreading about Sitting Bull's Hunkpapas like leaves dropped from the central tree. Young Miniconjou men challenged the Oglallas to snowball fights. Or the Nez Perce came charging down on the Santee camp, shrieking in glee as they pelted the Sioux with an icy barrage.

Hunting proved easy that first winter. The buffalo were plenty, and the back fat thick across the great humps. Hides were taken, meat dried, and the people rejoiced in their happiness. They were far from the danger of soldiers. Bear Coat Miles was long gone in the south across the medicine line. It was a time of singing and retelling stories of the great fights that glorious summer gone.

Even when a heavy, wet blizzard came just before the short-grass time, the people rejoiced. For they knew the deep drifts of everywhere-white choking the land would in a matter of days melt to feed the breast of the Earth

Mother. It was a time for family, gathering round their warm lodge fires, listening to the rattling of the icy buffalo hides against the lodge poles as the wind battered the Grandmother's land in one last gasp of winter.

"You both are to be scolded," White Cow Bull agreed with Monaseetah. "Your mother is right. Not one day passes but that someone comes to her lodge to complain of the trouble one of you has caused."

Yellow Bird looked carefully at the warrior's face. The eyes were not right, he decided. The Oglalla did not really intend to scold them. It was not in his heart.

White Cow dragged a knife blade back and forth, back and forth across the sharpening stone. Every night as the wind howled, he did this. It was like a religious ritual with him, sharpening the knife that had lifted many scalps two summers gone.

"I can remember a time when boys your age were sternly warned by their uncles to be quiet when older people are speaking," he said, noticing that Sees Red was about to speak. The boy clamped his mouth shut, chastised.

Yellow Bird was a bit braver, noticing something in the Oglalla's face that told him there was nothing to fear in this lesson.

"Are you my uncle, White Cow? Or, because you married my mother, are you no longer my uncle?"

He chuckled, the knife stopping on the stone. "I am your uncle, little Yellow Bird. I will always be someone special to you. Because you will always be someone special to me."

"Tell us more of the ways of your people when you were a boy, uncle," Sees Red gushed, emphasizing that last word.

The knife resumed its path across the stone. "Boys were not to be noisy or play in the lodge."

"Even when our mother tells us we cannot go out in the snow?"

"Yes, Yellow Bird. Even then. In the lodge an Oglalla boy was not allowed to pound on anything or knock a stick on anything." He leaned forward dramatically. "Especially, a boy must never hack at something with his knife in the lodge . . . nor tap a stick in the fire."

Sees Red dropped the twig into the flames, leaned back, and gazed at the warrior intently. "What might happen—if he did do wrong?"

Back and forth the knife wheezed across the surface of the stone. "Such things would cause the boy bad luck. He may even cut off a finger with that knife."

Yellow Bird swallowed, imagining the pain, having wondered many times on the ritual practiced by the women of his tribe and among the Sioux. So many in this camp had cut off one or more fingers in the last two years, leaving gnarled, scarred nubs among the bony fingers of their hands.

His trembling fingers secretly roamed to his side, feeling for the security of his small knife, given him by an old Cheyenne woman the autumn after that big fight along Goat River. The small belt knife and scabbard had been taken off one of the pony soldiers who had been killed on the hill opposite the Cheyenne village. It was small, very much a boy's knife. He wondered once again, as the Oglalla went on, why a white man had been carrying so small a knife. Had a boy died along with the soldiers?

"As far back as I can remember, from the first time I understood what my father and his brothers said to me—I was taught how important it was to be brave. Not just in war against other tribes or in fighting the soldiers. But to be brave in the hunt, in catching eagles, in working with the ponies."

He gazed into both sets of young eyes. "I learned that there may come a time when, to save the women and children of my village, I might have to give my life in staying behind—covering their retreat."

"Like the Sore-Eye Moon fight with the soldiers?" Sees Red asked enthusiastically.

"Yes, when my Oglalla brothers joined your Cheyenne warriors to fight off the soldiers while we could."

Yellow Bird stared into the fire where Monaseetah fussed with her steaming, fragrant kettles. "How I wished you had your warriors there when Dull Knife's camp was attacked the winter before we crossed the Medicine Line."

He looked up, finding White Cow Bull gazing at him with sympathy. "Yes, little Cheyenne." His eyes rose to look with love at Monaseetah. "If I could have been there."

"Please, uncle—tell us more of becoming a young man," Sees Red prodded, nudging White Cow Bull, trying to draw his attention back again.

"Boys are always treated better than girls." He stopped when Monaseetah laughed softly behind a hand. "Boys are treated better because they may one day have to die for their people. So they are given the very best of beds."

"I have always given my sons the best of beds—because they are my sons."

The Oglalla laughed easily. "Yes, my sweet young grass. And you have given White Cow Bull the very best bed of all—where you sleep, warming me with your tender body."

She swung at him with a dripping ladle and swung a second time as he backed away, ready to rebuke him. "I have told you not to talk in this way around the boys!"

He held his hands up. "I am sorry! Sorry! But there comes a time in a boy's life when he must learn of girls—and *women* most of all!" He kept his hands up to defend himself, looking at the boys with great seriousness. "Especially the women—oh, the pleasures of a woman. How special she can treat her warrior."

Monaseetah swung again, but this time he snatched the ladle from her hand.

Wide-eyed and slack-jawed, Yellow Bird watched them wrestle for a moment, until his mother's closed fists relaxed, her fingers stroking her husband's face. He could not understand the words they were murmuring to one another across the lodge among the rawhide boxes, robes, and blankets toppled and strewn asunder. But he had a feeling that one day he too was going to like looking into a woman's eyes the way White Cow Bull was looking into his mother's at this moment.

In wonder he watched, feeling the first stirring of something within, something that yet had no name. Knowing he would one day hold a woman as the Oglalla held the woman called Monaseetah. Certain of it.

Hoping that his woman would be every bit as beautiful as his mother was at this moment.

As the short-grass poked its head through the moist breast of the land, the bands slowly migrated east toward the

Cypress Hills, following the buffalo. With the retreat of the cold, the buffalo wandered north, back across the Medicine Line. But the herds remained small as the days grew longer.

More hunters this season. Fewer buffalo.

The fear rested on many a heart like a cold stone. Yet no mouth spoke of it. For now there was enough meat and robes and hides to trade for those necessary things, for those pretty things they had lost to the white man during the time of struggle and flight.

For now it was enough to live north of the Medicine Line, where the bluecoats dared not come.

The bands who had come to the Grandmother's Land had been putting their lives in order once more. The women always had work. Yellow Bird's mother was no different. Hauling wood and water. Building fires and dressing meat. Cooking the many meals and scraping the hides of game brought in by White Cow Bull. For her a woman's work was never done.

Still, Yellow Bird watched the change in his adopted father in those days as they drew closer to the end of the Moon of Fat Horses. White Cow Bull was truly no different from the Hunkpapa or Cheyenne or Miniconjou or Nez Perce warriors among the scattered camps erected down the creek.

The men had grown restless this short-grass time. With no warpaths to ride, was a warrior expected to hunt all day long, day in and day out?

White Cow Bull had been gone for many suns without explaining. And his mother had been angry, sullen, not talking to her sons for those long days flowing into summer—until she, like the other women, stood outside their lodges in the bright sunlight one morning, watching the twenty young warriors come riding back over the hills, coming out of the south. Leading many fine horses through the center of the village.

The Oglalla had slapped a friend on the shoulder, then reined his pony over to Monaseetah's lodge, where Yellow Bird's mother stood, arms crossed, her lips as tight as the mussel shell he had collected with Wind two summers ago.

The warrior dropped to the ground, holding open his arms, his head back with laughter at her worry for his safety.

And he felt that nameless thing inside him once more cause him warmth as he watched his mother lunge into her husband, wrapping her arms about the man. Swinging, swinging—the Oglalla danced round and round, rubbing his face all over Monaseetah's while he told her of the dozen new ponies he had brought her as a gift from the white man's settlements south of the medicine line.

"Mon-tan-nah," Yellow Bird tried the word on his tongue, the word White Cow Bull had used to describe where the warriors had found their American horses.

Later that day Sitting Bull's camp police came through, scolding the warriors who boasted of their raid. The harsh words did not last long, though, for the great chief and his *akicita* could not stay angry at those men who had only done what each and every one of them longed to do at the core of their beings.

"All the harsh words are not yet spoken," Monaseetah said to him that night in the dark lodge, when she must have thought her sons asleep.

"What words, woman?" White Cow Bull asked then, a bit breathless as his hardened flesh slowly softened between the woman's legs. He had been many days without her, and waiting for the boys to drift off to sleep had been such sweet agony.

"Ssshhh," she scolded him quietly, listening to Yellow Bird roll beneath his blanket.

In the dark his mother could not see that he had rolled, feigning sleep, so that he could better hear their talk. The coupling sounds he knew by heart already. But their words—those, he hung on every one.

"The redcoats will come soon."

"Let them come," he sighed, rolling from her. "I am weary and going to sleep."

She hrrumped, and continued, as a woman will do. "The Americans will complain, and the army will argue with Walsh again—and the redcoats will come to make things hard on us once more."

"They will not send us back," White Cow Bull mumbled.

How could he be so sure? Yellow Bird did not know, lying there, tingling with the fear of it beneath his blanket.

"The redcoats will come for the ponies," she said, gushing it all out at once the way the water broke over a beaver dam he remembered Sees Red breaking when they were much younger.

"Then they will come for the ponies. Go to sleep."

"You will let them take back the ponies?"

He was a long time in answering, and Yellow Bird longed to hear the Oglalla strongly say he would defend his new herd.

Instead White Cow Bull sighed. "If I don't—"

"There can be much trouble, for us all. I came across the Medicine Line to get away from trouble. For me—for Yellow Bird. No one must know—"

"My heart will not like it—but I will let them take back the ponies." He gave in totally.

"We do not want to fight the redcoats too."

"Yes, woman," the warrior mumbled as she curled round his back. "This is a new day. The Sioux need to have some friends. It is not—not as it once was. These ponies . . . they can have them back when they come for them."

"Sleep well, my husband."

"Sleep well, woman. I may wake you later—to have you again. It was a long, long journey after those ponies I will have to give back."

"Wake me, White Cow Bull. Mine was a long wait for you, not knowing when my husband would return. Not knowing—if I still had a husband, or if he too had been killed."

"I am not leaving you, woman. Now, sleep."

Yellow Bird listened as their breathing became more regular as the small fire's light slowly died away to a dull crimson glow on the smoked hides above his face. A summer wind gently rattled the lodge skins against their poles. Outside the night sounds buzzed and chirped with the voices of the tiny creatures from the grass and trees, along the narrow creek nearby.

As he had rolled over in his blankets, his mind rolled to the recent sun dance that the pony raiders had missed during their sojourn in the land of the south. It was not like before, those summers when many men paraded before the crowds dressed in their war paint and finest costumes, feathers aflutter and bells ajingle with every step. It was not like before, when Sitting Bull sat below the great painted pole as one hundred bits of flesh were slashed from his bleeding arms. It was not like before, when the people prayed, giving thanks for the past year, and begged the Great Mystery for another year of blessings.

This sun dance saw few come to hang themselves from the prayer pole. This sun-dance time found too many empty lodges, and too many remembering the empty bellies and that long march north for anyone to cry out too loudly in thanksgiving.

It had been a muted sun-gazing celebration that summer, what with so many of the men missing on the horse raid and worry for them as well. So many of those left behind had their hearts instead on the richness of those old days in the land to the south long gone now.

Yellow Bird listened, riveted, when any person talked of those times gone before him. He hung on those words, their magical pictures dancing in his head while the magical feelings leapt in his heart whenever the old ones talked of the buffalo hunts and the pony raids and the scalp fights and the swirling combat of those days beside the Rosebud and the Greasy Grass.

When life was a young man's to seize and hold onto with all he was—because it was a time of life for a young man, filled with buffalo and rifles, and pretty women and coupling, a time of watching your children grow strong to follow in the tracks of your moccasins. When the air was cold and the water sweet.

Why gone those times? he asked himself, swallowing the sour knot and realizing his eyes stung with hot tears—there, beneath his blanket, as the summer wind huffed past his mother's lodge, on its way east to the white man's settlements at Fort Walsh.

He clenched his eyes, knowing those times would never be again—convinced now, having heard with his own ears a strong, courageous Oglalla warrior admit he would give back stolen horses to the Americans south of the Medicine Line.

That secret someplace inside told him now that he might very well be the last generation to know the feel of the free wind shouldering its way across the wild prairie, know the sting of dust in your nostrils during the chase, know the smell of blood on the field of battle after the warriors have done their killing and time had come for the squaws and old men to work on the bodies of your enemy.

How could he not know now that all things had changed, now that the world was turning on its head and he feeling so dizzy for it?

How could he, Yellow Bird's heart cried out in the silence of that blackened lodge—how would he ever know the glory, the honor, the bravery of a warrior—when those times had gone the way of lodge smoke on the winds?

CHAPTER 25

Spring, 1879

THE wind had shifted out of the north early that year, bringing on its back the snowy breath of the arctic itself. The great encampment broke apart as small bands scattered across the extent of the Cypress Hills, each under a different chief. More than five thousand all told prepared to winter in that one region alone. Each warrior attempted to feed his family as the cold hand of time squeezed the land.

Game was already scarce. One blizzard on the back of the next buried the lodges and kept the families close to their fires for days on end. Bellies began to pinch. Hearts filled with the first bitter tang of despair. And as the mind often does in times of trial, it remembers the fair and sunny days of the old life on the plains, faithlessly forgetting what had been two generations of broken promises, fleeing from the bluecoat soldiers, and buffalo gone the way of breath smoke.

"You will go?"

White Cow Bull stared at the ground between his thick

buffalo-hide winter moccasins. He could not take the apprehension so plain in her eyes. He nodded. "Yes, I am going."

Monaseetah sighed. "It is no use talking you from it."

"Many of us are going this time," he said, looking up, an arm sweeping the horizon dotted with small camps where as many as a third of the men prepared to ride south across the Medicine Line in force. "We can kill many buffalo, butcher them, and be back here before the Bear Coat's soldiers know we crossed the Medicine Line."

Yellow Bird's heart leapt in his chest, caught between the hope of one day going on a buffalo hunt of his own, and the fear he felt now for his adopted father, riding into that land of death they had fled two years gone.

"Young men will always be made bold by dreams of glory and honor," Monaseetah grumbled as she stepped into the bulk of him wrapped warmly for a long journey on the prairie in a hooded blanket capote and buffalo-fur vest and leggings.

His chin touched the top of her hair, where he drank in the smell of her, enough to hold him many, many nights alone in his single robe. "There is little glory anymore, Monaseetah. Gone are the days of dancing and feasting and fighting and loving. . . ."

Then his eyes found the boy's boring into his. The Oglalla's face softened as he held out an arm for Yellow Bird.

He embraced his wife's son, then knelt to him. "It will not be long—two summers perhaps—when you are ready for your vision-quest."

"That long?" Indeed, it seemed forever since they had come here, two summers now. Not that many more to wait?

"Yes," he said, rising. Monaseetah handed him the Winchester repeater when he had crawled atop his pony and taken up the halter to a pack animal strung behind him.

Yellow Bird looked at the rifle in the warrior's mittened hands: no longer like a powerful weapon, more like an old, forlorn tool of a bygone day.

He watched the warrior gaze down at his mother.

"Next year, woman," White Cow Bull promised, "next year will be better for us all!"

As strongly as his adopted father said it in reining his pony away through the deep snow, Yellow Bird knew there was no ring of certainty to it. Nothing more than a brassy declaration of hope, tarnishing with each day it lay exposed to the immutable march of the sun.

He watched his adopted father join others, the rumps of their war ponies and pack animals ambling away from the browned lodges that seemed like squat ticks buried in deep snow. The ponies' noses were pointed south toward the Medicine Line, the buffalo, and the land of soldiers. It was not the first time Yellow Bird wondered if perhaps they all had done something gravely wrong in coming here—where the land did not look familiar, where it did not feel or smell or taste like home. Perhaps they had done something wrong in running here for safety.

It was as if they had caused the Everywhere Spirit a great anger at them all—severe enough to punish his people with a hard squeeze of a long winter lasting late into spring when the buffalo returned at last, grazing their way north in the annual migrations that crossed the medicine line. Yet this year it was as if he had held down his great hand and turned back the beasts in their northward march.

But Yellow Bird knew better. Those who had journeyed near the great stone pillars marking the Medicine Line in the days before last winter brought back word of the boiling pillars of smoke and the stench of seared prairie. The land itself had burned, as far to the east and as far to the west as the scouts could see before turning back to the Cypress Hills with their reports.

With no grass to eat, with nothing to entice the great beasts north, the buffalo had not returned.

"Bear Coat."

With a hiss Yellow Bird heard White Cow Bull whisper the soldier's name to his mother late one night last autumn.

"Bear Coat's soldiers have set fire to the land. When the buffalo don't come—our bellies will pinch with hunger. Then a man has only feeding his family on his mind. He no longer remembers the lies and the killing. He thinks only of food for his family. I will join the men going south—to find the buffalo where the buffalo still feed. That is where my heart knows the Bear Coat will have his soldiers waiting."

White Cow Bull knew there would be trouble now after the hunters returned from the land of the Americans.

Sitting Bull wore his pride on his shoulder, as if daring any man to look crosswise at it. With summer already mellowing beneath long days of sunshine, the great Hunk-papa chief had carried his anger like a badge of courage ever since the Bear Coat had caught the buffalo hunters in his trap south of the Medicine Line last spring.

Nearly five hundred hunters, and women who had come along to butcher, had marched south, slipping past the great stone pillars at night beneath a cold, full moon. Better than riding into the land of the bluecoats in the light of day.

It did not take them long to find the herds, stretching across the great, wide valleys the buffalo had always haunted. Not content to nibble at the new green grass poking its head through the scorched earth farther north— no, *pte* had instead chosen to eat among the tall, rich grasses of the Montana prairie.

Shouting the old words of encouragement to one another, the hunters had lunged at their work. They could not miss, as if the spirits of the buffalo were telling the people they would be rewarded if only they crept south to capture the rich prize. When the shooting ended, the prairie was blanketed with the great carcasses while the herds moved on east, spring winds nudging their wide rumps, leaving behind the trilling, laughing women who came streaming onto the killing ground with their knives and travois and renewed spirits.

Much meat was loaded onto the pack animals and laid in the great drags pulled by the winter-poor ponies. Men had pulled off long slices of raw liver and sprinkled it with the bitter, yellow gall. Their faces red, the women splattered in blood—joy was as infectious as the white man's spotted disease in that great hunting camp while they prepared to begin their flight for the medicine line.

But the Bear Coat's Indian ears had heard the echo of so many guns. In secret, behind the hills, their eyes had widened to see so many hunters and women and the loaded drags.

Miles's soldiers caught them marching north toward the great stone piles. A handful escaped on fast ponies to reach the camps in the Cypress Hills with their desperate plea while the rest of the hunters turned about, covering the retreat of the women and what meat they did not have to leave behind in their flight.

Four Bears, White Bird, and Sitting Bull were as one heart. They had given their word to White Forehead Walsh that they would not cross the line. Yet they had time and again turned their backs and pretended not to know of the others who had gone south in search of food to feed the hungry families. Now the riders came, and the chiefs spoke with one voice.

It brought a lump to White Cow Bull's throat each time he remembered the wave of warriors washing past the long line of women and their travois hurrying north. The sight of so many Lakotas must have given Bear Coat's soldiers pause—for they chose to fight no longer that day. No American bullets followed the warriors as they gathered their wounded and limped north, past the gray stone pillars.

White Cow Bull had the same feeling that day, retreating north, as he did this early summer day, following Sitting Bull, Four Horns, Black Moon, and others past the outer buildings of the Wood Mountain post. It felt like a hand choking the spirit of him.

"Tell White Forehead we want provisions," Sitting Bull announced as some of the redcoats eased forward, apparently eager to learn the purpose of this unscheduled visit of the Sioux headmen. "There is no game. Little bellies have gone empty. So many—even the Grandmother must hear their cries."

Walsh appeared at an open door, drawing the warriors' attention. "What is this?" he asked through an interpreter who loped up, buttoning his red tunic.

Sitting Bull's entire party slid to the ground in stony silence. Walsh still stood there beneath his porch awning, unmoving, waiting for his answer as the interpreter asked the question a second time.

The feeling trapped him again as White Cow Bull

glanced around at the redcoats. Funny how things had changed. Where before, the reception for Sitting Bull's chiefs would be a grand occasion of polite posturing and protocol of meal and pipe, now the handful of Canadians seemed unconcerned at best, haughty at worst.

"Perhaps they no longer fear us," whispered an old man in White Cow Bull's ear.

"These Red Coats should always fear us."

"We are poor," continued the old man, his rheumy eyes filled with the yellow glare of fear. "When we are poor, they do not fear us. And when the Red Coats no longer fear us—they will not respect us."

So Sitting Bull asked again. "We come for food. Anything the Grandmother can give us to feed my people." He crossed his arms. It was as if he intended to make as strong a showing of it as he could.

Walsh came forward, his eyes taking in the delegation quickly. He smiled ruefully, "I have nothing to give you, Sitting Bull. You are not the Grandmother's children."

The Hunkpapa waited through the interpretation before the look on his face soured.

"We are your children—we are here—and we tell you to give us something to eat."

White Cow Bull watched some of the policemen ease backwards through the doors of the log buildings. He knew it would be a matter of moments before they would point the muzzles of their guns at Sitting Bull's party from the darkness of those nearby shadows.

"We have nothing to give you—"

"The Americans have done their magic on the buffalo," Sitting Bull's voice rose slightly. "They keep our food from us."

Walsh stepped off the rough-plank porch, onto the earth left damp from a summer thunderstorm just passed. "It was something I was going to leave until later," he began, letting it out slowly, "but since you've brought up the matter of the buffalo, Sitting Bull—I've got a few words to say that can't wait—about the journey your warriors made in crossing the line."

"We had families to feed."

"Not on that side of the line—you can't hunt there."

"We will feed our families on the buffalo," the chief's tone grew strident. "Our brother, *pte*, does not know of this Medicine Line. We are called on to not know the line as well."

Walsh smiled without humor. "The Grandmother has been told of the fight you had with General Miles. There is much bad talk of it already. You broke your promise to me."

"My hunters," Sitting Bull attempted to explain, for the first time his eyes going to the ground, "I could not keep them from going to feed their families. That is why I am here today."

"It is simple enough to me, Sitting Bull. You made a promise to me and the Grandmother, and because of that promise you will be responsible for all your people—to keep your men on this side of the line. If any cross over, they will have to stay south of the line and suffer the American soldiers."

"What does the Grandmother say?"

With the interpreter's translation, Walsh flared. "*I* am the Grandmother's tongue here, Sitting Bull! I am telling you that you broke your word to me."

The interpreter grew anxious, hearing the angry murmurs from the delegation.

"You will not give us food because we went in search of food?"

"I will not give you food because you are not the Grandmother's children!"

Sitting Bull's fists clenched, his lips pressed in a thin line of sudden loathing. "We will eat! What you do not give us," he shouted, waving his arm at the handful of redcoats standing about, "we will have to take by force!"

As the interpreter's words and Sitting Bull's tone battered Walsh, the major took a few steps back, stopping at the porch. "Go now, Sitting Bull."

"We came here for food. We will not return empty-handed!"

"I said *go!*"

Sitting Bull advanced on the Canadian, one arm clutching the blanket, his right imploring Walsh.

"We came here to this land, seeking only peace—"

"Take your men and get off this military ground immediately!" Walsh growled.

The interpreter rasped his words, hurrying back against
the porch.

"We will not leave until you give us food for our little
ones."

Walsh flared, his voice climbing. "If you don't mount up
and ride out of here immediately, I will be forced to throw
you in my lockup!" He flung out an arm, pointing at the
ugly squat log hut, iron bars striping its windows and only
door.

Sitting Bull's eyes slowly tore from the hut, glaring. "I
come asking for food, and you threaten me with your log
prison?"

"Go now—or I will put you in irons!"

As the words tumbled from the interpreter's lips, Sitting
Bull advanced on the post commander, his hand slipping
beneath his old blanket. Many of the chiefs and warriors
shouted out in warning. Redcoats barked their orders at
the same time as the Hunkpapa's pistol flashed into the
early summer sunlight.

With a swift upward motion of both hands, Walsh had
the chief's wrist penned, wrenching the pistol from Sitting
Bull. As the weapon tumbled free, the Canadian brought
his open hand slamming down against the Hunkpapa's
barrel of a chest.

Sitting Bull stumbled backwards off the edge of the
porch, sprawling on the damp, trampled soil.

Suddenly enraged at the show of the pistol, Walsh acted
like a wronged lover. Leaping off the porch, he lunged
toward the chief and with his boot shoved Sitting Bull onto
the ground again.

Rifles clattered, muzzles poked from every window and
shadowed doorway. Along the banquette at the wall, four
more riflemen aimed their weapons at the Indian delegation
preparing to storm the redcoats.

Suddenly Sitting Bull rolled from Walsh and with a
grunting roar got to his feet, pulling his scalping knife from
its sheath. He lunged once at Walsh, who backed away two
hesitant steps. Three of the policemen surged forward with

their pistols leveled at the Hunkpapa chief, surrounding their superintendent.

Yet the redcoats arrived a step too late. White Cow Bull and Black Moon were there a heartbeat before them, pinning Sitting Bull's arms at his back, gently prying the knife from his grasp as the chief spit out his hatred.

The two Lakotas struggled with the chief as Walsh ordered his men inside their quarters, bolting the doors. White Cow Bull shouted his own oath at the White Forehead.

"You have betrayed us!" He did not wait for the interpreter to explain, hurling his words at the Canadian as he struggled to hold back the hot-blooded Hunkpapa chief. Sitting Bull was dragging him closer and closer to the log building that served as Walsh's office. "We want only—"

Sitting Bull lunged forward suddenly, hurling Black Moon against Walsh's isinglass window, shattering it loudly.

"We do not want to be at war with you, White Forehead—but if you wish it, let this be war!" spat Sitting Bull.

At the interpreter's garbled words, Walsh halted, quickly sizing things up. "I too do not want war. The rest of you—take Sitting Bull back to his lodge, where he can cool his temper. You explain to him that I cannot feed your people. You must live on the buffalo, White Cow Bull. Your people must live on the buffalo. Now take him out of here before I change my mind about putting him in irons."

The Lakotas hissed and cried out for blood as Sitting Bull whispered something to the men who held him prisoner. They immediately released him as Walsh's men laid two long poles on the ground between the Indians and the police. With the bark of his order, Walsh brought his redcoats to back him in number.

"See this line, Sitting Bull?" Walsh asked. "This is a line you cannot cross. If any man among you crosses this line, I will have him arrested. If any of you attempt to stop us arresting that man, the rest of you will be shot."

"There may be blood on the ground this day, Walsh—but it will not be only Lakota blood!"

Walsh's face slowly drained of tension. "Sitting Bull, take your anger, and your men. Go home. Take your weapons into the hills. Hunt game to feed your families. If you cannot survive here in the Grandmother's Land—go south to your agencies in the United States. The Americans will feed you there."

"We would be prisoners there," White Cow Bull said, taking up his reins.

"If you went, no more would you have to hear the cry of your hungry children," Walsh said. "Go south. Return home—to your reservations. This hunger, and the anger it breeds, is turning your proud people into beggars."

CHAPTER 26

Summary, 1879

S TILL licking their wounds from the attack by Bear Coat's soldiers and scouts, the bands drew together on the slopes of Wood Mountain for their annual sun dance later than normal that season.

A nearby band of Canadian Slotas, French Indians, possessed a powerful horse with a wide reputation for never losing a race. Despite the best efforts of Sitting Bull's camp police during the sun-dance celebrations, a hundred ponies disappeared from the Slota herd, among them the long-legged racer. In the midst of the praying and singing and bleeding that was the sun-gazing dance, Major Walsh rode into camp with a half dozen of his redcoats.

"I will ask which of my young men have been gone from our camp," Sitting Bull told White Forehead when he was informed that the Slotas had reported their horses missing and suspecting the nearby Sioux. "Among them will be your horse thieves."

Walsh and his men sat down to wait, watching the nonstop ceremonies of self-punishment that marked the annual rite of prayer giving for the Lakota people. Yellow Bird hung close to the Canadians, always fascinated by their blood-colored uniforms, the brilliant buttons, and those tall boots much like those worn by American soldiers come to the Goat River battlefield three summers gone. And the hairy faces of the Canadians—great droopy mustaches, like that straw-colored mustache worn by the soldier who had been his father. Yellow Bird squatted close, wanting to know more about these white men.

By late afternoon the *akicita* returned with their report for the Hunkpapa chief. Sitting Bull fumed, growling in rage at the news brought him. He trembled, as if trying to contain a summer thunderstorm within, then ordered his police off again. He stomped over before the Mounties, his face set in stony distress.

"My men have found the horse thieves, White Forehead," Sitting Bull began, his voice on the edge of quaking, speaking very quietly, as if struggling to control himself.

"They will be brought here?"

The chief said, "Yes." His eyes found another place to land.

Walsh grew suspicious. "There is something you are not telling me?"

Sitting Bull listened to the interpreter, then glared at Walsh. "Because of the temptation of those horses owned by your Slota Indians—my young men were driven to stealing. It has long been the way of our people—for a young man to prove himself. We no longer have a way for a young man to prove himself. Now I learn that Gray Eagle led the young, thoughtless horse thieves. But I am angry most at you for coming here, causing me to do this. Then I turn, angry with Gray Eagle for stealing those horses to bring you here." He stepped away a short distance, his back to Walsh.

The major leaned close to his interpreter. "Who is Gray Eagle?"

The interpreter whispered his reply, "Sitting Bull's brother-in-law."

Walsh slowly got to his feet. He strode over to the Hunkpapa chief, weighing his words.

"Sitting Bull, these thieves must be punished. Even your brother-in-law."

As if stung the chief wheeled on the Canadian, pain etched in his face. His eyes flicked to the interpreter, then back to Walsh, showing he understood how Walsh learned of Gray Eagle.

"Yes, they must be punished."

"Will you do it—or will I, Sitting Bull?"

The chief gazed past the Mountie, watching some of the older warriors at the sun pole, straining at their rawhide tethers, recalling the pain of that torture three summers ago. It was as if he were lashed to the pole of this dilemma—with no way to free himself. The sun dance was torture nowhere as painful as what he felt at this moment. He looked back to Walsh.

"What punishment do the Red Coats hand out for this crime?"

When the superintendent had spoken, Sitting Bull asked the half-breed interpreter twice to explain the Canadian's words. Even a third time the description rang clear.

"The redcoats have an iron horse. Its back is as sharp as a knife blade. The guilty men will be placed on the iron horse, and they will be cut in two."

With each translation, Sitting Bull never winced. Yet Yellow Bird was sure the great chief must feel a great stab of pain. When he spoke to Walsh, his voice rang clear, determined.

"We will punish our own—by the laws of my people."

"Very well, Sitting Bull. May I stay to see punishment carried out?"

He nodded, turning from the Canadians to issue his orders.

By sundown Gray Eagle and the rest of his thieves had been gathered before Sitting Bull's lodge. A gentle old mare was brought forward. The chief handed the rawhide rein to his brother-in-law.

"This pony you will ride to that far bluff."

Gray Eagle looked across the prairie, then laughed nervously. "This old mare will never make that ride, brother."

"Pray she does," the chief answered. "Now mount."

Gray Eagle hesitated. Sitting Bull waved a hand, and two dozen of his police moved in, tightening their noose. The horse thief leapt atop the mare.

"You can begin any time you like," Sitting Bull said, signaling the police to mount.

"They will follow me?" Gray Eagle asked, pointing to the two dozen warriors.

"No—they will chase you." He turned to his warriors. "Run Gray Eagle to the top of that far bluff. Do not give him or his pony rest. If he falls—kill him. Yet if he stays atop the mare until he reaches the crest—we will let him live."

With a hard slap to its rump, Sitting Bull sent the mare on her chase. The warriors followed, whooping, slapping Gray Eagle's mount with their quirts, kicking up dust. All eyes were on the chase, the only sound in camp the beating of the sun-dance drums.

At the far edge of the rimrock, Gray Eagle brought the winded mare skidding to a halt spare inches before the pony would have carried her rider over the edge to certain death on the rocks below. The two dozen police fired their rifles into the air, signaling the village in the distance that Gray Eagle had survived his test of skill.

He was allowed to walk back to camp on foot, ahead of Sitting Bull's soldiers.

"You must now bring forth the other thieves, Gray Eagle," the chief commanded, watching Walsh's intense interest in the proceedings.

"I must tell you their names?"

"You must."

"That will shame me in front of all my people—to tell of the others."

"I am waiting, Gray Eagle."

Smoldering with hate, the warrior named three more. Each was called forward. The first two cowered and were shoved roughly into the council ring by the chief's soldiers. At Sitting Bull's order the *akicita* buried eight lodgepoles in the center of the camp circle. All four thieves were stripped. Each one was then tied between a pair of poles, hung by his wrists from the top, his ankles lashed so that his toes barely scraped the dust below him. A pair of Sitting Bull's warriors were to guard each of the thieves.

"If these men are freed before I say they can be cut down—or if a member of a family comes to feed one of these men," Sitting Bull threatened, "the soldiers guarding that thief will be hung up on poles to be punished alongside the thief. For a week these four will hang here."

Horror crossed the thieves' faces. The wailing of their families grew louder still.

"Each sunrise my police will tie the four to their poles. Only water will be given them through the travel of the sun, from horizon to horizon. At sunset my police may cut them down so they can return to their lodges. For a week these four must hang and think about what they have done to shame our people before the Red Coats who have allowed us to come north of the Medicine Line."

"It is no crime to steal horses!" Gray Eagle shouted.

"No more!" Sitting Bull whirled on him, a fist raised, trembling. His brother-in-law began to cower, but the hand stopped inches from the side of the warrior's face. "No longer do we have the old life to live. Gone are the dreams and the dancing and the powerful visions that have led our people for many generations. Now we pray just to have enough to eat, pray so that our children do not starve. Now it is enough just to live."

His eyes touching each of the four thieves one last time, Sitting Bull strode slowly past Major Walsh without another word as the camp soldiers began stripping the criminals, readying them for their punishment. A severe punishment, for sure, Yellow Bird figured, something within telling him Sitting Bull was in as much pain as the four combined. A look of undisguised hatred come over Gray Eagle's face.

"We have come to this—great chief, Sitting Bull?" Gray Eagle shouted as his breechclout was stripped from his waist and his arms jerked high in the air. "Punishing a man for stealing a horse? When not that many seasons ago, such a coup earned a man great glory! Will you now be a chief of a fallen people, Sitting Bull? A people with no honor? Ground under the heel of the white man?"

For the first time Yellow Bird thought he understood hate. He sensed the warrior would long remember this shame and pain brought him by Sitting Bull, his own brother-in-law.

The autumn wind slashed through the saddle cut of his long coat as he tromped across the muddy parade toward the mess hall. Harley Fagen figured he would find a cup of hot coffee there. No self-respecting mess sergeant would be caught not having a pot of hot coffee warming at the back of the stove, anytime, day or night.

Two summers back he first came to these plains of Kansas. But winter had closed in on him before he had scratched up anything worthwhile in finding the white scout who might hold the key to the woman's whereabouts. Then last summer Fagen had prodded and pleaded with post commanders and old files alike, from Fort Riley over to Harker, across to Hays and finally down to Dodge. It was there he had come across a scrap of a clue that had led him to a dead end by the time he made it out to Fort Wallace on the Denver Road just as winter was closing the land again. With the going of autumn went the hope of finding Ben Clark.

He returned east, facing another winter of chasing bail jumpers in the bitter cold of a lakefront Chicago, just to keep himself in the room three flights up. That, and buy his rye, along with the snuff. Those important things in a man's life.

But here he was again, down in the territories themselves now. At Camp Supply, a place first established by no less than General—by God—George Armstrong Custer himself back in the year of eighteen and sixty-eight when he marched his soldiers down here to hunt for Cheyenne and Kiowa. The same campaign, as Benteen told it, that Custer came up with a Cheyenne concubine for an entire winter.

And pregnant to boot! Less than two months after Custer captured her with the rest in Black Kettle's camp, the young gal squeezed herself free a simon-pure Cheyenne boy-child. Eyes and hair blacker than sin on a starless night. Still Custer kept the woman with him for the rest of that winter, through the spring, and right on into the beginning of summer before Mrs. Custer rejoined her "Boy General" at the Big Creek encampment near Fort Hays. Custer hustled the Cheyenne captives off to Camp Supply that June, from there back to their assigned reservation.

Rumor had it from Benteen and others, however, that the young Cheyenne gal Custer sent back with the rest was already swelling up again. With child. A condition which made for something a prim and proper lady from Monroe, Michigan, could never set by.

Fagen brooded over his cup of steaming coffee. It was burnt and a might too hot, but it did the trick of cutting the icy chill of that sleeting rain hammering the parade at Camp Supply into a quagmire of wagon tracks, hoofprints, and steamy horseapples quickly freezing as the sun sank beyond the blackjack oaks.

Each time he limped back into Chicago for the winter months, Fagen telegrammed Mrs. Custer a coded message. And both times he received a reply the following day, stating time and date of their next meeting. A week later she would slip into Chicago and check into a nondescript hotel, waiting for Fagen's visit. For hours he pored over his notes and vouchers with her, going over every inch of territory he had covered, more amazed each time at the passion the woman put into her search.

Had she been brought up more of a physical specimen, perhaps a little wiser to the ways of men and animals, Harley Fagen believed Elizabeth Custer just might have taken on this task for herself. Oh, her breasts were ample to excite a man, and her hips had a gentle roundness to them still, but as it was, she was a thinnish sort, built more along the line of a tomboy who had never been allowed to jump from the mold of prim daddy's girl. Still she had learned to enjoy something of the outdoors and the plains and the possible cruelty of the frontier during her years with the general. Harley Fagen gave no second thought to the fact that Libbie Custer chose to oversee every detail of his semiannual reports with an intensity little known to the Chicago detective.

As he set there, drinking coffee during his third day waiting for Ben Clark to show up at Camp Supply, Fagen knew he'd have the lady's attention come this next reunion in Chicago.

Ben Clark usually brought his wife and passel of half-breeds in to Camp Supply about this time each fall, just before first snow, so he was told by the post commander. If a man was patient, so the story went, a man could get a chance to meet the chief of scouts who rode with Custer that winter his Seventh Cavalry slashed their way through Indian Territory.

Who better to ask about an army general and a Cheyenne gal? Who better to ask about the child she might be rearing for that arrogant dead bastard who got himself killed up on the Little Bighorn?

Yellow Bird watched the ponies and travois, men, women, and children, until all twenty-five lodges disappeared over the rounded hills above White Mud Creek. As soon as the weather broke after a week of winter storms, the Lakotas had sadly broken camp. They had decided to return to the agency south of the Medicine Line rather than face starvation with another winter bearing down on the Sioux camps.

"So long as there is a gopher to eat, I will never go back," Sitting Bull had declared to Walsh and his Canadian delegation during a great council held during the last full moon.

The redcoats had come, calling for a formal talk with the leaders from all the bands. They came, bearing a message from Bear Coat Miles that said the Americans would be patrolling the border more heavily than ever now with the onset of winter. Hunting would not be allowed in any way. The Grandmother's government had no choice now but to keep a much closer eye on the Sioux camps. The Canadians would punish any who left to cross the Medicine Line.

Even a boy of nine summers could see that life in the land of the Grandmother had become desperate, strung with hope on a thin whang of rawhide about to break under the strain of too many mouths and bellies, with too little buffalo and game. Every day brought colder weather. Every day he had to go farther and farther for firewood for his mother's lodge. Each time he returned to camp, dragging his deadfall and warming his fingers where they broke through the holes in his blanket mittens, Yellow Bird heard more tongues wagging.

No longer enough food in the villages—food both to fend off the hunger stalking each small camp and to maintain the independence of the mighty Lakota nations. Where the buffalo went, so went the Sioux. For as long as he could remember, Yellow Bird figured the buffalo had been roaming south of the Medicine Line. Perhaps one day soon the Lakotas would have to return south as well.

Always there came the whispers of the old men who had the yellowed eyes of too many lodge smokes and many winters. Old men who talked of the dwindling herds. And spoke of the coming day they hoped never to see—a day when the buffalo would vanish like a man's breath smoke in a blizzard.

No more buffalo. No more their old way of life. And no more Sioux.

Each time Yellow Bird had listened to the old ones, hanging on their words as he hunkered down, back in the shadows of the lodges or in the lee of the trees, watching the gnarled hands reverently move along the stems of their pipes. He enjoyed the way the smoke curled around their lined and grizzled faces.

More certain each time that their old, far-seeing eyes were the same yellow as the wolf that had many times stared into his soul.

CHAPTER 27

Winter, 1879–1880

THE blizzard outside had snapped another smoke-flap pole as the wind yanked and battered the icy-stiffened buffalo hide when it was urged back into place by White Cow Bull.

The thought of that pole brought back to Yellow Bird the vivid picture of those four warriors strung up for seven long summer days. He longed for some of that heat now as they huddled round the fire that struggled to keep at bay the frost from the inside of the hides. They had to conserve firewood. Few if any men braved these brutal storms to go in search of firewood. Three days now.

It became a winter of deep snow and pinched bellies.

White Cow Bull lunged back through the doorway, bringing a swirl of buckshot white in with him and a blast of hoary winter's breath on his heels. He joked that at least a man could eat his fill of snow—if only to keep his mouth and belly busy until the wolf of winter had moved on.

Yellow Bird pulled his blanket up past his chin and stared at the red coals near his feet, thinking back to the warmth of summer, and those bad feelings begun by the stealing of the horses.

When the four thieves had been cut down at sunset that final day of their punishment, Walsh had been there. He had come to witness the freeing of the criminals as much as he had come to show Sitting Bull's headmen the letter he had received from One Star Terry.

A feast was given by the camp police for the four, as if to show in the way of the Hunkpapa that the thieves' debt had been paid and the four warriors were once more in good standing. Sitting Bull's soldiers gave presents of clothing, furs, and finery to the four who had endured their punishment. While Gray Eagle, White Bird, Good Crow, and White Cow Walking sat filling their bellies, Walsh explained the marks on the piece of paper he had brought to show Sitting Bull's headmen.

The telegram from General Alfred Terry, an interpreter explained, was in answer to a letter Walsh had addressed to One Star months ago, early that spring. Walsh had asked the American soldier-chief if he would be allowed to keep a gray horse given him by Four Horns. A gray horse bearing the unmistakable brand of the U.S. Seventh Cavalry.

White Forehead had asked Four Horns to keep the horse among his ponies until he received permission to accept such a gift. Now he had come bearing just that permission to accept such a tangible prize of the Lakotas' great victory over the bluecoats on the Greasy Grass.

It seemed so long, long ago—that day. How many fires had he sat by since that bloody day, Yellow Bird wondered. A day when it seemed the nations were at their zenith, streaming like shooting stars across the heavens with more than enough fire and fury to last generations to come. So much joy and celebration and thanksgiving.

Now tongues whispered only prayers for deliverance from the despair and hunger and death that stalked every lodge in every camp along every creek in the Cypress Hills. Increased talk of lodges going south if they could make it. Perhaps too late now. Was it better to die here, or on the trail south toward the Medicine Line, better to die at the agencies where they could eat again the white man's flour and his bacon and his skinny spotted buffalo?

Each time he heard the talk, Yellow Bird sensed with growing certainty—the people could not go on much longer. Not starving as they were. Not begging from the Metis and redcoats. A proud people brought to the point of killing off the old and feeble among the herds of their once-fine ponies. Simply to feed the children.

He shuddered, not so much with the cold, but with the vision of watching the women and old men at work over the still-warm carcasses of the ponies they butchered every few days to supply a handful of meat for each lodge. How those whimpering, hungry people fighting over the bones and steaming gut-piles reminded him of a pack of wolves busy at a hamstrung mare.

Wolf packs, always guarded over by a solitary leader. His jowls bright with the blood and gore of his feast, his nose raised into the wind to scent his enemies, his yellow eyes constantly scanning the horizon.

The boy would never forget those yellow eyes that returned to haunt his night dreams almost every night now.

The same yellow eyes that haunted even these winter days of despair for the once-mighty Lakota.

Fagen watched a tall, gaunt man push through the plank door, then stand there waiting as the swirl of snow settled round his boots, slowly pulling the thick blanket mittens from his tanned, veiny hands that reminded the detective of some wrinkled broughams he had been forced to wear through mud and snow in the war.

The war down south, that was. The war of rebellion. That bloody scrap with the Confederacy.

Harley had been reminded of that time and again by these soldiers stationed out here on the plains. They were fighting a war every bit as much as the armies back east had fought. There were bullets and an enemy and blood and terror here as well. Harley had to agree with them. One thing was certain, this war kept grinding on and on, with no end in sight.

The tall man yanked the buffalo-fur cap from his long graying hair. He used it to knock the wet snow from his thigh-length mackinaw beneath a buffalo-fur vest. Kicking his heels together to dislodge more slush, the newcomer measured Harley Fagen with a look of amused curiosity as he marched over.

"Your name Fagen?"

He rose clumsily from the crude bench, scooting his big china cup aside. His hand came out.

"You must be Ben Clark."

The scout looked down at the older man's hand, then took it in his. He eased himself down on the bench opposite Fagen. "You mind getting me a cup of that stuff? I can't see no sense in a man poisoning himself alone."

Fagen chuckled as he lumbered over to the crude table at the end of the hall. He snatched up a cup and hurried to the stove, where he poured the thick brew from one of many waiting pots. As he settled back on his bench and drew his coat about him, the detective found himself liking the scout already.

He waited while Clark blew steam from his cup and sipped at the scalding coffee. The scout set it down, cradling the cup between his cold hands.

"I'm told you wanted to see me."

"For some time now."

He smiled wryly. "I'm told that as well. This your second trip out to Indian country?"

"Third, if you count the summer of seventy-seven when I talked with Captain Fred Benteen up at Abraham Lincoln."

Clark pulled again on his coffee. "Benteen and now me—hmmm. This wouldn't have anything to do with Custer's Washita campaign, would it?"

Fagen found himself straightening. Surprised at the man's insight, yet he immediately remembered that a good army scout made his pay by keeping his intuition well honed. Clark was cut of that cloth.

"That's right, Ben. May I call you Ben?" He waited until Clark nodded. "The Washita winter. I like the ring of that myself."

Clark eyed him severely a moment. "Something just struck me as well, Fagen. You can't be military, don't have the cut for it. Someone's got you asking around about something. So goes my suspicion."

That intrigued the detective, almost as much this man of the plains. "What would that be?"

"I figure you're here about the Elliott matter."

"Elliott?"

"Major Joel Elliott," he repeated, his eyes narrowing again, his voice not sounding so sure of it.

"No," and he shook his head, feeling disconcerted. "Wasn't he the one who got himself and his men killed while Custer's men cleaned up Black Kettle's village?"

"Yep." Clark went back to his coffee. "That's not what you came for?"

"Why, no. It's not."

"You've done your homework on the battle, I take it."

"Everything I could get my hands on. Newspapers mostly."

Clark smiled. "There you go, believing all that white-wash again."

Fagen leaned in. "It's another kind of whitewash I'm interested in uncovering." He watched Clark glance in both directions before leaning in on his own elbows.

"The army's full of its own dirt. No one much cares anymore. A man's drinking, perhaps he's a little too randy with another officer's wife—that sort of thing. Men at war and all that. It'll never change."

Fagen's eyes lit for perhaps the first time that day. "You're perhaps the only one left who can tell me the real story of that winter."

"Nawww, lots of 'em left. The boys with Benteen—up on Reno hill. A good portion of 'em served with the Seventh—"

"No one else would have known about Custer's whore."

He watched how his interruption drew Ben Clark up like a short lead on a lip halter. The scout slowly set his cup down, his eyes shrinking to slits.

"That what this is about? You gonna ask me about a dead man's dalliance with an Injun squaw?"

"Wait!" Fagen said a little too loudly as Clark began to rise from his bench. He felt foolish, noticing a handful of soldiers at other tables glance over at them.

"I won't let you drag a man—"

"Captain Benteen led me to believe you weren't in the Custer camp."

"I'm not, Mr. Fagen. Far from it. But I'm a decent enough sort, despite what I've seen in my thirteen-odd years out here on the frontier."

"I was told you live with a Cheyenne woman."

Clark pulled his wrist free of the old man's desperate grip. "That ain't got anything—"

"You'd be the one to know how to peer inside Custer's guts, then—wouldn't you?"

"What you mean by that?"

"You're a white man, living with a Cheyenne—"

"She's my wife, mister."

"Living with a Cheyenne wife," he repeated, settling once again, nervously. "Please, Mr. Clark. Give me a chance. I've waited so long—to get this chance."

Clark pushed the cold coffee aside. "None of this makes any sense to me, Mr. Fagen. Suppose you start from the beginning and tell me what it is you want to know, and why the hell I should tell you."

He nudged his china cup aside, making a steeple of his old hands before him as he leaned forward. "I want to know everything you can tell me about Custer's, his—"

He glared at the detective. "Don't use that word *whore* again. My wife ain't no whore just because she chose a white man to marry. And from what I knew of that woman Custer took up with—she was the farthest thing from a whore a Cheyenne could get."

"Tell me about Cheyenne women. Are they . . . of questionable morals?"

Clark shifted uneasily. "You might be treading on dangerous ground here, Mr. Fagen. The Cheyenne come closest I know to protecting the virginity of their women."

"You can't be serious, can you? Why, the woman Custer took up with was carrying another man's child at the time she first bedded the general."

Clark wagged his head again and said, "You do have a lot to learn. She divorced her first husband before she found out she was carrying his child."

"This, this Monaseetah?"

"That's her," Clark answered.

"Then she was Custer's, the general's concubine before her first child was born."

"Pure Cheyenne, he was."

Fagen squirmed. It was all he was hoping it would be. "The fact that you mentioned the woman's first child being a pure Cheyenne leads me to believe her second might not've been pure blood."

Clark scratched at his beard. "Benteen told you that much. You had to know that much to even come looking for me. It's something else you want to know, ain't it?"

His mouth went dry. "Yes. You live down here in these parts with the Cheyenne. I want you to tell me where I can find this Monaseetah—and her son. The *second* one."

Clark smiled coldly. "The one with the light hair, and Custer's blue eyes?"

Fagen reminded himself to stay on the bench and not leap across the table to grab the scout's buffalo vest. "Yes!" he rasped anxiously.

"You've made a long trip. Probably waited a mighty long time to come to this, Mr. Fagen."

He watched Clark rise, hefting one leg off the bench. "Wait. What—"

"I can't tell you where the woman is. Or her son."

"Why—you mean you *won't* tell me?"

"I can't. Don't know. Simple as that."

"Benteen told me—but you're a scout for the army—married to a Cheyenne woman."

He laughed, hard and short, like the pounding of a blacksmith's hammer on a cold anvil. "The woman up and disappeared several winters back."

"How long?"

He gazed into middistance, as if dusting off a corner of his recollection. "Some time . . ."

"Before Custer's disaster on the Little Bighorn?"

"Yes. Before that—certain of it."

"Where could she have gone?"

"Looking for Custer."

Fagen felt gut-shot at the news. "What do you mean?"

Clark sighed. His eyes threatened to mist over. "She had it in her head that Custer promised to return for her."

Fagen's eyes widened as his jaw dropped a bit. His

mouth was still dry. What he needed was a strong drink over at the sutler's. But it could wait a bit longer. "He promised to come back to her?"

"And—and his son."

"Custer told you?"

Clark wagged his head. "Custer and me? No. He never would tell me nothing like that. She did."

"When?"

"Winter before she lit out to find Custer."

"How she know where to look for him?"

"She didn't. All she had is what I told her."

"How to find him?"

Clark nodded now. "That he and his Seventh was reassigned faraway up north. Where you run onto Benteen."

Harley Fagen sagged a bit on the bench, running a sour tongue over his teeth the color of a pinewood chips. "I'll be damned, Ben Clark. Now how about that? Suppose you can't tell me where to find her, but I'll bet you could—"

"Tell you *how* to find her?"

Fagen bobbed his head eagerly.

CHAPTER 28

Spring, 1880

THE snow lay in shrinking, greasy patches as far as his red eyes could see. Here or there in a muddy knot lay the bleaching bones of a horse they had sacrificed through the long winter. A gaping skull, perhaps a rib cage spreading fingers of sunlight and shadow on a patch of muddy, ocher earth, maybe even what leg bones had not been dragged off by wolves or the Lakotas' own half-feral dogs.

The camp stank of death and dying.

Yellow Bird's eyes seeped with a sickness he and other survivors suffered that made their gaunt faces all the more deathlike. This foul yellowish ooze he wiped from eyes and nose and sometimes found crusted at the corners of his lips. So many of them had it after eating the rotten meat all winter, no one thought anything of it now with the warming of the skies.

They were alive. And that was all. Having been half-wild in hacking at the carcasses through the long nights of winter while the wind howled and the icy shards of snow's fury battered the camps. They began occasionally butchering ponies for food. And by the time winter had arrived in its full might, the Lakotas found themselves searching out one by one the horses that had not foraged well enough, the animals the Lakotas found frozen in the snow where they stood, unable to move to feed themselves as the snow deepened, and deepened.

The meat of those animals long dead smelled like death itself. But to live, Yellow Bird and the rest closed their eyes and nose, forcing themselves to swallow again and again. An empty belly forgets the fetid taste after a while. It was that winter Yellow Bird learned that the wolf of hunger had no eyes nor ears to the cries of the dying.

Many died, already weakened from hunger, when sickness came an unwelcome visitor to every lodge, not one left untouched. So afraid were they of the dying and the despair that Monaseetah and White Cow Bull dragged their lodge through the snow one terrible morning, setting it up far, far from the camp circle. Afraid to watch friends slowly die. Afraid more of the spreading unknown.

They kept Sees Red and Yellow Bird in the lodge, going out only to relieve themselves, or to fetch wood with Monaseetah, or water with White Cow Bull. From the side of their hill, they could look down and watch the rest of that once-great circle. And notice how the burial scaffolds multiplied each day. Bodies frozen, lying above the earth, far enough from the wolves that prowled the camps come each twilight when the Sioux hid like deer mice within the circle of their tiny lodges, forgetting the wind that scratched insistently at the door, rattling the frozen hides against the lodgepoles. Every one of them tried to shut their ears to the snarling, snapping, keening cries of the wolves sweeping down on the camps with the falling of the sun like long-toothed, yellow-eyed messengers of that long night's winter visitation.

Yellow Bird did not like the feeling in his belly, looking down at that muddy, snow-patched village below, watching the people move slowly about as if they were half-dead now. The sun still traveled low in the south but was bringing longer days nonetheless. That gnawing feeling clung to his belly, making him think more each day about

the things his mother and adopted father spoke of when
they believed no one else listened.

Then there were the nights when no sound but the track
of the cold moon across the sky was rent on his little ears.

In the blackness of the lodge, back in the deepest nights
of that winter, he had awakened often and noiselessly, lying
breathless beneath his robe and blanket, listening for the
whispers of the adults or the coupling sounds. At the
coldest times he put off what needed doing. He hated
disturbing his warm cocoon, hurrying out of the robe and
blankets, shivering with the cold's first, sharp bite even
before he heaved back the frozen door flap and stepped
outside onto the pale, blue snow. For yards in all directions,
the surface of the deepening snow had been beaten down
by incessant moccasins.

Yellow Bird had his favorite spot where he would stand
shivering, quickly pulling up the long tail of his shirt,
yanking aside his breechclout, then hurriedly spraying the
snow so he could scurry back to his robes like a rabbit back
to its burrow. Yet he stood there, this was a night not like
those gone before. Down below, a shadow caught his
attention. A dark shape quietly emerging from Gray Eagle's
lodge.

There beneath the sliver of a moon that cast an eerie pall
over the camp below, the shadow slipped away from Gray
Eagle's doorway, creeping soundlessly uphill toward the
nearby burial scaffolds.

In that milk-pale moonlight giving everything a cold,
blue luster, he watched Gray Eagle bring out the flash of a
knife and cut quickly at the rawhide binding one of the
dead. The shadow struggled over the scaffold body for what
seemed like a long, breathless time to the boy. Then the
warrior wheeled to hurry downhill, disappearing into his
lodge without a sound to betray his evil.

It was what the young Cheyenne had seen Gray Eagle
carrying back to his lodge that had sickened Yellow Bird and
made him afraid of telling even his mother. For weeks he
carried the awful burden of it inside him, until it became
difficult to eat what little Monaseetah could set before him.
At last he could contain it no longer, waiting only until Sees
Red was away before whispering his secret.

"You saw Gray Eagle do this once?"

The boy stared at the wriggling red coals in the fire pit. Shaking his head was all he could do.

"How—how many times did Gray Eagle visit the burial scaffolds?" White Cow Bull asked when Monaseetah was unable to speak, hand to her mouth in utter awe and revulsion.

"Many," he answered, eyes begging for understanding, for someone to grant him some absolution from the horror. "And others."

He explained that, after that first time, sleep rarely came without the recurrent nightmare of dead, frozen bodies helplessly crying out to him from their burial platforms as the half-living hacked off arms and legs to feed the starving. Yellow Bird often came out to the cold, hunkering in his robe back in the shadow of the lodge, waiting. Watching, and by that simple act eventually feeling as if he himself were every bit as guilty of complicity in the evil as the others—simply because he knew and had not stopped the evil.

White Cow Bull and Monaseetah argued that they did not know whom to trust, whom to tell of the horror. Monaseetah urged him to go to Sitting Bull. But he could not. White Cow Bull said he was not Hunkpapa, while Gray Eagle was the chief's own brother-in-law.

Despite how White Cow Bull's heart bled for young Yellow Bird, despite how Monaseetah pleaded with the Oglalla to tell, he remained resolute. An Oglalla warrior, married to a Cheyenne woman, could not easily go to Sitting Bull's lodge and tell him what his half-breed Cheyenne son had seen the great chief's brother-in-law do in the darkness of those long winter nights.

It was as if that winter they became outsiders, if not prisoners, in this great, yawning wasteland north of the medicine line. Nowhere could they escape the horror, the sadness of what had reduced a proud people to robbing the burial platforms of their human flesh—friends and family not alive to greet the warmth of spring.

Meat was meat when the wolf of winter came to stay.

"Do you really think we will know something soon, know if the woman, her child—if they are dead?"

Elizabeth Custer turned from him, the hem on the long black dress slurring the rug beneath her.

"From what Ben Clark had to say," Harley Fagen replied, absently drumming his fingers on the wing chair's worn arm.

She went to the window, looking down on the noisy street below. Libbie had purposely opened the window, not only to let in the cool May breezes coming off the lake, but so she would not feel so cooped up, a prisoner with the man she despised yet so depended upon. The sounds of commerce and traffic clattered along below her window in this run-down hotel as she went back to him, pushing a curl of stubborn hair back behind an ear.

"What all did he have to say? This—Mr. Clark."

"You knew him, ma'am?"

"No. Only what Autie spoke about him, wrote of him in letters, and the book."

Fagen rubbed a fingertip over his teeth a moment. "He told me what she looked like."

"Does it sound like the woman I saw for myself at the stockade—Fort Hays?"

"The one who gave you her baby? Yes, ma'am. Mona-seetah's the one with that simon-pure Cheyenne for her firstborn."

She winced at the stab of pain, whirling her skirts back to the window, if only to catch a breath of the cool air nudging the curtains aside. The smell of the detective grew stronger every visit, the frontier coming back with him every time, mixed generously with Fagen's rye and pungent snuff, his nose more red and weepy than normal.

"And the other child. A boy as well? What did Clark have to say about him?" She knew he was staring at her back. Libbie felt his marblelike eyes searing a hole between her shoulder blades.

"He gave me a good idea how the boy would look, Mrs. Custer."

"Anything resembling Autie?"

"The boy's hair."

"Blond?"

"Not exactly."

"Close enough to make him stand out, I assume."

"Yes'm," Fagen answered. "It's the eyes, mostly."

She turned. "Autie's eyes?"

"Clark told me—he's seen the child—the boy has them pale eyes the general had. That blue, mixed with his pure-bred Cheyenne mother's eyes, they give the lil' mongrel what Clark called something close to a yellow-eyed, wolfish look."

She found herself biting her lower lip for a moment, finally realizing the pain. "How old would he be?"

"Clark figures something on the order of eleven or twelve years now."

"You have your boarding ticket to—?"

"North Platte, Nebraska, ma'am. From there I'll let me a horse."

"You have enough?"

He rose from the seat, looking every bit as anxious to be gone from her, as Libbie was anxious to be rid of him.

"More'n enough." He patted his coat's breast pocket.

She watched him step to the door of the tiny room. "We will know something soon, Mr. Fagen?"

"I figure we're nearing the end of the chase, Mrs. Custer. Clark said the woman could have been among those who made the break from Fort Robinson a year ago last winter—them as was killed by the soldiers or died along their escape trail north."

"He wasn't sure, was he?"

"No, not 'sactly. But Clark knew she wasn't among the survivors he got a look at not long afterward."

"The boy?"

"Him neither."

"Dead," she whispered, perhaps without all the hope she should have hoped for his death. She went to the window again. "Somewhere out there, on that vast wasteland—where Autie roamed and died—their bodies lie unmarked and nameless."

"We'll know something soon, ma'am. I'll wire you soon with when we can arrange for our next meeting. Good-bye, Mrs. Custer."

She listened while he pulled open the ill-fitting door, then waited for the secure, solid clunk of the heavy latch catching once more. Libbie sighed. Staring out the window, feeling not the damp breeze of Lake Michigan on her cheeks, but the dry wind of the high Dakota plains.

Hearing not the street vendors and hack drivers and bustling merchants at their commerce below her window, but the shrieks of eagle wing-bone whistles and the grunting war songs and those keening cries of the widows mourning their fallen warriors.

Her eyes looking far beyond the brick and sooty chimneys and crude signs, beyond even the far lakeshore. Her eyes finding farther yet the high prairie of Montana Territory, and a sun-washed hill where her beloved Autie's spirit lay prisoner still.

Gophers and deer mice.

Sitting Bull had boasted that as long as he had them to eat, he would not return. Yet even he could not escape what had gone on around him last winter.

"For myself, my hand will never shake the hand of an American. But any who would go back to the agencies can go."

He had freed his people to return. Perhaps they would find enough to eat on the reservations. Surely, many argued, it could be no worse than their life had been in the north. No longer would Sitting Bull try to hold them here in the land of the Grandmother.

By the last nibbled moon of April, almost a fourth of his combined camps had headed south, each small band carrying a letter from the Mounted Police that would help should they bump into any roving detachments of the Bear Coat's soldiers.

For those who had suffered through that harsh winter, Major Walsh and his men could do little. The Canadians had ceased throwing away their scraps, even bones with the promise of life-sustaining marrow. The major himself turned his head when a few of his old veterans took to sharing their personal rations among the neediest bands of Sioux. He could not bring himself to punish any man for wanting to help, for seeking to stretch what the queen had put on their table. What the white men brought was not much, yet enough of something to carry to the stinking camps filled with sickness and death, something to put in the kettles of those still alive and not gone south.

Even the Quebecois trader who had himself founded the settlement at Wood Mountain had run out of supplies. With small hope of repayment from the queen's coffers, Jean-Louis Legare had emptied his shelves for Sitting Bull's Sioux through that terrible winter. Many of the Lakotas felt a bond with the trader for it. But as the spring trading season began, Legare had nothing to offer. It did not matter much. The Lakotas did not have much to trade.

"I will be the last to go, I think," Sitting Bull repeated, some of the spirit lost from his words. "The Americans will kill me when I go south, I think. I do not want to die like Crazy Horse. Let me die like a warrior."

Walsh listened respectfully that nineteenth day of May when the great Hunkpapa chief and eight others grumbled of their shrinking hopes. In so undramatic a way, Sitting Bull shocked White Forehead when he finally came around to saying he was ready to end his war with the Americans.

"Will White Forehead talk to the Bear Coat and One Star Terry for my people?" Sitting Bull asked, his hands kneading one another, not accustomed to pleading. "I beg you to see the White Father of the United States. See that the conditions of my surrender will be carried out by faithful men."

Walsh recognized the inner struggle apparent in the great chief's eyes, knowing how difficult it was for so proud a man to admit so great a need. The major knew Sitting Bull had recently watched an old friend tear himself away and take his small band south toward the agencies. Gall, the fierce warrior-chief of the Greasy Grass fight, longtime friend and counselor to Sitting Bull.

Something even more personal still scraped at the Canadian's strong sentiment. Over the recent years he had come to share a common respect, indeed a friendship, with the Hunkpapa chief. It was something Sitting Bull had rarely experienced with white men. James Walsh remembered what he had written in a report bound for Montreal not that long before.

In my opinion he is the shrewdest and most intelligent Indian living, has the ambition of Napoleon; and is brave to

a fault; he is respected, as well as feared, by every Indian on
the plains; in war he has no equals; in council he is superior
to all; every word said by him carries weight, is quoted and
passed from camp to camp.

Now Walsh struggled for control as he found the words to
explain. "I will try what I can for your people, Sitting Bull,"
he said, rising from his chair, coming forward to stand
before the Hunkpapa delegation. "I am not a big chief
among my people. You ask me to speak to your leaders, but
among the Americans I am no chief at all."

"You speak to the chiefs for us," Sitting Bull repeated.

Walsh wagged his head. "It may be too late for any of us
now, my friend. I am leaving Wood Mountain."

"You are going east to speak for us?" The Bull's voice
rose with hope.

"No, Sitting Bull. Perhaps my chiefs are not happy with
the job I have done here."

"Not happy?"

"My chiefs are transferring me to a post far away.
Qu'Appelle."

Sitting Bull's face went slack as the interpreter's words
sunk in. "There will be another come to sit in your chair,
White Forehead?"

"Crozier," he answered, unable to look into the Sioux
eyes, thinking about the less than two hundred lodges left
in the once great encampment.

"Do you know anything of this man Crozier?" Sitting
Bull begged. "Will he help my people?"

Walsh shook his head, his mouth trying to form some
words. At last he said, "He has worked for me here. But he is
a different man. I can only pray Crozier will try as I have
tried."

Sitting Bull did not know white men, but he understood
enough to read the Canadian's face. In his heart the
Hunkpapa chief knew the new man would spell the death
knell for his people.

The great chief of the once-mighty Lakotas laid his face
in his hands, overwhelmed with more despair than ever
before. "I am thrown away."

CHAPTER 29

FOR the last two years L.N.F. Crozier had served as Walsh's second in command, and post commander at Fort Walsh itself. Now he vowed to hold the reins of the Cypress Hills more firmly than had his predecessor, beginning immediately to deal with the lesser chiefs, symbolic of his clearly defined goal of undermining Sitting Bull's solitary hold on leadership of the Lakotas in Canada.

Five days after his arrival, Crozier went into council with Spotted Eagle, clearly the chief second in power only to Sitting Bull. Less than a week later, Spotted Eagle headed south for the Medicine Line and the reservations in the United States, taking with him more than sixty-five lodges, a full third of those who had survived the last winter with Sitting Bull.

It took five more months of wheedling on Crozier's part, but the agent finally convinced Oglalla chief Low Dog that he too should lead his people south to their traditional agency. Still, it was not until Sitting Bull himself promised Low Dog that he would go part of the way as well, if only to test the American waters and see familiar country, that the Oglalla finally gave the order to his people for them to tear down their lodges and load the pony drags.

Yellow Bird rode behind White Cow Bull that winter morning late in the moon the white man called December. Sees Red rode atop the second of only two ponies left the family. Monaseetah chose to walk beside the travois bearing their lodge and few possessions. She said she did not mind walking, as long as her feet stayed warm in the thick buffalo-fur winter moccasins.

A few flakes of snow lanced out of the gray sky, yet the ground was blown clear and hard beneath the ponies' hoofs. Only sixty lodges remained with Sitting Bull's camp, following Low Dog's band out of the clay hills in the Wood Mountain district, pointing their noses for the tall stone pillars that marked the sacred Medicine Line. Low Dog's Oglallas crossed first, then the Hunkpapas. The women keened lowly beneath the harsh scut of wind whipping along the ground. The old men sang their prayer songs.

Back in the land of the white enemy.

As each new day crawled by without trouble, the travelers grew more gay. Many knew great joy in recognizing familiar landmarks as they journeyed south across the high plains once their homeland. They had been marching for better than three weeks, approaching the new phase of the Moon of Cold Nights, when early one afternoon Low Dog's forward scouts came back to report some happy news. They had just returned from Gall's village of southbound refugees, finding them camped just ahead.

"Why have they gone no farther?" Monaseetah asked White Cow Bull as he and Yellow Bird trotted back along the caravan with the news.

"There has been some sickness," he replied. "I believe Gall had his people stop to hunt, to gather their strength before going on into their reservation."

She looked at the gaunt faces of her two sons. Another might not recognize them. "What about the soldiers? Don't they patrol anymore, looking for us?"

White Cow Bull pursed his lips. "The soldiers told Gall he had to be into the post they call Fort Buford by a certain day."

"Will they make it, as weak as his people are?" she asked.

"Gall told Sitting Bull that ordered day has come and gone."

Yellow Bird watched the hardening come to his mother's eyes. "We must all sleep light from now on," she whispered apprehensively. "I remember the warnings from soldiers before. They do not care that our people are too weak or sick to move quickly. The soldiers come—and old ones die."

"Pray we have not done wrong in following Sitting Bull back to the land of the bluecoats, Monaseetah," said the Oglalla warrior. "Pray."

Yellow Bird whirled at the sudden rattle of rifle fire booming behind the low hills not far ahead.

"The soldiers!" White Cow Bull shouted, immediately helping Yellow Bird slip off the war pony.

"You left Gall's camp just in time, my husband!" Monaseetah shouted as she hurried off to join the rest of the women, children, and old ones heading for a low bluff where they would attempt to make themselves small.

Yellow Bird stood alone on the prairie, watching the few warriors left to Low Dog and Sitting Bull put heels to their ponies while the others scurried toward cover. The wind whipped the threadbare blanket coat that had become too small for him a long time ago. It whistled and howled at his cold ears with the familiar bite of a winter-gaunt wolf.

Not heeding his mother's voice to follow her, he set off at a trot, following the men over the top of the first rise. From there he could see the first lodgepole spirals in the distance that marked Gall's camp of refugees. Beyond the lodges the open meadow blossomed with puffs of dirty white smoke, followed seconds later by the dull, delayed booms of the soldiers' wagon-guns.

He was frozen there atop that low rise, watching the mounted warriors rise and fall with the kneading land as they galloped to aid the besieged village. With his heart trapped in his throat, he watched the gauntlet of white gunsmoke blossoms tighten round the camp circle. To the east streamed a line of black ants. The women and children. At the center of camp, more black ants scurried backward among the smoky brown of the lodges, slowly retreating toward the oncoming reinforcements.

Still, the warriors of Sitting Bull and Low Dog were no match for the combined forces of infantry and cavalry, in addition to the steady bombardment of the Hotchkiss guns.

On the cold, dry air of that second day of January, 1881, Yellow Bird first heard the loud, booming hiss of those terrible instruments of destruction that could fire fifty rounds per minute. Each wagon-gun sent a resounding message of death through the shredded lodges of what had once been Gall's camp.

He fell to his knees in wonder at their power, listening to the distant cries of the wounded, at times swallowed over by the loud bellow of orders given the gun crews, followed by the whispering boom echoing and reechoing from the low, frozen hills about him.

Alone there, until the pounding of pony hooves awakened him as if from a nightmare trance. He stared transfixed into that low valley until White Cow Bull's voice startled him.

"Come, little Cheyenne!" he shouted, reining up on the cold, bare earth. "We must fly. Get your mother—all the rest."

Yellow Bird held up a hand, pulled himself behind the warrior. "Where?"

"Low Dog has decided to stay and surrender with Gall."

"Are we surrendering to those soldiers?" The boy's voice had never held so much fear.

White Cow Bull bent an arm behind him, cradling the youngster against his back as he kneed the pony into a downhill gallop. "No, little warrior. Sitting Bull will never surrender to soldiers who attack a village of women and children with their murderous guns! Our chief has told us to escape across the Medicine Line! *Aiyeee!*"

Throughout the remainder of that winter, the snows came and went, and with them, the game. There were times of meat. There were weeks of famine. And always there was the remembering of the hard winters gone before when the ponies died and many of the people gave up their spirits to walk the star road.

Twice more during elaborate feasts, agent Crozier attempted to convince Sitting Bull to take his remaining lodges south to Fort Buford where the others had gone. In the end the Canadian's patience ran dry, and he physically threw the Hunkpapa chief off the post, shouting, "I don't want to see any of you again—I've had far too much trouble with you already! You can all go to hell!"

White Cow Bull had not needed an interpreter to understand the superintendent's message. All hope faded for a permanent reservation of their own in Canada. Time and again they had been told they had a place waiting for them in the United States. Now there would be no more rations from the sympathetic Mounties. Crozier forbade it.

Their only hope for lasting a free people remained the short Quebecois trader, Jean-Louis Legare, founder of the Wood Mountain trading house. Perhaps because Sitting Bull's people had been a financial drain on Legare's resources and he realized he could no longer stay in debt to his own creditors, or perhaps because he sensed that there might be some widespread recognition to come of being the man who brought about Sitting Bull's surrender—no matter what the reason, the little trader gathered what he had left in the way of supplies and called for a council with all the men left in Sitting Bull's camp.

After a grand feast held before his trading post, and after the pipe had been passed round the circle four times, Legare rose to welcome his guests. He then spoke eloquently of the ones who had already abandoned Sitting Bull.

"The mention of the names bring their faces before your eyes," he reminded them. "White Bird. Spotted Eagle. Gall. Low Dog. Do I go on, Sitting Bull? I think you and your people hurt enough, knowing you have been left behind by your friends and your families. Just look at you. You are poor! Begging at the door of my trading post for flour! Time was, your proud people would cut open a bag of flour and pour it on the ground, saying it was poor white-man food. Now—now your children lick their fingers and suck at the flour to give their gnawing bellies something to end their torment."

Legare watched their eyes. Instead of what he figured

would be contempt for his harsh words, the trader found only a blank look of acceptance.

"If you love your children, you will heed my words. Surrender and let the American agents feed your families."

Sitting Bull sat with the others, stunned by the seriousness of Legare's words. Finally White Cow Bull rose to speak.

"Many times before we have offered goodwill to the Americans, trader. Now you talk to us this way. Who are you? Can you give us a guarantee that if we surrender, that we will not be surrounded and cut apart as the soldiers cut down Gall's people with their powerful wagon-guns? How can you guarantee us that our surrender will not be our first step to being killed?"

The Oglalla stood there, listening to the grunts of agreement from the warriors seated round the council circle. He felt strong, putting the French-Canadian in his place.

Yet Legare's mind worked busily as he paced back and forth across the bare ground. Descended from a stalwart race of bandy-legged voyageurs, the trader was not about to admit defeat. He stepped before the Oglalla, smiling.

"Your people know I can give you no guarantee when it comes to the Americans—don't you, White Cow Bull?"

He smiled in return. "You cannot."

"But—before Sitting Bull and all these warriors—I offer to supply and personally lead a delegation to go to Fort Buford."

"To Fort Buford!" Sitting Bull exploded, lumbering to his feet with a limp. "The troops who destroyed Gall's village are stationed there!"

"Then that is the only place where your men must go to arrange for a peaceful, safe surrender," Legare explained.

"I will not go—not with you—not with any man," Sitting Bull grumbled. "Instead, trader—I will take my own delegation and go to Qu'Appelle."

"To see Walsh?" Legare asked, astonished. "White Forehead can do nothing for you now."

"He is my friend. And friends can always do something for me."

"Sitting Bull," Legare said, stepping right up to the

broad-chested man some ten years older than himself, "I am your friend. When will you trust me?"

A voice spoke out behind the Canadian. "I trust you, trader."

Legare whirled, disbelief written on his face as he stared at White Cow Bull. "You, Oglalla?"

"Yes, I will bring to you all those who would go to Fort Buford with me to arrange a surrender."

"Yeee-hooo!" exclaimed the little trader as he jigged round the merry fire. He leaped up to the Oglalla, taking the warrior arm in arm with him. "I'll begin tomorrow morning, supplying our party for the journey south. You'll see who your friends are now, Sitting Bull. You'll see."

Resolute in his distrust of the Americans, Sitting Bull took the rest of his people east to Qu'Appelle in hopes of finding White Forehead. Instead James Walsh was on leave in eastern Canada early that summer, attracting even the disgust of Prime Minister MacDonald with his steadfast pursuit of a reservation for the Sioux. The Canadian bureaucrat coolly toyed with the major, for fear that if he dismissed Walsh too soon, the police official would return to Qu'Appelle and stir up trouble with Sitting Bull, just when Crozier was reporting that trader Legare had headed south with a delegation intent on surrendering at Fort Buford.

By the time Sitting Bull's haggard band of hold-outs marched back to Wood Mountain in July with a guarantee from the Mounted Police of provisions for their return trip, Legare had completed his second trip across the Medicine Line. Already two groups had turned themselves over to the soldiers at Fort Buford. White Cow Bull alone remained, waiting for Sitting Bull's starving stragglers to march over the low hills ringing Legare's trading post.

He embraced Monaseetah, hugging both boys as if he had again been unsure he would ever see them.

"Sitting Bull is promised the Red Coats are bringing provisions to us," Monaseetah said, looking at him, hollow-cheeked, the sparkle gone from those sinful black cherry eyes.

"The Red Coats will never come with food for Sitting Bull now," White Cow Bull whispered into her hair, the boys clinging to his side.

"We have no hope but the trader," she replied sadly.

"No," the Oglalla said, sadder still. "Our only hope is that Sitting Bull will cross the line."

"Surrender?" Yellow Bird asked.

It was a question needing no spoken answer.

CHAPTER 30

July, 1881

T HE food promised by the Canadian politicians and
commanders of the Mounted Police never arrived that
summer. Game grew more scarce as summer droned on.
The camps stank and the children cried. Seeing they had
nowhere else to turn, the last four headmen visited Jean-
Louis Legare.

"Like those gone before I will take you and your families
to Fort Buford," he told them as they squatted on the
rough-plank floor of his trading house near Wood Mountain.

Sitting Bull, Four Horns, The Thunder, and Red Eagle
considered his offer, conferring among themselves while
some of the younger warriors looked on. Behind them all,
sitting beside a barrel of salt, hid Yellow Bird and Wind,
eyes wide and ears pinned back.

"We are willing to surrender, trader," Sitting Bull grudg-
ingly announced, then added, "—if we are given enough
time to prepare."

Legare clapped his hands, his big yellow teeth gleaming
round an unashamed smile. He had his victory. "I'll guide

you to Buford myself. Until then your families will have all that I can offer. Flour for the fry-bread your women make."

"You have no meat?" Four Horns asked.

Legare shook his head. "You have eaten me out of everything else. At least my flour will fill the bellies of your families until we start our journey."

The Thunder inched forward. "When are we to leave, trader?"

His eyes rolled to the low, rough-beamed ceiling as a finger tapped against his lower lip. "Five days from now."

Indeed it was on the eleventh of July that Legare readied thirty-five wagons and three red-river carts in the meadow before his trading post. A runner came from Sitting Bull early that day, saying the chief was sick and would wait a while longer.

"You tell this boy to go back to Sitting Bull with my words," Legare growled sternly. "We are not waiting." His eyes watched the horizon fill with men and women and children, families coming to his Wood Mountain post to begin their long journey. "Tell him the time has come to go."

As each group came in, reporting to Legare and his clerk who acted as interpreter, the trader gave them their choice of weapons, bullets, blankets, and some staples to see them on the way into the land of their old enemies. But as the morning wore on, two problems arose. As he counted noses, Legare grew more worried that he no longer had enough food to take along for all the Sioux he was about to lead South. Worse yet, Sitting Bull still had not cast a shadow on Legare's meadow.

The first problem was something his quick mind could cure. Calling forth his wife's two Metis brothers, Legare sent them with a message to the commander at Fort Buford that stated he was on the way with Sitting Bull's last hold-outs. He needed food and assistance. But mostly food.

With the messengers on their way, the trader turned back to the men, women, and children waiting in the meadow. The high-walled wagons and the two-wheeled carts were filled with animated and noisy little ones, sad-faced squaws, and the stony-eyed warriors. No one needed to explain to Legare that the adults were waiting for Sitting Bull.

As the sun pushed past midsky, he decided he could wait no more. The others were ready. Messengers were on their way and the animals had grown restive.

"We will go!" he shouted, waving his arm.

All up and down the meadow echoed the interpreter's order. The men slowly returned to their wagons, preferring to walk beside them. This journey was a thing hard enough to do without riding in a wagon. They were men who had ridden the plains atop grass-fed ponies, following in the wake of the mighty brown beasts. Stealing horses and lifting scalps. These men who had counted coup on Red Beard's soldiers on the Rosebud, beaten Reno's soldiers back across the Greasy Grass in a wild stampede of death, then crushed the others who charged down Medicine Tail Coulee. Only five short summers before these men trudging along in the dust kicked up from the creaking wooden wheels of those rickety carts had taken ammunition belts from the Custer dead.

Then the procession stopped. As suddenly as if the shadow of a hawk's wing had passed over a burrow of mice. Many pointed. Some jabbered. Most sat silent, waiting for the trader to see.

"What is it, White Cow Bull?" Yellow Bird said, poking his head over the side of the high-walled freight wagon. He squinted into the high prairie sunlight. In the distance the dim figures swam and danced.

"It is Sitting Bull, little warrior." He turned to the others, raising his battered Winchester high in the air. "Sitting Bull has come!"

As if to recapture the magic and joy of a long-ago time, all round them rose the throaty cheers and high-pitched trills of the women. Old men quickly tore the covers from their hand drums. Some of the younger children beat iron ladles and tent stakes on the sides of the carts. The racket caused the old mules and draft horses to dance in their harness and tug at their traces anxiously.

From the crest of the hill, the Hunkpapa chief moved out of the trees, into the open with his two wives and many children. Three tired ponies dragged travois, each pole tip kicking up a small storm of dust swirling around the many moccasined feet pointing toes into the meadow.

As this last family drew close to the trading store, Legare stopped dancing round and round with his clerk, breathing hard. He stood still as a statue, only his wide brown eyes moving, watching the chief's face as Sitting Bull limped past within an arm's length.

This mighty chief of the Hunkpapa band, spiritual leader of the Lakotas for many years, the vision-holder of the great victory on the Greasy Grass—Sitting Bull looked into the face of Legare for but a moment as he passed. Only his eyes moved as well. Nothing on that face changed. Remaining implacable. Stony resignation.

Yet the eyes said something more: the Hunkpapa chief knew he had been bested by the little trader, beaten by the winters without end and crushed beneath the starvation that no man could count coup on. Those dark, brooding eyes said in that flicker of a moment that he realized surrender would cost him his life. If not tomorrow, then perhaps the day after.

If not then, surely the day after that.

Legare's weary caravan limped into Fort Buford on the nineteenth of July, 1881. Built at the mouth of the Yellowstone on the Missouri River, the fort stood barely seventy miles south of the sacred Medicine Line that five summers before had saved Sitting Bull's people.

The banquettes along the stockade walls were lined with blue-shirted soldiers and an array of civilians as the procession hoved into sight and went into camp just below the fort walls. Inspector A. R. Macdonnell arrived from Wood Mountain to officially turn the Hunkpapas over to the Americans the next day as the bacon grease lay warm in their Lakota bellies.

"Ho, all you people!"

Yellow Bird looked up with the rest, seeing the half-dozen interpreters riding into the center of the tiny camp circle on army horses, wearing parts of soldier uniforms.

"You listen now!" the interpreter went on. Each of the six held an army Springfield butt locked on his thigh as the group rode cocky into the crescent of poor lodges. The riders stopped behind the speaker.

"You women—ho! All of you—keep your children back now. Stay with the little ones and do not interfere with this man's business. Stay back—back away from your warriors!"

Sitting Bull's men rose slowly, muttering to themselves. From the fort gates emerged a column of infantry, arms at their shoulders, marching between the horns of the camp circle, where they halted on the order of their company commander. The soldiers split into two groups, each column lining a side of the road. Silently waiting.

"Warriors line up—be quick now!" the interpreter shouted again, waving his rifle. From time to time he pointed it at one of the women or children, scolding them for getting in the way. The other five half-breeds acted much like herders to the warriors on foot keeping them funneled until Sitting Bull and the rest stood at the end of the long gauntlet of bluecoat soldiers.

Down the center of the gauntlet strode a single soldier, followed by two more. He stopped before the warriors, saluted, then presented his hand to Legare.

"I am Captain Walter Clifford, U.S. Seventh Infantry. I understand you are the gentleman responsible for bringing Sitting Bull in?"

"I am," Legare dusted off his rusty English.

"The government of the United States owes you a great debt for bringing this chapter of our Indian wars to a close, monsieur."

Legare blushed. "I am in hopes your government will accept my claim to them for the provisions and supplies required for these past four trips to your fort."

"That? Oh, yes. It has already been forwarded to General Miles's desk. I am certain our Congress can free something from the treasury for the man who single-handedly brought Sitting Bull in to surrender." He strode past Legare a few steps. "Tell me, which one is this Sitting Bull?"

Legare turned, smiling broadly. "You can't tell, Captain?"

Clifford cleared his throat, biting on a lip as he looked over the bunch. "Why, no. To tell you the truth, I'm

disappointed in their appearance. They all look so much—
like beggars. Hardly what I had supposed they would—a
proud, savage race of thieves and warriors. The finest light
cavalry in the history of the world—all that, you know. But
these—this bunch of dirty beggars, dressed in rags and bits
of worn, greasy buckskin. Among this motley collection—I
cannot tell the leader from the lowliest."

"Sitting Bull has the eagle-feather fan across his left arm,
Captain."

Clifford eyed him, doubtful. "I see. This is the man who
stalemated Crook, then a week later butchered the cream of
Custer's cavalry? That squat old street beggar?"

Legare hurried to the soldier's side. "I think it fortunate
these Hunkpapas do not know English, Captain. If not
Sitting Bull, then any one of these warriors might like
wetting their skinning knives on the guts in your belly."

Clifford blanched, stepping back toward the safety of his
troops. He yanked on the wrist of the interpreter who had
been barking orders, whispering his instructions now into
the half-breed's ear.

"Ho—you warriors!" began the interpreter, walking his
pony down the line of Hunkpapa men. "Drop your guns on
the ground before you. Do not be slow—the soldiers are
waiting!"

Yellow Bird stood with Monaseetah and Sees Red,
watching. Four Horns was the first to drop his Springfield,
taken from the Reno fight. More weapons clattered to the
ground, mostly a collection of old muzzle loaders and
cap-lock pistols laid in the dust at the warriors' feet.

Clifford hollered his orders. A sergeant brought up a
squad to scoop the rifles and pistols from the dirt. The
weapons disappeared through the fort gate as the captain
gave his next command to the interpreter.

"You warriors—each one of you throw down your bow!"

Yellow Bird felt his mother's hand tighten on his shoulder. Many of the Hunkpapas straightened, standing a little
taller, swelling their chests and jutting their chins in
defiance.

Quiet muttering buzzed up and down the line as Sitting
Bull fanned himself, his eyes in slits that stared straight
ahead without looking at the nearby soldiers. Legare's

interpreter whispered in the trader's ear. He in turn hurried to Captain Clifford's side.

"These men own sacred bows. They have performed the special medicine on them and the arrows. Sitting Bull's warriors will never throw these weapons in the dirt at your feet."

"Superstitious savages," Clifford murmured, eyeing the haughty, hungry warriors. "Some religious significance to their weapons, eh?" He turned eventually, barking his command to his interpreter, coupled with more instructions to a pair of soldiers who trotted from the fort gates.

"Hunkpapa warriors, you will lay your bows and quivers on the blankets the soldiers spread on the ground before you," came the orders as Clifford's men stepped back into line. "Many of you will get your bows back—to hunt with come your return to your reservation."

The men eyed one another. White Cow Bull glanced over his shoulder at Monaseetah. Yellow Bird watched her smile bravely, tears coursing silently down her cheeks.

The proud Oglalla warrior slowly pulled the bearskin quiver strap from his shoulder, over his head, and held it before him a moment. Sadly he knelt, laying down the special weapon that had served him well for years, taking much meat and many buffalo, driving the life from many a bluecoat soldier along the Greasy Grass.

He rose, glancing at Monaseetah for but a moment more so she could see the look of humiliation and defeat in his eyes.

"Will he cry, mother?"

"No, Yellow Bird. A Lakota warrior does not cry. In grief he calls out with his pain. But he does not cry. Your adopted father—he came here to give up his body to the bluecoat soldiers. But White Cow Bull never realized he would have to give up something more to these white men. Stand up straight, Yellow Bird!" she whispered sharply as the boy fought to choke down his tears.

"It is hard, mother." Yellow Bird watched the soldiers roll up the army blankets laden with the bows, arrows, and quivers. It was a hard thing for the boy to witness, this shaming of these last proud warriors who had once roamed the freedom of the high plains.

"You must, Yellow Bird!" her whisper snapped at him as he shuddered in grief. "White Cow Bull, and all the rest—they are counting on us to be brave with them."

"Brave?" he cried out in a small voice, sounding hurt and alone beside her, watching the soldier-leader turn the Lakota men aside, leading them like the white man's cattle out to their small pony herd.

"How can I be brave now, mother?"

"You must be brave, my son." The tears cascaded down her cheeks now as she stared straight ahead at the walls of the stockade. "You have a soldier's blood in your body. You have the spirit of a warrior in your heart."

"Mother—"

"You . . . will . . . be . . . brave."

BOOK III

YOUNG MANHOOD
1883–1884

CHAPTER 31

Autumn, 1883

H<small>IS</small> legs ached fiercely.

Yellow Bird had been crouched here in the shady pit for so long, he was beginning to worry his muscles would never let him crawl out. For a moment as he came awake slowly, it seemed as if he had been here as long as he could remember. It scared him to think he would be staying here, cramped and breathing the still, hot air, for the rest of his life.

Just over his head were breaks in the spindly branches and dry leaves he gazed through to scan small patches of the clear, cold sky far above. The old white woman teacher at the school said this season was known among her people as fall. He laughed. White people were still amusing to him. Of course it was fall. That's just what the leaves on the cottonwood and alder had almost finished doing—falling.

The pains were less sharp now. Almost every day he had been having them in his legs, sometimes in his arms. And much of the time, it was as if he did not know his legs and arms to begin with. They conspired against him, doing strange things to him when he was not expecting. As if he were no longer familiar with his body. Growing like it was. No longer was he a boy. Now he stood to look eye to eye with his mother.

His fourteenth summer had come and gone. Winter was hurrying autumn out of its way. Still, there would never be any winters here on the Pine Ridge like those they had suffered in the land of the Grandmother.

Sky above was clear. Not a smudge of cloud to mar its cold clarity. Nor was there any sign of an eagle yet. No great, wide-winged bird swooping high overhead to spot the skinned and bloody rabbit carcass he had tied to the branches of his pit cover. With their eyesight, the great birds could spot the carrion from far, far overhead. He hoped it would not be much longer that he had to wait.

Hoping for an eagle and feathers. He needed feathers to carry with him to the top of the faraway bluffs in the badlands. It was there that White Cow Bull told him many young men had gone for generations to suffer through their vision-quest.

There were no more sun dances. The agents and soldiers and missionaries had seen to that. Last summer had been the first time in any man's memory that the Lakotas had not held a sun dance. The black-robes had come in earnest last summer, to replace the dancing and thanksgiving to the sun with their Bibles and their stories of the son of God who was hanged on the bare tree.

To Yellow Bird it sounded an awful lot as if the son of God were a warrior who had been captured and tortured by his enemies before he was hung from the prayer pole of sun-dance lodge.

Yellow Bird felt his muscles ease, not aching so badly, easing like solid ground gone to mud under a relentless spring rain. He relaxed within his growing body, eyes drooping as his breathing grew more regular. Thinking on the two winters he had lived at Fort Randall with his mother, brother, and White Cow Bull—sent there with the last hold-outs.

For the few days the Hunkpapas had remained at Fort Buford, most of the talk among Sitting Bull's people was in anticipation of going to the place the white man called

Standing Rock. Since other Hunkpapas had been assigned to that agency, they were hopeful of being sent there under the watchful eyes of the Fort Yates soldiers.

But when they were herded aboard the frightening paddle-wheel steamers to begin their river journey south, they had passed right on by Standing Rock Agency. These hold-outs under Sitting Bull were taken instead to Fort Randall, south of the Rosebud Landing on the Missouri River. A place far to the south in what the white man was calling South Dakota. Far from the land these men and women had roamed as a free people.

Wind, Sees Red, and the other children had joined Yellow Bird at the boat's railing that first day, watching muddy water foam past the first deck as the belching, smoking monster that had a voracious appetite for wood hurtled them downriver like prisoners clinging to a piece of bark in spring runoff. He remembered what his mother had told him.

Yellow Bird bit his lip to keep from crying out, blinked his eyes free of stinging tears, and he was brave.

There were trees and good water and open clearings in which to erect their camp circles at their new home the soldiers called Fort Randall above the Niobrara River. Summer was at its peak when they arrived, so it gave the women time to patch the torn lodge skins and replace lodgepoles broken on the long journey south. The men asked for the return of their bows so they could hunt, but the soldiers told them to wait. For the time being they would be given rations by the agency: hard-bread and salt pork and some flour. The women became good at frying the flour in boiling fat. He and his brother enjoyed watching the flour-and-water paste his mother dropped into her kettle as it spit and popped and grew swollen into a sweet, puffy bread.

From the first morning after their arrival, every day became one of simple, quiet routine. Not long after a breakfast of fat pork his mother fried and the hard-bread she let soak in the same grease, the soldiers came down to the camp circle and counted Sitting Bull's people. Each lodge had to stand together, no one allowed to talk, while the soldiers walked slowly by, speaking among themselves and pointing, one soldier scratching marks on his paper.

In the way he had learned to count from his mother, there were ten-times-ten, plus half that again almost every day in this camp of Sitting Bull's hold-outs. The count rarely changed. One morning an old one who had died through the night would be dropped from the soldier's paper marks. Then a few days later, the soldiers would add another mark signifying a new child born to one of the families.

Life went on into autumn, and autumn slowly froze itself into winter before the Oglallas were allowed to join their own on the Pine Ridge. But winter on the reservation left nothing for the men to do except grow more sullen and argue among themselves and with their women and children. The children brought water and the women found firewood. But there was no longer any hunting. The men had only to show up on ration day at the post to collect their allotments.

He watched sadness etch dark circles round White Cow Bull's eyes as each day crawled relentlessly into the next. It was a deepening sadness that one day slipped into despair—the day the Oglallas watched the young boys of the band return from the agency school with their braids cut. The men had set about howling in grief and rage at what the white teachers and Christian missionaries had done. They had accomplished what the bluecoat soldiers had failed to do: destroying the warrior code for the Lakota young. A warrior's hair meant everything to him. He preened and brushed, then braided it, and hung conchos or stuffed birds or coup feathers in his hair.

When the braids were gone, so was the last hope for the people. Their young.

Those were the white men and women who came with their black books and spoke down to the Indians, pounding on their books, preaching that everyone must look out for his neighbor, taking care of the weak and the ill and the crippled. Yellow Bird began to understand something of the wide gulf between the white man and the Indian. The Shahiyena and the Lakotas both were peoples who cared for one another without the threat of damnation in eternity's pit of fire. They were a people who took in the survivors of the Sore-Eye Moon attack and the Dull Knife fight, giving them food and shelter, clothing and ponies.

He had both bloods in his body and was beginning to have his eyes opened to that. With two dreams to follow, the young boy grew frightened of doing right by both. Of the two peoples who lived in his body, Yellow Bird began to wonder who needed the preachers more.

Many of the old ones who had been the last to leave the land of the Grandmother with Sitting Bull cried most of all with the deepest despair. Across the seasons Yellow Bird grew to understand these people who stayed close to the earth, practicing a reverence for those gone before. But the white man and his bluecoat soldiers came and forced them to move from their ancient lands, forced the people to leave behind the bodies of their ancestors. No more could the daughters and sons and grandchildren visit the funeral scaffolds of the old ones gone ahead on the road through the stars. A grief rumbled through the old people like the rumble of an empty belly that had nothing to fill it.

There was a despair that had no end.

Some tried digging in the ground with the tools the agent at Pine Ridge gave them. White Cow Bull gave up digging at the earth and took to smoking willow bark and tobacco when he had it in the shade of the lodge, smoking willow bark when there was no tobacco to be had. So Monaseetah took up the hoe and canvas satchel of seeds. There were no more harsh words between them after that. They rarely spoke to one another or to Yellow Bird when both of them were about. Only when alone with Sees Red or his brother would one of the two adults have something to say.

He knew his mother felt shame for starting her husband down this long, terrible path. The time long ago when she had told him he must give the horses back.

From that time on there was no turning back for the warrior. When a man could no longer hunt buffalo or go on the warpath, when a man had to return the horses he had stolen to prove his manhood and worth—then that man became a little thing when no longer a warrior.

In the little corral behind the lodge, White Cow Bull kept his pony and the two skinny spotted cows the agent had given him one ration day. Each man took his stock home to his lodge, each dwelling separated from the others. No more could the chiefs keep their people living in a sacred camp circle, what had kept them strong through so many of the dark days behind them. Now, instead, the people strung out along the creek the white man had come to call Wounded Knee.

But it went against everything Scabby and White Cow Bull and the old ones had taught him. The people were meant to move from place to place. To allow the game to come back to an area, to allow the land to heal from their passing. To allow the predators to come in to pick the land clean of what the people had left behind in their journey across the face of the seasons.

Now the people could not move on. They stayed. And stayed as the seasons shuffled past them. Each new sun no brighter than the last.

The circle lay broken.

"I've asked you not to come here anymore," whispered the sawbones doctor as he wiped his hands on the bloody apron he had lashed about his ample girth. In disgust he eyed the burlap sack hung at the end of the detective's arm.

"You haven't done anything about the messages I been sending you," Harley Fagen hissed, his eyes watching those around them in the parlor that served as the physician's waiting room.

"For good reason," replied the doctor, anxious. He wagged his bloody hand for the detective to follow.

He led Fagen back through a long corridor, past a series of rooms where waited a cast of ills and wounds for his treatment.

"Still like the blood, don't you?" Fagen asked as the doctor closed the door to a small room behind them.

"Just finished setting a fella's leg, Fagen," he explained, looking at the blood drying in dark crescents under his fingernails. "A messy job. Got himself run over by a freight wagon up on Rush Street."

"How 'bout it, Doc?"

"This will be the last, I say."

"No it won't," Fagen threatened. "You and me ain't done."

He wagged his head, his neck shrunk back into his shoulders with a weariness of long hours. "I am—"

"You like my money too much, Doc. Need it. And need me to keep my mouth shut as well."

"That all happened so long ago—"

"Not so long that a Pinkerton don't remember."

He glared at the little detective. "You aren't a Pinkerton any longer—and I'm not the same bumbling fool I once was, Fagen."

He waited a moment before pressing his case again. "Still don't answer the matter about the money."

The physician studied Harley's face. "It's not your money, I'm sure of that."

"No matter whose money it is—it will always be mine to pay you for your powder."

The man pursed his lips, then finally shrugged his shoulders and turned. From under his bloody apron he produced a small ring of keys, selected one, and used it to open a plain-faced wooden cabinet hung on the wall among many others. Whitewash and oak doors, a room filled with but two colors and textures.

He pulled down a large apothecary jar. "How much?"

Fagen licked his lips with the pink tip of his tongue, beads of sweat beginning to break out on his forehead. "You got plenty of that, don't you, Doc?"

"You're not the only one needs it—and you damn well know it, Fagen. Now, how much this time?"

He wiped a hand across his dry lips. "What will—let's say, a hundred dollars buy?"

The doctor squinted, eyeing the little detective. "You damn well get most of the candy store, Mr. Fagen. That's what a hundred dollars will buy you. You bring your tins?"

"Right here." He patted the small burlap pouch suspended at the end of his arm.

"Give them here and let's be quick about this."

As Fagen opened the sack and pulled forth the first of

the nondescript tin containers, the physician slid the glass stopper from the apothecary jar and began spooning the white powder into the first of tins.

"That should about do it," the physician muttered when he watched Fagen put the last of the small tins into his dirty burlap satchel.

"Not quite, Doctor." He pulled one last one from his coat pocket, pulling its top off. "Fill it up."

"You have quite enough already—"

"You want your hundred or not, Doc?"

He filled the tin up and stared at the floor when he was finished, unable to look the detective in the eye.

"You like my money as much as I like your—these headache powders of yours, my good doctor." He handed the physician five double eagles, clicking them individually into the man's palm.

"How long you gonna keep taking that widow's money, Fagen?"

He watched the physician's hand stuff the coins into a pants pocket behind the dirty apron. "Until I find where her dead husband's Injun whore and bastard son are."

"You're no closer now than you were two, maybe three, years ago, are you?"

He grabbed the man's dirty shirt. "What difference it make to you, Doc?"

The doctor shoved the fist from his pleated shirt, revulsed. "You told me the angle you were working on in Nebraska turned up dry some time back. Since then there's been nothing but you touring the plains, looking for someone might as well be a ghost."

"They're not ghosts—I know it," Fagen hissed, feeling as if he could use some of his snuff right now but needed to hurry back to the small closet of a room he let during those months he returned to Chicago like this.

"The general's widow sure picked the right man for this job, didn't she, Fagen?"

"What you mean by that?"

"You've become every bit as obsessed with finding the squaw and her boy as the Custer widow is herself. Aren't you?"

He considered it, his heart pounding more and more

loudly in his ears. Harley needed to return to his room. Needed to—

"Yeah," he finally whispered, turning to grab the dirty knob on the door. It protested noisily as he pulled it open. "I s'pose I am a bit obsessed with it at that."

CHAPTER 32

GENERAL Philip H. Sheridan tugged aside the window curtain and peered into the drizzling icy sleet drenching Chicago's lakeshore. The pair of matched grays pulling his coach made sodden sounds with every step as they clattered along the graveled bridal path extending for miles through the countryside along the shore of Lake Michigan.

"Good," he said to himself as he pulled his nose out of the cold and leaned back against the leather cushion.

He pulled out his watch and discovered that he was himself two minutes late as the coach driver eased back on the reins and eased into the brake. "At least he's punctual," he muttered.

There was no one else to listen. He sat alone inside the chilly comfort of the high-wheeled coach. For a reason.

"Lovely day for a ride along the shore," a voice called out from the wall of gray sleet.

"Maybe it is for you, sonny," the coach driver grumbled. "No matter, I'm soaked to marrow up here. You ain't out here riding for your health, are you?"

"No, sir. I'm supposed to be meeting a very important gentleman."

Sheridan pulled back the curtain and hurled his voice into the icy rain, "Any man calls Phil Sheridan a gentleman deserves to stay out in the rain. Get in here, Captain."

As if lit with fire, the young officer emerged from the wall of sleet, splashed across the graveled path, leaving his horse tied to a bush beneath a tree. He stood for a moment beside the door Sheridan held open, saluting.

"Goddammit," Sheridan growled, pulling the cigar from his lips and saluting. "Get your wet ass in here, Tripp."

"Yessir." The younger man scrambled into the coach.

Inside he pulled the dripping cloak from his shoulders and laid it on the floor at their feet, where several puddles were already growing. Sheridan eyed him carefully, comparing some of the young officer's physical characteristics with information in the man's military file.

"General Sheridan—"

Philip held out his small, toughened hand. "Call me general and no more sir out of you. This may be one of the few times you'll ever get me face-to-face, so let's start out as friends. From then on—it's up to you to keep us that way, understood?"

"I'll try, sir. . . . Sorry, General."

"I'll make this brief. It's cold, and I goddammed well never liked the cold. Last time I really had to bivouac in it was down in Indian Territory in sixty eight—sixty-nine, thank God. That was a time campaigning with Custer . . . well—." He cleared his throat. "I asked my aides to come up with a man I could depend on in a tight situation. Are you such a man, Tripp?"

"I've never been in combat, General. But I'm sure—"

"I don't need you to fight, goddammit. I'd rather have someone with a head on his shoulders. I looked over a lot of men before I decided on you. Judge Advocate's office thinks highly of you."

"I've tried."

"Well, in this job, Tripp—trying won't begin to shake the dew off the lily. In the army, so the saying goes, only results count. So I'm going to expect results out of you. That's why I've had you reassigned."

"Reassigned, General? To your staff here in Chicago?"

He wagged his head, smiling in the midst of his dark beard as he dragged another lucifer across a dry plank of the coach floor and rekindled his stub of a cigar. "Not exactly, soldier. As far as your orders read, you're assigned to General Terry's staff. Have you ever met the man?"

"Once, General."

"Good. He doesn't know of you, however. I'll take care of seeing that he knows your name, at least. But if you get in a tight spot—don't count on Terry to pull your ass out of the fire. You got that? All right. You're on your own, Tripp. You're working for me, but if anyone throws it up at me that you have your ass over the fire, I disown you. I don't care who it is—Sherman or Terry—hell, especially those goddamned newspaper people. I've never so much as heard of you."

Tripp gulped, then nodded, wiping some dripping rain from an earlobe. "I had a suspicion it would be something—"

"Strange, Captain?"

"Yes. When I was ordered here from Washington, with sealed instructions waiting at my hotel to rent a horse from a certain livery and meet a coach here along the lakeshore at this hour of the morning—"

"No one but us chickens up, is there, Captain?"

He smiled. And Sheridan liked that smile, the first one the young officer had ventured since stepping into the coach. The air had begun to warm slightly so that the two soldiers were no longer making gauzy clouds between them when they spoke.

"You're denying any knowledge of me, yet—I take it you must want me to perform something damned important—excuse the expression, General."

"I figured I'd like you, when I saw you here on time, Tripp. And the more I hear you talk, the better you get. Damned right, you'll be doing something important for me—and for the nation as well. If we succeed, we'll be heroes in the press—you and I. Together, Tripp. If you fail, you'll hang alone. Still in?"

"You haven't given me a shred of anything to hold onto,

yet you want to know if I'm going to risk my career on this—"

"It's a damned fool's errand is what it is, Tripp. Here," and he presented the captain a cigar from the leather case he pulled from his tunic pocket. "Just about the finest. Sam Grant doesn't know tobacco from horse squat, but these are good."

"Thank you," he replied, eyeing the general over the end of his cigar as Sheridan lit it for him. "I suppose every condemned man gets a last smoke, doesn't he, General?"

"By shivers, you'll do in the trenches, Tripp! Now, are you on for this wild ride into hell and back . . . or do you want to go back to your nice warm office, with your nice warm secretaries and streetwalkers in your nice, comfortable Washington City?"

"Good cigar, General. Cuban?"

"That's right, Tripp. I asked you a question, goddammit."

"I'm in. Suppose you tell me what it is that I'm not going to be doing for you—and why it is I'll be doing it alone."

"You ever have opportunity to know General George Armstrong Custer?"

"No, sir."

"His wife, Elizabeth Custer?"

"No, but I have an associate who has handled a claim she had in the War Department following Custer's death."

"You're best at working with witnesses, I'm told."

"That's what they have me doing with the Judge Advocate, General. Interviewing witnesses in our—"

He waved a hand, shutting up the captain. For a long time they sat silent. Sheridan brooding, staring out the crack in the window curtain. Tripp sat smoking his cigar, listening to the hard, icy rain batter the side of the coach. Every now and then the horses grew restless, nudging their traces until the muttering driver calmed them once more.

"I brought you here because you're savvy, Captain Tripp. You'll do just fine in working with the witnesses I'm sending you to interview. And you'll enjoy doing a little detective work of your own."

"Detective work?"

"That's what I'd call it when I send you out to find some folks."

"Here in Chicago?"

He shook his head, jabbing with his cigar toward the window. "Out there."

"West?"

"You're earning your pay already, Captain."

"Speaking of that, who will I be paid by, General? For funds I'll need—"

"I've set up an account at the Chicago Mercantile and Trust in your name. All you have to do before you leave town is stop in and ask for a Mr. McGuire. He'll have you sign some forms so they have a copy of your signature. He will give you a code as well. Something to use when drafting on the account. From then on I'll be sure the account has in it what you'll need."

The captain leaned back for the first time, realizing his shoulders had been tense ever since seating himself across from the old soldier. "Sounds like I can have a pretty good time of it, General."

"You do, I'll send some of my bloody Indian scouts after you. And there won't be enough of you left to mop up a dirty barroom floor with."

"Yes, General."

"This is no lark, Tripp. I picked you because I expect results. It could make your career. Perhaps jump you to lieutenant colonel. Maybe even colonel before your head stops spinning."

He shook his head, disbelieving. "Suppose you tell me what it is you want this red-haired detective you've hired to do."

"There's an Indian woman I want you to find. For the last year or so, I've been getting reports in from division commands about some snooping around someone's doing. Asking a lot of questions, stirring some folks up—in general, just making a mess of things. Don't you make a mess of things, Tripp."

"I'm supposed to get on this fella's trail and—"

"No, Tripp. I hope you'll be able to find the Indian woman before this washed-up detective who's sniffing around does. Or before an old friend of mine finds her."

"An old friend of yours?"

"Name of Ben Clark. He was chief of scouts for me back in the winter campaign of sixty-eight. If he's on this scent too—as I hear, he's gone and put his nose to the ground—Ben Clark is the one I'm more worried about."

"You want me to be the first to find this squaw."

"An Indian woman, Tripp. Here, take another cigar with you."

"That's all? All you're gonna give me to go on?"

"When you see McGuire at the mercantile, he has a sealed manila packet for you."

"McGuire can be trusted with it."

"He fought for me in the west before I moved with Grant to fight in the Shenandoah. McGuire chose to stay with me to Appomattox—took three chunks of lead watching out for my ass in that Virginia campaign. And he's paid his dues out west in Custer's Seventh."

"I see."

"No, you don't see. McGuire can be trusted. The rest of it is up to you to find out now, Captain."

"Am I to be in contact with you, General?"

"Only when you have something solid to report. Otherwise, have a good hunt, Captain."

"No matter how long it takes?"

"No matter, Captain. I want results."

He watched Tripp sweep his damp cloak from the floor and button it at his neck before he bent to step from the coach.

"One more thing for you to think about from here on out, Captain," Sheridan added, holding the door open so he could talk in muted tones to the soldier standing in the driving sleet, his gloved hand holding down the brim of his wide hat.

"You find the woman—you'll get to be a major. Count on it," Sheridan said. "You find her half-breed, blue-eyed son for me—I'll see you make colonel."

"Be he Shahiyena or Lakota," White Cow Bull spoke in soft tones to him beneath the soft rustle of the new leaves on the cottonwoods above them, "no man can succeed in life without power of his own. With that power all things are made possible."

The gentle breeze of spring moved the short-grass around them. They sat alone beside the creek, more than a mile above the lodge where they left Monaseetah behind with her chores earlier that morning.

"See where I point," the Oglalla said. "The country is called the badlands. That is where you will find your power, Yellow Bird. For some men it comes easily. Like water rushing over the ground in a storm. For most, power comes as a difficult thing. You must pray and give of your flesh."

"We cannot pray to the sun any longer. The soldiers say we cannot dance—"

"You are not going to dance, Yellow Bird. You are going to ask for a dream. In the way warriors have asked for dreams of power far beyond any man's memory."

He felt the chill drop of fear and dread spill down his spine as he stared into the eyes of his adopted father. They sat cross-legged, their knees touching. White Cow Bull had across his lap his pipe bag, and from it he had taken his pipe, tamper, and a small pouch of tobacco mixture. Something he saved for special occasions.

"You have done this with Sees Red?"

"No," he answered, tamping small pinches of tobacco into the redstone pipebowl. "Sees Red apparently is taking another path to manhood. He has his friends, and the trouble he gets himself into. But you—your mother has long been hoping that you would have your own vision quest by your fifteenth summer."

"This will be my fifteenth."

"Then you are ready?"

"I am," he answered watching his adopted father take the char and tinder from a belt-pouch. With flint and steel he lit the char, then caught the tinder he laid in the pipe bowl. The pipe came to life with a soft hiss, glowing hot and red.

"Smoke, Yellow Bird. Offer a breath from your body to the earth, and the sky. Then one each to the four winds. Six in all, with a new prayer for each breath." He gave the pipe over to the youth.

Accepting it in both hands, the youngster felt a surge of wonder and awe at the power of this ceremony. A connection, a bonding with the ages—this ceremony of smoking with an older warrior. Preparing for the trial that would make him a man in the eyes of all Sioux men.

He prayed to the sky, drawing on the pipe stem and nearly choking with the strong, pungent mixture as it seared the back of his throat and burned his nose. It brought tears to his eyes, but he would not allow himself to cry.

A second puff, more controlled this time, to the earth, blowing smoke across the ground before he drew on the short stem four more times and prayed to the cardinal directions. By the time he was done with that part, the tobacco made a pleasing taste in his mouth, numbing his tongue slightly.

"From this day you will leave your mother," White Cow Bull recited.

His eyes widened with fear, staring into the seamed face of the Oglalla. "White Cow—"

"Take heart, little warrior. You go on living with us until you are ready to have a lodge of your own—with a woman of your choice." He was smiling.

It calmed much of his fear, here so confused between boyhood and manhood. Not wanting to leave his mother, but admitting to himself he watched the girls more often as they went to the creek for water or tried to sneak away to go swimming. He knew the girls knew he was looking when they bathed. How they loved to show their budding breasts and their hips rounding in womanness like his mother's. They knew, as surely as he knew, feeling his manhood grow swollen and hard when he gazed upon them. Knowing someday . . .

"I want to stay with you and my mother."

"I am speaking of your spirit. No longer will you have the spirit of a boy. From today you will walk upright like a man. Now finish the pipe—all the tobacco in the bowl. Pray that the Everywhere Spirit Above gives you strength for what you are about to do. Pray he is beside you when evil comes stalking your spirit."

Later as White Cow Bull scraped burnt tobacco from the

bowl then separated stem from the bowl, Yellow Bird leaned back on his elbows, light-headed.

"Now, my little Cheyenne—you have the next five days to think on."

"Five?" he said, sitting upright again.

"Today we are going into the badlands together."

He looked about. "We have no ponies."

"They are no good to you. Besides, on foot we can stay away from the soldiers who watch for us leaving the reservation."

He sensed the fear again. "What awaits us in the badlands?"

"My friends. Old ones. They are building a sweat lodge for you, Yellow Bird. To seek your spirit powers—you must be purified. The stones will be hot for you by the time we reach the foot of the red bluffs."

The boy stood with the warrior, staring north into the unknown. "And—for the next four days following that?"

"You will stand alone against the wilderness and the sky. Alone against the spirits, both good and bad. They will test your strength, and your will, Yellow Bird. I pray your Cheyenne blood will make you strong. I pray your white blood will not make you fail this trial of your soul."

CHAPTER 33

Spring, 1884

I T was late afternoon by the time they reached the small clearing by the narrow creek leading out of the vastness of the red bluffs. The nearby fire had long ago gone to red coals, baking the stones to a searing heat. Around the fire sat four old men who rose when White Cow Bull led Yellow Bird from the trees.

The oldest began to chant and shake his buffalo-scrotum rattle as the other three moved toward the boy. With White Cow Bull's help, they removed all Yellow Bird's clothing, then rubbed every inch of his flesh with sage. Then the four men quickly stripped off their breechclouts and moccasins, entering the low-domed sweat lodge one at a time.

"See the mound of dirt," White Cow Bull said when only he, the oldest man, and Yellow Bird remained outside. "It is from the fire pit inside. Makes Crazy is an Oglalla spirit dreamer. All his dreams are of wolves."

"Wolves?"

"Many times in the time I have known you, Yellow Bird—you have told me and your mother of the wolf you see. Makes Crazy does good wolf medicine. Perhaps it will be your medicine as well."

The old man shuffled forward, chanting and shaking the rattle, kicking up scuffs of dirt with each foot-dragging step. He stopped before the naked youngster, moving his rattle up one side of Yellow Bird's body and down the other.

"You will follow this path between the mound of dirt and the sweat-lodge entrance, Yellow Bird. It symbolizes your path in search of a vision. Once you have gone into the sweat lodge and I have passed the stones inside, I will shut the door off to this outside world. When you emerge after your purification, look first to this path."

Yellow Bird looked down at the smoothed earth leading to the sweat-lodge entrance as the old man continued.

"Pray that you will see the tracks of your spirit helper on this path, Yellow Bird. It means he has visited your sweat ceremony, blessing it for you."

"If there are no tracks, Makes Crazy?" the Oglalla warrior asked, concern in his voice.

The old man looked into the boy's eyes. "Then—your vision-quest will be very difficult. The boy will be on his own—without a spirit helper."

"It can be done?"

"Not all. Very few. But it can be done. Go now, Yellow Bird. The sun is falling fast. You must complete your sweat before the full moon rises. By its light we will look for the tracks on the path. Tonight you climb the bluff." He pointed above them.

"In the dark?"

"Yes," White Cow Bull said. "I will wait here for you to come down in four days."

Inside the sweat lodge he settled onto the bed of sweet sage the old men had spread like a fragrant robe around the fire pit. Makes Crazy passed in the first hot stone, carried on a forked stick. He dropped the stone into the pit, where it hissed with a protest against the moist earth. The door flap closed once more, plunging the lodge into total darkness.

"Repeat after me, Yellow Bird," said one of the old men from the dark warmth. "This stone is for all my relations. Those living, and those gone before."

He repeated the words, his voice cracking slightly, eyes straining at the darkness until the flap was pulled back and a shaft of day-end light burst into the lodge. A second stone was dropped into the pit, and the flap again covered the door.

"This stone is for all the winged creatures of the air."

Again he repeated. Then as if Makes Crazy were waiting for his cue, the door opened and a third stone was brought in. Now the small dome was becoming close, warmer than a hot summer day with no breath of air sighing.

"This stone is for all the creatures moving on legs across the Mother."

His third prayer given, the door opened a fourth time, and the final rock was delivered to the steamy pit.

"This stone—say it, Yellow Bird—this stone is for all the crawls on their bellies."

"This stone is for all the crawls on their bellies," he repeated, his head swimming as one of the men in the darkness began to slowly pour a dipper of water on the rocks, releasing clouds of stifling steam. Beads of sweat seeped from every pore until he felt he was swimming in his own juices.

"We will sing a song now," the old man across the pit in the darkness declared.

With each of four dippers of water poured on the stones, four different songs were sung. He recognized White Cow Bull's voice beside him, the other voices reedy and less strong—the voices, he thought, of old men. Four songs. Four dippers of water. He wished to be out into the cool of the evening. Yet he dreaded the climb up the sharp face of the red bluff, which loomed in his mind every bit as much as it loomed above the sweat lodge.

"Please . . ."

White Cow Bull's hand found Yellow Bird's bare thigh, gripping it securely, paternally. "We are almost done here. Be strong, Shahiyena son of Monaseetah. Be strong."

"In the old days we worried not of the coming of soldiers," an old voice on the other side of him began. "Today, with many giving up on the old beliefs and turning to the missionaries and their black book—we are forced to sneak away to practice our prayers and thanksgiving. The soldiers, and their preachers—they do not like us to hurt ourselves to give thanks. They do not like us to bleed except with their bullets. We bleed and give of our flesh to the spirits, for it is all that is truly ours. Our clothing, our weapons, any other gift is not truly ours. Only your body—only this can you give on top of the hill, Yellow Bird."

"You are ready to give of your body, Yellow Bird?" a new voice asked from the steamy darkness.

He thought he was going to pass out, fighting it as best he could, feeling he might throw his stomach on the ground before him. The steam was all he could see in the darkness, all he could smell, all he could taste.

"You are ready, Yellow Bird—to give your body?"

"I am ready—to give my body over."

The door flap suddenly flew back, allowing in a rush of fading sunlight from the horizon, allowing a rush of steam to issue from the door that dazzled his newborn eyes while they grew accustomed to the light.

"You must go first, Yellow Bird," White Cow Bull whispered at his side, gently urging. "See—see for yourself if there are tracks of a spirit helper on your path outside."

Crawling clumsily toward the low open doorway where the light beckoned, he was surprised how small the sweat lodge was, illuminated now in the fading sunlight. Yet there was a sense of symmetry to that thought, for during the long ceremony it had felt as if the sweat lodge were wrapped tightly around him, almost a part of him, suffocating him with its closeness.

Just outside the doorway sat Makes Crazy, crouched, his withered arms hung inside his knees as he peered into the young man's face. He gestured to the path.

Becoming frightened, Yellow Bird crawled forward a few more feet, straining to pick something out of the smooth, brushed earth that stretched some twenty feet to the mound of dirt.

Nothing! No footsteps.

"What do you see, Yellow Bird?"

He shook his head sadly, it sagging between his shoulders. "Nothing, White Cow Bull."

"There are no tracks, Makes Crazy?"

"There are none here for the boy," the old man answered.

Yellow Bird's heart grew smaller with the words of it, and with the sigh coming from behind him. White Cow Bull's disappointment was no less than his own.

"Go on, Yellow Bird," he instructed.

The youth crawled from the doorway and stood, the cool evening breezes chilling his naked body that, moments ago, had been warmed to a rosy tint by the scouring heat.

The old ones dressed him in his breechclout and moccasins, speaking to him in hushed tones all the while, instructing on how to find the path to the top of the bluff, each hand and foothold. Telling him too what he would find when he reached the summit. The cedar bower they had built earlier in the day for his four-day stay atop the butte, where he could stare down on much of the country for miles around.

No water and no food. Alone.

White Cow Bull waited patiently as the old men finished their instructions on what to do as the sun rose each day, what to do as it set each evening. What prayers to say and what powers to invoke.

Then the Oglalla embraced the youth in his strong arms as he had never done before.

"I may not be there with you, my son," he whispered in the boy's ear, using that word for the first time, "but my heart will be at your side."

He stepped back, clutching Yellow Bird's hand before the youth began his climb. All the old men stepped up behind the warrior, watching Yellow Bird begin pulling himself up along the jagged rocks at the base of the bluff.

"*H'gun! H'gun!!*" one of them shouted, giving praise with the Lakota courage word.

"*Hopo! Hopo hey!*" another yelled his encouragement.

Tears streamed down White Cow Bull's weathered cheeks. His chest filled with pride and yearning. "My heart goes with you, my son!"

The sharp rocks cut his hands and bare feet, scraping hide from his slim chest and flat belly as he dragged himself ever upward.

Once he dared to look down, seeing the fire far below like a faint red dot of flickering dancing light, and tiny figures blotting it out for but a moment—like the flight of the firefly across the sky before his eyes. He clung to the rocks as the sky blackened. Above him the stars began to swirl in the deepening of twilight's purple blessing on the earth. Below, there was nothing but an opening, yawning, unfilled void.

He was afraid to go up. He could not see to go down.

Yellow Bird cried, clinging to the side of the cliff until there were no more tears and the pain became a dull reminder that he had lived with fear before. Winters before he had awakened to the attack of soldiers. The frightening white-bellied fish bodies of the dead soldiers on the bloody hillside beneath a glaring summer sun. And winter after winter of starvation and despair spent far to the north in the land of the Grandmother.

There were no more tears. No more reason to be afraid. And no more reason to stay here in the darkness, like a bat clinging to the rocks, waiting for a juicy moth to come winging by in the darkness before swooping down on its prey. He climbed.

Hand by hand, foothold by tiny foothold on every slight outcrop, Yellow Bird inched his way to the top of the great wall.

As he pulled his chin over the rock lip, a gust of wind whispered past his sweat-plastered hair. It smelled sweet. Like the high plains themselves. With the smell of no man. Only the fresh, virgin fragrance of being here the day after the Great Everywhere Above had made all things.

But there in the pale light pouring milky from a sliver of moon, he saw he was not the first. The old ones had come before him. A willow bower large enough for one man to curl himself into had been built by tying the long limbs together to fashion a crude dome. Over it they had pulled the leafy fronds of squawbush and hawthorn to give him some shelter. Around him the ground had been cleared for some distance. Not a stone nor a twig nor a single growing plant. The hard earth pounded to a smooth consistency of polished granite.

He sat, relieved, at the front of the tiny shelter while the moon tracked overhead. From his right hand to his left shoulder. Sat thinking on what he had come here for. Dreaming of food and water and sometimes the young girls he watched bathing, but mostly he thought on what it might be to go without those things. He had done so before. More so the food. The water . . .

He would not think of that anymore. His mouth shriveled like guts drying on the parched ground from game he had shot, leaving the insides for the predators. His tongue felt twice its size after all this time. On hands and knees he groped, feeling his way about until he found a small pebble, barely the size of one of his fingernails. He put it in his mouth, gagging at the dusty taste of it. But soon it helped stimulate the flow of saliva, enough that some of the ache in his tongue went away.

From time to time as he sat, watching the slow whirl of the stars in a great dance overhead, Yellow Bird believed he heard a small animal in the brush and grass nearby. He tried to see it, straining his eyes in its direction. Tried to smell it even more, to pick out its peculiar scent. He figured it was a night hunter. And night hunters were either lost, or stupid, or dangerous. He found he still preferred skunks and gophers and chipmunks to badgers and weasels and snakes.

"After the sun finds its place of rest," he remembered his mother's story as if she were talking to him once more, sitting right beside him here on top of the bluff, "I go from place to place, looking for something to fill my little belly. If I chance upon a trail of some other animal or even man himself, I will follow it. Perhaps it will bring me to food faster that way," she used to tell him and his brother when they were tiny babies.

"Sniffing, hoping, looking for something to eat, I force myself to keep searching until the sun has come back out in morning. Then I find a place to lay my head for the long day. My eyes are closed, but my ears must be awake," she whispered to him again in his dream. "I wait until it is time again to go in search of something for my little belly."

"What am I, mother?" he had asked her as a tiny child, his little fists clenching and unclenching.

"You tell me, Yellow Bird. What are you?"

"Am I a badger?"

"Could be—but no."

"Am I a fox?"

"Good guess, but no again."

He often bit his lower lip in consternation, thinking hard. "Am I a skunk?"

"Yes, you are a skunk! Very good for you, Yellow Bird!"

It made him a little less afraid of the rustle in the dark to think on the skunk hunting for food in the dark, to dream back to his mother's animal stories as she rocked him to sleep, caressing his forehead and cheeks with her fingertips roughened with hard work.

He was glad she was with him here in the darkness this first night alone. He could not remember ever having been so alone before in his life.

This aloneness was a feeling he disliked more than the feeling of fear itself.

CHAPTER 34

"AWAKEN, Yellow Bird!"
He jerked at the sudden alarm he felt with the voice, his gritty eyes blinking into the darkness. His tongue more swollen now than it had been the first night, despite his sucking on the pebble constantly now. How long . . . ? This was his third night.

"I am over here, Yellow Bird!"

The deep, ringing voice called out again as he tried to focus. His eyes strained into the sky, figuring from the position of the stars it would not be long until morning. Sunrise coming and another hot day broiling here, high under the sun.

"You cannot find me?"

"No, I can't see you," the boy answered.

"Your voice shows some fear."

He realized that it had. Better to admit it. "Yes. I am afraid—but only of what I cannot see." Yellow Bird felt that would be a good answer.

"Do you believe in what you cannot see?"

"If the Everywhere Above calls out to me—I believe. If you are here to do evil to me . . . then go away. I do not believe in you."

The voice laughed loudly then. "This is good, Yellow Bird. Do you not remember my voice?"

"Should I? Who are you?"

"You know me, Yellow Bird. I have been with you always. Though you were frightened, I am always with you."

"Have I seen you?" he shouted into the darkness, standing slowly, testing his weary limbs grown flaccid from lack of use and weakened by three days of fasting.

"Many times you have seen me, Yellow Bird," the voice replied.

As it did, the voice seemed to move around the young man, slowly, as did a predator circling its prey.

"The first time you went hunting with your little bow and you chanced on meeting me in the timber."

"You are the wolf!" Tangibly his skin prickled with dread, perhaps great anticipation.

"I was there when your mother dragged you to the top of that bloody hill to look down on the face of your father. All along that ridge I was there to exact my revenge on those who had to make their blood atonement to me."

"You helped kill those soldiers?"

"No, Yellow Bird. The warriors did not need my help that day. But I was there to drive them on when they became tired. I was there to keep them from turning back when they became weary of the killing. I was there to be sure that no man among the soldiers was left standing. If a warrior acted as if he were not ready to kill every living thing on that ridge, then I fought at his side . . . lifting his bow . . . firing his rifle—wielding his scalping knife.

"I am the wolf of war."

"Why have you come here to trouble me during my vision-dreaming?" He wanted to turn his back on the voice. But every time he did, the voice seemed to move with him so that always it stayed in front of him, no matter how he wheeled. Finally Yellow Bird crumpled to the hard, pounded dust, feeling the sting of hot moisture at his cheeks.

"You have dreamed nothing yet, Yellow Bird. Only children's dreams. You have been turning away the visions of a man."

"I am a man . . . will be—when my spirit helper comes."

"He is here."

"Where?" he asked, suddenly afraid as the word tumbled from his chapped lips.

"I speak to you. Don't you hear me?"

The rasp of the voice, like the grating of something rusty dragged across a rock, hissed all about him, reverberating into an ominous silence. Then all he heard was the breathing.

"I'll come closer, Yellow Bird."

Of a sudden he felt the hot, dank breath of the creature as the hair rose on his arms, his nostrils widening at the fetid stench.

"You are my spirit helper?"

"You have known for some time, haven't you?"

"Why can't I see you now? I saw you before—"

It was as if the moon were rising when the great, looming creature opened its eyes above him, before him, all around him, both as yellow as the moon itself ascending off the bowels at the far eastern edge of the earth.

He gulped, more frightened than he had been on the climb, wondering if it would have been far better to have fallen from those rocks, dashing the life from his body on the granite below, near the sweat lodge where he had been prepared.

"I came here to meet you," he said bravely, swallowing down the fear, shuddering, but then suddenly made bolder as he conquered the wave of terror and aloneness here confronting his most secret despair.

"Why are you so afraid of me? I am your helper."

"No," and he shook his head violently. "You cannot be. My helper would make tracks outside the sweat lodge."

The wolfish creature laughed aloud again, the thunderous roar of it rocking the flat ground like the crash of two great stones about the boy. "That is the way for others. Not for me. I wanted to see if you believed you would fail—because you were on your own. But you came on.

Alone. Without help you came on. Knowing down in your belly that you would have to stare face-to-face at me all the time you climbed—knowing that you would have to face your two bloods."

"I am Shahiyena!"

He heard the breathing hiss inch closer, the heated stench of it searing the side of his face. "Your mother was a Cheyenne who laid with Yellow Hair, a white warrior. Remember the times you looked into the still water, Yellow Bird? Think back—then remember the faces of the white men you have known. Soldiers, agents, the Black-Robes and teachers and traders—think of them."

He did not want to think of them, like something burning in his gut, warning him. "Where . . . I don't know what you mean—"

"They cut your hair like the other boys who go to school. Dress you in their missionary clothes. Whose son will you be then?"

"I will be Monaseetah's!"

"No!" and the creature gushed a laugh. "You were Monaseetah's boy when you were born and when you ran from the soldiers in the Sore-Eye Moon and when you crawled to the top of that summer-blood hill beside the Goat River and when you ran to the land of the Grandmother with Sitting Bull's people. But you are Yellow Hair's son now. The moment you became a man—no longer is Monaseetah your mother—"

"She is my mother!" He collapsed to his knees, shielding his eyes with his hands, keening with the growing pain of it deep in his belly.

"She gave birth to you and had you named Yellow Bird. But when you climbed this rock, you were coming to me, coming to be changed, weren't you?"

"I am to become a man," he whimpered, reluctantly pulling his hands from his face, staring upward into the hot breath of the presence.

"That's why I am here. To take you away from your mother. To take you away from everything that you have known before."

"No-o-o!" he whimpered, falling forward, suddenly weak, unable even to stay on his knees.

"It is the way with every man who would be a man. He must come and stare himself in the face, leaving his family behind. Leaving his mother and others. No longer can he belong to them. No man belongs to his family. Hear me and look upon what it is that I am going to show you."

"You are part of my dream," he whispered to the presence. "That is all. You are here to test me—"

"Open your eyes!" the voice thundered round him, shaking the ground, rattling the dried limbs and branches on the nearby bower. "See what a man must see, for you have undertaken a life that will be most difficult."

Slowly he opened his eyes, raising his cheek from the hard, pounded earth. The great beast opened its moist jowls, and there against that gaping blackness of his pit, Yellow Bird saw himself, easing down the face of the bluff until he reached the bottom, where the old ones rejoiced, slapping him on his back. Where White Cow Bull stood back, waiting until they were done, admiring this new adopted son he had. So changed.

"Is that—"

"It is you, Shahiyena. When I am finished with you, then you return to the others."

"I look—I am so different."

"Is not a man much different from a boy? Is not the frog different from the tadpole? The blizzard different from the first snow of winter? A boy was named Yellow Bird. You will no longer be a boy. No longer are you Yellow Bird."

"Who?"

"Stone Eagle," the presence whispered, like the feet of ghosts moving through the dry grass. "Your mother keeps the eagles your father wore into battle like bits of war stone, the eagle with its wings spread in flight. She has them for you. When you see her next, ask for them—Stone Eagle."

"Stone Eagle is my new name."

"Every boy who climbs high and is granted his vision—that new man is given a new name, signifying the new person he has become. So it is with you. Look upon the east now, where the sun will be rising soon, and see what the future holds."

He turned slowly, rising slightly, staring at the narrow bloody band of light tearing itself along the far horizon. A star emerged, like the sun itself, glowing and growing until he recognized the tall conical hide lodge, recognized the others gathered around it. A tall young man emerged from the doorway, stood in the morning sun, the breeze tousling his hair.

"It is—it looks like Ghost."

"It is."

"He looks, so different now."

"Ghost has grown older. Like you."

"Older than me."

"This is the future, Stone Eagle."

"How far into my days?"

"Three summers," the spirit helper answered.

He watched, captivated, excited with the feeling, like a voyeur peeking in on something no one else knows of, watching Ghost walk round the lodge toward a pair of women. One old, Ghost's mother, he recognized. The other he had a strange feeling for, something light and fluttering in his breast.

"She looks familiar."

"Ghost's sister."

Stone Eagle could not believe it. "So beautiful. I knew her the summer of the—that fight with the soldiers along Goat River."

"She is but a season younger than you, Stone Eagle."

"I had no idea she would . . . when she was so skinny before."

"She has grown up as well."

"Why do you show me this?"

"Wait."

Yellow Bird concentrated on the starry glow along the horizon, squinting his eyes until the scene came into focus once more. A tall young man rode into the clearing beside the creek, dogs barking at his pony's and pack animal's heels.

"Who is he?"

"That is Stone Eagle."

"Me?"

"You will see."

Ghost called out to the new arrival who led his packhorse toward the lodge. He slid from the pony's bare back, tied the animals, then began freeing the bundles from the packs.

"I will call my father," Ghost said, smiling. "He is who you must give your presents to. Not a woman's brother!"

Stone Eagle watched the vision, seeing how he spread out on blankets what he could afford in his eighteenth summer.

"I am—asking for a wife?"

"Ghost's sister."

"Double Woman? I marry her?"

"You have seen anything to doubt it?"

"No," he answered quietly, a rush of unknown feelings flooding over him, stirring him across the loins. "She is so very beautiful. I never thought she could love—anyone like me."

"She has—from that summer you met her along the Rosebud."

"Show me more, spirit helper. These days to come show much happiness."

Indeed, the presence instructed Stone Eagle to turn to the north, where at the fading tip of the Big Dipper he saw a vision of the birth of his firstborn. A son. Light-haired but just as black-eyed as his mother. He watched the man he would become take the wriggling, squirming body into his hands, raising it above his head in praise.

Then he was told to look to the west, where it was the darkest yet, concentrating on a spot of white growing out of the inky film of night-going. It became a woman's white dress, her dark buttoned shoes holding his attention, fascinated as she walked closer and closer, beneath her arm a bundle of schoolbooks. Her hair was rust-colored, texture like cottonwood seed, soft and loose like his. Her eyes green, like nothing he had ever seen. Yet it was the way she looked at him, it was like the look Double Woman had in her eyes when she gazed up at him as they were making love in his dream, lips moistened, opening for him.

The green eyes held his, taunting him, luring him, filling him with foreign longings.

"Who is she—this white woman?" he asked, dry-mouthed.

"She is your teacher."

"My teacher?"

"One day you meet her."

"She stirs me—something in me."

"Her spirit talks to your white blood, perhaps, at the same time her spirit wants to experience your Indian blood, Stone Eagle. But I fear it will be her body you want to possess. That will be the curse of your white blood—this hunger to possess her, to own her and keep her from all others."

"I feel attracted . . . danger at the same time."

"She will be there near the end."

"End of what?"

"Look south now, Stone Eagle."

He turned, where the sky was brightening. It hurt his eyes with its vivid power. Stone Eagle had to squint, realizing the ground was white with new snow, given a dazzling brilliance by a new sun rising over the valley. He knew the valley, recognized the trader's store, the steeple on the church far away. But there were soldier tents in orderly row upon row below him, two wagon-gun emplacements along the low bluffs overlooking an Indian encampment.

From among the hundred canvas lodges, he recognized one. "There's Ghost's lodge."

"No. You are seeing the lodge of Ghost's parents. Beside it, there stands Ghost's."

"He has a family of his own now."

"He will—and he gives a home to his sister."

"Double Woman? She is to be my wife—what of our son?"

"They are both with Ghost this winter."

"Why? What happened? Why am I not there to protect them?"

"Look, and see the future."

The air about him suddenly erupted with explosions, the profane stench of gunsmoke and sulfur. Rifle fire. Shouts of men. The screams of women and the cries of babies. Ponies neighing, crying out in terror and pain as the huge guns on the bluff opened up, spitting flares of orange light. Soldiers cursing, walking blindly through the fog, shooting blindly through the gunsmoke at anything that moved, looming out of the dazzling white light of that snowy morning.

Yellow Bird stood unable to move, riveted to the hard ground beneath him as he watched, his eyes unable to tear themselves from the bloody scene as women and children darted for the shelter of the creek banks, a few men standing to fight. It was a scene he had witnessed time and time again.

"Where? Where are they?" he asked, his voice barely audible, cracking, painful to talk when the last shot echoed off the ridges.

"All dead."

"My family?"

"It is for you to decide, Stone Eagle."

"Take this away from me!" he cried out, like a wounded animal.

"I cannot. Some things can be altered, to be given another man's life. But this, it remains your making. This you must endure. There is more afoot already than just the life of one man, Stone Eagle."

He shivered with cold, sensing the strong wind wolfish across the snowy battleground at last, a wind that carried on it a great cold, a stench of blood and burnt powder. In the distance, canvas and lodgepoles smoldered. Out of the smoke and fog of the battlefield a figure walked toward Stone Eagle, limping slightly.

"Who is this?" he whispered to the spirit helper.

"Stone Eagle!" the stranger hollered, holding up a hand. "Do not be afraid to ask it of me. I am your grandfather."

"My mother's?"

"Yes. Little Rock was my name. Yellow Hair, your father, killed me. As he killed many more of our people a cold winter day like this—a day when he took your mother away from our people and made her his own. This was a time before you were born. And now you have his blood in you."

"My mother told me it is a warrior's blood."

Little Rock nodded. "It is. Come a time you must decide on your blood. Red or white. Come a time of cold."

A sudden, unexpected bolt of phosphorescent electricity shot out of the clouds over the bluff, shaking the ground where Stone Eagle stood.

"Look at these," Little Rock demanded, his hand spreading the fog so that his grandson gazed upon the bloody, riddled bodies lining a narrow trail as far as he could see, stretching to the distant horizon.

"These did not listen, Stone Eagle," the presence instructed. "They did not heed the lessons you are now granted."

With a wave of his hand, Little Rock disappeared in the fog.

Thunder clapped, so loudly Stone Eagle cowered from it as the sound rang in his ears. And with that clap of thunder, it seemed as if the entire underbelly of the sky itself had been gutted. Rain came in pounding sheets.

"Stand and gaze upon this final vision," the presence ordered.

Stone Eagle shook slightly, wondering that the rain did not strike his skin, pelting only the ground about him. He felt himself rise from the hard ground, lifted as if by the wind until he realized he was standing in the sky, looking down on an old, weathered lodge.

Gazing down through the smoke hole, he saw small figures. Men, all covered with hair, like wild animals. About each of their tiny heads hung a halo of pulsating red stars. Their eyes sunflower bright, like a wolf's with its prey in sight. From their heads extended the huge antlers of an elk, and from their shoulders quivered the great folded wings of a golden war eagle.

"Few men have ever seen what I have shown you," the spirit helper hissed at his ear.

"Why me?"

"If you are to learn of your two bloods, you are given this vision. The animals you encounter, they will speak to you alone. That will be your power to have and to use."

"You have already spoken to me," Stone Eagle replied, looking at the presence of the wolf.

"I am a spirit helper, living only between earth and sky. The rest will be animals."

"What does this mean—these little men?"

"You are shown this so that you will know to give away all that is given to you."

"All my goods?"

"That is required of you. And never forget what you have seen. Unto you much is given. For much will be required. All the animals lived before the Everywhere Spirit Above put man on earth. They have much to say to help you."

Another sudden gust of wind roared across the flat of the bluff, and with it came the rising of a gray sun behind the rain clouds that suddenly enveloped him as he was hurled back upon the hard-packed earth. The ground cut him. The driving water slashed at him, soaking him.

"Stand, Stone Eagle. Stand before your grandfathers!"

Slowly he stood like a clumsy child unaccustomed to his new body. Bleeding, drenched with the driving rain, his hair streaming in his eyes, blown by the gusts of wind cruelly cutting across the top of the bluff, the young man raised his face to the clouds above.

"Go now. And remember what you have been shown."

He clung to the slippery, rain-drenched rocks as he began his descent. Shivering with more than the cold, wet wind brutal against his naked body. Afraid and alone once more. Without his spirit helper. Without his mother now.

A solitary, naked man. More alone and frightened than ever before.

BOOK IV

ALL THE GHOSTS RETURNING
1887–1890

CHAPTER 35

Autumn, 1887

Iᴛ surely wasn't the first wagon he would ride in, but it had to be the very best. Those wobbly carts and creaky freighters Sitting Bull's hold-outs had taken south of the line better than six years before had been a shameful way for a man to ride. But this newly painted, high-walled Pittsburgh freighter was about the prettiest thing he had seen in some time.

Down at Pine Ridge or east over at the Rosebud Agency, Stone Eagle had rarely something so bright and beautiful—painted a bright green like new grass bursting through the soil on the spring prairie, tall wheels as red as the shimmering clusters of new buds on strawberry blite. And those black iron tires welded tightly to their wheels with barely a scuff on them. He hadn't seen anything so new and frankly unused in all his life.

He glanced at White Cow Bull and his brother. The three of them stood on the porch at the back of the granary behind the trading post at the Cheyenne River agency. Over two hundred miles they had plodded on some worn-out plow horses the trader at Pine Ridge had given them to make the trip north to the Missouri River depot. Sent here by White Cow Bull's employer to fetch the new wagon just arrived from downriver, come all the way to the landing at Fort Bennett from a faraway Pennsylvania factory.

Come the gray of first-light tomorrow morning, the three would put the Cheyenne River Agency behind them, heading south by west, back toward the trader expecting his new wagon that he would keep busy traveling between his Pine Ridge and his Rosebud trading posts, at times supplying Mosseau's post up on the Wounded Knee. What with the growth of the trade in the recent years, the trader had flat worn out one wagon already.

The two-hundred-some miles up from the trader's place on White Clay Creek had taken them better than a week. They figured it would be every bit as long going back, if not a bit longer. Two of the horses were harnessed in tandem, the third strung out behind the wagon or ridden bareback by one of the two youngsters. Stone Eagle hoped the weather might treat them more kindly going back than it had on the journey down, following the trail from White Clay Creek to White River, downstream to the mouth of Wounded Knee Creek, then overland past the Cuny Table, skirting the badlands where three summers gone he had suffered his four days and nights before seeing the wolf. North of the badlands they had reached Sage Creek, following it down to the Cheyenne River. From there it had been merely a matter of staying with the Cheyenne all the way to the agency, situated just south of where the river gave itself to the Missouri.

The journey going back with the empty wagon would likely mean a chance of snow, if White Cow Bull's foot were right again. It always complained at him for a few days before a big storm rolled in. But Stone Eagle figured the snow would at least mean a warming break in the temperature that had been hovering near zero for better than a week already, ever since they pulled away from the Pine Ridge.

"You're ready, boys," announced the white man as he stepped from the trading-post door, folding a sheaf of papers. Clerk for the trader at Cheyenne River Agency, he had handled the signatures needed to send a new wagon south into Indian country with three Indian men aboard. "This will keep you boys safe enough from arrest by the army."

"What does he say?" White Cow Bull asked haughtily, his eyes squinting.

Stone Eagle took the papers from the clerk. "He says these papers will keep the army off our backs."

"It is good," Sees Red muttered, sullen as a wet hen because he knew little English. And his young brother knew enough. "I do not trust any white man."

"Neither do I," agreed White Cow Bull as they turned toward the wagon together. "I would prefer to be hunting buffalo, or fighting soldiers. But the buffalo are gone, and the soldiers are everywhere. You and your mother are my family. My family needs to eat. We can starve on the rations the agent gives out to each family—or I can work to provide better."

"White Cow Bull is right," Stone Eagle said, helping to back the horses into their traces.

"Your word means nothing to me," Sees Red grumbled. "Nor to any true Indian. I would expect you to agree that working for the white man is a good thing. You are half-white yourself."

Sees Red had never taken to the schooling or the learning of the white man's tongue. Instead he and his sullen band of friends preferred fishing or roaming the hills looking for something to occupy them to sitting in a classroom listening to an old white woman drill them on letters and vowels and all those numbers to cipher on their dusty slate tablets. The way Stone Eagle took to it.

"I think something in your father's white blood makes you want to sit inside that schoolhouse instead of riding out under the big sky," White Cow Bull had often teased Stone Eagle these last three winters since the youth climbed down from the vision butte and told of his powerful dream.

For three years Stone Eagle had watched events swirl slowly around him while he dutifully attended the school where the teacher and agent tried to chop off his long hair the first day of school following his vision-quest. But they got no closer with the huge clippers than an arm's length before he explained to them in broken English that he would learn their speech and their counting, but the length of his hair had no bearing on how smart a student he would prove.

"It is the way of the white man," they had tried to convince Stone Eagle.

"The white men I have seen, they would be prettier with long hair," he had told the old schoolmarm. "My hair stays—or I go."

She had let him stay. And the hair as well, perhaps recognizing something in the youngster's spunk that merited this blister in her otherwise unwavering policy of teaching the Indian children to be white.

"As long as you aren't a troublemaker, Stone Eagle—like that brother of yours—you can keep your hair down to your shoulders. But no longer."

"It is agreed," he said in Lakota, nodding to her as she once more approached him with the clippers.

She had been good to her word and cut off no more but what would brush his shoulders. Yet as the weeks rolled into months, and the seasons into years, the old woman had not really paid all that much attention to the fact that Stone Eagle's hair was growing long every bit as much as he was growing tall.

Almost from the time he had climbed down from the vision butte, he became a real source of irritation to his mother as well. If for no other reason than Monaseetah could not seem to keep him in moccasins. If he wasn't wearing them out, better were the chances that his toes were nudging through his mother's sinew-sewn seams. And those legs of his, once like long, thin lodgepoles, now became sturdy trunks, every bit as strong as they were tall. It seemed as if his mother were always sitting around the lodge fire at night, sewing up new leggings for him, until this last spring she gave her son his first pair of used leggings. They fit as if they had been made for him.

"I remember when your mother made those for me," White Cow Bull had said with admiration. "It was with the approach of winter in the land of the Grandmother."

Stone Eagle was ashamed at times of how he felt when the older folks talked of their cherished memories north of the Medicine Line. He remembered some good times. But more often he recalled the hunger and cold and the despair and the dying. Weeks upon weeks of holding out until spring melted the everywhere snow. Many of the old ones talked about the happy days of roaming and hunting buffalo without fear of the bluecoat soldiers. But try as he might, Stone Eagle could not remember much happiness in their days of taking refuge north of the stone pillars.

He felt most ashamed of the feelings that had come over him after coming back to his mother's lodge from the badlands. Walking beside White Cow Bull into their camp, finding Monaseetah waiting for their return. The moment she had spotted Stone Eagle, his mother had come rushing toward him. Then slowed and stopped as she drew near, gazing at her son with a queer look on her face. As if she might be looking upon a stranger.

"Woman, you are acting as if you do not know this man beside me," White Cow Bull had said as the three of them stood there, an uncomfortable silence settling over them as the dogs came up to sniff at Stone Eagle. "Before you stands your son—but he is a new man."

She had started to move toward him, to embrace her second born. Then stopped, putting out her hands instead, not wanting to embarrass the young man. "Who is this I gaze upon?"

"I am Stone Eagle, Mother."

He had watched her gasp, putting a hand to her mouth before she found more to say, eyes moistening. "It has been many winters since I have heard those words used."

"When?" White Cow Bull asked, embracing his wife.

"Long ago—I showed my young son, Yellow Bird, the tiny stone eagles I had taken from his father's shirt that day Yellow Hair's soldiers came to attack our camp on Goat River."

White Cow Bull looked at Stone Eagle, admiration in his eyes. "It is as you told me on our way home, my son. You are to ask your mother for one of the eagles she took from your dead father."

"This was in your vision?" Monaseetah asked.

"Yes, mother. You are to keep one, giving me the other."

She nodded, reluctantly, as if by that nod she were

agreeing that his tearing away from her was to be complete. In the early winter of her year of sorrow, she had given birth to him, the first time he had torn himself from her. Time and again her little Yellow Bird had come back to her arms, to the circle of her love. But at that moment, staring at the new Stone Eagle, she had grown afraid, seeing a different son before her.

A little older, perhaps a little wiser, if not in the ways of men, then perhaps in the ways of nature. He was a young man from that moment on, she realized. Knowing it was truly up to her to let him go one last time.

"Come, Stone Eagle—we will eat to celebrate your vision-dreaming," she had said uncertainly, turning away with tears pooling as she tried out her son's new name. His manhood name. "We will talk of what you have learned while you have been away from us, alone. And I will give you something from your father—something I am sure he would wish you to have to remember him."

From that day of returning to his mother's lodge, it had not been the same as when he had been a boy. For now, almost every day, Stone Eagle thought on those things his father had left him. More than the small eagle, its wings spread in challenge, with the sharp pin on its flat back. Each day he thought on his hair, his eyes, his skin, his very blood. And wondered at times if he were not more white than Indian in his soul. His fears of it were enough to make him remember the future visions shown him on top of the butte.

Through the march of the seasons, Stone Eagle had worked hard at his lessons with a handful of other children whose parents allowed them to attend the agency school. Until at last the Pine Ridge agent had enough of the stiff-backed Oglalla and threatened that any family who did not enroll their children would not receive their bimonthly rations. Soon enough empty bellies filled every chair in the tiny classroom. In their midst Stone Eagle remained one of the few who wanted to be there, learning.

Then this past summer White Cow Bull had been at the agency store with his adopted son, trading some of Mona-seetah's moccasins for some extra coffee and sugar when the agent asked in broken Lakota mixed with English if the older Oglalla warrior would want to work from time to time for him—hauling supplies between trading posts, helping count and unload incoming supplies, assisting with the hundreds of families come each ration day.

White Cow Bull and Monaseetah had talked of it into that night, and at the first gray of dawn, the Oglalla had started walking back toward the trading post to give the sutler his decision. It had been a happy day when he returned to their lodge at the edge of the clearing by the creek, bearing a few gifts from the sutler for his new man's family. Some flour for fry-bread along with some salt. In addition, a few sticks of hard candy and a tin of raisins.

Sees Red did not agree with working for the white man and continually reminded White Cow Bull that the Oglalla had always claimed he would never shake a white man's hand, much less work for one.

"Times have changed, my son," Monaseetah said, jumping to her husband's defense before anyone else could open his mouth. "The buffalo are gone—and a man must find a way to feed his family."

"Then I will not have a family. I will remain alone—as a warrior should."

Stone Eagle remembered the hurt look on White Cow Bull's face, recalling that the Oglalla had remained himself a bachelor for many winters, devoting himself to the defense of his people, taking Monaseetah for his wife only when they had escaped north of the medicine line.

"Perhaps someday, Sees Red," Monaseetah said as she served them steaming bowls of *tipsina* soup, "a woman will change your heart for you."

"Never," the young man had growled, slurping at his hot soup.

"Never is a long time," said White Cow Bull.

The new freshly greased wheels on the long green wagon hummed easily as they bumped down the rutted road leading west from the agency. The sun warmed his neck, though the air was chilled with the threat of a coming storm. Small cascades of fine dust kicked up by the spinning wheels glittered like gold in the morning sun as White Cow Bull turned off the road, following a narrow trail into the trees.

"Where are we going?" asked Sees Red, forever sullen and sucking on a sore tooth.

"I have a friend among the Miniconjou," White Cow Bull replied. "Touch the Clouds. I have not seen him in a long time—I want to talk of the old days with him before we begin our long journey back in earnest."

"I would hurry back without delay," Sees Red argued.

"So you can join your young friends in your mischief?"

He glared at his adopted father. "I do not like these Miniconjou."

White Cow Bull slowed the horses as they neared a small grouping of lodges gathered at the edge of a clearing. Dogs barked their notice of newcomers. "We will not be long."

Stone Eagle heard the call of a familiar voice.

"Yellow Bird! Is that you?"

It was his friend, grown even more in the last winters since their return from the land of the Grandmother.

"Ghost—I do not believe you are so tall!" he shouted, jumping from the rear of the freight wagon as it rumbled to a stop. The two sprinted into one another's arms, slapping, pounding, thrashing one another in boyish exuberance.

"I am not the only one grown tall!" Ghost replied. "Look at you, little Cheyenne! You are now a great Yellow Bird."

"My friend," he whispered, his eyes glancing quickly for any white man who might be in camp, "I am no longer Yellow Bird."

Ghost regarded him a moment. "You have had a vision-quest of your own?"

"Three summers gone now."

"Has it been that long since we have talked?"

"Yes, Ghost. It is good to see you."

"And good to see you. What is your name, my tall, handsome friend?"

"I am called Stone Eagle."

A smile brightened the Miniconjou youth's face, as bold as summer sun, his eyes twinkling with a faint mist. "My, but I knew you would be something special one day."

"From that first day we met along the Rosebud, playing shinny?"

He threw a long arm around Stone Eagle's shoulder, holding him in a fierce embrace. "Come, my old friend. I want my mother and father to see this little Cheyenne who has grown into a tall man while we have been apart! You are—how many summers now?"

"Seventeen."

"And you have not taken a wife yet?"

He stopped suddenly, mystified with the suggestion. "No—I have not. Have you?"

Ghost reared back in laughter. "Yes. And you will meet her. But first you must come see my father's family—they all will remember the little Cheyenne."

"I am little no more, eh?"

"Little no more," Ghost added quietly, hugging his friend as the others gathered near. He turned, and introduced his family. "You remember my mother and father? This is my friend who used to be the Cheyenne boy known as Yellow Bird."

Stone Eagle bowed his head in respect.

"You are given a man's name now?" asked Ghost's father, High Pipe.

"Stone Eagle."

Ghost tugged on Stone Eagle's arm slightly while a dog nipped at his heels. "And you will remember my young sister from long ago."

His breath caught in his chest the way he held it when he dived under the cold water in winter, searching for the beaver kits. Like a hand that would not let go as he looked upon her. Once homely and all bone, usually caked with dirt from head to toe—Stone Eagle could not believe he now looked upon a young woman every bit as beautiful as his mother.

"Double Woman?" he said as she shyly looked into his eyes.

CHAPTER 36

Winter, 1887–1888

Nᴏɴᴇ of these godforsaken frontier posts kept any heat going in their records sheds. Colder than blazes, that wolfish wind howled outside the rickety, groaning clapboard building threatening to topple over and take off on its own with the next strong gust.

Captain Preston Tripp stuffed his wool gloves beneath his armpits to warm his fingers as he read down the pages of medical report. Looking for familiar names, more so a particular name—anything out of the ordinary. He reluctantly drew one hand from an armpit to turn the page, quickly returning the fingers to their cocoon of warmth. From time to time he wriggled his toes inside the cold-stiffened boots, wishing he had taken the size bigger when it had been offered to him by a supply quartermaster at Fort Riley last autumn.

"Room enough for three pairs of socks, Captain," the old soldier suggested. "You'll want 'em come winter—you go down there in Indian Territory."

"That old file was right," he muttered to himself.

Squatting at the base of the Arbuckles, Fort Sill was about as cold as a man could take it come winter's full blast across the prairies. He had heard tell of how cold things could get up north, at Fort Abraham Lincoln. No, sir. This was as cold as he wanted it. Damp as blazes too. Sleety, bone-cutting, windy cold. So much of it the last two weeks here that Tripp wondered why he just didn't tell Sheridan he had had enough.

He stopped his reading down the page. "Because if you do—the old man will see you turned into parade-ground fodder, you dumb chucklehead," he murmured to himself sourly.

Sheridan would at that. A man give up on something like this, after this long. Hell, he'd spent the last three birthdays away from his family in southern Indiana, Friendship. The letters these past two years had gotten fewer and further between. Not that he was consumed by the search—far from it. Preston Tripp simply hated getting bested.

He had interviewed Major Edward Godfrey, a lieutenant during the Washita campaign. Tripp found the man a real joy to listen to for hours at a time—all those stories he had to tell of service during the Indian campaigns. The Seventh's attack on Black Kettle's village, the whole of the Sweetwater campaign. Along with the matter of Custer's steadfast belief that Major Joel Elliott and his men had become lost and were heading back to Camp Supply—instead of accepting the fact that they had galloped themselves into trouble and had been fighting for their lives at the very minute Godfrey tried convincing Custer he should ride to Elliott's aid east of Black Kettle's village.

Tripp could see it in the major's eyes, clear, glassy gray that they were. Surrounded by wrinkles wrought of years on the plains where bright sun and dazzling snow meant a man was squinting all but in his sleep. Yes, Preston Tripp had seen that look come across Godfrey's face when he talked of it. The major could not hold the young captain's eyes—looking off instead somewhere in the middistance, his voice getting hollow.

As much as Godfrey admired Custer, thought the sun rose and set by the man, and stood by Custer's actions as he

led five regiments down into the valley of the Little
Bighorn River, Tripp realized Godfrey could not reconcile
the general's actions that cold day back in eighteen and
sixty-eight with the untarnished image he had of Custer. It
was like a smudge. Perhaps more so like Lady Macbeth's
bloody hands. No amount of washing would ever cleanse
them to suit Major Godfrey.

So Tripp was consigned to stand here in the cold, poring
over records at this outlying frontier post, named that
winter of '69 by General Sheridan for a friend of his killed
in the Civil War, Joshua Sill. Trying still to find some
corroboration to the sworn testimony he had been given by
Captain Frederick W. Benteen. Following his sessions with
the crusty gray-head, Tripp had wired his first coded
message to Sheridan in all the time he had been working
this secret assignment—telling the general that Benteen
was not the only one who had spoken out on the subject of
Custer's liaison with the Cheyenne girl that winter so long
ago.

More than one man had done more than wink and smile
and give a suggestive nod when it came to agreeing that
Custer's Cheyenne concubine was with child when the
general sent the captives back to Indian Territory. More
men than Benteen had suggested the young captain have
himself a look at the Fort Sill medical records for that first
winter in Indian country.

So it was that Captain Tripp found the detailed records
of one army physician's treatment of lonely men on the
frontier for a common malady.

The post surgeon, in his crude, frosty tents those first
few days after establishing a camp, had entered the names
of several soldiers among the U.S. Seventh Cavalry seeking
help for a urinary condition that the surgeon diagnosed as
syphilis. The remedy was purely a matter of choice, for not
every man decided in favor of taking the mercury cure for
the disease. Some figured it would take care of itself.
Others figured they could drown it in whiskey. But Custer
himself, brother Tom, and several others stoically came
forward to endure the excruciating pain of that dreaded
remedy for one's sexual indiscretions.

Tripp copied word for word that nineteen-year-old report, even misspelling those words the surgeon or his steward had scribbled down incorrectly. Perhaps it might have some future bearing on this matter of Custer's peccadillo with the Cheyenne girl. If he had caught the disease from her . . .

No, he decided. The timing was all off. From what he had learned, Custer had not taken the girl into his robes until sometime after he would have contracted syphilis. But she would have been in the final month of her pregnancy with her first child while Custer was on the Sweetwater campaign. Tripp wondered, for what little he knew of such things, if the woman had not contracted syphilis herself, but had been carrying the disease at the time her first child was born, would the boy she had still be alive today? He cared not to think about it.

It was her second child he was looking for.

Custer's half-breed son.

He was about ready to give up and go back to the mess hall where he would find a cup of coffee, the kind old line soldiers liked to drink, when he spied the notation of a newborn child being brought into the fort from the Cheyenne reservation that early winter of 1869.

A young woman, reportedly of eighteen summers, most attractive, appeared wanting examination from the post surgeon. I complied and examined the woman, who brought into my examination room a small bundle wrapped tightly with a piece of blanket shroud. She appeared to have suffered a mild case of syphilis in the past. From what source of infection, she cannot tell me, through the post interpreter who I had stand on the other side of a blanket partition so that I could converse with the woman. One thing was certain, I told her. She would not have any children.

That's when she informed me she had one son, born last winter. January as far as the interpreter was able to make out. Still alive she reported. When I told her she would have no more, she asked if I meant no more after her second son. Then the woman peeled back the blanketing from a newborn male child.

He was the oddest specimen I have seen among half-breeds on this frontier during my years of service to both soldier and Indian alike. His skin a much lighter color than his mother's, hardly Indian at all. And his hair, instead of possessing the blackness of the raven's wing, the child had a brownish blond hue, with highlights of red that shimmered below the light of my examination lamps. Yet most startling of all was, upon examining the child at the mother's request, the boy awoke and began to protest my machinations. Squinting up at me were the most handsome pair of blue gray eyes I believe I've ever seen on a young male of the Cheyenne race.

Preston Tripp looked up from the page, realizing his chin had dropped to the buttons on his wool coat. Quickly he glanced over his shoulder, feeling like a spy, blew on his frozen fingers, then read on.

Through my interpreter I informed the woman that he looked well enough, for its mother having suffered a terrible disease. Likewise, I informed her she would in all likelihood not be able to have any more children. She explained that would not be a complication of her marriage. That her husband would more than likely be pleased to know she could not bear any more hungry mouths.

When I inquired how the hunting was for her husband that winter on the reservation, she smiled at my stupidity, then explained that the husband she had referred to was not a Cheyenne warrior. Instead he was a soldier-chief, assigned to a post somewhere in the north (from the direction she indicated—perhaps Kansas or Nebraska).

"A soldier-chief . . . in Kansas—that winter of 1869." He chewed on it the way as a boy he had chewed on a stalk of tall grass. "Damn! It couldn't have been Custer she was referring to," he muttered on, recalling his knowledge of the general's career. Disappointed, he began to read on, more carefully this time, until something struck him, causing Tripp to gaze up from the page.

"But as far as the woman would know, Custer would still

be at the Fort Hays Big Creek encampment of the Seventh."

He shuddered. His belly wanted food, and his mind required more of that nerve-jangling coffee waiting him in the mess hall.

"Of course she would have no idea Custer was on an extended leave—without his beloved Libbie—among the famous and wealthy of New York society. Sometimes, Tripp, you can be a chucklehead."

He busily scribbled the last of the physician's entry for the visit from the young mother, word for word in his cramped, cold hand, a hand he continually blew upon to warm it, keeping the inkwell from freezing beneath the fold of his coat. Then he carefully folded up his pages of script and stuffed them away in a section of his leather case, heading for the door, the wind, and the cup of coffee he had coming.

"Got you now, General," he said to no one in particular, a wry smile crossing his face.

"Looks like Sheridan's hired help is ready to track down those scouts—Milner and Corbin—come spring."

His heart sank like a heavy stone pitched into the middle of a rain puddle left behind in the passing of a summer storm. Standing there in the shadows of a deepening twilight this spring night, watching a young Miniconjou man pay court to Double Woman outside her lodge. More galling still, a half dozen more waited patiently in line for their turn to talk with Ghost's beautiful sister.

Fireflies danced above the waving grass in the meadow. He hugged the darkness of the trees so he would not be seen.

Stone Eagle cursed himself now for coming all this way north to the Cheyenne River Reservation. Like a fool he had thought of nothing else all winter, waiting for the breakup of the rivers and the warming of the land. Until the boiling of his own young juices could be denied no longer.

When he took off on the old horse White Cow Bull had loaned him for the journey, the young man had believed he knew exactly how a bull elk or buck deer felt in the rut.

Ready to take on all challengers for the right to the female.

But here now, watching the dim figures outside Double Woman's lodge, his fighting ardor drained. He felt more fool than warrior, awash with trampled pride. Either he had seen something in her eye last autumn that was not really there, or she had expected him to return earlier and gave up on the waiting.

He could not blame her. He was mortally afraid of coming back. She, his first love. Speaking to no one of the ache in his heart for the Miniconjou girl. Wanting to talk with his mother of his burning love for Ghost's sister so many times through the long darkness of winter nights when he was tortured into sleeplessness by her vision before him. Biting his tongue and turning his face to the lodge skins instead of giving voice to his unrequited love. Until one night he could keep from bursting no longer.

"Your mother is right, Stone Eagle," said White Cow Bull. "Even I had to ask again and again before she said she would marry me!"

"I cannot!" he gasped. "Once only—and only if I am sure she will have me. If she does not—then I will not bring her father presents."

His mother had smiled. "Stone Eagle, I do not think that Double Woman's father will expect ponies and blankets for his daughter."

"Why not?" he asked, bristling with young pride. "She is worth anything!"

"She is at that, Monaseetah!" the Oglalla agreed.

She swung at her husband playfully. "Looking at the young ones again, eh—old man?"

"What I meant—Double Woman is pretty enough for our son."

She had gazed at her second born a moment. "If you want a woman—you must tell her. Not only once. Many times—convince her of what you feel inside for her in any way you can. Do not waste time, Stone Eagle. Your days with her are so very precious."

"Your mother is right again," the old warrior echoed. "Think of the years I was without the warmth of your mother's body next to mine at night when the wind howls outside our lodge. All the days we wasted not being together."

He looked at the two of them then, smiling at one another and oblivious to his being there across the fire. They were in love. They must know.

"I will go." He had to say it a second time before either of his parents turned back to look at him.

"You find out if she loves you as much as you love her," White Cow Bull suggested. "If she does, I will work double hard to make enough money to help you buy her father fine presents."

"You must be careful," Monaseetah warned her husband. "The white man tells us we will be punished if we give presents for a woman."

"It is the old way," Stone Eagle protested.

"It is the new law," Monaseetah reminded.

White Cow Bull patted the young man on the leg. "We will keep everything from the eyes of the white man, my son. It will be like the old days for me."

Stone Eagle had smiled that last night in his mother's lodge, barely a week ago before he began this trip to Cheyenne River. No young man in love could ask for better help than that of White Cow Bull's.

Yet there he stood in the shadows as twilight flowed liquid across a spring night, warm stars dusted like flour spilled on a dark walnut floor. Waiting until there was but one left in Double Woman's line of suitors. The last young man moved up, talking low now that he and the beautiful girl were alone.

Stone Eagle stood back some from the splash of light spilling out the lodge door, a blanket pulled over his head, watching Double Woman and the suitor. The couple kept looking back at him.

"I am tired," Double Woman said quietly, to them both. "If you would return tomorrow night."

The suitor took up her hand and squeezed it between his, looking over his shoulder at Stone Eagle. "Sorry you are too late. Perhaps you can stand in front of me tomorrow night."

"I will not be here tomorrow night," said the Cheyenne.

Her long, delicate fingers leapt to her mouth in aston-
ishment. "Can it be?" she asked. "Stone Eagle?"

"Have I come too late?"

She glanced at the suitor, then stepped past the tall
Miniconjou youth, stopping almost toe-to-toe with the
Cheyenne.

"No, you are not too late, Stone Eagle. I have thought of
you so many times. And each morning Ghost comes to ask
me if I have accepted one of the suitors who came calling
the night before. He tells me, every morning, that he prays
me to wait. I did not believe him when he said you would
return."

Suddenly she put her fingers to her lips again, afraid.
"Oh, Stone Eagle—I am so sorry. Perhaps . . . oh, you
came to see Ghost and you didn't—" her voice caught
suddenly.

"I came to see you," he said, sweeping her hand away
from her breast.

"I will return tomorrow night." The suitor stepped up to
them to speak.

"Perhaps you will," Stone Eagle asserted. "Yet perhaps
you should court someone who will marry you instead."

"We will see," the suitor huffed, whirling away among
the handful of lodges.

He gazed back into her eyes. "I am not too late?"

"No," she answered, then dropped her eyes demurely.
"Have you eaten?"

His stomach suddenly very empty, he realized he was
ravenous. "It has been days since I have thought of
anything other than you, Double Woman."

"Come," she said, dragging him by his arm playfully
toward another lodge, away from her parents'. "Ghost will
be glad to see you. His wife will warm you something to eat
and spread a robe for your bed in their lodge tonight."

"You will stay for a while?"

"For a while," she answered, her face lit with the rising
of the moon above the tall trees lining the creek. "And
tomorrow we can sit in the new sun and talk of many
things."

"Yes," he replied, wishing it were sunrise already.
"Tomorrow."

CHAPTER 37

Autumn, 1888

R ATION day came but twice a month
This was to be the first for Stone Eagle as the head
of a household, the male leader of a lodge registered on the
rolls of the Pine Ridge agent.

No matter that it was only he and Double Woman.
Theirs was a family.

Most families struggled to stretch their allotments from
ration day to ration day. Most months many of the adults
went without for the last few days so that their children had
something to fill their bellies.

Both Stone Eagle and Double Woman were young and
strong. He helped White Cow Bull with the freight work.
And she pitched in with Monaseetah's chores in their camp
of six lodges along the creek. They did not suffer so badly
as did others during the hard times. And every week when
it came time for the trader to pay his Indian help, Stone
Eagle and White Cow Bull converted their coins into
foodstuffs before walking home. Each trip found them
arriving home with less and less, simply because they gave

away more and more to help others through the lean times between ration days.

Funny how the people so looked forward to those two days each new moon—flour and old beef, coffee and sugar, sometimes a thin army blanket or some used clothing would be distributed as well. And funny how that sense of excitement and anticipation wore off so quickly as the men carried their meager allotments back to their homes and families. Most of them were ashamed to bring home so little when once a man took pride in providing well for his relatives.

The white man cut off the school boys' hair at the same time he was successfully castrating their fathers of their manhood.

"Take away the buffalo," White Cow Bull had said many times since those hard winters in the land of the Grand-mother, "and we will have to eat from the white man's hand—like begging dogs."

"I will never beg," Sees Red grumbled each time.

"Nor I," the Oglalla replied. "But as a man I have a responsibility to my family. I cannot watch them waste away and grow sick until their spirit wants to leave their bodies—as many other men have watched their relatives slowly starve. It is just too hard for a man to see that with his eyes and his heart."

Beneath a bright autumn sun this ration day, the men gathered in small knots in front of the agent's storehouse, waiting for the white men to finish their marking on papers before they would come outside into the cold to set up their table and chairs. Each head of the household would be called forward, shown where to put his mark down in the book before receiving his rations. Some of the Oglalla sat talking, others smoked at their pipes filled with willow bark and buffalo berry. Few could afford the high price of the white man's tobacco now that there were no buffalo robes for the women to tan for trade.

A few sat in the shade, their blankets wrapped about them, solitary and ashamed. Mostly the older ones, former warriors who remembered the glory days when they swarmed over Fetterman's soldiers, the good times of chasing buffalo and riding out to whip Red Beard Crook's troops. Most of these remembered the soul-stirring call of Crazy Horse as he led them galloping up the north slope against Long Hair's last pony soldiers swallowed up in a red wave beside the Greasy Grass.

It was hard for such a man to be treated like a child, forced to wait until he would be given less than what he deserved, now that he was kept from providing for himself and those he loved. White Cow Bull tried his best to put a good face on things for the others.

"Each time I come here to stand before the agent," he said loudly before his fellow Oglallas, "I am made happy once more that my wife is Cheyenne and that she has no relatives living near us. There would be more mouths for me to feed!"

Most of the men laughed. Some easily, others nervously. Some refusing to show any emotion here on this ground of shame. Eager to take the white man's handouts and be gone from this place.

"You need a second wife!" a man shouted to White Cow Bull. "It might be good for you to have another mouth to feed!"

"No. Another wife soon means little mouths to feed!"

That laughter and joking at their condition proved to be the only tonic available for most. Still, the laughter infuriated others.

"Perhaps your adopted son could ask the white man to give each of us a little more today. He speaks the white tongue, I have heard."

White Cow Bull and Stone Eagle turned toward the old man who sat sullen and wrinkled, wrapped in his blanket with his back against a tree.

"He knows the white tongue—"

"Let me speak for myself," Stone Eagle interrupted his Oglalla father. "You think because I know their tongue that I can help us?"

"Why did you learn the white man's tongue if not to help your people?" asked a second older man who inched closer.

"I learned because I love to learn. We are asked to live with the white man—live by his ways now. It is right that some of us learn his tongue."

"Do not criticize young Stone Eagle," said a round,

full-faced older man who stepped close to the ring. "He cannot help himself. It is his white blood that makes him the way he is. Stone Eagle has forgotten his people. You see, he does not even live with the Cheyenne down in the territories. They do not want him."

He leapt toward the fat one, restrained by White Cow Bull and another before he could reach the old man.

"Perhaps Rattling Drum is right," a new voice was raised. "This white man's tongue he has learned is no help to us. Why don't you go back to your father's people—your own people, Stone Eagle?"

"He grew up among the Lakota!" growled White Cow Bull.

"Please, let me speak for myself," the young man asked. "My mother left her people long, long ago, for there were no close relatives left among her tribe."

"Of course, Stone Eagle. They were killed by your father—the Long Hair!" joked a man, his words causing a twitter of laughter among some others.

"She did not leave because she had no relatives," the fat man shouted. "She left because she was searching for your father. He was your only relative!"

"I am his father now!" White Cow Bull hollered, fists clenching and unclenching at his sides.

"I never knew my father," Stone Eagle said quietly. "But what he left me was a warrior's blood—"

"Ha, Stone Eagle. You mean he spilled enough warriors' blood, don't you?"

"Long Hair did not put us on this reservation," he replied. "My mother says he only came marching after those of us who wandered off the reservation."

"Your mother saw him through the eyes of a woman. Not the heart of a warrior."

"Let your Indian blood do something for your people, Stone Eagle," declared one of the group tightening their ring about him. "Forget your white side and truly feel your Indian blood."

"I have a wife. Full-blood Miniconjou, Double Woman is. I am not a white man like my father."

"Would you fight the soldiers if the time came that you

had to protect your family and all that you own from the white man?"

Stone Eagle glared at the questioner. "I would fight any man who came to take away what was mine."

"Your father came to take it!" another shouted.

He lunged for the man, restrained once more. "I am not my father! I am not white! I am a Cheyenne—who speaks Lakota and has married a daughter of High Pipe, of Black Horse's band. One day we will have many children who will learn their father is an honorable man!"

"What will they learn of their grandfather, Stone Eagle?"

He stared at the ground a moment, the anger seeping from his body like milk from a cracked blue bowl. "They will learn that my mother loved him very much."

"Loved the killer of women and babies?" shouted one of the group.

"No," replied White Cow Bull this time. "Monaseetah loved a man different from the killer you call Long Hair."

"There is only one Long Hair!"

White Cow Bull shook his head, looking at Stone Eagle before he went on to explain. "Monaseetah did not see him as a killer of her people. She saw him only as a man— perhaps a powerful warrior. But she looked at him with eyes of love. The way your wives look at you."

"How does your wife look at you, Stone Eagle?"

He turned round to face his questioner. "I hope she looks at me with the same love in her eyes as there is on my mother's face when she looks at White Cow Bull."

A sharp, chilling blast from a bugle signaled that the allocations were to begin. A small soldier detail had arrived to keep everything orderly among the men, who hurriedly shuffled for a place near the front of the long line. White Cow Bull and his adopted son were left alone as quickly as they had been surrounded by the accusing glares of their attackers.

"I am happy to know that you have noticed how your mother looks at me," the Oglalla said quietly as they inched up at the back of the line.

"It is the truth. I would have Double Woman love me as much as Monaseetah loves you."

"Then you are very happy about the child coming."

"Child—a child coming? What do you mean?" He felt the words seize in his throat.

White Cow Bull smiled, looking confused. "Double Woman is carrying your child, isn't she?"

He wagged his head, finding things so hard to contain right now. "No. We haven't . . . she hasn't—"

"I am sorry then. Perhaps I should have waited. Monaseetah thought that you surely knew."

"My mother knew? Double Woman told her?"

He laughed gently. "A woman does not have to speak it to another woman. They can always tell without words. Monaseetah spends more time with your wife than you spend with Double Woman. She has noticed the small changes in your wife. And sees Double Woman grow sick every morning now."

"I haven't seen—"

"Because we men don't know what to see." He laughed easily, pushing Stone Eagle ahead of him as the line inched up toward the table.

"A baby?"

"Monaseetah is going to be a grandmother," White Cow Bull said, wagging his head. "I can't believe I'm married to a grandmother."

He paid no attention to his adopted father, moving ahead only when nudged, for his thoughts were far, far away. Afraid he would not be ready to be a father when the time came.

"I have a pretty good idea what Joe told you," said Jack Corbin.

Captain Preston Tripp had finally tracked down the former army scout working out of Fort Smith, Arkansas, for the federal court into Indian Territory. Twenty years ago next month, Jack Corbin and Moses "California Joe" Milner had helped Ben Clark's Osage scouts lead George Armstrong Custer's Seventh U.S. Cavalry to Black Kettle's Washita camp. Tripp judged Corbin to be in his mid- to late forties as he sat in a patch of autumn shade on the veranda looking out on the wide expanse of the Arkansas River. The scout's hands were what most intrigued the captain.

Gnarled with arthritis. Probably from the brutal, change-able weather of this land.

Tripp had tracked Milner down to west Texas after chasing after word of him from Fort Chadbourne to Fort Concho, from there to Fort Sumner in New Mexico, down to Fort Bliss and finally cornering the old veteran of the Mexican War at Fort Davis, the army post located dead center between the Pecos and the Rio Grande rivers. Milner kept moving to keep himself employed. And he kept himself employed doing whatever a post commander needed him to do—just so Joe could keep himself in what he called his tanglefoot.

A mixture of grain, red peppers, and strychnine was what Captain Tripp called it. But California Joe nursed a lot of pain away with his deadly elixir, sucking dry all his memories of his high times on the plains in the process.

"Joe didn't tell me all that much, Jack," Tripp replied. "Sounded doubtful on most things. And on the rest it sounded like he was taken to doing a lot of bragging."

Corbin chuckled and swabbed the droplets of coffee from his long mustache on the greasy bandanna hung round his neck. "Don't doubt it, really. Joe's been that way for the last twenty-odd years I've knowed him. So you come to look me up? Joe put you on the trail?"

"I would have come no matter what Milner had to say. And no, he hadn't the foggiest where I could find you."

"Funny, ain't it? How we lost track of each other after all those winters riding together."

"Sometimes I would suppose folks can have a falling out."

Corbin smiled beneath his shaggy graying mustache. "Suppose you're right, Captain. So you want to know all about that winter campaign of Custer's back to sixty-eight?"

"Not rightly, Jack." He scooted his chair closer to Corbin's. "Just want to know about Custer's dalliance with the Cheyenne woman."

Corbin eyed him from the corners for a long moment, then eased his chair back on two legs, settling the ladder-back against the clapboard wall without a sound. He let out a long sigh and stared off at the river below the bluffs.

"Joe wouldn't be a damn bit of help with you on that,

Captain," he finally said after a long spell. "Him and me out riding herd on them Osages for Ben Clark or carrying messages for Sheridan back and forth. Matter of fact, I don't know all that much myself."

"Custer did keep the woman with him all winter long."

He grinned widely, teeth like pale pinewood chips beneath the cat's whiskers. "Isn't a man marched down the Washita and west to the Sweetwater with Custer gonna tell you any different. The general made no bones about it. Hell, what man would blame him? She was a looker. Best damned lookin' Injun woman I ever see'd in my life, Captain. And she had eyes for Custer, that's for sure."

"What about her son?"

"He was Cheyenne. No doubt about that. Weren't Custer's."

"Are you talking about her second?"

He wagged his head. "Now her second was another man-child. And that was Custer's—no doubt in hell of that."

"That was rumor?"

He shook his head. "That was the word from the Cheyenne camp. Custer never owned up to it—and took his Seventh right on outta Kansas not long after shipping her back down to her own folks in the territories."

"Everybody knew?"

He looked away toward the river for a long time. "It was Custer's business. Weren't none of mine. Man's dead now—a long time gone. Whyn't you folks leave 'im be?"

Tripp pursed his lips, sensing he was losing this witness the way he would occasionally lose one on the witness stand. It had always reminded him of the feeling of some strong tug on his line, knowing he would not last getting the fish in to creek bank before that line snapped and his catch was free.

"You served that winter with the blessings of General Philip H. Sheridan, didn't you, Jack?"

Corbin eyed him severely, those hard, dark plainsman's eyes below the shaggy eyebrows, wrinkled lids like old boot leather.

"I served for Sheridan many a time."

"I'm here on account of the general. He asked me to talk with you special."

"Me, did he?"

"Said you could help me—and keep yourself quiet about it as well."

He stared back at the river for the longest time, then rocked forward in the chair, settling all four legs before he stood, holding out his hand.

"Tell you what, Captain Tripp," Corbin said quietly. "Sheridan's right. Jack Corbin do keep his mouth shut. And you ought'n go find the man who can answer all your questions."

"Who would that be?"

"He was a scout and interpreter hired on by Custer—the one the general put in charge of the Cheyenne prisoners that day we burned Black Kettle's camp into a greasy patch along the Washita."

"What's this man's name?"

"Romero—the Mexican. As a child he was stole from his folks and raised by the Cheyenne."

"Where can I find this Romero?"

"Chances are you need to start looking in some Cheyenne camps, Captain Tripp."

"Why Cheyenne camps?"

Corbin looked off at the clouds gathering in the west, lead-bellied with snow. "Just before Custer sent his left-hand woman back to her people to have his half-breed son, ol' Romero headed out with his Cheyenne wife."

"He had a Cheyenne woman as well?"

"There, you see? Ain't no better man to tell you about Custer and that Cheyenne gal of his. None better to tell it than Romero."

CHAPTER 38

Spring, 1889

"You keep pacing up and down like that, your moccasins will wear a trench in front of my lodge, Stone Eagle."

After he had said it, White Cow Bull laughed along with the other men who were gathered outside Monaseetah's canvas lodge here along Wounded Knee Creek where she and her Oglalla husband lived, some eighteen miles from the Pine Ridge Agency. Her son had arrived here late last night after the falling of the moon, bringing his wife with him from their camp many miles away.

Frantic with her first hard contraction, Stone Eagle had hoisted Double Woman atop the bony back of their old horse, borrowed another, then hurried as fast as prudence would allow along the cold, muddy roads of this Moon of First Eggs. He kept thinking of the word the white man used for this time. May. Thinking it was right his firstborn should come in the spring when all the ponies foaled and the wild animals bore their young.

Afraid, he had come here to the lodge of his mother. She

would know what to do, he realized. Monaseetah did exactly that—taking control and shooing the father-to-be away along with White Cow Bull.

At least they would not be bothered by the glum countenance and caustic words of Sees Red. He now lived many miles away with some others in a cabin close by the agency. A big change, this living in a white man's structure, but no more dramatic than was the fact that Sees Red was now a Pine Ridge policeman. He kept his badge polished and his guns well oiled. It was the guns he liked most of all being a metal-breast with the other policemen. Sees Red could finally order folks around and ride a horse and brandish his guns, threatening to use them at the drop of a feather. He was truly happy now.

By late afternoon a small group had gathered to await the arrival of Stone Eagle's child. From inside the lodge came the grunts and screams and heavy, labored breathing that told the experienced men that Double Woman's time was at hand. But not soon enough for Stone Eagle. Back and forth he had paced, scuffing a trench in the rain-softened ground in front of his mother's lodge.

"Yes, White Cow Bull," one of the old neighbors agreed. "It is a good trench though. Something you and Stone Eagle can be proud of. Something either one of you can trip and twist your ankle in!"

The rest of the group roared with more laughter, passing round the little bottles of red whiskey White Cow Bull had brought out. He told everyone he had been saving them for a long time. Many winters since first going to work for the trader, saving them for this time when he would first become a grandfather.

"I am too young to have a grandchild," he exclaimed again, hoisting one of the small brown bottles into the air.

"But a good one you will make," another old friend cheered.

"I think Stone Eagle needs another drink, White Cow Bull," someone suggested.

"He does not, but I do!" the old man said, then drank from the long-necked bottle. "Come. Sit, Stone Eagle. The child will come no quicker with you making a wagon rut of

White Cow Bull's camp. Here, we have saved you a special place in the sun."

Stone Eagle reluctantly settled into the short, green, fragrant grass with the others. The ground was warm this afternoon.

"When a boy grows to be twelve summers," began Makes Crazy, "that boy's grandfather will begin to talk with him about how the boy should live."

"Will you do that for your grandson, White Cow Bull?"

"I am proud to do that for Stone Eagle's son."

"It may be a girl," Stone Eagle said. "Double Woman said the old women felt her belly and told her it was to be a girl."

"What do they know of such things?" White Cow Bull retorted. "A man's firstborn should be a boy!"

"*Hau!*" shouted some of those who agreed. Many hands reached for the brown bottles being passed around as they waited out the birthing in Monaseetah's lodge.

"White Cow Bull will instruct your son in all his manly duties, Stone Eagle," said Makes Crazy, the fire tender during young Yellow Bird's medicine sweat. "He will show your son that it is right for a boy to listen to his elders and do what they say. If he is sent to fetch something, he must go at once."

"That is right," another of the old ones joined in. "The boy must be taught to do nothing bad in camp, to have no fights with the other boys."

"I will teach my grandson that he must never let the sun catch him in bed. In the days of my youth, we were to be in the hills before the sun came up—bringing our horses down to water and fresh grass."

"If your son grows up to be a good warrior like his grandfather, Stone Eagle—he must learn not to be boastful. To go about bragging to others of all the brave things he has done is most unseemly conduct. He will learn that his friends will sing his praises. He must not paint his deeds too gloriously."

"If my grandson listens to the advice of his elders, he will grow up to be something of a man."

"The way Stone Eagle has become a good man," Makes Crazy said. "A man who will provide for his family and keep them safe from harm. Doing them no wrong and protecting them from the bad ways of the white man."

"Stone Eagle is a good man," White Cow Bull agreed. "And he will make a good father. It is important to teach my grandson not to lie, especially when talking to his elders."

"Will you teach your grandson about the ways of women, White Cow Bull?" asked one of the old ones as many in the group laughed soundly at the verbal challenge.

"Who better to teach him?"

"You?" another old one asked. "You who were about to go to your rest as an old bachelor bull before Monaseetah took pity on you?"

They enjoyed their joke at White Cow Bull's expense.

"I waited, my friends," he replied. "And look what happiness I have now with the beautiful woman who is Stone Eagle's mother."

"Did White Cow Bull teach you about women, Stone Eagle?"

"He taught me much, yes. But—Double Woman taught me so much more."

They hooted and passed the pipes and bottles around once more as the laughter died.

"We must teach my grandson never to run off with a woman. It is not a good way to begin a life together. A man is to give horses and not excuses. That makes for a long life together. When a couple runs off, they are talked about, and that is not good for either of them."

"Did Stone Eagle ever hunt buffalo in the land of the Grandmother?" Makes Crazy inquired.

"He was not old enough before we came south with those left in Sitting Bull's band."

"It is sad then, Stone Eagle," the old medicine man said, his tongue licking across his fevered gums. "When a young man hunts his first buffalo, it is a sacred time for him. The young hunter must seek out an old man among his people, someone who holds some special powers, and offer him the best portion of that first buffalo."

"I remember when I gave my meat to you, old man," White Cow Bull said, pointing.

"Yes. You have benefited through the years from my

prayers and my giving thanks for that buffalo meat, have you not?"

"You have been there for me always, uncle."

Makes Crazy turned back to Stone Eagle. "The old man chosen by the young hunter would be taken to the buffalo carcass, where he would pull it around so the head faced east. Then he would slit the buffalo down its spine, pulling out the right kidney. The young hunter was to take it and hold it to the east, then south, then west, and finally north. Then he would hold it toward the ground and then to the sky above before he lay it on a buffalo chip."

"That is when the old man offers his prayer for the young hunter," White Cow Bull advised.

"I would say, 'May this boy live as many winters as I may live, having each summer the luck of good hunting. May he have a large family with many sons, and may they all have plenty to eat.'"

"After that prayer you walked with me back to camp, Makes Crazy. Praising my name—telling all of my first buffalo."

The old man smiled. "It is good that our people should know of a young man doing a brave thing."

"Many of our ways to show bravery are gone now," White Cow Bull said. He freed the long tail of his cloth shirt from his belt and pulled it up, showing the white pucker scars on his breasts.

"Yes!" an old man shouted, leaping to his feet. "We who have prayed at the sun pole should not be afraid to show our scars." He pulled his shirt off, while more of the old ones rose unsteadily to their feet, stripping off their shirts in the afternoon sun.

"It is something all the people can see and remind them of the old days when we were a strong people!" Makes Crazy said, smearing a dribble of whiskey on each of his six scars.

"Can't a man offer himself to the sun now?" Stone Eagle asked.

White Cow Bull shook his head vehemently. "No! The agent and his police will find out. The white man forbids our sun dance—for over four winters now."

"There would be much trouble if we buried a sun pole in the middle of any of our camps now," Makes Crazy said.

"Are you all become old women?" Stone Eagle asked quietly, instantly snagging their attention as if he held their heads on invisible strings.

"We are Lakota warriors!" some shouted. Others howled like wolves or started chanting their old warrior-society war songs. A few stomped the old dances right there beside Monaseetah's lodge where Double Woman cried out in growing pain.

"Yes. We are all warriors," Stone Eagle agreed. "And a warrior does not turn away from a fight."

"What fight is this, my son?"

"To hold onto the old life." He gazed at his adopted father's eyes. "I want to hang myself from the sun pole. To thank the spirits for what they have given me—my beautiful woman, this child. I must give thanks and pray for the sun's blessing."

"We must keep quiet on this," said one of the old ones who stopped singing.

"Sun-dance time comes soon," another advised, a faint smile creasing his wrinkled face.

"I think we can do this," Makes Crazy whispered, signaling all the others in close. "Yes, we can have a sun dance for Stone Eagle. No one else must know. You, Rattling Drum—you have a daughter who is a virgin. Is she still?"

"If she has not lain with a young man while I have been here drinking to Stone Eagle's baby, she is still a virgin!"

"Good! She can select the tree. Go high, where the white man and his soldiers cannot chance upon you. Take four of you—from different camps, and bring the pole down the long way back of the ridge. Carry it far away to Medicine Root Creek. I am thinking of a small clearing many miles up from the mouth. There is a lot of red stone along the creek there. Do you know the place, Rattling Drum?"

"I know it. *Aiyeee!* It is the right place, Makes Crazy. We can help Stone Eagle give thanks to the sun there."

Makes Crazy turned with the others as the door flap to Monaseetah's lodge was yanked back. The men suddenly fell silent, as if only then realizing that the screams and torment of Double Woman had ceased.

A black head flecked with the first strands of iron appeared as Monaseetah bent forward, stepping into the late sun of spring. No man among them spoke; instead there came the muted gasps of surprise and amazement as the woman walked toward them silently.

She stopped before Stone Eagle, who was struck dumb, then pulled back the calico wrap from the tiny, reddened, pinched face.

White Cow Bull nudged his adopted son without a word spoken. Stone Eagle obeyed, nervously accepting the bundle from his mother. Monaseetah looked up into her son's face. The strain of the long night into the day showed red in her eyes, yet that weariness was softened by the moistness glistening there in the falling sunlight.

"I am a grandmother, Stone Eagle," she said quietly as the old Oglalla warriors drew close. "I don't think I've felt any richer than I do at this moment."

"Double Woman?"

"She is young and strong, Stone Eagle," Monaseetah said. "She sleeps now but wants you to be there by her side when she awakens."

"Yes, I will go," he said anxiously, never having held anything so small in his adult life—thinking of the tiny sparrows and wrens he had killed with his small blunt arrows when he was a child himself—how light they had been to his own tiny hands, weighing almost nothing more than a breath of smoke.

This too—his child—weighed like a whisper of wind in his hands. He started toward the lodge door.

"Wait, Stone Eagle," White Cow Bull said. "You have not told us. Do you have a daughter?"

He glanced at his mother, fear and embarrassment pinching his face.

"See for yourself, my son," Monaseetah suggested.

He gently pulled back the scrap of wool blanket, then the shroud of calico bunting, suddenly overwhelmed as he exposed the genitals. He looked up, his eyes pooling.

"Double Woman has given us a son!"

"*Hopo! Hopo!*"

"Hau kola!"

"Stone Eagle has a son!"

"We must all ready ourselves as warriors!" Makes Crazy shouted above the clamor of the old men crazily circling one another in their war dances, pounding on their old bellies like drums. "For this new father. Stone Eagle must give thanks in the old way. He must punish himself before the sun!"

The new father stood there as the old Oglallas continued to circle him and the newborn, swirling in and out in their old dance steps, chanting their songs. Just as it had been in the old days when these same men rode free across the prairie, the wind whispering through their unbound hair, driving arrow after arrow into the vitals of the great shaggy beasts. Every one of these same men had helped turn back Red Beard Crook and Reno. These were the same brave old warriors who many summers gone had pounded Long Hair Custer and his soldiers into the dust of a yellow hillside beneath an angry sun.

"I will give thanks in the old way!" Stone Eagle declared, sensing his new son turn slightly in the cradle of his father's hands. "For my son—I will give thanks in the way of the warriors!"

CHAPTER 39

WHEN it rose that third day, the sun no longer burned him.

He had purified himself with the old men in the tiny dome of a sweat lodge within sight of him now as his feet continued their hypnotic shuffle from side to side around the pole, forever from right to left in the path of the sun across the land.

That first day the old ones had escorted Stone Eagle from the sweat lodge to the foot of the sun-dance pole. There the aged Oglallas had laid him on his back and pierced his flesh without further ceremony. His blood flowed free and red, pooling in the dust beside him before they were done with the skewers driven beneath his pectoral muscles. He remembered it not hurting as much as he had feared it would through all those days before the old men were ready to steal out of camp and away into the badlands. Perhaps the steamy heat of the sweat lodge had had something to do with it, he remembered thinking as they pulled him out of the sticky dust and onto his feet, slipping the feather-decked eagle wing-bone whistle between his lips.

Quickly they had lashed the ends of long rawhide tethers to the skewers embedded in his chest, slowly nudging him outward until there was a slight pressure on the fresh wounds.

"Pull, Stone Eagle," said the old dance leader, Makes Crazy. "As you pull, sense the glory of your pain. With it comes your prayers to the Great Mystery!"

And they had left him to dance alone. These old men who day after day sat back in the shade of the nearby trees. Near enough to watch the pain on his face and admire his bravery. Far enough that he alone stood beneath the sun's high cruelty.

There was a flush of excruciating, delicious pain each time he jerked back on the rawhide tethers binding him to the top of the sun pole, where he kept his eyes riveted across the days and into the two nights he had slept on a bed of sage near the arbor. Throughout the days the old men took their turns at the drums and the singing, their voices croaking more as the days crept by, like that persistent rusty hinge on the old schoolhouse door.

He dreamed of her, the whiteness of her hands, the caked powder on her cheeks, where he felt he could peer into every one of her pores as she bent over his desk each time he needed help. Sometimes he remembered not needing help at all, but raising his hand still, calling the old teacher from her desk at the front of the room by that milky black slate board where she drew her numbers and letters— called her to his chair just so he could smell her.

The old school woman smelled so different from his mother. Even in his dream he could still smell her. It was not something wild and fresh. More so, something strangely forbidden and sinful, kept bottled and for use only by the elect. Like the white man's whiskey he had tasted once and not taken again. He did not know why, but the old woman's powder and lip rouge and lilac water gave her a smell of something far away from this reservation land of his.

Every bit like the whiskey his stomach would not tolerate. But Stone Eagle had enjoyed the smelling of her, the nearness of her ample white flesh. Her fingers always

laid softly on his shoulder as she bent herself over his tiny
desk to work through ciphering a problem with him.
Sometimes, he thought, he had come day after day to her
school simply to smell her—thereby learning much of his
white man's knowledge by absorption if not by desire.

"Today you must pull harder, Stone Eagle!"

Makes Crazy's voice pierced his foggy veil, scattering his
dream of the old school woman like the beans he had
spilled across the hard plank floor of trader Mosseau's
storeroom two years before. Rolling, tumbling, clattering
hard beans pouring from the torn corner of the burlap
sacking. He was certain from that day he never found every
bean, just as he now accepted that he would not be able to
retrieve his fragment dream of the fleshy white schoolteacher.

"You must pray harder!"

Didn't they know how hard this was on his young body?
His muscles gave and stretched, yet resisted. Perhaps
another twenty years from now when he danced, he could
tear through his flesh much, much easier. But now . . .

He thought back to the first ration day of this first month
of summer the white men call June. The Indian agent had
received a small shipment of skinny cattle, smaller than he
had expected. Less than was needed to feed the families.
Perhaps in apology, feeling ashamed that there were not
more of the skinny cattle, the agent agreed to let the old
men chase plodding cows in the old way of chasing buffalo.

Yanking hard against the rawhide tethers, Stone Eagle
brought tears to his eyes as he bit down on the end of the
eagle wing-bone whistle and blew its prayer toward the sun.
But not all those tears coursing down the dust on his cheeks
were of the pain he had caused himself. Most welled from
his remembrance of that joy on the faces of the old men as
they gathered at the appointed hour between the agent's
office and trader's corral. The same old men who had been
with him at the moment his son was born. These who
waited in the shade of the cottonwood and alder for him to
punish his flesh and prostrate himself before the Almighty
Everywhere.

What exquisite pain it was to remember how they each
had hobbled to that corral, leading their old horses, every

man dressed in his finest clothing, quivers of arrows slung at their backs and their short, sturdy bows clutched in their bent and misshapen hands. Their iron-flecked hair spoke of many winters of survival, many youthful summers in the chase, hair now neatly combed and brushed, braided or tied with special amulets for success in the hunt.

The old women and the youngsters had gathered too, singing and trilling their tongues like chattering magpies, giving voice to their joy as the men completed their painting of the old plug horses they called their war ponies and buffalo runners. The white man did not allow them to own the sleek, hard-boned, wide-nosed cayuses of their youth. No, instead the army would provide these old men horses befitting the passing of their days of glory—horses marked on the left hip with a regimental brand. Marked on the right flank with the *IC* that few of the old men realized meant "inspected and condemned."

Instead of making bait meat or dog steaks from the horses, the army had made a grand show of presenting the animals to the Oglallas from time to time. Proudly splotched in earth paint now, feathers tied in manes and tails tied up in the old way—the plodding, ribby mounts were readied for their chase.

When the agent had given the go-ahead, some of the young men went to the corral gate, awaiting a signal from the riders. Other young men, who had never known the feel of the free wind in their unbraided hair as they whipped their ponies alongside a fat cow or aimed their arrow down into the heart of a strong young bull, gathered about the twenty-four old men. These young helped boost the lame, bent, and arthritic old warriors onto the bony backs of those condemned army horses.

Stone Eagle cried out with the vision of it now, his eyes misting enough to blind him to the bright afternoon sun, remembering how in that settling on the backs of those plodding old horses just how those old men had once more become young and vital and courageous warriors. And how for those old men those condemned army nags had mysteriously become the sleek, grass-fed, mule-eyed war ponies who had surrounded and hammered Long Hair's finest cavalry into the dust of a Montana hillside.

If only for an afternoon of joy and remembrance.

The signal given, the young men at the corral gate yanked back on the poles and began waving their colorful blankets and rattling small pieces of rawhide. It took some doing, but the bony, spotted cattle eventually snorted and bellowed in protest, lumbering past the shouting men and women and children, out from the trees and down the long, dusty, rutted Wounded Knee road leading east from the Pine Ridge Agency.

And with a whoop those old warriors drove their heels into the ribs of their buffalo runners, crying out in joy, feeling the wind in their faces one last time as the resistant pace of the army's condemned horses matched the slow, lumbering plod of the white man's skinny cattle.

One by one the cattle were brought down, accompanied by a shout and a prayer. And one by one the women and children descended on each still-quivering carcass. Old women instructing the young on the proper spreading of the four legs, slicing round the neck, then down the back. Though there was no hump, and no boss, no fleecy hump fat on these bony beasts, the women and children dived into their chores, bloody past their elbows, mouths and chins dripping with red as they sucked at the raw, warm meat and fought the dogs from the gut-piles buzzing with flies.

Unlike the bygone times, that day the dogs would not be allowed to root through the fragrant offal—all of it meat too precious to find its way down the gullet of any half-feral camp dog.

The looks on those wrinkled faces were what seemed like a prayer itself to Stone Eagle. Bright eyes glistening with joy as they brought their plodding horses back to the carcasses to join in the feasting along the white man's road. Sweaty, paint-smeared faces smiling gap-toothed at their successful hunt. One by one they dropped to the ground, hobbling bowlegged and hipshot to join the other old warriors in a passing of the ceremonial pipe of thanksgiving.

He felt the tearing on his right breast like a loosening. A moment later the pain seared through him like a hot coal as Stone Eagle realized he had torn himself free from one of the tethers. Without stopping to swallow down the hot tongues of pain, he redoubled his efforts on the skewer still embedded in his left breast.

A moment more and he became aware of the shuffling of feet around him, the smell of dried sweat and rancid grease in their snow-flecked braids. The old ones were surrounding him once more.

"Pull now, Stone Eagle!" White Cow Bull's voice rang at his ear like the chiming of the school bell on that small clapboard one-room building where the old woman taught him to speak the white man's words.

"Be strong, young one," Makes Crazy called at his other ear.

The drumming was almost deafening. He was certain they had drawn this close simply to numb him to the pain as he yanked, again and again and . . .

He sensed the tearing. Finally! *Grandfather Above!* his heart sang out as he sensed the slow, bloody ripping of his muscle and sinew and sweaty hide. Tearing himself free.

May our prayers be answered! he thought as he stumbled backward, unfettered for the first time in three days.

Perhaps we can dance back the ghosts . . . perhaps the buffalo will now return.

Flush with hope, he stumbled backwards and fell, sensing his muscles going completely, like meat so rotten it had turned to soup. At his back pressed the cool of the short green grass and the hard fists of bunch sage. Above him arched an endless canopy of blue.

Now the buffalo can return. . . .

By the time the sun-dance group returned to the camps on Wounded Knee Creek, Stone Eagle's celebration was swallowed by the growing excitement over the return of the Pine Ridge messengers who had gone west to see with their own eyes this Paiute messiah called Wovoka.

Late last year word had arrived on the reservation that the son of God had come back to earth as he had promised long ago. But this messiah had come to sweep the earth clear of all white people and make it a safe place for his Indian children once more. Even more astounding had been the fragments of rumor that claimed all those long dead would soon rise and live again, while those Indians alive to watch the miracles would live forever.

With the return of the ghosts would be a returning of the buffalo.

Could it be, Stone Eagle wondered, *that my words of prayer at the base of the sun-dance tree will come to pass? Will there come a return of the buffalo?*

Cloud Horse and Good Thunder had led the delegation to the far land of the Shoshone and Diggers to learn of this messiah firsthand, for it had been said that all miracles could happen if the people learned the dance Wovoka would teach them.

They returned, convinced they had seen and talked to and touched the son of God. And though he had the white name of Jack Wilson, he was full-blood Indian! At the messiah's knee they had learned the Ghost Returning Dance and the sacred medicine songs to be sung during the dancing. Word was spreading like prairie fire across the reservation: If man and woman alike would only dance the sacred dance and sing the sacred songs, they would see the spirits of their departed loved ones in preparation for the return of the buffalo that would again blanket the prairie.

Already the messiah declared the buffalo were coming from the land of the setting sun!

"Who are we to believe this Paiute? They are not warrior people!" asked some of the doubters of those who had returned from their long trek to visit Wovoka.

"He is a simple man who died so that the rest of us can live forever," Good Thunder declared. "He went to God's heaven where God prepared him to return to earth."

"He saw the Great Mystery for himself?"

"Yes. God said the earth is old and tired, and he wants to renew it. But this time he will make the earth without the white man. Only the Indian will live in the new world."

"How will this happen?"

"The earth will tremble and shake as our legends tell us it has shaken before."

"I remember those stories," many yelled.

"Won't we be swallowed up when the ground shakes anew?" prodded the doubters.

"No, not if you believe . . . and if you are a believer,

you must wear a sacred eagle feather in your hair when you dance. At the time the earth trembles, all those wearing the feather will fly into the air while God drives the whites back into the sea where they came from."

"We will be free to roam the prairies once more?"

"Yes!"

"There will again be plenty of buffalo to hunt?"

"Yes!"

"We can live our lives in the old way as warriors once more!"

"YES!"

CHAPTER 40

Autumn, 1889

H E hadn't smelled anything this bad in years.
For certain, Captain Preston Tripp had dug and filled his share of slip-trench latrines in his day. But this was something altogether more potent.

There wasn't a good spot for him. No place upwind where the whole Cheyenne encampment did not reek of filth and feces, rotting meat and slow death.

At least he could sit outside with the old Mexican as they watched the children play and the women of the camp scrape at the greasy hides begged from the agency's cattle herd.

"Corbin told you to look me up?" Romero asked as he settled on a nearby log dragged close to the smoky fire.

The air was thick with the expectation of snow. Smoke from a dozen nearby fires hung suffocating beneath the naked branches of the oaks where the small band of Southern Cheyenne had pitched their canvas lodges among the log shanties the white agents and soldiers had convinced the tribe to build for themselves as they walked down the white man's road.

"He figured you were the best man to talk to," Tripp replied, eyeing the drippy-nosed child who ran up to Romero, gave the old Mexican's knee a hug, then darted off again after the older children and a pack of ribby dogs.

"Talk to about what, Captain?"

"Your winter with Custer down here in Indian Territory."

The pudgy Mexican scratched at the back of his neck, coming away with a tiny white louse between his fingers. He squashed it between two dirty nails, then flicked it into the flames, where it made a faint pop. "What's so special about that time you want to come ask me now?"

"Corbin said General Custer put you in charge of the Cheyenne prisoners." Tripp found his eyes looking away apologetically.

"He did." Romero pointed to one of the stout women at work on her hands and knees over a greasy hide, swatting at any dog approaching too close to sniff at her scraping. Back and forth she dragged the iron tool across the skin, then poured a little more of a foul-smelling liquid on a small section, working it into the hide all the more while the skin steamed into the chilly air.

"You remember a young woman who was named Mona-seetah?"

Romero twitched slightly as he looked up at the captain. Finally he took his eyes away and went back to scratching at the ears of a hound that laid its chin on his thigh. "She the one you want to know about?"

"Her. And the boy."

Romero did not look up. "You know about him?"

Tripp decided not to bluster his way through it. The ex-scout and interpreter was forthcoming. He only needed to coax. "Some. Not as much as I want to know."

The Mexican stared at him with glassy eyes that moistened over slightly in the smoky, slanting light that cut through the low clouds overhead. "Just you? Or you finding out for someone else?"

"General Sheridan."

"The little general, eh? He hear rumors of the boy?"

"Now he wants to know if the rumors are true."

Romero dragged a pudgy hand beneath his drippy nose,

then rubbed it along his buckskin legging. "You tell Sheridan the story is true."

Tripp waited as the man went back to scratching the dog's ears and staring at the smoke spurting from the damp wood.

"That it, Romero? You've got no more to tell me. No more to say to Sheridan."

"General gonna be disappointed, won't he?"

"He'll be more than that if he figures you're holding out on him."

Romero finally grinned. "All right. You go get some coffee out of your saddlebags, and we'll talk serious."

"How you know I've got coffee?"

The Mexican snorted as he rose, striding over toward a dented coffeepot. "What good soldier like you gonna go riding around in this country this time of year without coffee in his bags?"

Tripp laughed easily with the Mexican. "We make coffee now."

"You got sugar?"

"As much as you want, Romero."

"Knew I was gonna like you, Captain—right off." Romero stopped a few feet away on his way to the little creek nearby. "We have coffee and sugar together. Then we talk serious on Monaseetah and her boy."

Tripp watched the stout bulk of the man fade into the smoky haze of shadow and shaft sunlight among the trees.

Without thinking he drank deep of the air, suddenly shocked as the stench belted his senses like those class-mates had repeatedly hammered his jaw at the academy during boxing class. But the mingling of so many foul odors no longer made him feel a revulsion. Tripp settled back to his log, sensing the ease of these people come over him as well.

Feeling close to some solid answers at last. Knowing Romero could put him on the right trail.

For the first time in all these years, sensing he stood close to the ghost of General George Armstrong Custer.

It had been some time since he had been here, walked up these steps, put his hand on this doorknob rubbed smooth by all the small hands come to touch it over the years.

Stone Eagle had reined up moments ago, atop the low hill overlooking the clapboard schoolhouse and the pounded-earth recess yard surrounding it, where grass refused to grow. It was so like the white man, he had ruminated. The whites built their houses and buildings to stay. And the earth suffered for it. He had nudged the old horse down the barren hillside toward the narrow valley, knowing nothing would ever grow in that no-man's-land, like a buffer, surrounding the schoolhouse.

Sad enough was the reason he had come back here after all this time. To the school where he had learned his English and learned to form his written words. Brought here to the empty schoolyard by the news that the schoolteacher had suddenly died.

He twisted on the hand-rubbed doorknob slowly, already sensing the seductive fragrance of her lilac water growing strong in his nostrils. The fresh, lye-scrubbed, talc-powdered headiness of her heavy-breasted softness as she strode purposefully up and down the rows of benches and desks, slapping the ruler in the palm of her big white hand while the class repeatedly went over alphabet and numbers and problems and stories together.

But the years exacted their toll, and now the woman had succumbed to both her years and the terrible winter they had just seen pass.

With her age and growing weakness, it did not take much of a winter's cold to turn itself into a case of pneumonia. But then he really never understood what carried some people away and why others survived. Ever since those winters of hunger and disease north of the medicine line.

The classroom was empty. No sound—except for the faint shuffling of a pair of feet across the hard floor in the small quarters behind the schoolroom. The place smelled strangely medicinal and closed. Almost suffocating in the way that sweat lodges had been suffocating in their smothering, steamy incense.

"I am too late," he whispered under his breath with a saddening realization that he found no casket here, slowly dragging his moccasined feet up the aisle between neat rows of desks. Stone Eagle surprised himself that he had spoken in English. Then realized this was a place where it was only natural that he speak the white man's words. His father's tongue.

She suddenly filled the narrow doorway leading to the living quarters at the rear of the schoolhouse, surprising him more than anything.

"You scared me for a moment," she said in a small voice, her green eyes widening as she looked him over, a pale, creamy hand held just below the brooch pinned at her throat.

"I came . . ." he began, still startled, but more so now with her auburn-haired beauty. "Hearing she died . . ."

She saw his hands flutter before him, trying to explain.

"Mrs. Nettleton? You came to see her?"

"Heard she died."

She turned, an empty hand gesturing to the old desk. "Her body was here for a few days. Her nephew came for her. He took the casket to the train just this morning. Heading back east where she'll be buried."

He stared at the floor, afraid for the longest time to look into the green of those eyes that reminded him of the electrifying power of the phosphorescent lightning of prairie thunderstorms. She took a step toward the desk, one more closer to him, inching into a shaft of sunlight that brought her hair ablaze with rust highlights.

"You were a student of Mrs. Nettleton?"

Stone Eagle nodded, afraid of the young woman's beauty. He judged her to be no more than ten years older than he. High cheekbones and wide, long-lashed, almond-shaped eyes that searched his every time he returned her gaze. It was not the first time he had been made uneasy by a woman. Yet it was the only time he had felt this way since becoming a man.

She came forward another step, her right hand coming up between them. "I am sure Mrs. Nettleton would have been happy to know you came to see her. I'm Avolea Rankin."

He stared at the white hand she held before her, then finally took it and wondered at its softness, shaking it twice, then dropped it as a child might drop a squirming spider.

"Your name?"

"Stone Eagle," he replied, resolving to look more directly into those powerful green eyes of hers, to match her steady gaze.

"Stone Eagle," she said with some measure of praise evident in her voice. "A powerful name, befitting such a tall and handsome Oga-lalla."

He shook his head. "I am Cheyenne."

"I can see that—yes. You really do not look like any of the Sioux here."

"You know something of the tribes?"

She smiled fully, tilting her head back into the shaft of sunlight, her teeth glimmering. "Some. What they could teach us back in the seminary where I studied to become a teacher. But I feel I've learned more in the past few days here than I did in three years of studies back east."

"You've been here long?"

"More than a month ago Mrs. Nettleton asked for help, saying that someone should come here to Pine Ridge to help her with the spring classes. She had been taken by a bad cold. I was here during her last days, as she began to fade, then take to her bed."

With self-assurance she stepped atop the platform and slid behind the desk, her skirt and petticoats slurring the floor as she sunk into the chair.

"Perhaps if I had known, I could have done something," he said finally.

"Are you speaking of one of your shamans?"

He wagged his head. "No. You are right. There are times when nothing can be done, and it is left up to God to decide who will stay. And who will go."

She rolled a thick cylinder of chalk between her palms while studying him. So uneasy did she make him feel that he stuffed the wide-brimmed slouch hat on his long hair and nodded slightly as he turned to go.

"Stone Eagle, you do not have to go."

"What do you mean?"

She seemed to be searching for an answer, then suddenly found her voice. "Have you finished learning?"

He retraced a few steps up the aisle between desks, filled with wonder and a little twinge of fear. Something inside him gnawed his soul with its fresh, foreign taste of danger. Curiosity. There was something about this woman who in every word, in every gesture, in the way she held his eyes and did not look away that told him this white woman knew her own mind.

"No, Miss—"

"Avolea Rankin."

"Miss Rankin, I can always learn."

"I am glad to hear you say that," she said, setting the chalk on the desk and rising as she smoothed out the skirt with her palms. "So many of the students will find it hard to adjust to a new teacher, I am sure. Would you help me?"

"I cannot sit with the children, Miss Rankin."

She smiled again. "I don't expect you to, Stone Eagle. You can help me when you can during the regular school day. But what I have in mind for you are lessons that will take you far beyond what the children are learning. Your studies will begin when the children have gone home each afternoon. I can tutor you alone . . . here. How does that sound?"

He was not sure he was comprehending. "You can teach me more—alone?"

"Yes! You understand, don't you—what this can mean to you?"

"You will help me better understand the white man and his ways?"

She came round the desk toward him in a flurry of movement, a light brightening her face. "Yes, Stone Eagle. This is everything I have always wanted. An Indian student prepared to grasp what I want to teach him—oh, the glory of knowing that I have helped you successfully place your feet on the white man's road."

Perhaps this was the answer, he considered quickly. The dying of the dreams and the drums and the buffalo hunts and the old ways of the warriors. For the past few years he had stood resolutely with a foot firmly planted in the old ways and one foot tentatively snared in the ways of the white man. Perhaps now was the time to decide, what with all the crazy talk of Wovoka and his revelations of destruction to the white man.

Something inside him burned for this chance. Perhaps it

was his father's blood that made him even consider it—that whiteness he kept buried deep within his private self.

For a moment he wavered, thinking back on the vision-quest and the wolf-helper who had whispered its prophecy in his ear. He thought back on the sun dance to celebrate his prayers and the thanks he gave for a healthy son. But if the Indian God were truly strong, he would not have allowed his children to starve. The buffalo would still roam free, and his children would not be held prisoner on these refuges of despair.

The white man held the power to make mighty weapons of war—rifles and bullets and even cannons that killed many with one shot. Perhaps the white man's God was indeed more powerful than the Everywhere Spirit he had grown up worshipping.

Yes, he thought, those who sought to dance back the buffalo were like the willow leaf against the hailstorm. They too would be swept away before the white man's ways and the white man's God.

His best chance for survival lay down the white man's road.

"It is good, what you have to teach me," he said, his eyes staring into hers, steadily.

She stepped up close at last, taking one of his hands in both of hers, clasping it gently within that smooth cage of perfumed softness.

He looked down at her heaving breast beneath the cameo brooch, then up to the strange look of danger and fascinated attraction that lit up those green eyes, smelling of the lilac water and the talc and the lye-soap fragrance of her, letting it fill his nostrils and make him heady with the surging he felt in his loins.

"Yes, Stone Eagle," she whispered. "When shall we start?"

CHAPTER 41

Summary, 1890

WHAT a godforsaken land he found this.
Every sundown saw the rising of the deadly clouds
from all the damp places dotting the surrounding prairie.

Fort Buford sat sweltering in the early summer twilight,
breathless.

Very little life stirred, man or beast. Last night, his first
here on the Missouri River, the heat did not retreat until
well after moonrise. He had broiled in his juices, stripped
nearly naked, stretched on his army cot, awaiting each
reluctant breeze wafting through the tiny window in the
monastic cell they assigned him for his stay here on the far
northern plains.

It wasn't the mosquitoes at night as much as it was the
biting deerflies in the day. Them and the tiny red buffalo
gnats that crept under a man's stockings or dug beneath the
waistband of his britches, hiding under the collar of his
tunic.

He had wrestled all night with the heat and the bugs and
even the dread of failure, wondering why the government

and its army just didn't give these high plains back to the Indians. If the Sioux and their friends the Cheyenne wanted this land so badly, give it back to them. What business would a white man have here? he wondered, as a hot breeze found its way in.

Captain Preston Tripp had come here on a long and circuitous trail that had led him north from the squalor of Romero's homestead on the Southern Cheyenne reservation in Indian Territory far to the south. The Mexican had convinced him there was indeed a Cheyenne woman who had spent a long winter with Custer. The one Romero called Monaseetah.

As far as any of her tribal people knew, the woman carried Yellow Hair's child in her belly at the time Custer sent the Cheyenne prisoners back to their reservation.

"Do you know of a child born to the woman?"

Romero had looked at Tripp strangely, smiling that crook-toothed grin of his. "You mean a second child?"

"Yes," he had answered impatiently. "You've confirmed the story of the first boy. What of this second son?"

"In the autumn of that year."

"Sixty-nine."

"You keep better track of the years than I, Captain. In autumn Monaseetah gave birth to Custer's son."

"Where are they now? Are they here in the territories, among these people?"

Romero had said, "You're not that lucky, Captain. Have some hunting to do still. Monaseetah took her boys north in the fourth summer for the young one."

"Eighteen seventy-four."

"Like I said, you count 'em, Captain. I'm just drinking your coffee and sugar."

"Go on."

Romero had, telling Tripp that the bands had lost track of her for the most part after that, until some of the Southern Cheyenne had once more come back home after visiting their northern cousins for a few seasons. After the many troubles with the army following the destruction of Yellow Hair's soldiers along the Goat River in Montana Territory.

Word was she and Custer's half-breed son were in the

great camp when the Seventh Cavalry came riding off the hills, down the Medicine Tail Coulee to its destruction.

"From there they fled with Dull Knife's camp."

Tripp remembered that name. "The bunch Mackenzie attacked that fall? Were they killed, either of them?"

"Story goes they escaped."

"Where?"

"North to Canada."

That had boggled him a moment. "With Sitting Bull's people? No, I can't believe that. The idea's preposterous. Cheyenne—"

"Believe what you want, Captain. Some from many bands went to the Grandmother's Land with Sitting Bull. Sioux, Cheyenne, even Nez Perce."

Preston Tripp had pushed his reluctant escorts north as soon as winter released its grip on the land. Great was the captain's disappointment to discover the trail gone cold when he arrived.

Among the Mounted Police stationed at the various posts or over at Fort Walsh, he did manage to locate a handful who had served in the Cypress Hills while Sitting Bull's band wintered north of the international boundary. Nothing more than a handful of men who had served under Major Walsh and had some recollection of their American wards.

Two of them even remembered a light-haired, fair-skinned boy who grew up to be a gangly youth during those four years of despair and slow starvation in the land of the Grandmother.

"Were I you," one of the policemen had suggested, "I'd ride down to Fort Buford."

"Why Buford?"

"That's where Sitting Bull's bunch went when they found they could not survive life north of the line."

"Could any of the bands who lived with Sitting Bull still be living around Buford?" Captain Tripp had asked of his half-breed guide assigned him out of Fort Keogh.

The guide scratched his chin. "Not likely. I heard the government scattered Sitting Bull's bunch a'purpose."

When he finally stood before the commander at Fort Buford, Tripp had a chance to ask, "Where were they all sent?"

"All were loaded up for the trip south from here. Every last one that come out of Canada was boarded on the steamboat, Captain Tripp."

"Bound for where?"

"Few of 'em got pulled off at Fort Yates."

"The Standing Rock Agency?"

"Right. Where Sitting Bull lives now."

"And the rest? Where did they go?"

"Army shipped 'em on down the river to Fort Randall to remain under guard for a couple years as I remember."

"Any records of those who were ordered south with Sitting Bull?"

"We could find out."

"But finding out will take time. That what you're telling me, Colonel?"

The post commander nodded. "Only the ones the army figured to be possible troublemakers went to Randall. My money on it—I'd figure the Cheyenne woman and boy you're looking for stayed at Yates . . . if—"

"If what?"

"If they haven't already disappeared from Standing Rock."

"Disappeared . . ." he groaned, sinking back in the ladder-back chair.

"They're Cheyenne, you see, Captain Tripp?" continued the post commander. "They won't stay on a Hunkpapa reservation, now will they? Your best bet might be to follow what trail you've got to Standing Rock."

"Thank you, Colonel," he said, standing and saluting to end his time with Buford's commander.

The colonel held out his hand. "I wish you luck. By the way, Captain—why are you carrying some gold-plated credentials just to look around for some squaw and her boy? Can you let out who you're sniffing around for?"

"Sorry, Colonel. I can't."

"Makes no matter to me. Just wondering why this squaw's so important."

"One day perhaps we can talk about it. The whole world will know. But for now, Colonel—I'm obligated to secrecy."

"Squaw's sake?"

He wagged his head, then swatted at a troublesome,

droning fly at his face. "No, sir. I'm no longer really looking for the Cheyenne woman. Now it's her half-breed son I aim to find—no matter what it takes."

Blind faith was the only thing left the Plains Indian.

He could not place his faith in the army, or the white preachers, much less the Indian Bureau with its system of agents and traders.

Only the previous winter the government had forbidden the Sioux from hunting the wild game on their own reservations. No longer able to supplement their meager rations with an occasional deer, the people grew as hungry as they had ever been those last two winters in the land of the Grandmother. The cattle given the bands to start breeding herds were butchered in desperation. No loss to the Sioux—most of the animals were too old to breed anyway.

Each bimonthly ration day the agents issued their low-grade cattle to their sullen wards. One steer was now expected to feed more than two dozen people until the next ration day. When they were available, green coffee beans and coarse brown sugar were handed out, but never the sweet, fine sugar they had learned to love nearly half a century before when the Sioux first encountered the white migrants taking their white-topped wagons west along the Holy Road toward the land of the setting sun. Occasionally the agents distributed weevil-laden flour to the bands. Handouts no settler would have accepted for his starving family.

But the Sioux had nothing else. Spring hailstorms came, followed by the curse of grasshopper plagues, then scorching winds and widespread drought saw to that.

Those summer winds had dried the grass for their stock along with wilting what few crops some of the Sioux had planted in blind hope last spring. Each day the sun had risen hotter than the day before. It became a summer that found white settlers giving up and fleeing the plains, returning east.

The Sioux had nowhere to run.

Scorching winds returned each morning to suck the lifeblood out of the withering plants along with the last dreams of the people. Sickness dogged the heels of the hunger and the heat. White man's magic, some believed— influenza, whooping cough, and measles swept through the reservations like unchallenged warriors. Young and old alike fell before the silent, deadly onslaught.

Despair spread like the cholera or smallpox of old, despair that infected all without immunity once the Indian Bureau cut the beef ration again at midsummer. For years now the people had obeyed the white agents who forbade the purchase of wives with ponies and other gifts, forbade a man in having more than one wife, forbade all rituals of the shamans and medicine men, forbade all feast days and all dances save the white man's favorite—the scalp dance.

Now in the Moon When the Geese Shed Their Feathers, August by the white man's tally, the Sioux had ceded back to the government over nine million additional acres of their shrinking reservations, newly opened to white homesteading. For more than a dozen years, the people had been ground beneath the heel of time, forged on the anvil of desperation, and ready once more for blind faith in their ancient beliefs.

On his way back to the Cheyenne River reservation, Miniconjou chief Kicking Bear brought the appealing news of hope to the Oglallas of Pine Ridge from the lips of the messiah himself.

"I do not know a word of the Paiute tongue," Kicking Bear told a growing crowd, "yet I understood what Wovoka told us. More wondrous still, many of the dancers went into a trance. When they returned from the land of the ghosts, some came back with buffalo pemmican clutched in their hands."

"But the buffalo are gone!" shouted some slow to believe.

Kicking Bear smiled. "The buffalo are returning. From the west. The messiah has told us this, and the dreams of the ghost dancers show us the truth of his words. The land will change, and the white man will be swept away forever."

"Show us this dance, Kicking Bear!"

"Yes! Show us the dance of ghosts!"

Assisted by Good Thunder, another who had made the pilgrimage to Wovoka's Paiute village, Kicking Bear went about preparing for the first Ghost Dance held by the Sioux of Pine Ridge.

The people journeyed up to the head of Cheyenne Creek, where White Cow Bull took Monaseetah to erect their beloved lodge among the camp circle of all the others come to join the religious festivities. No longer were these lodge skins made of buffalo hides. Nonetheless, the Oglalla joyfully raised their white canvas lodges toward the late-summer sky in praise of the old days. In the center of their circle stood the sacred tree, its trunk stripped of branches and painted red. Bright, colorful ribbons fluttered from the few spindly branches left at the top of the tall trunk.

After fasting for a day, the ceremonies began at sunrise. Kicking Bear directed men and women to separate sweat lodges where buffalo skulls sat staring eyeless at the entrances. When the dancers emerged naked from the purifying steam, they ran, plunging into the cool waters of nearby Cheyenne Creek. As they climbed onto the bank, each one had his or her face painted with the sacred red symbols: sun, moon, and morning star. An eagle feather was tied in the hair. When ready the dancers approached the tree, tying to it their small gifts of tobacco, earth paint, and bits of food as offerings to Wakan Tanka.

White Cow Bull and Monaseetah enthusiastically joined the dancers who sat in a grand circle facing the sacred red pole where the dance leaders stood. A young Sioux woman joined Kicking Bear and Good Thunder, holding an elk-horn bow and four arrows tipped with bone heads she dipped in bull's blood. These arrows she now shot into the four directions. Four young girls gathered the arrows and returned them to the center of the ring, where they were tied to the tree with prayers.

The archer now took the position she would keep throughout the rest of the dance, at the base of the tree, holding a sacred red pipe, the stem of which she pointed to the west. From the land of the setting sun would come the messiah and the ghosts of those who were soon to appear to the dancers.

Kicking Bear called to the faithful, giving directions. "Great Wakan Tanka, we are ready to begin the dance as you have commanded. Our hearts are good. We would do all that you ask. In return for our efforts, we beg that you give us back our old hunting grounds and our game. Oh, great one, carry these dancers who are in earnest to the Spirit Land far away and let them there see their dead relatives. Show them what good things you have prepared for all your people, then return them safely to us here once again. Hear us, we pray!"

Good Thunder passed around the circle a kettle filled with meat symbolizing the sacred buffalo the people had long eaten to nourish their bodies and their ancient way of life. When all had eaten a mouthful of the flesh, Kicking Bear called them forth.

"Stand, all of you! Stretch out your arms to the west, from whence the buffalo will come! And sing these words with me:

> "The Father says so, the Father says so.
> You shall see your grandfather,
> You shall see your grandfather.
> The Father says so, the Father says so.
> You shall see your kindred,
> You shall see your kindred.
> The Father says so, the Father says so."

Good Thunder and Kicking Bear showed them how to dance now in that shuffling step that moved the dance ring in the path of the sun, from right to left, slowly. Then, here and there, a few of the dancers began to bob up and down slightly, ever so slowly. After a time the movements mesmerized the dancers as their feet scuffed over the hard, sunburnt earth.

> "Someone comes to tell the news, to tell the news.
> There shall be a buffalo chase.
> There shall be a buffalo chase.
> Make arrows, make arrows."

For the better part of an hour as the sun rose full and mean out of the east, the dancers kept at their hypnotic ring until Kicking Bear suddenly yelled.

"Stop, my children! Weep for your sins!"

The warm air filled with their cries and wails. Some raised their arms to the cloudless sky above. Others fell to the dusty earth, pounding it with their fists, asking for forgiveness. Still more rushed to the center tree, laying small gifts at its base.

> "The people are coming home,
> The people are coming home.
> Says my father, says my father.
> The time comes, I shall see him,
> The time comes, I shall see him.
> Says my mother, says my mother."

White Cow Bull had nothing left to give. Yet he took Monaseetah by the hand so that they approached the tree together. There she followed him in removing her knife from her belt. Man and woman dragged the blades across a palm. Both watched their blood ooze up, then bead and trickle into a shiny flow. This they joyfully smeared on the sacred tree, while around them a few of the dancers began to faint in trances, others dancing fitfully as if possessed.

The Oglalla warrior who had gloried in the days gone to dust now brought his Cheyenne woman to the prayer tree where they could offer themselves and their blood—the last either had to offer in prayer.

Their blood was the last any of them had to give.

CHAPTER 42

Late August, 1890

BY late summer the chiefs who spoke out against the white man were basking in renewed glory among their people.

While the dances went on, gaining converts every week, the tired and the weak continued to die, the small ones continued to cry with empty bellies. And everywhere sickness still ruled.

Down on the Pine Ridge, Kicking Bear left the Oglallas with the songs and the dance before continuing home to teach the ceremony to his own Cheyenne River Miniconjou, already led by Hump and Big Foot, who constantly reminded their people of the goodness in the old life.

Despair reigned over on the Rosebud where the Brules had taken to crossing the Nebraska state line to reach Fort Niobrara. They begged food for their children from the army's garbage pits behind the mess hall or hung about the post's slaughter pen, hungering after the stinking offal that lay rotting beneath the hot sun.

Double Woman did what she felt best, feeding her son

first, giving the rest to Stone Eagle, then eating what was left. It was the way she had been taught from the time she was a young girl. But with each day her resentment grew, not only for the white man and his Indian agents and soldiers who kept them penned on the tiny reservation, but for her husband as well.

Something in Stone Eagle had changed in the past weeks as he kept himself away from their camp more and more, riding down to the agency at Pine Ridge more frequently, mumbling some excuse of seeing agent Gallagher, or telling her some white man had hired him for a bit of work here, some labor there. Each time he climbed atop his pony, he rode away from their White Clay Creek camp without a word, more sullen and distant than the last.

Each day it seemed he talked to her less, touched her less. Even turning from her many nights in the darkness of their cabin, where at sundown she returned after each day of dancing. At first she had tried not to think long on it, but she could no longer keep the wolf of doubt from her thoughts. Even with Stone Eagle seated across the fire from her, or back in the shade of their cabin porch, when he lay no more than the thickness of a blanket away from her in the darkness of those hot summer nights—Double Woman felt alone. More alone than she had ever been.

More and more she threw herself into the frequent dances to call back the ghosts, perhaps to attempt replacing what she felt slipping from her life each time Stone Eagle left. What had begun only as a ceremony held on Sundays, that great medicine day of the white man, now was reaching a feverish pitch among the Oglallas on Pine Ridge. They took to dancing any day of the week without pattern, beginning in the morning and lasting well past sundown, dancing and falling down in their trances to see the faces of those gone before and now returning with the buffalo to a renewed land free of the white man.

Those white settlers homesteading near the reservation feared they were watching the beginnings of a renewed war vigor among the Sioux and demanded agent Hugh Gallagher use his Pine Ridge police to stop the dancing by force. Under the agent's orders, twenty young Oglalla metal-breasts rode north to the White Clay Creek encampment on August 22. They were surrounded and told they were not welcome.

They returned to Gallagher on the morning of the twenty-third, with word from Torn Belly that another dance would be held the following day.

On that Sunday morning, the twenty-fourth, Agent Gallagher led his twenty policemen north eighteen miles to the dance camp. Along as well for the journey were interpreter Philip Wells and Special Agent E. B. Reynolds.

The police detail discovered a silent and empty village comprising a scattering of cabins and 150 lodges. At the center of camp, they found the Ghost Dance pole, from the top of which hung a sun-faded American flag.

"They found out we were coming," Wells said in a whisper.

"How?" Gallagher demanded, his voice filled with disappointment. "Did one of these police let it slip?"

"Gallagher!" shouted Agent Reynolds.

The group whirled as two Oglalla men emerged from their cover back in the trees, quickly dropped to their knees, and brought their repeaters to their shoulders.

"Don't just stand there—arrest those two bastards!" Gallagher ordered. "Tell them, Wells!"

Nervously the interpreter gave the order to the Oglalla police, then countermanded on his own initiative.

"You work for me, Wells," Gallagher growled. "But not for long, you keep—"

"I figure if you try to arrest those two," Wells interrupted, attempting to explain, "we'll be in for more trouble than you can imagine. Look around you at this camp."

"So?"

"Count the lodges and cabins. Those wickiups. There's better'n five hundred—maybe six hundred dancers here. Your policemen don't stand a snowball's chance in a sandstorm here."

"If these police won't live up to their badges, by God, I will do it myself." Gallagher nudged his horse toward the two riflemen.

Wells hammered his heels against his own horse, putting himself between the Oglallas and the headstrong agent. At that moment half-a-hundred more heads popped over the creek bank behind the first pair, each man brandishing a weapon.

Gallagher reined up, his horse shoved aside by the interpreter's mount. He sputtered, "What the devil do they mean, pointing these weapons at their agent—at me?"

Wells translated that question to the Oglalla warriors, then spotting the father of a good friend among the group, the interpreter added, "Father, I want you to obey me. Put down your gun, so we all may live."

The older man rose from the willow brush, laying his rifle down in the dust. "Yes, my son. I will do as you ask." He strode forward half the distance to Gallagher. Staring up into the sunlight, he demanded of the agent, "If you have come to talk to me in peace, why did you bring all these metal-breasts who carry so many guns?"

"I . . . I—"

"Stop your men, Gallagher!" Wells shouted at the sight of more Oglallas springing into sight, guns leveled.

"Draw your weapons!" Reynolds hollered boldly as Gallagher sputtered, his horse prancing in a nervous circle.

"No!" Wells shouted to the police, most of whom had already drawn their weapons at the sudden challenge from the willows and cottonwoods along the creek bank. For the space of three heartbeats, the lives of more than a hundred men hung in the balance. One finger twitch, one stupid mistake would have spelled disaster.

"Ho, my children!"

They all turned to find Young Man Afraid of His Horses shuffling onto the dusty dance circle.

"Who is this?" Reynolds asked.

"He is respected by his people," Gallagher whispered. "A fine Indian. A man who can be trusted."

"Let us hope he will see things our way," Reynolds muttered.

Wells explained to Man Afraid that the white men and the police had come only to witness the ceremony, not to stop it. With that assurance the warriors lowered their weapons, and the entire encampment emerged from hiding on all sides of the agent's police. Torn Belly himself ordered the ceremonies to continue when the haughty metal-breasts had moved from the dance circle. Gallagher and Reynolds joined interpreter Wells on the fringe of the dancers as the morning sun grew hot on their necks.

Among the twenty metal-breasts who had ridden in with agent Gallagher, Double Woman recognized Stone Eagle's brother. Pushing through the sullen, muttering crowd that surged around the police and continued with their prayers, she fought her way to his side.

"Sees Red," she whispered.

He looked over his shoulder, his eyes narrowing on her beneath the wide-brimmed black felt hat that had seen many a rainstorm. He appeared surprised. "Double Woman. My nephew is with you here?"

"Yes. You and the others must not stop this dance."

"You and these others must not dance."

She felt like crying of a sudden, here before the full-blood Cheyenne brother of the half-white man she loved—driven to tell Sees Red that their only hope was to dance back the buffalo and the spirits of the departed ones. To dance away the white men.

"I must," she sobbed. "I must dance for me and for my son."

"And for Stone Eagle?"

She could not hold his eyes for long. Something there told her he knew. Double Woman said, "I dance to drive away the white man. Perhaps the harder I dance—it will drive away the white man that is in him. Then the Indian that is in Stone Eagle will come back to me."

Sees Red looked at her, for a moment angry. Then his face softened. "You have every right to be selfish, Double Woman." He watched the dancers moving slowly, slowly around the pole as hot spurts of wind dallied with the bits of faded cloth and tiny bags of tobacco. "I pray that you can get him back."

"You do not believe I can get the Indian in him to return?"

Sees Red stared at her for a long time, his eyes smarting in the shade of his big hat. "Best you dance long and hard, my sister. Dance to bring the Cheyenne in Stone Eagle back. Dance to drive the white man from our land. But even more, you must now dance with all the strength left you—to drive the white woman from the heart of Stone Eagle."

* * *

A long summer rolled lazily into a reluctant autumn. The skies continued to remain clear for the most part, with little real cold and no hint of snow. It proved good for the worshipers at Pine Ridge, Cheyenne River, and Rosebud. Yet up at Standing Rock, Sitting Bull and the Hunkpapas were still uncertain in lending their wholehearted support to the spirit calling. To the south, however, the dancing camps continued to grow in size, and the new blood prayed in earnest for the coming of the new world under the messiah.

Word from the Miniconjou reservation trickled into the White Clay Creek camp from time to time. Most of that news Sees Red brought to Double Woman. He kept his ear open for any shred he could glean down at the agency.

"The great chief Hump has turned in his police uniform General Miles gave him years ago for a ghost shirt," Sees Red announced one evening as he ate supper with Stone Eagle's family.

"What of their dancing camps?" Double Woman asked.

"Both Hump and Big Foot have moved their bands away from the agency."

"Where have they gone?" She glanced at Stone Eagle's impassive face. He seemed not to care for a thing nowadays.

"Up the Cheyenne River, more than eighty miles from the fort and agent. Word has it their lodges are pitched where they can watch the white homesteaders who move onto the land right across the river."

"Land that once was ours, and given back to the white man," she added.

"You act like the white man stole it," said Stone Eagle, finally speaking.

Shocked, she found it hard to tear her eyes from his sullen, angry face.

Sees Red spoke up to fill the gnawing silence. "I hear that Big Foot's band grows and grows every day. They are dancing night and day since they no longer have to worry about the agent sending his police after them!"

She tried to laugh, but it came out forced and fell like a

weak thing to the ground. Then silence wrapped them once more as the cold autumn darkness swallowed the land.

By the middle of the Moon of Deer Rutting, November to a white man's reckoning, the Oglallas and Brules were told by Short Bull to gather near the boundary of their agencies.

The Brule apostle had himself journeyed to the land of the Paiute. Kicking Bear and Good Thunder gathered with the other faithful as Short Bull began haranguing the crowd.

"My friends and relations, I will soon start this thing in running order. I have told you that this would come to pass in two seasons, but since the whites are interfering so much, I will advance the time from what my father above told me to do, so the time will be shorter. Therefore, you must not be afraid of anything.

"Now, there will be a tree sprout up, and there all the members of our religion and the tribe must gather together. That will be the place where we will see our dead relations. But before this time, we must dance the balance of this moon, at the end of which time the earth will shiver very hard. Whenever this thing occurs, I will start the wind to blow.

"We are the ones who will then see our fathers, mothers, and everybody. We, the tribe of Indians, are the ones who are living a sacred life. God, our Father Himself, has told and commanded and shown me to do these things.

"Remember always, the Indian must not permit the white man to interfere with our last great dance. There may be soldiers around you, but pay no attention to them, continue to dance. If the soldiers surround you four deep, three of you on whom I have put holy shirts will sing a song which I have taught you, then some of the soldiers will drop dead, then the rest will start to run, but their horses will sink into the earth; the riders will jump from their horses, but they will sink into the earth also; then you can do as you desire with them.

"Now you must know this, that all the soldiers and that race will be dead; there will be only five thousand left living on the earth. My friends and relations, this is straight and true.

"Now, we must gather at Pass Creek, where the tree is sprouting. There we will go among our dead relations. You must not take any earthly things with you. Then the men must take off all their clothing and the women must do the same. No one shall be ashamed of exposing their persons. My father above has told us to do this, and we must do as he says. You must not be afraid of anything. The guns are the only things we are afraid of, but they belong to our father in heaven. He will see that they do no harm. Whatever the white men may tell you, do not listen to them, my relations. This is all."

Oglallas and Brules now flocked to the Pass Creek camp of Short Bull, yet a few remained behind on White Clay Creek, where Double Woman remained with her son. Stone Eagle refused to join in the dancing. Instead he would sneer at every mention of the prayers and ceremony, laughing at the very idea that the messiah was about to return for the Indian only when the white man had already proved the Indian religion inferior.

"We have lost too many times already," he told her late one night in their cold cabin as the frost etched a crystal pattern on the single window near their bed. "I do not want to lose again, Double Woman."

She heard him roll over, then listened as Stone Eagle's breath became regular while he drifted off. That night, like many nights gone before, Double Woman did not sleep. Again she tasted the bitter gall that mocked her, convinced she had lost him.

Four days later the new agent, Royer, issued beef at the Pine Ridge. A Republican appointee, Daniel F. Royer had recently replaced Gallagher, the Democratic party's agent on the Oglalla reserve. Like so many others, he was a man who came to his job ignorant of the needs of his wards. Upon arrival he had even joked with army officers that he was seeing his first Indians.

What made that day worthy of memory was the veteran warrior, Changing Hawk, who chided the crowd as the bony steers and lean cows lumbered out of the corral to be chased by young and old warriors. The cattle did not run like buffalo, so the chase did not take long.

Arrows brought the animals down. Women and children were on each carcass before the last breath was taken, butchering, reveling in the still-warm flesh as in days gone long ago. Before noon the last animal of that two-week ration had been eaten—every bit of gut, fleece, and sinew. As the Oglallas sat there within sight of Royer's office, cracking open the bones to suck out the marrow, Changing Hawk intensified his Ghost Dance talk.

"Children! My friends! Are you going to wait until the white man is ready to feed you again?"

"What do you say, Changing Hawk?" asked an old woman, flecks of the greasy marrow shiny on her lips.

"There are many fine and fat cattle the white man raises for himself, while he gives us these skinny poor creatures to feed our children."

"Where are these fat cattle?"

"On the white man's homesteads and ranches, on what used to be our land!" shouted Changing Hawk, pointing suddenly into the four directions. "Everywhere you look, you will find food!"

Philip Wells had been watching and listening from the fringe until he grew alarmed and went to Royer. The agent burst from his office, dashing across the compound and into the Oglallas with a handful of his Oglalla police.

"Arrest that man!"

"The white agent will die soon anyway!" Changing Hawk shouted, turning to meet the challenge. "Better sooner—so let me kill him now!"

Sees Red and the rest of his police detail pulled their pistols with a clattering of hammers. Several of the Oglalla warriors scrambled for their rifles as women and children scurried for the timber.

"Sees Red!" Changing Hawk shrieked, wheeling on the line of policemen. He held open his wool vest brazenly. "See my breast. I do not wear that chunk of metal on it. Shoot if you must, Sees Red! Kill me today—for I will rise when all red men sweep the white man from this land. Kill me!"

"No! There will be no killing today," declared a new voice.

Double Woman saw chief American Horse hurry into the middle ground between the two groups.

"I am going to arrest this man for provoking these people!" Royer shouted.

"No, it is better that he go with his people. If you attempt to arrest this one man—the blood of many will darken this ground," American Horse said. "Perhaps your own, white man."

While Royer conferred with Wells, Double Woman gazed down at the stranger who sat beside her. Once her husband, now fully a man she no longer knew.

"Are you prepared to die for what you believe—like the old ones, Stone Eagle?"

He looked at her, his face impassive, as if not understanding.

"Is what you want something different from what the rest of us want, my husband?"

"I don't know," he answered, staring at the ground.

"What I want is a husband who cares for me and our son. A man who cares as much as that for his people. I have realized how your white blood poisons you more every day, Stone Eagle. It is choking the life out of you, and I cannot bear to watch it any longer."

He looked at her with glazed eyes. "My white blood—it gives me hope, Double Woman."

"Your white blood leads you astray, Stone Eagle. Go! I grow tired of this pain. Go to that white whore of yours!" She felt herself trembling inside as she swept her son into her arms, a few of the older women gathering around her protectively when Stone Eagle started to inch toward his wife.

He stopped where he stood, his hands moving aimlessly. "She . . . the woman—"

"Go back to your white whore. You are free. I do not want you anymore, Stone Eagle. I want a man of the people. Not a white man who lies and cheats and steals the very soul from me. You are free to go."

"Where are you going?" he asked, his words sounding numb.

"I am going back to my people now. Back to the Cheyenne River, where I can forget you."

She whirled, tears streaming, a stifled cry strangling her as she hurried into the crowd, leaving Stone Eagle behind.

CHAPTER 43

November, 1890

"BARKEEP!"

He was on the small size, compared to the well-fed reporters, many of whom tended to be rather portly. Yet because of his age or demeanor, Harley Fagen commanded his due of attention standing at the counter of James Asay's trading post.

To Pine Ridge had flocked the curious and the courageous. Soldiers and government officials of one color or another, along with a generous mix of half-breed scouts like Nick Janis and Sam Dion and Joseph Bisonette. And the newspapermen. James A. Finley's small hotel accommodated them all, sometimes six to a room, floor space only at a nickel a night. Other facilities would cost a man more, but at least a nickel bought him a piece of hardwood floor in a room filled with snoring, whiskey-fragrant bodies.

"Rye," he ordered at the counter, awaiting his drink.

Fagen rubbed his red nose before picking up his glass. Shoving his way past the milling throng, the detective plopped down in his chair at a corner table with his four new companions—reporters from Nebraska papers.

"What's he charge you for the rye?" asked Charles W. Allen of the Chadron *Democrat*.

"Too damned much," Fagen grumbled, sipping gingerly at the lip of his tiny glass, attempting to make it last longer by trying to taste it this time around, rather than throwing it back as he had been doing nonstop since midmorning. All five of them were well on their way to another rib-pounding night of it.

"Here's to expensive red-eye!" toasted Thomas Henry Tibbles, reporter for the Omaha *World Herald*.

There hadn't been much else for them to do for the past week or so. Wait it out here in the trading post or back at the hotel, expectant of any word squeezed out of army sources or pried loose from the interpreters and scouts who could be bribed with a glass of whiskey or a double eagle in the palm. Something, anything at all to feed the folks back east who hungered to learn all they could of this new "Indian war." Trouble was, there was no war when the newsmen began to thunder into the agency. Nonetheless, the eastern editors and their huge printing presses needed grist—so the reporters obediently supplied the copy.

Massacres of helpless homesteaders, battles between stalwart soldiers and screeching warriors, atrocities committed by the army against the peaceful villages spread across all four reservations in the Dakotas—the stories all went back home to enthrall and captivate the eastern reader.

Barely five days ago Fagen had arrived from Kansas, on the same train the army had contracted to bring the entire Seventh Cavalry from its home post, Fort Riley. Colonel James W. Forsyth, brother to George A. "Sandy" Forsyth, hero of Beecher Island some twenty-two years before, had come to command the operation. The regiment bivouacked on agency grounds, tenting outdoors in the mild autumn weather, and awaited further orders. Captain Allyn Capron with his Light Battery E from the First Artillery had been assigned to Colonel Forsyth's forces.

"Not a man here ain't stoop-shouldered with all the iron he's carrying," muttered Will Cressey, working for the Omaha *Daily Bee*. He glared at another trio of reporters shoving through the trading-post door, gun belts strapped over their hips and rifles in their hands.

Will Kelley, sent here by the *Nebraska State Journal* out of Lincoln, eyed the bulge under the Chicago detective's coat suspiciously. "You can't tell me you aren't packing a little iron yourself, Fagen."

Harley pulled back the flap of his duster to reveal two pistols, one in a holster, the other hidden for the most part in a vest pocket. "I'm not fool enough to go around showing it off like them other gun-cocks. But then, I didn't get to be as old as I am by being stupid neither."

The five all had a laugh and went back to their whiskey. Something to do, somebody to gossip about, anything at all until dinner hour rolled around and they could grumble about what innkeeper Finley would be serving for supper.

A few days back the Brule warrior called Two Strike had threatened to make General John R. Brooke the first casualty of the coming war, by stabbing the commander of the whole of the Pine Ridge operation in the heart with his scalping knife. But Two Strike had not dared come in to the agency. Instead he had halted his growing village of dancers at Wounded Knee Creek, some eighteen miles from Pine Ridge. The drama of that imagined confrontation between warriors and soldiers had commanded a lot of ink and newsprint for a time, until new reports leaked out that two of the most steadfastly dangerous chiefs had come in to give themselves up to Brooke. Little Wound and Big Road told the army their bands were on the way to make peace with the soldiers.

A commotion at the door drew Fagen's attention. The crowd of newspapermen surged, thronging toward the new-comers.

"Who's that?" asked the detective, watching two men part the crowd as the door slammed behind them.

"Tall one's named Remington," answered Cressey. "He's the artist-reporter for *Harper's*."

"No," Fagen growled. "The other one." He eyed the cut of the frontiersman who strode to the bar, where he laid a Henry repeater among the glasses and bottles.

"Name's Grouard. Frank Grouard. Half-breed," Kelley replied, leaning away from the table to attempt catching some of the talk at the bar.

"Hear he spent some of his boyhood with Sitting Bull himself," added Charles Allen.

Then, as Grouard wiped the drops of whiskey from his
lips and turned to eye the room, the trading-post patrons
fell respectfully silent.

"Boys, Mr. Grouard here's got some news for you!"
shouted James Asay from behind his bar. "Seems Two
Strike is on the march!"

When the hooting and the gun rattling quieted down,
Grouard began. "Army just got word that Two Strike is
marching down Wounded Knee Creek."

"He's running from a fight, boys!"

Grouard waited for the laughter to die. "Taking his band
north. On the way he's been thieving the friendlies blind.
Burning the cabins of those what come into the agency for
protection already. Driving off any cattle they got left."

"Where's he headed—you know?"

Grouard said, "My guess is he's headed for the badlands
with his bunch."

"How many he got with him?"

"Hard to figure that too. But we do know Short Bull's
followers from White Clay Creek have joined up with Two
Strike now after they run off the agency herd down at the
mouth of Willow Creek."

"Give us a guess, Grouard. How many warriors that
make?"

"Over five hundred lodges, easy."

"That can make fifteen hundred warriors!"

Grouard wheeled on the reporter as the room filled with
stomps, whistles, and hoots. "You said it, boys. Not me."

Fagen sipped at his rye as the action quieted down, men
slapping Grouard on the back, buying him another round.
The excitement over for the moment, many of the reporters
scribbled key phrases in their notebooks, which they
stuffed securely into pockets before once again picking up
their half-filled glasses.

"Believe I'm going to stay with the Seventh from here on
out," remarked the detective, licking his lip.

"Figure that's where the action is gonna be?" asked
Cressey.

He nodded. "This is Custer's Seventh, goddammit.
Don't you ever forget that. You may look out there at that
huge tent camp and see nothing but peach-faced boys,

but—by God—there's officers in that regiment still remember the bloodthirsty war cries of the Sioux they held off for three days beside the bloody waters of the Little Bighorn River." He threw back the rest of his rye and pushed away from the table. "Best you remember them same warriors running amuck out there right now are the same that wiped out the good half of the Seventh Cavalry."

With it said, Harley Fagen shoved past the mob at the bar, out the door, and into the crisp air of twilight.

He had to admit that he liked having the company, but it ran afoul of him after a while. Too many men, quarters too cramped. He still found himself enjoying the company of soldiers better. Especially now that he had run across the Seventh Cavalry after all these years. Thirteen of them, off and on—years spent scratching for clues and hints and rumors. From Fort Abraham Lincoln to Fort Hays. From Indian Territory to the posts in western Kansas and northern Montana. Then, finally, he had reeled in a hopeful bit of news from Saskatchewan. News hopeful enough that the widow Custer had freed up another sizable chunk of money for the red-nosed detective.

A light-haired, light-eyed youth had lived with his Cheyenne mother among Sitting Bull's people for a time in the Cypress Hills.

He followed the faint trail of it to Fort Buford, learning where The Bull's people had gone from there. From Fort Randall and Fort Yates, he learned that the story claimed the light-haired youth had an Oglalla father.

"Where would a man find this Oglalla family?" he had asked at Standing Rock Agency.

"Down at Pine Ridge, of course."

As odd as things turned out, he had found himself a passenger on a paddle wheel heading south down the Missouri. Then he purchased a one-way ticket west across Kansas. At first he was aggravated to find that the K-P he was riding would be stopped at a siding near Hays City for the better part of a day. But while Harley Fagen consoled himself eating beef pie and hot coffee at a table pulled up to the station canteen's window, he was able to watch the Seventh Cavalry load its men and mounts and matériel onto that same train bound west—for Pine Ridge.

Didn't take long for him to make friends either, becoming the center of attention for some of the new recruits heading into what might be their first Indian fight.

"You know General Custer had himself a half-breed son, don't you, boys?"

He loved telling anyone and everyone about that, having the bunch of them soldiers gathered round him on the siding or in the box cars, all shut-mouthed and wide-eyed as he let it out, slowly.

"Cheyenne she were—the squaw Custer poked and got with child. He'd be . . . hell, that bastard son of General Custer would be some twenty years old this fall. Almost old as some of you fellas."

Walking back to Finley's this night, Fagen angled down the agency road, drawing deep the fragrance of the cold, crisp air, heavy with wood smoke from a hundred fires. For the evening he decided he would amble on over to the bivouac and look up some of the soldiers who hung on every one of his stories of searching for Custer's half-breed bastard son. Especially when those stories were told over a cup of coffee laced with Fagen's whiskey and were told by the detective who was going to be the one and only man to find that bastard half-breed son of no less than General George Armstrong Custer himself.

And tomorrow. Yes, tomorrow he had decided he would look up another of the ministers on this reservation filled with churches all trying to outdo each other with their savage flocks. See what he could dig up from the Bible thumpers. Never any shortage of excitement here on the Lakota stomping ground.

Following that he just might look up that schoolteacher he was told about earlier in the day. The young, pretty one.

Fagen figured there were two kinds of people who really knew where a man might find a certain light-haired half-breed. Preachers and . . . of course, teachers.

Avolea Rankin was her name.

Captain Preston Tripp stepped off the short porch in front of the telegraph office at Fort Bennett, stuffing General Sheridan's reply in his tunic.

He had Sheridan's orders to beef up his personal escort.

General Nelson A. Miles had been keeping Sheridan informed of all the latest developments, from Standing Rock down to Pine Ridge. Reports had it that Sitting Bull was sending word on the moccasin telegraph to bands as far north as Canada itself, coaxing them to journey to Bear Butte in their sacred Paha Sapa, the Black Hills. There they would make their sacred stand.

Friendlies were abandoning their homes. Some others who had been dancing were coming in to the agencies. White settlers, missionaries, and teachers leaving the outlying areas and seeking the protection of the army.

The country was afire, Sheridan wired. Increase your escort to twenty well-armed troopers.

Tripp strode across the parade, heading for the lamp-lit windows of the post commander's office, intent on securing his men now, so that he could head out before first light in the morning.

The captain had coded his message to Sheridan, telling him the time was running short. He had tracked the rumors and stories up and down the central and northern plains. Then finally found an interpreter he could trust and an old Miniconjou who would talk without demanding whiskey in return. The wrinkled warrior stated he had spent some time in Canada with Sitting Bull. That his youngest grandson had been childhood friends with a light-haired, light-eyed, half-breed Cheyenne boy in the land of the Grandmother.

But the icing of it all had come later, as the old Miniconjou laid out his story, Indian fashion, slowly, deliberately. Wandering here, then there, but always moving toward something. Looking back now, Tripp would not have imagined just what it was the old man was getting to, not for the life of him. But when the warrior told the white man about it, the story landed on Tripp's ears like a twelve-pound mountain howitzer shell plopping into his lap.

The cloudless December sky overhead held an untold treasure of winter diamonds as he passed the flagpole where a group of soldiers sat smoking after evening mess. Word on every lip was the coming war. Every paper from back east was devoured for news of what was going on right here. Some headlines urged kindness and philanthropy to put out the growing fire of Indian troubles. Other headlines screamed for vengeance, claiming only the blood of a thousand Sioux would stamp out the war fever on the reservations, once and for all.

Not much to celebrate these days in the two Dakotas. North and South had just been admitted to the union as the fortieth and forty-first, fully sovereign states of the grand republic. Yet even that big news was swiftly relegated to the back pages as reports came in rumoring of Sioux breakouts and the plundering of white homesteads. Word came that Big Foot's band of Miniconjous had taken to wearing bullet bandoliers across their Ghost Dance shirts up on the Cheyenne River. And Hump was thinking of moving from Cherry Creek to join up with Big Foot's dancers.

But Miles himself had seen to that contingency. The general sent a special emissary to his old friend, Hump. The two warriors went back many years, to the days when soldier-chief Miles enlisted Hump to scout for him in chasing the Nez Perce into the Bear Paws and when Hump led them to Dull Knife's village. This time Miles asked the old chief to remember their old days together—asked Hump to give up the Ghost Dance and settle his young warriors.

Hump never did again put on his police badge. But he did take off his ghost shirt and take his people back to the agency.

Which left Big Foot to stand alone among the Miniconjou leaders. With the rumors of armies closing in on his band from all directions, the chief took his disheartened people back to their cabins near the mouth of Deep Creek, below the forks of the Cheyenne River.

Perhaps that would show Lieutenant Colonel Edwin V. Sumner, who had been sent to that part of the country to keep an eye on Big Foot's band, that the Miniconjous really wanted no part of the coming war that seemed sure to ignite down on the Pine Ridge. At least that's what Captain Tripp could make of it as he climbed the steps and opened the post commander's door.

"You're General Sheridan's man, aren't you?"

"Yes, sir," Tripp answered General Thomas H. Ruger's question.

"What is it I can do for you, Captain?"

"I need some men."

"How many?"

"The general suggested I request twenty."

Ruger considered that, staring into the sheet-iron stove at his feet. "If Phil Sheridan says you're to have 'em—you'll have 'em." He looked at the young officer standing expectantly at the corner of the desk. "Where are you going with these men of mine, and when?"

"Tomorrow morning, General. I've got to get to Pine Ridge as fast as your mounts will carry us."

CHAPTER 44

Early December, 1890
Moon of Trees Popping

Stone Eagle reveled in the whiteness of her, the smell of her, the softness of her.

Whereas he had found himself growing weary of making love to Double Woman more and more ever since last winter, he had been delighted to discover that he became like a heated stallion with a receptive mare when it came to Avolea Rankin. For months it seemed his wife had put him off whenever she could, complaining of her fatigue with her chores of raising their son, tending the stock, and keeping up with all the rest of the things to do around the cabin. The schoolteacher, on the other hand, had nothing to do, day or night now. No classes since the Oglalla parents had refused their children to go to school when the trouble started weeks ago.

He rubbed his palm across the rumpled sheets she washed and pressed every day. Four sets of them Avolea had brought with her to the Pine Ridge reservation. She changed them every morning after they had their breakfast

and dressed for the day. The clean sheets were something
he looked forward to every evening when he rode up to the
timber behind the schoolhouse, waiting for dark among the
trees where he unsaddled and hobbled his horse, then kept
to the shadows as he hurried to her door. The white sheets
seemed to symbolize something taboo and forbidden. Not
that making love to a white woman wasn't frowned upon,
especially now with all the trouble the hotbloods had stirred
up.

She washed them every day. Stone Eagle wondered if
she would wear out the sheets with so much washing, wear
them out before she tired of him.

Avolea snuggled more against him, kicking a white leg
out of the blankets and comforter.

He marveled at the color of her, so pale against his own
skin, and he wasn't dark as most, even for a half-breed.

Smelling deep of her fragrance, he watched the murky
light from the oil-lamp chimney dance against the far wall,
pulsating gently against some old, dated prints surrounded
by crude frames.

"You're not tired again?" she asked, her voice heavy with
sleep.

"No, I cannot put my mind at ease."

"I don't understand it, Stone Eagle. You take every bit of
strength from me. Yet our coupling only energizes you."

"Perhaps it is the white man in me that keeps me from
sleeping."

"No." She giggled against the taut muscles across his
chest. "I believe it is the Cheyenne warrior in you that
keeps us both from sleeping."

He rolled her on her side and stroked her small breast.
Against the alabaster skin, the rose of her nipple stood out
in the dim light. He bent to kiss it.

"You want me again?" she asked, trembling at the touch
of his lips on her flesh.

"No, not yet."

For a long time she lay against him, running her fingers
across his chest, before she spoke. "What is it you really
want from me, Stone Eagle?"

"I have wondered what you want from me, Avolea. You
say you do not want a husband."

"No, not just yet."

"And he won't be Indian, will he?"

She pushed up on her elbows, staring full into his eyes. "No, you and I will never marry. But we will share each other, for what time we have together."

"How long will that be?"

"As long as we want it."

"How long, Avolea?"

She stared at the rumpled sheets, smoothing them with one hand. "Perhaps we are clinging together because of the uncertainty of the things going on around us now. You are real to me, whereas so much that has happened is not. I do not want to lose you yet. I need you so desperately."

She sought his mouth and pressed hers firmly against him. He sensed her fingertips gently moving down his chest, across his belly until her hand surrounded him firmly, kneading him into readiness. Stone Eagle rolled her off and mounted her, satisfied with her gasp of surprise as he drove himself within her heated readiness.

"It will be morning soon," she whispered to awaken him hours later.

His eyes slowly fluttered open. He was struck by the darkness to the room, the gray light seeping in around the window shades she pulled down each evening. The lamp had gone out long ago. And the damp smell of their lovemaking was heavy on the ironed sheets.

"I will go now."

"Not yet," she whispered, pressing his shoulders down into the mass of goose-down pillows. "Please. Talk to me. Tell me you would buy me if you could."

"Buy you?"

"Yes. Tell me you would buy me before all the others—bringing expensive presents to my father's door: fast ponies and thick blankets and your hands filled with shiny beads."

"Yes, I would buy you before all—"

"And tell me you would take me to your lodge and have your will with me, Stone Eagle."

"Yes, Avolea. I would have my way with you. You would be my wife."

"Then why did your Indian wife leave you, if you could have your way with her?"

He turned from her, facing the window, wondering again himself why he had let Double Woman go.

"Perhaps it was for the better that she went. She called you my whore."

She gasped quietly. "Am I your whore?"

He refused to look at her. "You are not my whore. A whore is paid for—"

"What about the old warriors who used to give their woman to a white man for a night. Were those women whores?"

"No."

"But the men were paid for those women—in trade goods, weren't they?"

"Yes, but that was something—"

"And what about your mother, Stone Eagle? Was she a whore for sleeping with your father—because he was a white man and they were not married?"

He rolled toward her suddenly, pinning her shoulders to the bed, eyes glowering. "They were married, Avolea."

"Like you and me, huh?"

He studied her face for a long time. Finally he read something in her eyes as they softened. He did not like the pity there either. "Yes. Just like you and me. Married in a bed like this."

"Then you have found me out, Stone Eagle. We are married like all pagans. Your people worship many gods, so you can never be truly Christian."

He released her and twisted up, settling to the side of the bed. "Are you Christian, Avolea? Is this your mission—to drive me crazy with desire for you, bed me, then go off when you are done with me?"

"I am not Christian, Stone Eagle. I was when I came here. But no longer. Once I met you . . . oh, damn! I don't know what I am anymore."

He pulled her into his arms, cradling her across his lap. "It is good," he said finally, smoothing her red-tinted hair. "You Christians fight among yourselves. There are so many different churches."

"You have many bands—yet you all call yourselves Sioux," she tried to explain.

"But we all have one religion, Avolea. We . . . ," and

he realized he had used that plural word. He was angry with himself, confused and angry with the growing despair. "What's one more god to us, schoolteacher? We have many now—one more means little to our lives."

He felt the hot tears trickle across his leg as she sobbed quietly.

"We must by example lift up the child of savage parentage from the degrading atmosphere of superstition and barbarism that surrounds him from birth," she murmured, repeating the doctrine drummed into her before coming west to teach on the agency.

"Am I a child of savage parentage?"

"Yes, Stone Eagle."

"Then I should no longer try to become more white, Avolea."

She clutched at him fiercely, so much that it frightened him. "You must, yes! As much as I must tell you of the strange little man who came here."

"A white man?"

"Yes. Polite enough at first, he asked me all sorts of strange questions. Things about a fair-haired, fair-eyed young man who would likely be twenty years old."

He pulled her away from him. "Why? What did you tell him?"

She shook her head, frightened. "I told him nothing. Nothing."

"Why was he looking for this man?"

"Isn't he looking for you, Stone Eagle?"

"I must go." He pulled away and grabbed for his wool britches and long handles.

"You tell me why, Stone Eagle—tell me why he would be looking for you. What have you done?"

He refused to admit it. "It doesn't have to be me."

"Why, Stone Eagle?"

As he yanked on his boots, he scowled. "My mother told me about them coming. Someday, she warned me. Someday they would come looking for me. She warned me—that if I had much to do with the white man, it would be the white man who would betray me."

Stone Eagle jerked on his mackinaw coat, pulling his hat over his long hair. "That's a joke on me, Avolea. My mother had it figured that a white man would betray me. That's why she told me to stay among the Indian people. But I had no way of knowing it would be a white woman who would betray me in the end."

She lunged at him as he strode to her door. "I did not tell him a thing! Nothing, Stone Eagle. I would never betray you—believe me!" Avolea clawed at him, desperate to have his arms around her. "Hold me! Hold me! Tell me you'll come back tonight!"

His arms eventually snaked about her, pulling her against him fiercely. He felt trapped. Knowing she likely would be the death of him. Certain that through her the white man would learn about his existence. The death of him for sure.

"Yes," he whispered into her fragrant auburn hair. "I'll be back at sundown."

Double Woman felt sorry for Big Foot. At the same time she felt something else she was unable to sort out, so she simply tried to forget it after all these days since coming north to the Cheyenne River where her Miniconjou people were dancing back the ghosts.

He had been like an uncle to her, the old chief Big Foot. And now he was trapped between two armies. The soldiers of Lieutenant Colonel Edwin V. Sumner and the chief's own young hotbloods he was struggling to control. From Sumner's "camp of observation," soldiers had kept an eye on the Miniconjous since the previous spring.

When trouble began heating up down south, Hump abandoned the Ghost Dance and went back to the army as a scout. And Big Foot took his band home to their cabins. So much did he yearn for the old life that he had fiercely hoped the Ghost Dance would bring about its return. But his hopes withered and died like the crops they had tried planting last spring before the drought and drying winds. He all but abandoned the ceremony himself but allowed the faithful to continue their prayers and trances and marathon dancing under the leadership of the zealot Yellow Bird, who kept the Miniconjous shuffling around the sacred red pole.

Indeed, the medicine man did more than keep them

dancing. Yellow Bird kept things stirred up. Time and again Big Foot's warriors cried out for vengeance against the white men who had stolen their land just across the river from their dance camp. Yet the old chief held them in check, telling Sumner that the Miniconjous had only peaceful intentions. It was not through his past prowess as a warrior that Big Foot held power among his people. Instead it was his political savvy, his ability to bring disparate parties together in compromise.

About the time Double Woman and her son arrived at the Cheyenne River camp, Oglalla runners brought Big Foot a message from the Pine Ridge chiefs offering him one hundred ponies if he would come to their agency and restore tranquillity among the troubled bands. After a long council with his advisers, Big Foot announced to his people he would go to Pine Ridge to help the Oglallas. But first they would wait for ration day before starting their long journey. The Miniconjous began their trip downriver toward the agency.

On the evening of the seventeenth day of December, the Moon of Trees Popping, Big Foot led his people into a camp across the Cheyenne River from Cavanaugh's store, barely twenty miles above the mouth of Cherry Creek. That night an old Miniconjou brought news from Fort Bennett that soldiers were marching their way, headed upriver.

Yet it was the arrival of two visitors the next morning that frightened Double Woman most.

Two Hunkpapas limped into camp, much the worse for their trek on foot south from the Standing Rock reservation. One still carried a bullet in his leg.

"Sitting Bull is dead!" the crier shouted as the Hunkpapas were helped into the camp circle.

Miniconjous swarmed over the pair, offering food and water, clean bandages and blankets, but demanding information in return.

"Killed by the agent's police?"

"Sitting Bull? Killed by the Sioux?"

It was unthinkable, that a detail of metal-breasts would have rousted the ancient chief from his bed in the middle of the night, intent on taking him back to the agency and Fort

Yates. Many of The Bull's people had gathered in the yard to prevent the police leaving. Angry words flared between the Hunkpapa police and the Hunkpapa warriors who had remained beside Sitting Bull throughout the roaming years on the high plains, the refuge years in Canada, and now the quiet years on the reservation.

"They pushed Sitting Bull forward . . . he struggled to hold onto his blanket . . . it was cold," one of the Hunkpapa refugees said, speaking around some jerked beef.

"I do not know how it happened next," the other refugee added. "One of our friends shouted to the police—saying he would not let them take the chief."

"Then a shot was fired."

"One of the police shot Sitting Bull in the back."

"Did the bullet kill him?"

"No," the refugee answered. "But before he had crumpled to the ground, another bullet was fired into his head."

"A police bullet?"

"Yes, from behind."

"*Aiyeee!* Sitting Bull has been killed by his own people!"

The wails of many pierced the cold air of the Cheyenne River country while Double Woman cradled her young son in her arms, rocking back and forth on the frozen ground.

What had become of her people? she cried out in her heart. That they should turn guns on one another. Surely the white man has won!

Not only does the white blood in her husband make him crazy, but the white man has divided her people.

"We are surely done—the white man has won!"

CHAPTER 45

December, 1890

"Is Brooke gonna just sit here on his ass, or is he going after them red bastards?" Harley Fagen asked the knot of soldiers who sat drinking coffee and brandy with the Chicago detective.

"Right now he's not letting anyone know what he's going to do," replied one of the older noncoms. "Especially them reporters who—"

"It were up to me, I'd march up there to them badlands and put the fight to 'em," Fagen interrupted. "Yank Two Strike and Kicking Bear out of there and string 'em up."

"Yeah, make an example of 'em for sure!" cheered a soldier.

Already the strain was beginning to show among the troops of the Seventh Cavalry at Pine Ridge. It was general knowledge that the two chiefs had joined up to make a stand on a flat tableland that vaulted itself between the Cheyenne and White rivers for several hundred feet. The warriors knew this plateau well. There were few entrances among its steep sides. Up at the far northeastern edge, near a narrow strip of land some three miles long, is where the bands chose to make their stand. The Indians called this smaller plateau "The Stronghold." Brooke's scouts and Oglalla police had told the general he would have a hard time launching an attack against the hold-outs. They had their own scouts out in the badlands, and they had gone back to their dancing.

Now more than ever it was time for them to dance in the new world.

"Boys, I'd love to be in your shoes about now," Fagen said. "To have me a crack at them warriors."

Some of the heads nodded. Most only gazed into the fire.

"You're Custer's regiment, by God!" he prodded them. "Think back—you weren't there, but you've heard the stories."

"I cain't cotton to shooting the women," said one young soldier finally.

Fagen whirled on him. "Then you better talk to some of the old files, sonny boy. And find out for yourself it was the filthy squaws who did the cutting and gutting on them brave soldiers left dead atop Custer's hill."

"Not the bucks?"

"The squaws, goddammit! They cut the tongues out and their balls off. It was the filthy bitches did the pretty work on them soldiers."

"Maybe it's about time someone finally evened the score," said one of the older men, a corporal, without looking up from his cup of coffee.

"Yeah," replied another, more strongly. "I don't recollect ever hearing that one Sioux buck or squaw ever got what's coming for their part in that massacre of Custer's boys."

"Right!" Fagen prodded them, raising his cup. He felt that tomorrow would be soon enough, a good time to visit that schoolteacher again. From his first meeting with Avolea Rankin, he sensed that she would be easy enough to break down eventually. His cup sloshed enthusiastically. "To Custer's ghost, boys!"

"Here, here!"

"To Custer's ghost!"

* * *

"Where are you going—dressed like that?"

Stone Eagle regarded Avolea Rankin in the dim light of predawn that seeped in around the window shades. He went back to wrapping about his ankle a lace that would hold the buffalo-fur winter moccasin in place.

"These are the clothes of my people."

She swallowed hard, pushing one of the rust-tinted curls from her eyes before tugging the blanket about her naked body as the chill finger of realization scraped itself down her spine the way chalk would grate on her schoolroom blackboard.

"Your people? I thought you were going to stay with me."

"Until what, Avolea? Until the white man has rubbed all sign of the red man from this land? Or until you don't need me anymore to fill your own loneliness?"

"Isn't that what you came to me for, Stone Eagle?"

"That's why I came, but that's not why I stayed as long as I did."

She took a step toward him, then whirled back, dropping to the edge of the bed. "You're going back to her," Avolea whimpered.

Stone Eagle stood, finished with the moccasins. "Yes. To her and my son. To my people."

"I'm your people—just as much as she is. You're half-white, Stone Eagle."

"If I could, I'd pour out that half of my blood right now. Here on your floor, to show you how much I hate everything it stands for."

The tears came slowly, silently, gently seeping down her rouged alabaster cheeks. He knelt before her, suddenly sorry that in his haste he had used her body again and again in the darkness of this room last night. Already decided on going—but ravaging her anyway. Last night he had grown frightened of the desperate strength driving him when he had entered her, roughly the first time, not delaying to remove their clothing. Instead Stone Eagle had thrown her against the door as he slammed it closed, yanking up her crinoline dress, tearing at the undergarments until the soft, white fleshiness of her legs drove him ever wilder.

He rutted with her there against the door, finishing in a gasping breathlessness before he dragged her to her bed, where he slowly finished undressing her before making long, and slow, love to her a second time. They both fell asleep.

Twice more he awakened her, for he found himself tortured by something allowing him no rest. Perhaps the warmth and smoothness of her body, its whiteness under the pale glow of the distant lamp all kept him awake. Those, and the memory of his mother's words long ago in telling of his father's first wife. A white woman with skin as pale and almost as translucent as breast milk.

Sorry now, for the guilt shamed him in what he had done. Using the teacher's pale, soft body so unlike Double Woman's. Using it to exact revenge on his father. One pale white woman was the same as another, he had always felt. Seeking to shame the spirit of his dead father by defiling the white woman's body with his seed.

The way his father had defiled his mother's body with his white seed.

"You are not to blame," he tried to explain as she pulled away from him, hiding her flesh now.

"I feel . . . so dirty—what you've done . . . and now you're deserting me."

"I can't abandon what I never had, Avolea. There never was any chance for us. We just filled some need in each other while we could. But I did leave a wife and a son—like my father did. Yet the difference is that now I can make up for my wrong. That bastard never came back to my mother and me. That bastard abandoned us for good."

"Go! Go to your Indian squaw!"

"Yes," he said quietly as he stood above her, finally releasing her pale hand. "I should have gone long ago, but instead I got lost in hurting myself through the pain I've made for you."

"You're a pagan savage—like all the rest of them!"

"Yes, and I'm leaving everything white behind. Burn it—it might make you, both of us, feel a lot better if you did. The clothes and those boots. I feel shame for ever trying to be white like you."

"You never can be, Stone Eagle."

"You're good at what you do, teaching. I refused to learn—but you finally taught me that important lesson. I'll never be white. I'm going home to my people. Good-bye, Avolea."

Stone Eagle swept up the hooded blanket capote as he tore through the back door, into the dusting of new snow, racing toward the timber where he kept the horse.

He had it saddled and a buffalo robe tied behind him as the sky turned rose to the east. Stone Eagle walked the horse from the timber, then leapt to the saddle. He sat staring south along the Rushville Road, thinking of all those soldiers from his father's regiment camped in their tents down at the agency. The Seventh U.S. Cavalry.

The sound of muted hoofbeats beyond the bend in the road spurred him into motion beneath the growing light of dawn. The horse snorted in protest of his hard use of the rein, sending a gauze of vapor from its nostrils.

In his hurry to be gone from this place before first-light drenched the valley, Stone Eagle moved the horse into a lope, hardly noticing the older man he passed on the road. A man riding an army horse, saddled with an army rigging.

A small, thin, tight-faced easterner who loped his horse toward the Pine Ridge school of Avolea Rankin.

On the nineteenth of December, the Moon of Popping Trees, Big Foot led his people across the Cheyenne River because the grass was better for grazing their animals. They camped near James Cavanaugh's trading post.

Double Woman was staying with her brother and his family. Two wives and five children now lived in Ghost's lodge. There was nothing to be done for the time being. It would be many weeks before Big Foot's band was back on its own land, after their journey to Pine Ridge. Then Double Woman could find a place of her own to live out her life and raise Stone Eagle's son.

Ghost's heart ached to see his sister in so much despair in losing her husband. Yet he wanted to give Stone Eagle a chance to explain himself before he became angry with his old friend. He remembered the day they met, back on the morning Sitting Bull had his prophetic vision—that summer so long ago, in the year of the soldiers falling into camp.

He would wait to give his old friend a chance to tell his story.

As the women erected their canvas lodges, some of the men went to the store with Ghost. In sign the tall warrior told Cavanaugh's two grown sons his people were hungry. The white men called their father. Cavanaugh immediately made out the gist of the subtle Miniconjou request. He gave Ghost's men some flour, along with coffee and sugar.

Ghost looked down at the sacks Cavanaugh piled on the rough counter.

"We have no beef," he signed, putting his crooked fingers on either side of his head, then rubbing a hand over his empty belly.

The trader knew when he had himself boxed in a corner.

"There," he said, and pointed out the door. He tried out some of his rusty sign language with a few words of Sioux thrown in. "You people go kill a calf, in the corral."

The white man did not have to offer them the calf a second time. Ghost's men swept the sacks from the counter and hurried out the front door, while Cavanaugh and his sons lumbered out the back and into the woods on foot.

"Let them go," Ghost said when one of the young men suggested going after the storekeepers, capturing them, and tying them up.

"They will go to the soldiers and tell lies about us."

"It does not matter," he replied. "We won't be here that long. They won't make it to the army soon enough to catch us."

The trade goods and skinny calf did not stretch far, but it was enough to stop the little bellies of the children from hurting so much, and it was good to give the sick and the old ones a bonemeal-and-blood soup to make them stronger for the coming cold journey.

Ghost did not stay in camp long enough to wait for the meat to cook. Big Foot selected ten young men to go in search of more refugees from Sitting Bull's camp.

Not long after sunrise on the twentieth, the men located a group of Hunkpapa women hunkered around some smoky fires, shivering without blankets, wearing only the clothing they had on their backs the night Bull Head's police came to arrest Sitting Bull. Their throaty voices were raised in wails and death-songs for their chief and the men killed in the fight with the white agent's metal-breasts.

"There are no men with you?" Ghost asked.

"They are in the village across the river," answered a Hunkpapa woman.

"Your men went to Hump's camp? We will go collect them and return here. Big Foot offers you food and blankets—not words you cannot eat."

Ghost led the nine across the Cheyenne into the village, where Hump was in council with his advisers and the Hunkpapas.

Hump leapt to his feet, his face filled with hostility. "What is it you men want here in my camp?"

The tall young Miniconjou looked about, then spoke. "Big Foot sent us to find these Hunkpapas, to take them to our camp, where we can share our food and blankets with them."

Hump whirled on the Hunkpapa men, his face reddening, trembling with anger. "These men are Big Foot's ghost dancers—they will get you into trouble. Already your chief is dead. Do more of you wish to die? You and your women should stay here. We will take you to the soldier fort, where you will not have to worry about bullets."

"Soldier fort?" asked a Hunkpapa, suspicious.

Ghost came forward. "Hump is a mighty chief of our people. But he has chosen to walk the white man's road. If there are Hunkpapas here who are still Indians, I say let them cross the river with us."

The squat, muscular chief stomped up close to the young warrior, staring up into Ghost's face.

"You will not take these men and their women into Big Foot's camp. *I* will take them to the agency. You people want to fight, so I will go to Bennett and bring some soldiers back to help you with your wish. Then you will have your fight."

For a moment Ghost felt like clawing the chief's eyes out for the insult. But he was outnumbered and outgunned here in a hostile camp. Hump ordered his warriors into a ring circling Big Foot's emissaries. The hammers on many rifles clicked back in the cold, dry air, like the snap of many twigs underfoot.

"Wait, Hump!" shouted one of the older Hunkpapas. "I fought alongside Crazy Horse on the Rosebud and Gall along the Greasy Grass. I am Sioux—like these men from Big Foot's camp. I will never work for the soldiers."

"These men are making trouble," Hump protested. "I will show you what I do with troublemakers."

"If there is to be blood here on this ground," the Hunkpapa warrior growled, "let our children know we died helping Big Foot's men!"

Most of Sitting Bull's warrior refugees clambered to their feet, enveloping the ten emissaries from across the river.

Hump sputtered and blew, angry that he had been bested by the young Miniconjous. "You who want to go—go now and do not look back. The army will be on your trail—and I will be leading them!"

As Ghost and his men started down the icy river to rejoin Big Foot, only thirty-eight of the Hunkpapa refugees left Hump's village. One hundred sixty-six men, women, and children chose to stay behind and follow Hump in to Fort Bennett.

Yet what made Hump more angry than anything is that thirty of his own warriors chose to go with Ghost.

"Better to die in the footsteps of our grandfathers," the young Miniconjou warriors said as they left their families and friends behind. "Better than walking the white man's road."

CHAPTER 46

December, 1890

HARLEY Fagen had to admit he liked that look of utter surprise in her eyes when she opened the door to the schoolhouse so that he could shove his way past her into the cold classroom. He would remember that look for a long time, and the way she clutched that heavy blanket about her as she threw open that door, a look of expectancy on her face as the words tumbled from her lips.

"No, I'm not Stone Eagle. Expecting someone, ma'am?"

She flustered, surprise tightening her features. "No, I'm not. Something you want?"

"To talk with you again, Miss Rankin. It's Harley Fagen," and he ripped the soiled hat from his head.

"Isn't there a better time, Mr. Fagen?"

"No, I don't think there is."

Then something new crossed the woman's face. Something Fagen had rarely seen on any woman's face. Though he could not admit to getting that close to all that many women. This was almost a mystery in itself, the look of control that suddenly came across her features.

He recalled now how she pulled the door back, smiling in a calculating way.

"Why don't you come on in, Mr. Fagen? I'll start some coffee, and then we can talk. I have some news that might prove helpful to you.".

She was every bit of that and more. While the Pine Ridge agent, he was awful closemouthed about anything. But then, Daniel Royer had his hands busy with all the stir of late. And none of the Catholic priests or Episcopalian preachers were any help either. Concerned over the welfare of their flocks come fluttering in from all corners of the reservation, with the troublemakers still out on the loose and looking to get something started.

"The previous teacher, Mrs. Nettleton, told me of a former student of hers who matches the description of the young man you asked me about last week."

"Why didn't you tell me about him when I was here last time, ma'am?"

She looked up from her coffee cup. He could tell she was going to tell the lie to him straight-faced even before she opened that pretty mouth of hers.

"I'm sure it happens to you all the time. You're doing something else when . . . I just remembered it this morning."

"You happen to know his name?"

"Stone Eagle."

"You have been doing some thinking about this lately, haven't you, Miss Rankin?"

She poured a bit more coffee to warm his cup.

"And here all this time, I had reason to believe I was looking for a man named Yellow Bird."

Her eyes widened, filled with a little consternation if not fear. "Heavens, no. The one you want is named Stone Eagle. He has long, light brown hair—not at all straight like the rest of the males. And his eyes."

"Tell me about them—those eyes, Miss Rankin."

"They're light."

"Blue?"

"Not exactly. More a blue gray, like the clouds that roll in over the horizon with that first honest-to-goodness winter storm."

"You ever see a wolf, Miss Rankin?"

"No, never have. Why would you ask a strange question like that?"

"Just them eyes you described—they sound for the life of me like you just described the eyes of a wolf."

She had rocked back in her cane chair beside the small table that stood by the tiny stove, sipping at her coffee.

"Perhaps they are, Mr. Fagen."

"Still, I ain't so sure we're talking about the same man. I've been tracking him for years now."

"Oh?"

He set his cup down. "The young buck I want is called Yellow Bird." Fagen rose to leave. "Thank you for the coffee, Miss Rankin. And the story about this Stone Eagle."

"Wait, Mr. Fagen!"

He pushed ahead to the door, more convinced than ever the woman had an ax to grind with this fellow Stone Eagle, whoever he was. Perhaps what they always said about a woman scorned was true after all.

"Mr. Fagen!"

"I've fish to fry, Miss Rankin."

"Stone Eagle is the one you're looking for—believe me!" she pleaded, catching him at the schoolhouse door after dashing down the aisle between the desks.

He turned about on her, almost feeling sorry for a woman who was so out for a man's blood. But then, he knew just what that emotion could do to you, wanting someone's blood. "Thank you for your time, Miss."

"Listen—just listen to me," she whispered huskily. "Stone Eagle himself told me his father was a high-ranking army officer. His mother was a Cheyenne squaw. Doesn't that fit the description of the man you're looking for? The bastard son of an army officer and a Cheyenne whore?"

He studied her face a moment before speaking. "I'm confused here: I thought you said the previous schoolteacher—Mrs. Nettleton—she was the one told you about this half-breed." That made her squirm a bit, biting a lip. "Now you're saying this Injun told you these incriminating details himself?"

"Does it matter?" she snapped caustically.

"Yes," he replied coolly. "If I'm to figure out who to believe. I'd like to get this search over and done with."

"To do that, you must believe me."

"All right," he whispered, his mouth gone dry, just the way it did whenever he was about to crack something wide open. "All right, Miss Rankin. Suppose you tell me where I can find this Stone Eagle of yours."

"He's riding north. Left this morning for the Cheyenne River."

"Left from right here?" Fagen remembered how her eyes had dropped to the floor, filling with shame. Harley Fagen was the last to allow a woman shame. Before she got around to answering, he continued, "You ain't the first woman's wanted to roll around in the blankets with one of them Injun bucks, Miss Rankin. Likely won't be the last, neither. Especially the good-looking ones—I hear they're a might like a fine racing thoroughbred."

Her eyes implored his suddenly. "Maybe you can make up time on him. It hasn't been that long."

"What's up north he's headed for?"

"The Miniconjou reservation—Cheyenne River—where he's going for his wife and son."

"Tell Big Foot I don't approve of him helping these Hunkpapas," scolded Lieutenant Colonel Edwin V. Sumner.

"If I may, Colonel?" replied Captain Preston Tripp. "I think you should listen to Big Foot's explanation."

Sumner let out a long sigh. "All right," he instructed his interpreter, Felix Benoit. "Tell the chief I'll hear him out."

"The soldier-chief must know I cannot turn away any of my brothers who come to me with empty bellies—their feet sore from a long journey to reach my camp—nearly naked as well."

Sumner looked past Big Foot, measuring the two trail-weary Hunkpapas. "This pair is pretty much as he describes they are, Captain."

"I expect they have nothing more than what they had on when they ran from their beds the night the agency police shot Sitting Bull."

"Very well." Sumner motioned his adjutant over. "I want

the command made ready to march. We'll about-face back to Narcelle's ranch and make camp there." He watched the lieutenant go as he drew over Felix Benoit, his interpreter. "With all this trouble, tell Big Foot that I can't allow him to go into the agency right now for his rations. He will have to take his people back to their homes until this Ghost Dance madness is over."

"It is good," Big Foot agreed. "My people are nervous about the soldiers marching upriver in our direction. We would not want to bump into them and some mistake to happen."

"Colonel Merriam's forces," Sumner said aside quietly to Captain Tripp.

That night the Miniconjous and their thirty-eight Hunkpapa guests, the entire group now numbering 333 men, women, and children in all, made camp at Narcisse Narcelle's ranch on the north side of the Cheyenne River, their village surrounded by Sumner's forces.

Edwin V. Sumner had compiled a distinguished service record as an Indian fighter and was known as one of the soldier-chiefs who coupled compassion and wisdom with military daring. When the whole Ghost Dance disturbance began, the army had assigned Sumner to watch over Big Foot, the chief regarded as one of the potential troublemakers. Over the past six months, the Miniconjous had come to respect the soldier-chief, while Sumner had come to trust the word of Big Foot.

Trouble was, he had trusted Big Foot once too often for the good of his career. Not long after the Miniconjous had guaranteed Sumner they were not looking to make any trouble and were heading back to their camp, the lieutenant colonel received word that the commander, General Nelson A. Miles, was counting on him to arrest Big Foot if the occasion was to present itself. About the time Sumner was realizing he had made a grievous error, Captain Preston Tripp and his twenty-man escort showed up, heading south, double time, for Pine Ridge.

Because of the heightened tensions in the air, Tripp and his escort threw in with Sumner's forces: C and I Troops of the Eighth Cavalry, along with C Company of the Third Infantry and two Hotchkiss guns. The lieutenant colonel immediately jumped onto Big Foot's trail, spending the next night at Narcelle's ranch. The next morning, the twenty-first, the soldiers had set out to make the last twelve miles to the Miniconjous' camp.

Yet Big Foot's scouts had learned of Sumner's march. The soldiers had marched only a few miles down the Cheyenne when they were surprised to meet the chief, one of his headmen, and the two Hunkpapa refugees who had carried word of Sitting Bull's death to the Miniconjous.

It was that meeting between an anxious Big Foot and an exasperated Sumner that Captain Preston Tripp witnessed.

A feast hosted by Sumner's men later that night at Narcelle's ranch went a long way toward easing the fears of the Miniconjous anxious at being encircled by so many soldiers and the two big wagon-guns. Double Woman ate little of the army food, giving most to her hungry son. Her loneliness and agony filled her. A broken heart was all she wanted to feed upon.

Yet when morning brought a resumed march, the anxiety returned to stir among her people like the restless, hissing warning of a rattlesnake. The soldiers had decided that, instead of dropping off the Miniconjous at their cabins, they would push them on, escorting them to Sumner's observation post, dubbed Camp Cheyenne. Yet that was not the last of the bad news that morning.

The soldiers were harsh when they issued their order of march for the day. Sumner had loaded all those Indians without ponies into the several rickety Miniconjou wagons. Packed mostly with women, children, and the old ones, these wagons were then divided into two groups, each with its own company of cavalry for escort. Ghost and the other mounted warriors were directed to ride behind the wagons. Captain Philip Reade's infantry brought up the rear of the march.

Tempers simmered before the march even got under way, emotions just below a boil while many Miniconjou voices grumbled that they had done nothing to warrant being placed within such a tight noose by the soldiers. It would be but a few miles of travel before the soldiers noticed more and more of the warriors had painted themselves and were now openly brandishing their rifles. Captain Tripp admired the coolness of Sumner's men under the circumstances.

"Many of them can't help but be frightened," Tripp said to the lieutenant colonel as their advance guard passed through a narrow gate marking the far boundary of Narcelle's ranch.

"I'm not all that much at ease myself, Captain. For the most part my men are untried. Their nervousness makes them tight as catgut on a fiddle."

The commotion of neighing horses and shrieking women immediately drew their attention to the rear. While guiding the second group of wagons through the gate, one of the old wagons snagged a wheel on a fence post, effectively hobbling it from moving. Anxious soldiers shouted at the frightened women to keep the column moving. Some of the women jumped from the wagon, some pushing, some pulling in the confusion, succeeding only in scaring the horses and further tangling the animals in their traces.

A cavalry officer from behind the wagons loped up to the scene, waving his arm angrily at the confused women, sternly ordering them to pull the wagon free. The tone of his voice accomplished nothing but scaring a few of the women into sneaking off toward the timber while some of the warriors came tearing up to the scene. Black Fox, son-in-law to chief Big Foot, leveled his Winchester at the officer's chest, sending the soldier galloping off in retreat.

Black Fox led the rest of the young men in a shrill war cry as they shook their weapons in the air. Most of the men milled about aimlessly, while a few dismounted and helped the women free the wagon. As soon as the gate had been cleared, the mounted warriors streamed through, rushing like water through a broken dam for the advance guard of the soldiers.

"Lieutenant Duff!" Sumner shouted. "Bring your company about and stand to skirmish formation!"

Up and down the advance guard the orders of old sergeants rang. Horses snorted as they were brought about-face, and carbines were dragged from scabbards with loud squeaks like protesting buggy springs. Leather creaked and bits jingled as the sergeants wrangled their men into line, to face the oncoming warriors, painted and armed, pouring from the gate like an amber flood from a whiskey-keg bunghole.

"Load! Arms at ready!"

The carbines were leveled at the charging warriors.

"Hold, men! Hold! Don't fire until I give the order," Lieutenant Duff shouted, loping up and down his long line of troopers.

Black Fox was the first to break, reining up in a splatter of mud and melted snow. The others turned about, leaving Ghost alone in the middle of the road, staring down the muzzles of those carbines.

More angry at his fellow warriors than the young, fear-eyed soldiers down the road, the tall Miniconjou brought his snorting pony under control. Then he slowly turned about and deliberately kept his animal at a walk while he rejoined his people.

"Well—I'm glad that's over, sir," Duff exclaimed.

Tripp turned to Sumner. "I'm afraid there'll come a time these warriors won't give way to your soldiers, sir."

For a moment the lieutenant colonel said nothing, then finally replied. "God help us all if they don't, Captain. God help us."

CHAPTER 47

BY early afternoon Big Foot's people crossed the river, escorted by the army, and came within sight of their cabins. The air filled with a dangerous expectancy as the women and men shouted back and forth among themselves.

"We will stay here!" growled the young men.

"We cannot. The soldier-chief said he is taking us on farther to his soldier camp," replied one of the women, afraid of provoking the army further.

"I will die here!" Ghost shouted. "Here—this is my home!"

Double Woman dragged her young son into her lap, frightened of the angry talk of the warriors after the soldiers' show of might near the gate earlier that morning. She felt trapped between the two groups of warriors—like nothing more than a prisoner, knowing prisoners suffered the whims of their keepers.

Yet this time when the painted warriors dashed along the columns, heading for the advance guard with shrill war cries, the soldiers parted and gave way, shouting orders, their rifles at ready.

Many of the women wailed and moaned, causing most of the children to cry as well as their homes came into sight. Big Foot loped past on an old horse, holding a wrinkled hand over his mouth as he coughed into a scrap of rag. While he conferred with the soldier-chief, the women hovered close to the wagons, ready to unload. The men raced their ponies about, hollering to work themselves up, preparing one another for battle.

When Big Foot came back along the column, the soldiers were already yelling their orders up and down the line of march. The walk-a-heap soldiers split as they moved past the wagons, then disappeared into the trees with the pony soldiers. In a matter of moments all was quiet once more.

Ghost whooped wildly. "We have won! The soldiers have gone away."

"Do not think we have won so quickly," Big Foot reminded his people sadly. "I merely bought us some time."

"The soldiers did not make us go on to their camp—we can stay here among our homes!"

"Yes, Ghost. But I had to strike a deal with the soldier-chief. I told him I would go to his camp—but that there would be trouble trying to force our women and children, cold and hungry as we all are, away from our homes. I told him to his face that these are our homes, where his government has ordered us to stay. I reminded him that none of my people have committed a single act requiring him to remove us from our homes by force."

"He saw we are ready to do battle, yes? Saw we are ready to die for our homes and families?"

"Yes," Big Foot sighed. "He agreed that if the soldiers tried to push us on to their camp, many would die, and he would look the fool to his chiefs for killing many women and children on the land of their homes, where they are doing harm to no man."

"Do you have to leave us to go with him now?" Double Woman asked the chief.

"No. The soldier-chief said I could stay if I promise to

come to his camp tomorrow for a council. I am to bring all our Hunkpapa friends from Standing Rock with me."

By early afternoon of the next day, Big Foot and his head men had grown agitated, if not frightened. Sometime in the night the Standing Rock Hunkpapas had slipped away and were not to be found. The chief ordered a few of his young men to go in search of them, to convince the refugees there was nothing to fear in going to parley with the soldier-chief. Not long after the searchers were dispatched, a white rancher from the area rode out of the timber, stopping near Big Foot's cabin.

"Red Beard! You have come to trade perhaps?" Ghost greeted local rancher John Dunn. In a moment the half-breed interpreter Felix Benoit emerged from the timber behind Dunn. Ghost's eyes narrowed suspiciously as they went back to the rancher. "So, what is this, Red Beard? You ride for the army now?"

Dunn appeared nervous as women and children gathered about the two horsemen. "He came along from the soldier camp with me. The soldier-chief wants me to talk you people into going on back to the Cheyenne River Agency. You will be safer there."

"We are here among our homes!" Ghost replied, trying to put the best face on it.

Benoit leaned over and whispered something to Dunn in mumbled English that Double Woman could not understand, though Stone Eagle had taught her many words over their time together.

Dunn straightened. "The Hunkpapas are gone?"

Big Foot pushed through the milling, angry crowd. "Yes. They disappeared. I have men out looking for them now. All will be fine, and I will come to talk to the soldier-chief when the Standing Rock Indians can come with me."

Dunn shook his head angrily. "It will be too late for you, Big Foot. Unless you go to Fort Bennett tomorrow morning, other soldiers will come down here to make you go."

"All of these people?" Big Foot asked, his eyes burning with betrayal as he coughed into the filthy rag.

"All of them must go. Not just you."

"And if we don't?" Ghost demanded.

Dunn turned on the tall warrior. "The soldiers will make you go. They will shoot you if they have to."

Big Foot turned to the soldier-chief's personal interpreter. "Does Red Beard speak the truth? Will the soldiers shoot if we do not go to Cheyenne River Agency?"

Benoit nodded to Dunn, his face passive and not betraying the fact that for some unexplained reason the rancher had lied to the Miniconjous. "Red Beard's words are straight."

"My people will talk," Big Foot said. "Go tell the soldier-chief I will talk with him soon."

As the two horsemen disappeared into the timber, the Miniconjou grew excited, shouting from anger and fear. Their chief quieted them.

"The best we can do is not to provoke the soldiers. We will stay here in our homes and see what comes next."

"No," Black Fox replied, giving voice to the opposition. "We now have the army on two sides of us. Before we left, there were soldiers coming upriver from the agency to the east. Now there are soldiers camped close by on the west of us."

"Perhaps we should do what we planned all along," Ghost said, stepping forward. "The chiefs at Pine Ridge want you there to help them end their trouble. Let us go to the Oglallas—and thereby show the army we mean them no trouble, if they mean us none as well."

"We should stay near our homes," Big Foot said, grappling with it. "There, up Deep Creek. We will go hide."

Immediately the women broke away, hurrying to their cabins to load wagons with bedding and cooking utensils, lodgepoles and canvas covers.

Ghost stepped beside Big Foot. "We will see now if the soldiers come to shoot our women and children."

A courier from Fort Meade had reached Sumner's camp on the twenty-second, the night before, carrying a wire from General Nelson A. Miles headquartered in Rapid City, alerting the lieutenant colonel to rumors that more than two hundred Indians were loose and roaming western North Dakota, having corralled a troop of cavalry in a fierce fight. While the general felt the story to be nothing more than rumor, Miles wanted Sumner to use his forces to shield the white settlements on the northern fringe of the Black Hills in the event more outbreaks occurred.

"Damn!" Sumner muttered, rattling the telegraph flimsy in his hand. "He's got me in the jam now."

"Who, sir?" asked Preston Tripp. "General Miles?"

"No," and he sank to the cot in his headquarters wall tent. "Big Foot."

"What's Miles want you to do? Take the whole of them in to Fort Bennett now?"

Sumner shook his head. "No. He thinks I've already got Big Foot and his headmen under arrest. He says, 'Be careful they do not escape, and look out for other Indians.' Miles wants me to take the Miniconjous into Meade before we march on down to protect the Black Hills."

Tripp settled to a canvas stool, the coffee warming his hands in the chill of late afternoon, the sun sinking on the treetops. "You wired him yesterday, so Miles will know from that message that you don't have Big Foot in custody."

"You can see I'm in a deuce of it now."

"Everything will turn out well—Big Foot promises he and the Hunkpapas are coming in to talk with you today, Colonel."

"Pray they do, Captain Tripp. If I have to go in search of Big Foot, that might provoke a fight. And if I have to arrest the old man, the young bucks will break for it—spreading trouble all over the surrounding country. I don't agree with Miles—who feels I should arrest Big Foot. The best path lies with keeping the chief with his people for the time being."

"I understand," Tripp agreed. "Big Foot's the only one likely to keep a lid on his young warriors. Like you I doubt they'll go south to Pine Ridge. I figure they'll either go to Fort Bennett as you've told them—or they'll turn on us and fight."

"Yes, Captain—pray the chief comes in to talk. Pray for the sake of us all."

By noon Big Foot had not shown his face in Camp Cheyenne. As Sumner was sitting down to a tasteless midday meal, his adjutant escorted a white rancher into the lieutenant colonel's tent.

"Yes, I live nearby," John Dunn admitted to Sumner. "My place is over on the Belle Fourche, just a few miles from here."

"I'll make you a deal, Mr. Dunn—since you know these Miniconjous of Big Foot's. I'll buy all your eggs and butter, plus a handsome day's wages, if you'll go to their camp with my interpreter, Felix Benoit. Convince them they should journey in to the Cheyenne River Agency."

"Tomorrow."

"Yes, start tomorrow."

"What if they bow up their backs, as they're likely to do?"

"It's up to you, Dunn. You've traded with them some. Talk their language. Get them to understand they're safer up there on their own agency. I can't have them roaming south—straggling out toward Pine Ridge."

"Lot of trouble they could get into between here and there."

"Yes," Sumner admitted. "Too damned much trouble for my little outfit to handle on its own."

Within two hours Dunn and Benoit were back, telling Sumner that they had witnessed the women loading wagons as they were leaving.

"Making preparations for their trip to the agency?"

Felix Benoit nodded. "Yes, Colonel. I think so. We left one of your scouts near the village to see what he could."

"Good. Send your other man back to Big Foot. Tell him he must not leave his camp until morning."

In less than an hour, Benoit was back at Sumner's tent accompanied by one of his scouts. The interpreter stood in the late-afternoon light, rolling the soft brim of his hat between his hands.

"They what?" Sumner growled.

"Headed south, Colonel," Benoit replied softly.

"Pine Ridge, goddammit!"

"Are you afraid Big Foot will join the rest of the rebels in the badlands?" asked Preston Tripp.

"Wherever he's going—and whatever he's planning on doing, it makes little matter to me now," Sumner admitted after Benoit left. "The die is cast now—Miles expects me to have the chief and his troublemakers under arrest."

* * *

That night in the low hills along Deep Creek, south of their cabins, the Miniconjous made a fireless camp as the temperature fell and the silver moon climbed above them.

Shivering uncontrollably, Big Foot called his anxious leaders together for another council. Throughout the debates and posturing, the chief had little to say. It was easy for Double Woman to see that his strength was beginning to wane, his frame wracked with pain each time he coughed into the blood-soaked rag he kept over his mouth.

"The soldiers have not come," Black Fox spoke the obvious. "Perhaps we can slip around them and make a run for The Stronghold where our Oglalla and Brule cousins will make their stand."

"It is not a good idea to try running the gauntlet of so many soldiers," Ghost protested. "We are more than warriors, Black Fox. We have our families with us. We must think of them first."

"I am thinking of my family. I do not want them killed like the white man's cattle caught in a holding pen at Fort Bennett."

"What I suggest is not a trip to the soldier fort, but to go where our chief has been asked by the Oglallas."

"No," Big Foot said, clearing his throat. "I believe we should stay here—near our homes. For the safety of our families. After all, I have promised the soldier-chief, Sumner. Told him I would not be going south to Pine Ridge."

"The Oglallas promised you one hundred ponies if you would come to help them make peace," Ghost reminded.

"I am too ill to make that journey to Pine Ridge," Big Foot admitted at last, pulling the red rag from his lips. "If I am forced to go anywhere, I prefer that we go downriver to our own agency."

On and on they argued among themselves for hours while the moon climbed ever higher and the air grew ever more cold. At last the great majority of the men supported Ghost. It made sense to stay with their original plans to mediate the crisis at Pine Ridge.

"Awaken the people," Big Foot said, resigned to the journey that stared him and the Miniconjous in the face. "Have them make ready for our trip."

"Now?" someone asked.

"Now. If we are to make it to Pine Ridge without any trouble from the soldiers, we must cover some ground, quickly."

Well after the quarter moon had reached its apex, the people were on the march into the darkness.

An hour later the rear guard shouted out their news, halting the slow, rambling column of wagons and those on foot. A half dozen of Big Foot's out-riders brought in Charging First, a Brule Sioux who scouted for Felix Benoit and Lieutenant Colonel Sumner.

"The soldier-chief is looking for you, Big Foot," announced Charging First as he looked down on the old man stretched out on a pile of blankets and robes in a slab-sided wagon. "Your nose is pointed south, though you gave Sumner your word you would not go to Pine Ridge."

He coughed up the shiny red phlegm. "I wanted to go to Fort Bennett, as the soldier-chief asked me. But my people wanted to journey south to help the Oglallas. I have no choice but to do the will of my people."

"So it is," Charging First replied, silent for a few moments. "What would you have me say to the soldier-chief for you?"

Big Foot struggled up on one elbow, some of the blankets sliding from his shoulders. He had a scrap of wool cloth tied around his head like a kerchief, knotted just below his chin.

"Tell Sumner—say everything will be fine now. We are not going to cause any man harm. I am going to Pine Ridge to put an end to all the trouble."

CHAPTER 48

December 24–27, 1890

CHRISTMAS Eve day.

Charging First rode in while Sumner drank his first cup of coffee. It could do little to warm the cold knot of anger and apprehension in the lieutenant colonel's belly.

Instead of hurrying after the Miniconjou band, however, Sumner hung back, worried still of the reports of hostile activity to the north. He realized he could not do both: capture and detain Big Foot while also protecting the settlements on the northern fringe of the Black Hills. Instead he marched his troops back to Camp Cheyenne, where a courier from Fort Meade awaited him.

"General Miles?" asked Preston Tripp.

"Who else is going to keep me on such a tight rein, Captain?"

Tripp went back to his coffee while Sumner quickly eyed the telegram.

Rapid City, 23d.

To Colonel E. V. Sumner,
Commanding Cheyenne:

(Through Commanding Officer Fort Meade)

Report about hostile Indians near Little Missouri not believed. The attitude of Big Foot has been defiant and hostile, and you are authorized to arrest him or any of his people and to take them to Meade or Bennett. There are some 30 young warriors that run away from Hump's camp without authority, and if an opportunity is given they will undoubtedly join those in the Bad Lands. The Standing Rock Indians also have no right to be there and they should be arrested. The division commander directs, therefore, that you secure Big Foot and the 20 Cheyenne River Indians, and the Standing Rock Indians, and if necessary round up the whole camp and disarm them, and take them to Fort Meade or Bennett.

By command of General Miles.

Maus
Captain and Aide-de-Camp

"Glad I'm not in your shoes, Colonel."

Sumner ground his teeth. "Miles won't like finding out that Big Foot's slipped past me."

"He must be mistaken about the number of Cheyenne River Indians. There's more than two hundred out there now, somewhere. Not twenty."

"Twenty or two hundred, Captain—I've got to bring someone else in to help me on this. You said you needed to get to Pine Ridge, and in a hurry."

"That was the idea all along. But if Big Foot has his warriors roaming around, I can't ask my escort to ride a suicide detail to get me to Pine Ridge."

"I've just thought of a way to get you a bit closer to Pine Ridge, Captain. And to help me as well." Sumner leaned over the small field desk, studying a crude map of the area south of the Cheyenne River. He placed a finger almost due south of his present position on the Cheyenne. "There—at a base camp where Rapid Creek empties into the Cheyenne. You'll find Carr's Sixth Cavalry."

"Carr?"

"Colonel. Eugene Carr. Good man. Hero of Summit Springs back in sixty-nine."

"I didn't learn much about that one, sir."

"Carr and his Fifth Cavalry were led to the Cheyenne by Buffalo Bill Cody."

"Buffalo Bill Cody—the showman?"

"Cody was an honest-to-goodness army scout before he became a master showman. The Sixth caught Tall Bull's camp of bloodthirsty Dog Soldiers sitting on their asses— put an end to Cheyenne troubles on this part of the plains for good."

"So now Carr's asked to do the same for the Sioux."

"His troopers are scouting east and west from their Rapid Creek camp, which is just north of the badlands. Carr's the man to do it. There's no man in the army—besides Nelson Miles himself—who has as much experience as Carr."

"With all respect—what's this Carr got to do with my getting to Pine Ridge?"

Sumner grinned. "Looks like we're going to help each other, Captain. I'm sending a message to Carr, alerting him that the Miniconjous are heading south. If he can march his forces east quickly enough, he just might stop Big Foot before he gets to Pine Ridge. My messenger can ride along with your escort. If you keep to the river, I'm certain you'll be far enough to the west to avoid Big Foot's warriors."

"It's not Big Foot you're worried about, is it, Colonel?"

"No, Tripp. It's his hotbloods. And those ghost-dancing medicine men. In all probability Miles wants my scalp now for losing Big Foot. Sitting back in his plush office over there in Rapid City, he's got himself convinced Big Foot is the one most dangerous man in all of this."

"Not the way I've seen it. The chief seems easy enough to convince of what you want him to do."

"Exactly, Captain. But Miles is convinced the best idea is to take Big Foot away from his people right now."

"Be a shame, Colonel—as it would leave no moderating influence among the Miniconjous. Big Foot's warriors and the hotheads will have their way without protest, won't they, sir?"

Sumner looked Tripp in the eye for a moment, a

fractured smile coming across his face. "Truth is, what we need is the War Department to send more levelheaded men like you out here, Captain. So—someday, when this is all settled down—you're going to have to tell me what the devil a savvy young officer named Preston Tripp is doing running secret errands for Phil Sheridan—when you could damn well be helping me keep the peace with these Indians."

After a horse-punishing ride up the Cheyenne River, Captain Tripp, his escort, and Sumner's messenger arrived at Carr's camp near midmorning.

The full-bearded veteran of the Indian wars immediately ordered to saddle the four troops of cavalry not already roaming the country. By nightfall the colonel's men had pushed to the fringe of the menacing monolith of bluff and canyon known as The Badlands, dragging their pair of wheeled Hotchkiss guns behind them.

The night seemed all the colder for the fact that it was Christmas Eve. Yet for Preston Tripp the stars shown that much brighter above their camp on the middle fork of Sage Creek. The light of the moon among all those stars lit up the frozen alkali ponds in the area Carr selected for his camp.

Dawn came slowly out of the east. During the night two more companies of Carr's Sixth rode in after couriers had taken them word of where to rendezvous with their commander. Few of those six troops of soldiers had captured any sleep beneath their saddle blankets through the freezing night. Instead they kept themselves company or kept themselves busy hauling in wood for the many fires.

"Not like all the soft, cushy comfort that junior colonel Forsyth is enjoying himself at Pine Ridge, is it, Captain Tripp?"

He looked up at the smiling, wrinkled eyes of Eugene Asa Carr that Christmas morning. "His lot is nowhere near as tough as yours, Colonel."

Carr sighed. "No one's worked harder than these boys of mine. For the last thirty days we've been on the jump day and night. I just hope the Sixth will have a chance to make a fair showing of it in the coming scrap."

"You think trouble is certain?"

"There'll be a fight of it, Tripp. Too many hotheads out there stirring the pot now. Something's bound to spill into the fire sooner or later. All this talk of the white man's days being numbered and the dead coming back." Carr studied the captain. "These secret orders of yours taking you to Pine Ridge got anything to do with this Ghost Dance nonsense?"

Tripp concentrated on the crackling fire while the front part of his body broiled, his back and buttocks like blocks of river ice. "No, sir. Nothing as full of intrigue as that. Looking for a man."

"Indian, eh? One of the troublemakers, I'll bet."

"I can't say, sir. Just someone I've been tracking for a while now."

"Very well," Carr said, his shoulders hunching as he shivered. "Phil Sheridan was always a closemouthed fella. No sense in the little general spilling beans to me about this secret mission of yours anyway."

"If it's all right with you, Colonel—I'll stay with you long enough to make sure my escort won't run into any of Big Foot's warriors before we push on south."

"Splendid! I'll enjoy your company while I have it, Captain. Not often I find a man with whom I can talk Homer or Shakespeare."

Beneath the full light of sunrise, Carr divided his command into two battalions and spent Christmas day scouting north toward Bull Creek across a wide area without success. Not a sign of Indians.

"I'll miss having you at tonight's fire, Captain Tripp."

"Likewise, Colonel." He saluted Carr.

"You'll be careful, won't you? It appears Big Foot's slipped south of us—right where you and your men are headed."

"We'll be careful, sir."

"Send me word when you arrive at Pine Ridge, so I know you're safe."

"Merry Christmas, Colonel." He found it hard to say.

"Merry Christmas, Captain Tripp. Even more, I wish you good luck and . . . good hunting."

* * *

Big Foot had slipped east of Carr during the long night of the twenty-third. Those women drivers in their rattling, creaky wagons covered more ground than any of the army officers thought possible.

Late the next afternoon, as cold scuts of wind whipped alkali dust into their faces, the Miniconjous reached the forbidding three-hundred-foot-high wall that bordered The Badlands for ninety miles. Almost due south of their beloved Deep Creek, near the eastern rim of the wall, they struck a pass that had seen little use in recent years. It was not an easy decision for the men to make, but to go in search of another pass down into the White River country at the northern edge of the Pine Ridge would have delayed them a few more days and possibly subjected them to army patrols.

They headed slowly down that trail of torture, inching the wagons along, digging their way through the underbrush and rock with spades and axes. At the same time Carr's men had been shivering in their Christmas Eve camp, Big Foot's people were starting their fires on the south bank of the White River, just inside the Oglalla reservation.

Their chief lay confined and cold in his wagon, unable to move, coughing up more and more of the bright blood onto his blankets. He was no longer able to make himself warm.

At dawn the next day, Big Foot sent three young men to ride on ahead with a message for the Oglalla chiefs at Pine Ridge, informing them that he was on his way, and though very ill, he expected to arrive soon. Then leaving three sentries on the White River to watch their back trail, the wagons creaked on to Cedar Spring. On the day after Christmas, after Big Foot endured a slow, jolting ride of only four miles, the Miniconjous camped on Red Water Creek.

Double Woman could not stand to look at the old chief when it was asked of her to feed him the hot bonemeal soup. Nor could she stand the smell of decay and death that hovered over Big Foot's wagon.

That night on Red Water Creek, Double Woman realized she could not rid herself of that stench merely by leaving the dying chief. Instead the smell of death seemed to be in the air, everywhere. It clung to her tattered, filthy clothing. In her hair. On her tongue.

Dawn of the twenty-seventh came bright, signaling some warmth to the camp the Seventh Cavalry had erected, its tents spread across the road from the trading post of Louis Mosseau along Wounded Knee Creek. Back in November when trouble started boiling, the trader had abandoned his store for the safety of Pine Ridge and General Brooke's troops.

The day before, Brooke had learned of the messengers Big Foot sent to the Oglalla friendlies, announcing his impending arrival. The general promptly dispatched the Seventh to intercept the Miniconjous and escort them in for disarming: companies A, B, I and K, along with a platoon of E Battery, First Artillery to handle the two Hotchkiss guns they were bringing along under Lieutenant Harry L. Hawthorne.

Major Samuel Marmaduke Whitside, commanding, was no desk soldier sent to do this man's job. He had learned all of his Indian savvy down in the Apache campaigns of Arizona.

As he drank his coffee and shared a tug or two at some fruit brandy with congenial civilian Harley Fagen, Whitside ordered his scouts under John Shangreau out to search for signs of Big Foot and his band.

"General Brooke offered those scouts twenty-five dollars to the man who found the chief," Whitside said.

"I hear Tibbles and the rest of the reporters up at James Asay's place put up another twenty-five dollars to the man who finds that Miniconjou bastard," Fagen replied, leaning back, his feet to the stove in Whitside's tent.

"Brooke doesn't like those reporters at all. Can't stand them creating their own war news when there's no war."

"Yet, Major. No war—yet."

Whitside regarded the Chicago detective. "I trusted that you weren't a newspaperman when I let you come along, Fagen. I bought this detective story of yours, whole cloth. You're not going to let me down, are you?"

He snorted, in his friendly way. "No, I won't, Major."

"Good. Because I want you to look at that small leather field case over there in the corner."

"I see it. Why?"

"You go look inside, you'll see the balls of the last sonuvabitch who tried to get around me."

Fagen found himself gulping. He tried out a weak grin on the officer. "Read you loud and clear, Major. I'm just here to find one of the troublemakers myself. He's said to be heading north, and you told me you were marching in that direction."

"Until we get Big Foot."

"Surely," Fagen sighed. "I'll push on from there myself, knowing the country is cleared by your boys."

"Don't like the idea of living to be an old man, eh, Fagen?"

That drew him up short, like Whitside had just grabbed hold of his balls and was tugging on them, testing them for stout.

"Major—I'm open to suggestions, you know that."

"I believe until everything's been put to rest with those hostiles penned up in the badlands, and we have Big Foot disarmed and shipped off to a new home—I figure you best stay close to my coattails."

"You don't mind my company, Major?"

He wagged his head, his eyes going gray as a spring thundercloud. "No, Mr. Fagen. I don't like civilians one goddamned bit. But I do like your brandy. I do, I do." He looked up as the tent flap rustled.

"Major, sir."

"Come in orderly," Whitside said, taking the message from the soldier. "This just arrive?"

"By heliograph, Major. From General Brooke."

A series of signal mirrors had been erected on every hilltop between Whitside's Wounded Knee camp and Pine Ridge some eighteen miles away. This newest order came from the general's aide-de-camp.

Major Whitside:
 I am directed by the Commanding General to say that he thinks Big Foot's party must be in your front somewhere,

and that you must make every effort to find him and then move on him at once and with rapidity. There must be a solution reached at the earliest possible moment. Find his trail and follow, or find his hiding place and capture him. If he fights, destroy him.

Whitside carefully folded the message and stuffed it into his tunic pocket before hoisting his cup of coffee laced with brandy. "Mr. Fagen, would you care to join the Seventh Cavalry on a little march in the field?"

He slapped his knee. "I knew it! You're out to capture Big Foot, aren't you?"

"In a manner of speaking, Mr. Fagen. And while you're at it, don't be so stingy with your brandy."

"It will be an honor to be in on that red bastard's capture, Major." Harley splashed more brandy into the officer's cup.

"Oh, this will be more than his capture, Mr. Fagen. This will undoubtedly prove to be Big Foot's destruction."

CHAPTER 49

FOR three suns now he had been riding south as fast as the bony army horse would carry him without protest.

On the day before the white man celebrated the birth of his messiah, Stone Eagle found himself among Hump's Miniconjous. The day before that, the twenty-third, he had ridden through the deserted camp of Big Foot's people.

Filled with a growing despair, he had hurried across the Cheyenne River to find someone, anyone, who could tell him where the band had gone. Hoping they were not among the Sioux who were huddling together in The Stronghold, bristling and dancing their spirits back, ready to fight.

Stone Eagle vividly recalled the long wall of steep, rocky cliff standing some three hundred feet above the valley floor where White Cow Bull had taken him to begin his vision-quest. Where he had once again listened to the whisper of the wolf. For something close to a hundred miles, that tall, irregular stretch of stony wall ran roughly east and west, eventually passing the place where the old

men had taken him after the birth of his son, there
secret, far from the prying eyes of the army and white m(
alike, to give his flesh and sacrifice his blood to the sun
prayer and thanksgiving.

He prayed now that he had done no harm to h
medicine, feeling a cold stone on his heart every time l
thought about how long it had been since he had seen tl
wolf. Or heard that frightening whisper of his voice.

What seemed like many winters now.

Not that he thought it wrong to believe in what tl
chiefs and the others had to say about adhering to the o
ways. Just the opposite. Over the last few days of ridii
through the cold and wilderness, skirting settlements ai
white homesteads, Stone Eagle had had himself a lot
time to think on the mess he had made of his short life. 1
think he had almost deserted the people who had taken hi
in and raised him, teaching him everything he had ev
known—it scared Stone Eagle to think he had come
close to taking up the cross of the white man's messiah ai
walking that white man's road.

Even more he prayed he had not lost his wife and son
the process of sorting things out, as long as it had taken. H
heart had been cold for many moons already. Yet he fe
empty just thinking of all the misery visited upon Sioux ai
Shahiyena families. Perhaps, after all, there was a real j(
he himself could share with them in the Ghost Dance. I
knew not of a family left untouched by the loss of a lov(
one to a soldier bullet. No family without the loss of a litt
child or old one gone now due to the white man's disease
the great hunger haunting the reservations.

No one remained immune to that pain of loss.

Perhaps after he had his family back together, Stor
Eagle decided, then he would go out on his own like in tl
old days. To fast and give of himself to the spirits. The
perhaps—the wolf would come to whisper to him on
again.

Just once more he yearned to talk with the wolf—if on
to assure himself he had done right in rejoining his peopl
in returning to the blanket.

Across the Cheyenne River from Hump's camp (
Cherry Creek, Stone Eagle stopped to buy himself a plug

tobacco and a small bag of coffee. For some time he stared at the shiny, oiled Winchester repeaters suspended on pegs behind the storekeeper at the stuffy mercantile in Cheyenne City. A time or two he thought of asking just to hold one of the Colt .45's on display beneath the heavy glass, a handful of shiny brass shells in a careless spray around the wood grips. But he had his own old black-powder pistol out in his saddlebags. That and the heavy Henry he carried at the end of his left arm were enough if trouble reared its head between here and The Stronghold.

He stood, just looking at this, then that, for the longest time, waiting for the clerk to come over. It was something more than embarrassment that he felt for the middle-aged white storekeeper who had no one else to wait on but the long-haired Indian youth who had been patiently biding his time.

"That comes to—six bits."

Stone Eagle handed the man a single eagle.

"This all you got, boy?"

"It is."

He walked away grumbling about having to break the ten-dollar coin just for some plugs of tobacco and a few coffee beans. Stone Eagle figured he was grumbling in doing it for an Indian.

"This your money, eh, boy?" the clerk asked caustically as he came back.

"Mine, legal—if that's what you mean."

Stone Eagle liked the look that put on the man's face as he accepted the rest of his money and stuffed it in the belt pouch he had hung beneath his blanket capote. He was halfway to the door when the clerk hollered out.

"Where you bound, boy? Down river to Bennett, or up to where all the ruckus is?"

"Looking for my family. They've moved off with Big Foot's band. Folks told me I would find them in the badlands since Big Foot didn't go back in to Fort Bennett like the army wanted him to."

The clerk snorted. "You know your English pretty good, son."

"Had a good teacher. Two of them, matter of fact, mister."

"Well, then you might be happy to know your folk aren't in no danger, 'cause they aren't gonna be mixing i with them troublemakers hiding back in them badlands."

"Big Foot's band isn't going to The Stronghold?"

The clerk came round the counter, dusting off his hand with his apron. "Word has it up and down the river— moccasin telegraph too—that Big Foot's bunch is headin straight for Pine Ridge."

"Pine Ridge? Why does he go there?"

"What Injun chief would pass up a hundred ponies?"

"I do not understand, mister."

"He'll get the hundred ponies for helping them Oglalla make peace with the army down there."

Stone Eagle's heart leapt. There was a chance, a rea chance now. If Double Woman stayed away from The Stronghold, the odds were pretty good nothing bad woul happen. No accidents, no stupid mistakes by warrior o soldier that would start the shooting. If Big Foot got in t Pine Ridge, he could convince the army and the agents o his worth to them to help make the peace.

He stepped up to the clerk, shifting the big Henry bac to the left hand as he held out his right. "Thank you for th news, mister."

The storekeeper shook, nervously, then smiled mor genuinely as Stone Eagle reached the door. There th young half-breed held the big brass knob, for a momen remembering the schoolhouse door and all the jumble memories that place had come to mean to him.

"Merry Christmas, mister!"

"Have a Merry Christmas yourself, boy! A real Merr Christmas!"

Yesterday found Big Foot's people still camped on Re Water Creek as the chief's pneumonia worsened. To Dou ble Woman it appeared the old man hovered between lif and death, fighting the pain as only a warrior of the old day would. She wondered how long he could fight, knowin how all his people would grieve in his death.

The night before, one of the chief's messengers ha returned from Pine Ridge with word that soldiers wer camped on Wounded Knee Creek near the trader's store

Later that morning of the twenty-seventh, another emissary, Bear Comes and Lies, returned with a Pine Ridge Oglalla, Shaggy Feather. They reported to the expectant crowd of Miniconjous who gathered around Big Foot's wagon that the bands in The Stronghold had grown convinced of the wisdom in surrendering.

"Short Bull has me tell you he and Kicking Bear will arrive at the agency in two days."

"This is good," Big Foot replied, grimacing in terrible pain. "They have heard I come to make peace for them."

"Yes, they want you to time your arrival at the agency so you get there when they do."

He shook his head. "No, it is too dangerous. We will run into soldiers."

"Kicking Bear has asked that you do this," Shaggy Feather pleaded. "I can guide you. You are to take your people to the east and south before turning back to the agency."

"No. I have decided. I am too sick and do not want to wait that long to reach the Pine Ridge. It is best that I take my people right to the soldiers."

"To the soldiers?" Shaggy Feather said, astounded.

"If I go to them, they cannot think I am running. They will see I am a man who means his life for peace."

The sun had reached midsky by the time the Miniconjous were ready to resume their march. They traveled slowly, the young men ahead carefully choosing the route of their travel for Big Foot's comfort, other flankers out as scouts to prevent any surprise meetings with the army. As twilight darkened the winter sky, they paused to warm their kettles on Medicine Root Creek. After reloading their upper supplies, the Miniconjous pushed over to American Horse Creek.

It was nearly midnight when the order came that they should stop and make camp just ahead. An open meadow afforded enough room for the wagons and old horses, along with the lodges the women would erect in the dark for protection against the great cold. Wearily they slid to the frozen ground next to the pine-log schoolhouse that had once been used by Oglalla children.

Nearby, Little Wound's village was as empty as the ribs

of a buffalo carcass after a year of bleaching on the prairie A cold night of fearful waiting.

By the time the sun crept off the far edge of the earth on that twenty-eighth day of December, Big Foot had his people on the march once more, south by southwest climbing up the divide from American Horse Creek, eager to reach the soldier camp, hoping there to find some measure of comfort. At the top of the divide, the advance riders began their descent into the valley of Porcupine Creek. Below them along the streambed, they spotted four of the army's scouts, watering their horses.

Baptiste Garnier, better known to the Sioux as Little Bat, his half brother called Old Hand, and two Oglalla scouts were held in the center of a ring of Miniconjou warriors while the wagons came down the slope to the Porcupine. At the chief's wagon Big Foot told the army scouts he wanted Old Hand and one of the Oglallas to take his message to the army commander camped at Wounded Knee Creek.

"Tell the soldier-chief I am coming to his camp."

As Major Whitside's camp of Seventh Cavalry was in the process of preparing their noonday meal, Old Hand and the Oglalla rode up. They babbled their story to the major chief of scouts, John Shangreau, who hurried off through the cavalry bivouac to tell Whitside.

"Gresham!" shouted the major. His adjutant, John C. Gresham appeared. "Sound 'Boots and Saddles,' Lieutenant."

Shangreau watched the grin spread across the face of the wiry civilian in a rumpled, soiled coat who sat on a stool near Whitside, busy at his snuff tin. "Major, all due—Big Foot told our scouts he was coming into camp. We may as well stay here till they come."

"Pure folly, Shangreau. Am I right, Mr. Fagen?" Whitside asked, turning to the detective.

"The major's right. Stick with what you do best. You're just a scout. Not a military man."

"See, John? Now, you know perfectly well that Major Henry's got his squadron of brunettes from the Ninth on cutting the countryside. What the hell would happen them buffalo soldiers of Henry's bump into Big Foot's boys?"

Shangreau shifted his weight. "Might be trouble."

"Might be is right," and he sloshed coffee into the small fire in front of his tent. "How about you getting ready to lead me back to where your boys found Big Foot?"

"As you say, Major," Shangreau replied, loping off.

Fagen licked the end of the green twig from which he had carved the bark before gently biting the end to spread the wood fibers. Repeatedly he dipped the twig into the German silver snuffbox that all but covered the palm of his hand. He brought the twig to his mouth, rubbing the snuff and powder mix back and forth across his gums as his eyes began to water and his nose started to run.

"You really enjoy your snuff, Mr. Fagen."

He smiled, feeling the hot prickling of nerve response awakening across his forehead. "Every man has his weakness. I just happen to have two."

"Snuff and?"

"Indians, Major Whitside. Lately I've grown quite fond of Indians."

CHAPTER 50

December 28, 1890

CAPTAIN Preston Tripp's escort had stopped to let the horses blow and stretch their legs upon reaching the dry wash of Pine Creek where it cut through the tree-studded foothills at the base of Porcupine Butte. No sooner was he lighting his pipe than one of the flankers rode up in a lather, pointing to his rear.

"We've got company, Captain!"

"Spread out!" Tripp ordered. "Horse holders to the timber."

He listened to the cursing of some of the old veterans and the young recruits alike as they plopped to the cold ground among the scrub oak and dwarf pine, waiting.

In but a moment three horsemen appeared downstream, picking their way along easily enough, without an apparent care in the world.

"Indians, all right," Tripp muttered to the lieutenant commanding his escort. "Let's hope there's not more of 'em."

"Captain, look yonder. There's more."

Through the bob and weave of the terrain and vegetation, Tripp recognized the movement of more men and horses some two hundred yards behind the trio of Indians.

"Volley fire, Lieutenant. On my command," he ordered, watching the officer nod and move off to spread the word.

The three came on. The two on either side of the middle rider were as dark as any Indian could be, braids and all. The middle light enough to pass for white. Tripp's mind snagged on the thought of it, wondering if he might be looking at Custer's half-breed son.

We're close enough to Pine Ridge, I suppose. A man never knows—

"They're soldiers, by God!" shouted one of his escort.

Cautiously Tripp and his lieutenant stood, gazing downstream at the column of cavalry, guidons snapping in the cold December air.

"Merry Christmas indeed, Lieutenant," Tripp muttered, realizing now just how hard his chest burned, how fast his heart thumped as he stepped forward, signaling the trio of riders.

John Shangreau had Old Hand and the Oglalla scout stay with Tripp's escort while he accompanied the captain back to the head of the column, where introductions were made all around.

"You're headed to Pine Ridge on army business?" Whitside asked.

"Nothing in the slightest to do with this current flap with the ghost dancers and all, Major. I assure you," he said, relief on every word.

Whitside shook his head, smiling that wolfish grin of his. "Good to have a soldier along for a change. Enough civilians back at Pine Ridge to keep Brooke stirred up for some time to come."

"He doesn't like civilians?"

"What army man does?" Whitside inquired. The tight-faced civilian in the rumpled coat who quietly sat his army rigging behind the major cleared his throat and hoisted his brandy bottle, from which he pulled a short swallow. Whitside flung his voice over his shoulder in the way of an apology. "Present company excluded, Mr. Fagen."

Tripp glanced at the man, sensing something of nagging

import with the civilian's name—more so wondering just what the solitary civilian was doing along with Whitside's Seventh: not a scout, hardly the type, nor did his clothing and physical makeup lend him to a life outdoors. A better guess would be a newsman, come along on Whitside's maneuver for an exclusive to his eastern readers. Still again, Fagen did not look the type. Perhaps nothing more than a friend of the major's, a curious spectator come to view his fill of Indians during the current disturbance—what the reporters for all those papers were billing as the last great Indian uprising.

"Introduce yourself, Fagen," Whitside suggested in that military tone of his.

"Certainly." He nudged his horse forward, shifting the brandy bottle and extending his hand to the captain.

"Harley Fagen. Of Chicago."

Tripp's eyes narrowed on the thin aquiline beak of a nose planted between the birdlike eyes. Chicago rang some distant alarm.

"Captain Preston Tripp. Adjutant general's office."

Whitside said, "You're a bit out of your league here, aren't you, Captain?"

"On assignment, Major—"

"Major!" John Shangreau whirled up, accompanied by his two scouts. "Have a look up there!"

Every head cranked up the gentle slope of Porcupine Butte, watching two horsemen break the crest of the ridge and hurriedly work their animals down toward the column.

"They're yours aren't they, Shangreau?"

"Little Bat for sure, Major. This could mean trouble."

As the pair reined up before the head of the column, the first of the Miniconjou warriors appeared at the top of the butte, moving slowly over the crest just vacated by Little Bat, inching down toward the soldiers.

"Little Bat! Good to see those Miniconjous released you. How does it look with that bunch of Big Foot's?" Shangreau asked as Baptiste Garnier reined up.

"They look plenty tough. All painted up," Little Bat replied. "We're liable to catch hell today."

Whitside asked some rapid-fire questions of Garnier, then gave the order for his column to move out.

After less than a mile, the major signaled another halt while they waited to see the disposition of the Miniconjou procession. Once the wagons were all over the crest, the warriors spread out in a rough front protecting their women and children. Whitside quietly gave Gresham the order for the formation of their own skirmish line. The Hotchkiss guns were run up and readied for firing by Lieutenant Hawthorne's artillery crews, while every fourth man serving as a horse holder took four mounts to the rear.

At the show of muscle by the soldiers, Big Foot's warriors grew more agitated, racing back and forth, shouting, brandishing their rifles overhead. Some dropped to the ground, tying up the tails of their ponies, saying their war medicine in preparation for battle. From somewhere behind the line of anxious warriors, an order was given, and the men milled to a halt. Behind them the wagons stopped, then two older men appeared on foot.

"Shangreau—go on out there and find out what those two want," Whitside ordered.

The scout rode out, talked for a moment, then accompanied the two back to a Miniconjou wagon, from which stood a long lodgepole. From it a white flag fluttered in the cold breeze that kicked up more of the stinging dust.

In a moment more the solitary wagon inched slowly through the protective line of painted warriors, crossing the open land between the two groups. Its driver brought it to a halt beside Whitside's command group as the front row of warriors echoed with the clicks of chambered rounds.

Shangreau pointed to the wagon. "Major Whitside, like you to meet Big Foot, chief of the Deep Creek Miniconjous."

The major peered over the tall, rough-boarded sidewall as the others inched up to have themselves a look. The chief lay so cocooned in dirty blankets that Tripp could see only a small portion of Big Foot's face. A steady ooze of blood seeped from his nose, despite the chief's attempts to dab at it with a filthy rag. The blankets and floor of the wagon were dotted with small pools of frozen blood.

At the same time, Whitside's young soldiers were every bit as anxious as the warriors. Some of the veterans calmed things, murmuring their reassurance that all a man had to do was to be ready. A small handful of the braver Miniconjou rode cautiously to the Hotchkiss guns. A single painted warrior slid from the bare back of his old horse, walked boldly up to the gun, and stuck his arm down the bore.

Satisfied, the tall warrior pulled his arm out, smiled, and leapt atop his horse, where he sat with his repeater across his chest.

Whitside shook hands with the chief. "Shangreau, tell Big Foot he must bring his people into my camp at Wounded Knee."

"Yes," the chief coughed in reply, barely loud enough to be heard by those surrounding the wagon. "All right. I was going there to see you anyway. Then I must go to Pine Ridge. The Oglallas have promised me a hundred ponies to make peace for them."

Whitside whispered quietly, "Shangreau, tell Big Foot I want their guns and horses."

The scout's eyes widened apprehensively. He shook his head. "You try to take the guns and horses from these men, there's liable to be one sonuvabitch of a fight, Major."

"I have my orders, Shangreau."

"It's the men you want, Major. If there's a fight, the bucks will bolt and get away, while some of the women and children will be killed in the shooting."

"General Brooke sent me his orders to dismount and disarm Big Foot's people, Mr. Shangreau."

"Might be so, Major—but I'm advising you to take this bunch into camp first off before your men disarm them there."

Whitside chewed on that, sucking on the inside of his cheek for a long time. His eyes finally came to rest on the expectant face of Captain Tripp. The major smiled as he glanced at his chief of scouts. "All right, Shangreau. Tell Big Foot to move his people down to my camp at Wounded Knee."

Bit Foot swiped the rag across his bloody mouth, then replied. "It is good. I am going down to camp. That is where I am going, soldier-chief."

He held up his hand to Whitside, and the two shook a second time.

The major waved his adjutant up. "Gresham, order the

ambulance brought up for the chief. I can see this wagon has no springs. Let's make the man more comfortable on the ride into our camp."

As a group of soldiers grabbed the bundle of blankets and slowly hoisted the ailing chief into the army ambulance, Tripp edged his mount up beside Harley Fagen, who was just putting his silver snuffbox back in a pocket.

"Mr. Fagen."

"Captain." He stuffed the peeled twig between his lips, chewing and sucking on it.

"I have the oddest feeling we've met."

Fagen regarded him beneath the narrow brim of his eastern bowler. "Can't say as I remember it, Captain. And I'm pretty good with faces."

"Just a feeling I had, Mr. Fagen."

Half of the mounted soldiers led off, pointing southwest for the creek called Wounded Knee. Near there, Double Woman knew, Monaseetah and White Cow Bull had their cabin.

Big Foot's ambulance fell into line, followed by the Miniconjou wagons and the warriors. The last of the cavalry and Lieutenant Hawthorne's guns brought up the tail of the march.

As she set her wagon in motion, Double Woman watched a pair of soldiers gallop away from the head of the column. She figured they were carrying word to the soldier camp. It was not long before the long line of heliographs were flashing their messages back and forth between Wounded Knee and the Pine Ridge camp of General Brooke in the late afternoon sun that did little to warm the winter air.

That sun was but two fingers above the western horizon when the procession crawled into the valley that measured three hundred to five hundred yards wide. Passing over the bridge that spanned the narrow stream itself, the column plodded south on the agency road. Wounded Knee Creek wandered almost due north through the valley at the foot of a tall ridge hemming the valley in on the east. On the west two separate ridges jutted to the east. Between them a dry coulee meandered to empty itself into the Wounded Knee. Not far past the coulee, the old agency road curved slowly to the west, streaming cross-country for eighteen miles to Pine Ridge.

After crossing the bridge some of the warriors dropped out of the procession at Louis Mosseau's store, which stood beside the small building housing the post office.

"I am hungry, mother."

She looked down at Stone Eagle's handsome son. "We have arrived. In a moment we will make camp, and I will cook something warm for your belly."

Double Woman did not want him to see the apprehension in her eyes as she looked over the row upon row of white army tents stretching along the right side of the road as the column rumbled by the soldier camp. The rows stood out stark and pale against the darker prairie here at twilight in the last days of the Moon of Popping Trees. Since that afternoon she had carried the cold stone upon her heart— fear she could taste like something tangible—ever since recognizing the war flags these soldiers rode beneath.

Sky blue and bright, blood red. Crossed long knives of silver. And the magical figure above those knives—a number 7.

Long Hair's soldiers.

This could not be good. The same men who had charged into Black Kettle's camp. The same soldiers who then found their own destruction on a sunburnt hillside beside the Goat River fifteen summers ago.

Monaseetah's father had died fighting these soldiers.

Monaseetah's son, her husband—the half-breed child of the man who had led his troops to their deaths. Long Hair.

"Come, my son," she called softly to him.

As the soldiers dropped off, returning to their tent city, and the scouts halted the first wagons, the young mother sat looking up at the hilltops above the flat, open ground the army had chosen for their camp. In the deepening twilight the dark figures of soldiers muscling their big wagon-guns into position stood out like nighthawks sweeping down atop their prey against the night sky.

Double Woman shuddered, holding out her arms to hoist her son to the ground. So many of the children cried as they tumbled out of the wagons into the cold, fading light. The mothers had been pushed and corralled and herded so much in the last weeks. Many lost their tempers and shrieked at the young ones or snapped at the slowness of the old ones who could be of little help.

Some of the young men still circled the camp, grumbling, waving their rifles, making war noise. The old men clambered out of the springless wagons, unsure on their spindly legs. One of the older ones, the medicine man called Yellow Bird, started his Ghost Dance chant. Pointing his finger here, then there at the soldiers surrounding their camp, passing his curse on them when the time came that the earth should swallow up the white man.

She knew the sight of those war flags would not let her sleep. The 7 come to trouble her dreams.

"It is good to see you again, Double Woman."

She wheeled at the sound of her name spoken by a familiar voice. "Sees Red!"

They embraced.

She found herself clutching to him too fiercely, perhaps because he was Stone Eagle's brother. "I am sorry, Sees Red."

He smiled down at her. "I am not. It has been too long."

"How did you know to find me here?"

"I knew you had gone to be with your people after the trouble with Charging Hawk. When the word spread five suns ago that the army was looking for Big Foot's band, I grew worried. I am glad to see you, and my nephew."

"I am Yellow Bird," the boy announced steadily, still hugging his mother's coattail.

Sees Red glanced at the woman, a question in his eyes.

"Yes, he was given your brother's childhood name."

The Cheyenne straightened. "It is good, Yellow Bird. A name that should live on for many seasons."

"How is it you are here?" she asked.

"I no longer work for the police at Pine Ridge. Many days ago the army was hiring some scouts. They came to the metal-breasts first. I have joined Lieutenant Taylor's Oglalla scouts. It is good work—and good pay."

"You always wanted easy work and good pay, Sees Red!"

They laughed easily as the camp went up around them. Not far to the east, close to the cavalry camp, some soldiers were struggling in the failing light to erect a large wall tent, complete with sheet-iron stove, both ordered for the comfort of the ailing chief Big Foot.

"Can I help you with your lodge, sister?"

"Yes, you and Yellow Bird collect firewood and build me a fire. I will see to the lodge. But the boy is hungry."

"Just like his father, Double Woman," the Cheyenne answered. "Always hungry."

CHAPTER 51

"PROVIDENCE had a hand in my running into Major Whitside's unit," explained Captain Tripp to the veteran cavalry officer at the fire. "Custer's Seventh, you see? There's six of you still with the regiment . . . six of you here: Varnum, Nowlan, Wallace, Godfrey, and Edgerly. Along with you, Captain. So when I learned that Whitside had asked Colonel Forsyth to bring up the rest of your regiment from Pine Ridge, I figured I could spend a day or two here at your Wounded Knee camp—interviewing all of you."

"Heard you talked with Ed Godfrey—some time ago wasn't it?" asked Myles Moylan.

"At Lincoln—yes. Years ago now."

The cavalry captain played with the coals for a moment. "He have much to tell you?"

"Not as much as I figure you can, Captain. You were Custer's adjutant during that Washita campaign, his capture of the Sweetwater Cheyennes. The whole long winter of it—while Custer was with this woman . . . Monaseetah."

"Don't know what I can tell you that will help."

"What you've already told me regarding Custer is a grea help in simply understanding the man."

"He was not just a good cavalry officer—the general wa one of the few men in all my life who liked me."

"I understand how he took you under his wing in sixty six."

"His memory—the good soldier he was and what th army meant to him—all that is the reason I've stayed in th army."

"Many a man never found a better home, Myles."

"Aye. No home better than the army for a file like me."

"So tell me—what of the stories, rumors even, of th child?"

"Child?"

"Monaseetah's second—the boy called Yellow Bird."

"I was with the general the night her first was born. simon-pure Cheyenne—what Fred Benteen called tha little buck." He paused a long while, dallying at the coals "I don't know anything of the second boy."

"Surely, as Custer's adjutant, you heard him mentio something about the woman . . . about the stories of he having a second child that fall of sixty-nine."

"Custer was busy then—back east or off on buffal hunts—in command, you see," Moylan explained.

"Did he ever talk about her again—after sending th Washita prisoners back to their reservation?"

Moylan's eyes climbed to Tripp's, held them for th longest time, then finally fell back to the squirming re coals.

"He talked about her a lot, Captain. A damned lot. Lik he never could quite get her out of his system."

He leaned forward, whispering. "Then tell me—wha did Custer ever say about his half-breed Cheyenne son?'

His eyes flashed. "No man can ever prove it was Custer son."

"Reddish brown hair, Myles."

"I've heard that said too."

"And his eyes."

"Heard they wasn't a bit like the general's eyes."

"Enough, Myles."

"Perhaps."

Tripp waited a while as well, sipping at his coffee as the coyotes began their nightly chorus from the far ridgetops. He finally set his cup aside. "You believe Yellow Bird is Custer's son, don't you, Myles Moylan?"

He nodded and swallowed hard. "I knew the general. He was never a man to retreat. And with that good-looking Cheyenne gal, once he charged in there—he was all but a goner. She had him—that much was easy to tell from the way they . . . hell, even the way they looked at each other. Damn—if only he'd laid back and left her be . . . not got so tangled up with her—it'd all been different today."

"What'd be different?"

"The boy—that Yellow Bird," Moylan said. He was a long time before continuing. A coyote called out. "That, and maybe even some of what he done on the Little Bighorn."

Tripp felt the hairs stand on the back of his neck for a moment. "This Cheyenne woman has some connection with Custer at the massacre of those two hundred men?"

Moylan's eyes pleaded, the soft Irish brown of them gone doughy as he looked at Tripp. "He might'a made a better decision, Preston. That's all I'm gonna say."

"Dammit, Myles. Don't go giving me the tease of it, then not come through."

"Captain Moylan!"

"What is it?" he demanded of the lieutenant loping up.

"Colonel Forsyth sends his greetings."

"He's arrived?"

Tripp pulled out his pocket watch and twisted it into the light. Half past eight.

"With the rest of the regiment, Captain. Also Captain Capron's second pair of Hotchkiss guns are going up on the ridge, yonder."

"Funny, you'd think I would hear the noise of that many men, horses, and wagons coming up the Agency Road," Moylan commented.

"They didn't," replied the lieutenant. "Came way 'round to the east, so they wouldn't frighten the hostiles any."

"I'm glad. These two companies I've strung around the camp are spread thin enough as it is."

"Them damned Oglallas are doing their best to stir u Big Foot's people, though," the young soldier explained.

"Oglallas?" Moylan demanded.

"Taylor's scouts. They're over there, other side of th ravine, hollering in to the Miniconjous—telling 'em abou Forsyth and the rest of the regiment pulling in."

Moylan looked at Tripp, then both men turned to the right at the distant clatter of horses and the creak of dr hubs on the Hotchkiss guns rattling into position on th high ground.

To their left on that open ground between the India village and the cavalry camp, there suddenly arose som shouting, the noise of a scuffle, and the muffled cursing c several men. As officer of the day, responsible for the camp Myles Moylan moved off like a shot.

Preston Tripp was on his heels.

Several soldiers were pulling other soldiers out of th mass of blue bodies. The handful of loud-mouthed, swea ing fighters were scuffling, refusing arrest by Moylan sergeant of the guard.

Suddenly one of the smaller figures broke free, whirlin on the newcomers. His hand flashed to his ankle, lifting u his pant cuff.

"Grab the sonuvabitch!" yelled one of the soldiers.

The pale winter light reflected for a heartbeat off th blued metal of the pistol.

As suddenly the figure drew down on Tripp, the muzzl spitting bright orange light on the snow between them a two soldiers wrestled to pull the man down. He felt a tea at his upper arm. A second time the pistol spat flame. Thi time the young captain heard the angry whine of the bulle passing his ear, raking an angry furrow alongside his head

"Who is that, goddammit!" Moylan shouted, in th middle of the fray, throwing himself on the gunman as th third shot went wild, into the air.

Tripp sat stunned on the snow, fingertips coming from the damp warmth on his left arm, touching the left side o his head where the bullet had left his scalp burning.

"I've got it, Cap'n!"

"The gun?"

"Said I got it."

"Give it here!" Moylan ordered, moving back. He looked over his shoulder. "You alive, Captain Tripp?"

"Yes, Captain," he answered, sensing his heart for the first time in the last few frantic moments. He struggled to his feet, feeling queasy at first. "First time I've had blood drawn like this."

"I'll get the surgeon—"

"No!" he answered stiffly, volving the shoulder. "It'll wait a moment. I want to see the man who shot me first."

"Are you bastards drunk?" Moylan demanded, grabbing one soldier's tunic.

"Drunk enough to kill us some Injuns!" shouted another as he spat at the man remaining on the ground, underfoot.

"My God—that's Big Foot!" exclaimed Tripp as the last two soldiers were yanked from the prostrate Miniconjou chief.

"I want to see that charges are pressed against these men," growled the army surgeon as he stumbled from the tent, a hand held to his bloody forehead.

"They jump you, Captain?" Moylan asked.

"Came in here, swearing and swaggering—boasting they weren't gonna wait until tomorrow. Wanted them Big Foot's scalp tonight. Him," and the surgeon pointed at the shadows, where two of Moylan's guards held the only man in the group not dressed in army blues, "he's the one did most of the cussing and is the one swung at me with a piece of firewood."

"And shot Captain Tripp with this little pistola of his," Moylan grumbled, brandishing the confiscated weapon. "He'll need you looking at his wounds."

"Have him come in the tent here when I get Big Foot settled," the surgeon growled as he turned on his heel. He and a soldier raised the ill chief and disappeared behind the tent flaps.

"Bring that one over here, Sergeant," Moylan ordered, indicating the fire kept glowing not far from Big Foot's tent.

"I want to talk with Major Whitside—immediately, sonny!" the civilian snarled as two young soldiers dragged his rumpled frame into the light.

"Who are you?" Moylan inquired.

"I said I want to talk with Whitside—or I'll have your rank, you mick bastard!"

"Fagen," Tripp whispered, stopping beside Moylan, his arm held in the right hand. He had a grim smile on his face, recognizing the thin man pulled into the firelight. "I just put it all together."

"Told you, Captain—we've never met. And you'll not hang a thing on me."

"I don't have to hang a thing on you," Moylan retorted. "Looks like attempted murder is good enough for me. You've done enough to hang yourself, mister."

"He led them others—the soldiers—in here to drag Big Foot out—sick as the old man is," one of the guards was explaining.

"Tonight—tomorrow . . . his scalp gonna be ours sometime!" Fagen hissed.

"But now your ass belongs to the army," Moylan said, stepping up to the civilian, stuffing the little pistol into his coat pocket. "By shooting Captain Tripp here—you've damaged some army property, uh . . . mister?"

"Harley Fagen," Tripp himself answered. "Self-employed Chicago detective."

The thin man jerked his face close to Tripp's. "No, I told you. We ain't met."

"Fired many years ago by Pinkertons."

"Trumped-up charges they were!"

"But I've known about you for some time, Fagen. We've been covering a lot of the same ground, don't you know?"

One marblelike eye squinted at him in the flickering light. "Same ground?"

"Looking for Yellow Bird." Preston Tripp watched that bring the detective up like a fistful of buckshot in the belly.

"I knew it, sonny boy. You looking for that half-breed too?"

"That's why I'm here, Fagen."

"I'll be goddamned and go to hell right here," Fagen muttered. "If that don't beat all: We've come to the same place, tracking that bastard sonuvabitch to this bunch of Miniconjous. How'd you find out he was supposed to be with Big Foot? That schoolteacher tell you?"

Tripp suddenly realized a red flag was waving before his eyes, the way it always did when he had a hostile witness before him on the stand. This sputtering, murderous drunk required some delicate maneuvering.

"No, Fagen. Wasn't the schoolteacher." He winced with the pain as a gust of cruel wind slashed across the open arm wound.

"Then how you know he was coming to find his wife and child with Big Foot's band?"

"Let's just say it was a little piece of detective work, and a lot of luck, Mr. Fagen."

"Can I take this bastard now, Captain Tripp?" asked Myles Moylan.

"He's all yours."

"Your time's coming, Captain!" Fagen spat. "You may have me—but you haven't got the general's son!"

"You'll file the charges in the morning with Major Whitside?" asked Moylan.

"It'll wait till then. Get him out of here now."

Moylan hurried the guards off with the drunken soldiers and the noisy civilian, then returned to Tripp's side.

"What's this you were hammering out with the civilian? Something about a half-breed. And the general. I knew any better—I'd think it has to do with Custer."

"Nothing, really, Captain Moylan."

"Has to do with Custer's son—the one you yourself called Yellow Bird, doesn't it?"

Tripp stared into the darkness at the distant lodges lit like paper lanterns hung at a society ball in Washington City.

"That drunken civilian may be a worthless pile of scum when it comes to being a decent human being—but he is good at what he does."

"Detective work?"

"Yes. Besides nearly blowing my head off—he just gave me the final piece in a very difficult puzzle."

"About this Yellow Bird?"

Tripp nodded, the hair standing at the back of his neck as the howl of a distant wolf shut off its little brothers, the coyotes on the nearby hills.

"Captain Moylan—I have every reason in the world to

believe George Armstrong Custer's half-breed son is in that village."

He awoke in the predawn darkness, feeling the hurt of the old bones and tired muscles that had taken such a battering in the ruckus over at the chief's tent last night. Harley Fagen was too old for such brawling anymore. Leave it to the younger and bigger fellows from now on. His head pounded as if he'd laid it for a hammering on a blacksmith's anvil. He decided he wouldn't go at the whiskey so hard next time around. Stick with his snuff and morphine mix he loved so much.

But last night when that Pine Ridge trader, James Asay, had come into camp with Colonel Forsyth and the rest of the regiment, carting along that big key of whiskey he popped for the officers, Harley Fagen was not about to refuse going over to propose a toast or two with Major Whitside. Knowing, as Fagen did, how the major was partial to his liquor.

Blinking his swollen eyes now, the detective dragged the iron chain between his ankles as quietly as possible across the frozen ground, sneaking close to the tent flaps lashed tightly together. Holding his breath, he raised the chains linking the iron bracelets clamped on his wrists and ever so slightly parted the flaps.

Outside he heard the footsteps of a pair of them, two guards stomping up and down across the frozen snow on either side of the tent, where they had put him under protective custody until the matter could be handled by Colonel Forsyth. Later in the day—after Forsyth no longer had more important matters on his mind. Like taking the horses and weapons from Big Foot's Miniconjous.

Through the narrow crack in the flaps, Fagen watched the graying of the sky lend some ashy illumination to the nearby bluff. A few thin spires of smoke climbed into the inky sky above the positions held by Captain Capron's E Battery. Having heard so much about their destructive power . . . Lord, did he wish he could see those god-damned guns in operation.

Maybe he would have to wait on that. What with that Captain Tripp warning Fagen he was taking him back to

Pine Ridge and General Brooke. From there to stand trial on some charges of attempted murder. Didn't matter—that young army scut would never learn the truth, Fagen decided.

He snorted a crude chuckle, reaching into his coat pocket for the snuff tin. He was relieved they hadn't taken that from him. His chuckle turned into laughter as he thought about Tripp's detective work.

Son of a bitch thinks he's got all the pieces put together to this thing. But Tripp doesn't have enough sense to know he should be looking for a half-breed buck named Stone Eagle.

His laughter wound itself tightly into a wild, hysterical cackle as he began cursing, shouting, rattling the chains that bound his wrists and clamped his ankles to a tent pole.

"To hell with that stupid Captain Preston Tripp!" he hollered.

"Quiet down in there, Fagen!"

"And to hell with the army itself—home to the powerful bastards of our dear republic!"

"Told you stay quiet!" shouted the second guard.

"Goddamn the general's lady—Libbie Custer!"

"You'll pay for that, Fagen!"

"—waking up the major, you bastard!"

Both guards were shouting at him . . . and beyond, from those rows upon rows of tents housing the Seventh Cavalry, came the oaths of Custer's soldiers.

"Most of all, boys—I curse Yellow Bird, the bastard son of George—Armstrong—Custer!"

CHAPTER 52

PRESTON Tripp hadn't slept well the night before.

Eager to have a chance to have a close-hand look at each one of those 120 warriors in Big Foot's village.

Following reveille, Colonel James W. Forsyth had laid out his plans for disarming the Miniconjou, explaining his deployment of troops—along with Lieutenant Charles W. Taylor's Oglalla scouts, some thirty strong. Due to the narrowness of the valley and the proximity of the hills, Tripp realized Forsyth's soldiers would be no farther than three hundred yards from the warriors when it came time to take their weapons.

By eight A.M., the colonel sent John Shangreau to summon the men to Big Foot's tent for a council. The interpreter instructed the Miniconjou crier, Wounded Hand, what to tell his people. It wasn't long before a few of the older men began shuffling up to the open ground around the chief's tent. Yet in the delay, as the soldiers deliberated on how to handle some details, many of the warriors milled back and forth between the council area and the village, restless.

"Shangreau, get the men settled so we can get started," Forsyth ordered.

His staff and regimental officers lined up on either side of the colonel, joined by the Catholic priest for the nearby mission, Father Francis Craft.

Within minutes Shangreau had the warriors gathered in a crude line facing the cavalry camp. They quieted for a few minutes while Forsyth talked, not knowing English. When Shangreau began his interpretation, the men became anxious.

"The soldier-chief says you must surrender your weapons. This is only temporary—for your own safety. You will be secure in the hands of your friends, these soldiers. No more will your bellies be empty. All your troubles are now at an end."

After a few moments of some excited debate, a few of the headmen decided to confer with Big Foot.

Tripp glanced over at the village. Some of the children ran about playing happily, their bellies full of bacon, grease still shiny around their little mouths.

Though his wounds hurt and Dr. Hoff suggested he rest out the morning, the young captain stood in the cold, suffering the brutal wind with the rest. He felt good about being here to watch this, knowing that soon enough he would be able to get a much closer look at each of the 120 warriors—anxious until he found the light-haired, wolf-eyed half-breed son of George Armstrong Custer.

Shangreau came back from listening to the Miniconjou conference. He bent over Forsyth to whisper. "Colonel, Big Foot told his men to give up the bad guns. Told 'em to keep the good ones."

In the meantime a few of the young men continued to move back and forth between the conference and the village. It didn't take a smart man to realize that the men were getting the women all worked up back in camp.

Minutes dragged by until the first group of about twenty of the warriors returned to the council area with but two busted carbines.

"These aren't the weapons they were carrying yesterday," Major Whitside growled. "They've got more—better too."

"Probably used by the children for toys, Colonel," Shangreau replied.

"Bring Big Foot out here, and let's get him to order his men to turn over their guns, Colonel. They'll listen to him," Whitside said.

"Very well, Major. Bring the chief out."

Two of Dr. Hoff's hospital stewards helped Big Foot from his tent. Many of the older men, the chief's advisers, moved behind Big Foot and settled to the cold ground.

"Captain Wallace, let's put a stop to this movement by the warriors back and forth to the village. Your men and Captain Varnum's," Forsyth ordered.

As the soldiers of the Seventh Cavalry were deployed, 106 men were surrounded in the council area.

"Fourteen must still be in the village now," Whitside said.

"Wells, come with me," the colonel said to his interpreter.

Philip Wells followed Forsyth to Big Foot's side.

"Tell the chief he must instruct his men to give up all their weapons."

"The soldiers at Cheyenne River stole and burned all our rifles," Big Foot sputtered, the blood oozing generously from a nostril.

"That's bullshit, Wells. You tell Big Foot that his Indians had many rifles yesterday at the time of their surrender—they were well armed. I am sure he's deceiving me."

"My men have only the guns you have found," Big Foot argued. "All were gathered up on Cheyenne River and burned by the soldiers there."

"That's fat in the fire," Forsyth muttered. "The old fellow gives me but one choice." The colonel ordered two separate groups to go in search of weapons in the village itself.

"Send Shangreau with Wallace's men. Little Bat goes with Varnum's detail. Be sure your men treat the women with courtesy," instructed Forsyth. "But remember the women are the ones now hiding the weapons the men don't want to give up."

As the two groups moved off in opposite directions, heading for the Indian camp, an old medicine man, the leader of the Ghost Dance zealots among Big Foot's people, the one called Yellow Bird, rose to his feet. In his knee-length deer-hide Ghost Dance shirt, tanned a creamy white and decorated with potent red symbols of the moon, sun, and stars, he danced side to side in a shuffling step, chanting his prayers and songs. At times he knelt to scoop up a handful of the hard earth, tossing his magic toward the cordon of troopers surrounding the warriors.

While Forsyth's thirty soldiers moved deliberately through the village, many of the nervous warriors attempted to find out what the soldiers were doing among their families. Others, mainly younger men, tried to muscle through the soldier lines.

"Major Whitside?"

"What is it, Wells?" the officer asked of the interpreter.

"That one—the old man dancing."

"What of him?"

"I figured you'd like to know he's making mischief with the others."

"Go tell Forsyth about this."

Tripp watched Philip Wells bring the colonel back to the gathering of wild-eyed, nervous warriors.

"Tell him to stop his dancing. Tell him I order him to sit down," Forsyth directed.

Wells translated the order, yet Yellow Bird kept on dancing, throwing his magical dust at the soldiers, chanting.

"He will sit down when he completes the circle," said one of the warriors to the interpreter.

Forsyth and the rest watched warily until the medicine man plopped to the ground and fell silent.

Pulling his watch from his pocket, Tripp found it just past nine-thirty as the search details returned from the village. The soldiers dumped half their weapons in a pile before Colonel Forsyth, the others taken to the hilltop gun positions.

"Not very many serviceable weapons, I would say, Major," Forsyth grumbled.

"A few Winchesters, but most of these are so old, they'd likely blow up in your hands."

"That means one thing only."

"Yes, sir. The weapons I saw the warriors carry yesterday can only be under their blankets."

Forsyth waved his interpreter over. "Mr. Wells, tell the men I will not search them. They are men—and men have their dignity. In return I will demand that they come forward like men and remove their blankets. Any weapons found under those blankets are to be left on the ground."

"*Hau, hau!*"

Tripp inched closer when two dozen of the older men agreed and stood. As they began to move between two groups of soldiers, opening their blankets, the younger warriors sat, their nervous eyes darting here and there. The medicine man rose to his feet once again, repeating his Ghost Dance songs, challenging the young men, pointing at the soldiers, and casting more handfuls of dirt in their direction.

As a few old pistols were placed on the ground, cartridges emptied into an officer's hat, the medicine man moved more vigorously, stirring more of the young men to their feet. They milled about anxiously, looking from the lines of soldiers to the hilltops where the Hotchkiss guns sat.

"You better get him to sit down now," Wells pleaded with some of the older men, pointing at the medicine man haranguing the warriors.

Behind him Tripp heard anxious muttering from many of the line soldiers. Glancing up and down the troops, he could read the tension and fear on most every face. They did not like the old man's troublemaking, nor the growing aggressiveness of the young Miniconjous.

"Be ready," Captain Wallace said quietly to his men. "Mark my word—there's going to be trouble."

"What's that one saying?" Whitside asked of Wells, pointing to a young warrior stomping around, boldly holding his rifle over his head and shouting.

"Says his name is Black Coyote."

"He anyone special to these people?" Forsyth inquired.

Wells shook his head. "Says his rifle is his—won't give it up. He paid a lot of money for it. These others say that Black Coyote is deaf—can't hear a thing."

"Colonel, I protest! We can't have that young buck

strutting around with that goddamned rifle—while we look like fools disarming these old men," Whitside growled.

"All right, Major. Get the rifle from him so we can settle things down." Forsyth wheeled, irritated at the growing noise from the medicine man. "And tell Wells to get that dancer to sit and stay on his ass. He's beginning to make me nervous."

While the interpreter went back to some of the headmen to ask them to convince the medicine man to cease his provocative dance, Whitside ordered a pair of his veterans to take the rifle from Black Coyote.

There was a brief struggle between the three men. In the space of four heartbeats, Black Coyote grappled with the soldiers, pointing his rifle up and down as they fought, six hands on the weapon.

Yellow Bird shrieked, pointing at the struggle, before he dragged a hand across the bare earth and flung the dirt high into the air.

It was like a nightmare that next beat of Preston Tripp's heart, falling back, stumbling—bumping into men with the bloody arm. Soldiers shouting, many cursing, a few shouting orders above the confusion. And in the center of it all the young men dropping their blankets, pulling up those shiny weapons: yanking pistols from their belts and levering cartridges through their repeating rifles.

He stared, fascinated as he tumbled to the ground over someone, something. Falling backwards as he watched, hypnotized by the orange muzzle flash of so damned many rifles.

Double Woman gave little Yellow Bird a squeeze, then let him run off to play with the other boys gathering at the lip of the dry ravine to play some shinny-ball. Their sticks scuffed tiny clouds of dust into the chill morning air, like the hooves of ponies racing through a herd of buffalo.

She sighed, turning back to her cooking fire outside their small lodge. Running her tongue over her lips once more, she still tasted the bacon grease that had fed them this morning, the strong burn of black coffee without the softening sweetness of sugar. Mosseau had little of the luxuries to offer the Miniconjous last night when Big Foot's band arrived.

She turned, listening to the distant, reedy voice of the camp crier, slowly working his way through the camp, calling for the men to come to a council with the soldiers. All the joy in a full, warm belly suddenly flew away like the yellow butterflies of summer. Double Woman glanced at the hilltop, backlit by the early sunlight, silhouetting the wagon-guns and the milling soldiers who had those gaping maws of death pointed down at the village. Down at her.

As more of the men, old and young alike, bound themselves up in their blankets and shuffled off to the east, she glanced over her shoulder at the ravine where the boys played, running back and forth, laughing, bacon grease still on their faces and little hands. A few dogs raced among the children, yipping and barking their enjoyment of the game as well.

By the time she had finished scraping the grease from the blackened frying pan and set it aside on a stone, Double Woman heard a stir at the eastern edge of the village.

"The soldiers are coming!" announced an old woman trudging through camp. "They want the guns!"

Many of the women hurried into their lodges, emerging moments later. Some stood haughtily by their lodge doors. Others sat on the ground, adjusting their cloth or hide dresses and heavy wool blankets about them, all awaiting the coming of the soldiers.

Double Woman swallowed hard at the hot knot that hung high in her throat. The fear grew into something she could taste.

Yet she told herself she was like a silly child to be afraid of the soldiers working their way into the village from two directions. She had no man. Her lodge hid no weapons. Only a pair of old skinning knives she used to cut up the salt pork or stringy beef they received as rations.

Most of the women suffered the searches in silence. A few chattered noisily or shrieked out their objections. Some called out to the men, wanting them to return to the village to help prevent the indignity of the soldiers combing through the lodges and personal belongings.

In and out of each lodge went some of the white soldiers,

hile others stood guard outside, holding what had been
nfiscated in the search so far, some playing with the small
ildren who hung about to watch the process, curious. The
eapons began to add up. Bows and arrows. A few repeat-
g rifles and pistols. Hatchets and large wood axes. Then
e soldiers came to Double Woman's lodge, led by an
ficer who carried a stone war club he had confiscated.

After several minutes inside, the soldier emerged carry-
g nothing more than her large butcher knife. He pointed
her waist. She looked down, finding the belt and
abbard and the knife Stone Eagle had given her father as
rt of the gifts brought when he came to ask for a bride.

"No," she said in perfect English, startling the soldiers
d shaking her head vigorously. "You cannot have this,"
w in Miniconjou.

The soldiers closed around her, one of them talking, his
outh moving up and down with nothing but nonsense
ords pouring from it. He had his hand out. She realized he
ould not touch her if he did not have to. She suddenly
arned to have Stone Eagle there to tell them in their
hite tongue that she needed her knife to feed her child.

"What harm is this little knife?"

His face changed, from kind to hard. Now his words had
rough edge to them, like the flint weapons of old she had
en.

Slowly she drew the skinning knife from the beaded
abbard and laid it in the soldier's palm. He passed it on to
other, then patted her on the shoulder. His eyes softened
ce more, wrinkled and warm the way her father's eyes
d always been. This soldier too had the iron in his hair of
any winters. She wondered how long he had been a
ember of these soldiers who belonged to the memory of
ong Hair and the Greasy Grass.

Had this soldier been there? When Stone Eagle was but
boy? And she so young herself?

The soldiers moved on, quickly completing their search
the village. While one group took their cache of weapons
ck to the council area where the men had gathered, the
her group of soldiers took their weapons to the top of the
ll overlooking the Miniconjou camp. They piled their
che near the yawning muzzles of the wagon-guns.

Some time passed, slowly with the sadness of giving
the gift Stone Eagle had given her. Double Woman fe
was one of the few things left to remind her of him. Yet
always had little Yellow Bird. Son of Stone Eagle. Grand
to the Long Hair who had struck fear in many hearts.

May her son grow to know peace, she prayed, pull
another sleeping blanket from the lodge. Shaking e
blanket in turn, and the robes. The stinging alkali d
coated her nostrils. It seemed the more she tried, the m
the wind kicked up the dust in this barren scar of land

She folded the worn blanket over her arm, placing
foot in the lodge door, when the loud call of a man's vc
stopped her. A Miniconjou curse—swift and harsh. T
more shrieks, then the frightening crack of a rifle.

Double Woman turned, slowly now, her foot still ins
the lodge as the roar of a hundred and more rifles split
still morning air as subzero nights would split the trees

Her eyes searched for little Yellow Bird, finding
running for her, his eyes frightened, tears streaming do
his face, his right arm bloody and useless. Calling out
her with that tiny black hole moving up and down in
dark face.

The earth opened up before her, like the shak
promised by their messiah.

CHAPTER 53

December 29, 1890

THE cold pink of dawn stretching out of the east had found Stone Eagle already moving up Medicine Root Creek.

Beneath the stars and sliver of moon of last night, he had come down one of the few passes in that cruel wall of The Badlands, finally making a cold camp, rolling into his blanket and single robe after rubbing down the old horse with some of the brittle, autumn-dried grasses.

He was back in the saddle beneath the gray light that beckoned him on, finding the trail of wagons and many horses atop the divide that led him down into the valley of Porcupine Creek. Still the trail continued, climbing once more as he realized the Miniconjou were not steering for Pine Ridge at all. Something had turned them toward the small settlement along the creek he knew as Wounded Knee. His mother and White Cow Bull lived nearby.

He knew the place well—enough times he had hauled freight from Pine Ridge to the Frenchman's store. Louis Mosseau would recognize him. Too, Mosseau would know

Double Woman if she came in to buy flour or coffee whe
Big Foot's band arrived.

Then he realized she would have to trade for everythi
now. Double Woman no longer had money to buy food f
little Yellow Bird.

He tried to hurry the old horse up from Porcupi
Creek, then stopped and dropped to the ground. He kne
over the hoofprints. Iron-shod. But it was not all those arm
horses that yanked a hot strip of sinew through Ston
Eagle's belly. It was those prints of so many boots. Soldi
boots.

That had him worried.

His concern grew as he descended into the valley of th
Wounded Knee. His eye was never far from the trai
studying it. Hundreds of hoofprints and wagon tracks h
followed, along with a few unshod horses he supposed son
of the young warriors rode.

A few miles out, Stone Eagle caught his first glimpse
faraway smoke smudging the horizon. Many fires. Th
winter wind drove the smoke from west to east across th
early blue of the morning sky. That smell to the win
reminded him of winters gone and never to hold agai
Winters of childhood, gone hunting alone in the timber f
his first kill to feed his family. Winters spent north of th
medicine line as the despair grew wide and ran deep, lik
the snows piling up outside the hide lodges.

The smell of winter with all its expectancy in the ai
Cold, dry air that hurt if a man drank too deeply of it. Th
aching blue of the early morning sky overhead, as y
untouched by the cotton flotsam of clouds. A sky too col
he realized, that no cloud would cling to it.

He stopped for a quick drink from the icy strear
allowing the horse its blow, a loosened cinch and a lor
drink in what water flowed this time of year down in th
central channel of the ice-bordered creek.

Time to go. Something pulling him on.

Pushing the old horse into a lope, Stone Eagle urged th
animal out of the timber thick along the creek, up onto th
narrow bench that ran south along the Wounded Knee.
was there he finally crossed with the Agency Road th

would take a traveler into the little settlement, or farther south and west to Pine Ridge itself.

He had to drink with shallow breaths now, the air so dry and cold. Though the sun was up, there was little warmth to the air. Smelling it, tasting it, sensing the woodsmoke of all those hundreds of fires with breakfast frying and coffee boiling. He pulled another coffee bean from the sack hung at his saddle-horn. Though it was strong and made his eyes water every bit as much as the cold wind, Stone Eagle sucked on the bean to relieve that coffee hunger.

Loping around a bend, the road took a dip into a low cut, then slowly rose. It was in riding out along the base of that ridge that he first saw them. Indistinct at first, shimmering on the dry, cold air in the distance atop the hills. As he drew closer and closer still, they shimmered apart, becoming half-a-hundred men.

Soldiers.

He stopped in mid-breath, his chest burning, when he saw the wagon-guns in the midst of those soldiers. The tiny figures suddenly darted back from the guns. There were puffs of white smoke belching from the muzzles, then long streamers of gray smoke slowly pouring from the cannons. And finally the rattling sound of destruction was carried to him from afar on the dry air.

Like the snarling, clattering teeth of wolves, working over the bones of an old carcass of downed bull.

The women and children in the northwestern edge of the village leaped into their wagons, careening up the road that would lead them to Drexel Mission.

Double Woman heard more shells coming in and knew they would not make the wagons.

She clamped off the scream in her own throat, lunging for Yellow Bird, sealing her hand over his mouth as her other pressed into the bloody shards of bone that had torn through his shirt and blanket coat. She carried him into the maelstrom of smoke and dirt, the black and brown of hell.

She had never heard a horse cry out before. But there were at least a hundred neighing and screaming, fighting their harness or the pin of a lodge where they had been picketed. Most already stumbled about, confused and in pain with their bloody wounds, or lay thrashing on the ground, legs kicking in their death-throes, their eyes wide and not understanding.

Confused, her one eye already filled with blood from a sharp splinter of lodgepole, Double Woman stopped, turning this way, then that, glancing at the hilltops where the soldiers went about their work with deadly efficiency. Up there—a large bear of a man hollered out his orders, stomping back and forth behind the crews in his huge red-lined cape aflutter on the wind, waving his arms.

Nearby a lodge erupted as if the ground had exploded beneath it, coming down in a clatter of smoking canvas and lodgepoles like so much kindling aflame, spewing ash and char and shrapnel over her and Yellow Bird. She started off, not knowing where to go.

"Stone Eagle!" she screamed, at the same time knowing he was so very far away, wishing he were there to tell her how to reach safety, what white man words to use to assure her of life for their son.

A wagon burst into splinters of smoking ruin directly in front of her, showering them both with deadly missiles as they plunged through the black cloud and towering pillar of spewing earth. It sounded to her like the cough of some huge beast each time the ground shuddered. She wondered if it were the Messiah come at last to drive the white man from this land.

Beginning to cry in shame, she realized she had forgotten to grab the eagle feathers in their lodge. Afraid now that she and Yellow Bird would have no way to fly above the destruction until the white man was driven beneath the belching, roiling earth and all was peace once more.

"No feathers, Yellow Bird," she whispered into his ear, feeling him go limp in her arms. "We must pray the words together and hope."

Looking down, she saw his eyes glassy as they rolled back in the boy's head. Then she sensed the dampness beneath her arms where he lay cradled against her bosom. The bright crimson spread like the slow ripples of a prairie pond she would throw stones into after a summer thunderstorm. Yet the blood steamed in the brutally cold air. Steamed as it spread down her front, with her son's tiny intestines beginning to spill from the terrible wound that had cut the child in half.

"Stone Eagle! Where are you?" She turned suddenly at the burning.

Reaching the ragged edge of the ravine, Double Woman went to her knees, spilling Yellow Bird.

"Mother?" he called out, his head slowly rising off the sandy ground, dirt and blood bubbling from his lips.

"I am here, Yellow Bird," she whimpered, pulling him into her arms once more, the burning growing like a living, angry thing in her belly.

She looked down at her own wounds, seeing her clothing smoking, smoldering, the way damp wool would singe when put to flame.

"Let me hold you, son," she whispered, mantling his tiny body with hers, the way the eagle mantled its young atop the far nests in the rimrock.

"Father?"

"He will come, Yellow Bird. Your father—"

The force of the explosive shells tore her body from the child's, yet even in the last spasms of death, with one desperate fist that would not loosen its grip, Double Woman clung to her son, afraid she would not be there when he died.

So afraid she would not be beside Yellow Bird now that the Messiah had called them.

A peace settled within her as the rattle of gunfire and the screams of women and the cries of children and horses, the obscene belching of the wagon-guns and the explosions of the earth gone crazy—all such noise faded, as if put out by the slow seep of her blood.

As the pain and emptiness and despair left her, Double Woman looked down, sensing more than seeing little Yellow Bird rising with her. Here above the madness of the smoke and blood, she felt a wondrous peace, like nothing she had experienced dancing back the spirits.

Something unhurried, something that gave her the time to pray for Stone Eagle.

He topped the hill just north of the Wounded Knee settlement, furiously kicking the horse down the slope toward the bridge that crossed the creek. As he clattered

past Mosseau's store, wagons burst from the thick curtains
of powdersmoke. They rattled past him, horses snorting
and straining at their harness, the wild-eyed women and
children clutching at reins or seat or side-board, crying out
as they clattered up the agency road.

Here and there through the nightmare of noise and
confusion and gray smoke, Stone Eagle saw the flitting blue
figures, moving about in masses, some singly, a few running
back for the splotchy white of the canvas tents. A few drew
up when they saw him, jerking around their weapons to
train the muzzles on him, hesitating for a moment. Long
enough for him to disappear into the madness and smoke
and confusion of all those bodies spilling across the valley
floor like beans from a torn burlap sack in the trader's store,
clattering and tumbling but never coming to a rest.

His chest hurt suddenly—Stone Eagle could not remember when he last had breathed. The feel of it foreign to his
chest, he drank deep and choked with the stifling, acrid
taste of it. Afraid suddenly now that he realized what he was
doing, where he was. Strangely unconscious of everything
but moving forward until that moment, he jerked the rein
hard to the right, spilling the old horse on its side.

The animal clawed its way back up on all fours, carrying
him with it as he tore into the open ground just past the
cavalry camp. Past the confusion and milling of soldiers in
formation, past the screams of the wounded and the
whimpers of the dying, Stone Eagle caught brief glimpses
of the smoking village beyond.

What few lodges still stood were like smoking towers of
ruin, funeral pyres torched by madmen.

In the pit of him, he knew they would be there.
Something had led him this far, past the other women and
their children. Knowing, with a growing fear.

The horse went down, surprising him, spilling him free
this time. With a single cry, it tried to raise its head once, then
no more. As he clambered to his feet, Stone Eagle felt the
pain spread all through the side of his body where he had
spilled. That burning drained from him, like the fire from his
breasts after the sundance, until all that was left was the hot
poker that had driven itself through the thick meat of his
thigh. And the flame each time he tried to breathe deeply.

He brought his hand away, watching the seep of blood bright and turning brown on the buckskin of his leggings. Tightening the muscle twice, he prayed it would take his weight. Slowly he climbed to his feet, into the madness again, feeling the pull of immediacy, the tug of need.

Dead men littered the ground as he pressed into the center of the nightmare. A soldier here and there, but mostly the old men, some young, wearing their blanket leggings and white man shirts, a few still clothed in their Ghost Dance shirts that the chiefs had claimed would turn the soldier bullets. Red moons and suns and stars on the white hides of those sacred shirts. Most with ugly red holes turning brown beneath the relentless, drying wind of the high prairie that was this land of Pine Ridge and the Wounded Knee.

The scream of the shells slashed the air about him, causing Stone Eagle to duck, tripping over a dead warrior. His chest hurt all the more as he crashed to the ground.

Behind him a tall Sibley tent erupted in a flaming tower of smoke. Some man in the tent cried out, screeching his deathsong then fell silent. As Stone Eagle clambered to his feet, some soldiers threw bales of hay on the collapsed tent and ignited them with brands from a nearby fire. They were going to burn the warrior alive inside.

On hands and knees he crept a few feet, then found the strength to struggle onto the bleeding leg, an arm clutched around him tightly. Headlong, he dashed through a splintered group of soldiers, bumping into a smooth-faced boy, freckles spilling across his nose. The white man's eyes were filled with more revulsion than fear. He dropped his weapon as Stone Eagle spun from him—away, away from the soldiers.

Directly ahead lay the village. He limped through it, calling out for her, calling out his son's name. Many of the lodges still stood, the canvas smoking into char and some of the lodgepoles smoldering. Others were no more than oily patches on the ground. On he pushed, until he found what was left of the small lodge, the burning canvas making for a gut-wrenching stench. Nearby lay the body of a horse, its belly torn open by one of those exploding shells from the wagon-guns, the gaping wound steaming into the cold air like breathsmoke from an exhausted man's mouth.

"Double Woman!"

He called her name, plunging into the gaping maw of the ruin of their lodge, frantically scraping at the blankets and robes, the refuse left behind by the white man's destruction. His foot kicked over a small rawhide box, spilling its contents on the scorched earth.

For but a heartbeat he stopped and looked down, past the leg oozing blood into his winter moccasin.

Crying out, he knelt, fingers digging, picking through her special things, gathering up the metal eagle his mother had given him so many long winters gone. It had been Long Hair's. This tangible bit of memory and medicine of his father.

The loud barking of orders and voices speaking his father's tongue yanked him to his feet, dragging more of the special things into both bloody hands, knowing Double Woman would want these things when he found her.

Stone Eagle burst through the smoking, smoldering gape of lodgepole and canvas, plunging into the center of the village, turning—darting to the south, putting the spewing orange flames of the wagon-guns at his back.

Across the ravine, a squad of soldiers scattered, shells whistling their warning descent above them. Fifty exploding shells a minute, each one bearing down with deadly precision on the village. Each one dredging up that deafening cough as it struck the earth, causing the earth to spit itself in a smoking tower.

Down in the shadows of the ravine figures darted, most running west, away from the destruction. Some women and children lay at the lip of the coulee, those having failed to reach its safety before the wagon-guns found them.

He stumbled, not seeing the gaping scar of a hole in the ground until he went down—his eyes locked only on their bodies.

"Double Woman!" he screamed, dragging himself to his feet again, heedless of the screeching, warning whine of the incoming shells.

"I have been calling you, Stone Eagle."

He jerked at the familiar, hissing, whispering voice—

looking over his shoulder, finding the burning yellow eyes like flame piercing the roiling clouds of oily black smoke that scudded across the cold ground, giving form to the creature's body.

"You are too late to help me," Stone Eagle whimpered, looking away, crawling toward the bodies. "Too late to help them."

Of a sudden, he felt cut in half, without pain. Strangely looking down to find his legs twisted, bone rammed through his bleeding skin from ankle to hip.

"Your power, spirit helper!" he called out, clawing at the earth, trying to pull himself out of the shell crater. "I need the power—help me now!"

"This is your power Stone Eagle," cried out the voice from the wolf-black smoke, yellowed eyes spewing their flames again and again. "It was the power of Yellow Bird—warrior son of the warrior known as Long Hair."

Stone Eagle turned, his arms reaching for them both, pulling himself along, blood streaming a sticky ooze across the frozen, blackened ground.

"My . . . my power now."

He collapsed over their bodies, sheltering them with his as the obscene eruptions walked in closer and closer on the edge of the ravine. Stone Eagle closed his eyes, satisfied that there was still no pain—thinking how much the coulee reminded him of the white man's grave.

How silly the white man was, having put his Messiah on the cross, torturing his very own chosen savior—sillier still that the white man buried his dead in the ground. Hiding themselves from the spirits of sky and water.

"My power now . . ." he repeated, as the barking whisper of the wolf faded from his ears, no more the cries of women and children and men and horses and the air filled with the whining whistles of death.

Knowing he had conquered.

Knowing the way of the warrior was to die here in the open—to let the birds and the animals at his flesh.

Letting the wind blow gently through his bones for all time.

EPILOGUE

January, 1891

DAMN, but won't it be fine, Captain Tripp!" Sarcasm
dripped from every one of Harley Fagen's words.
"We'll watch George Armstrong Custer's grand Seventh
Cavalry pass in review!"

Preston Tripp stared at the shackled prisoner astride the
big army draft horse, chains connecting the ankle irons
beneath the beast's belly. Fagen's mittened hands wrapped
about the saddle horn could not conceal the wrist cuffs. He
seemed almost proud to be a prisoner, now, after all this
time—perhaps at last with some good reason to give up his
search. No better reason than the trial and long prison
sentence that would undoubtedly keep Harley Fagen from
the outside world for some time to come—if not put him at
the end of an army rope.

"How fitting it is, my young captain," the aging detective had said last night at Mosseau's store where he had
been held after what the soldiers were calling the Battle of
Wounded Knee, "that it is Custer's regiment forcing me
from my quest. Nothing else, no other man could have

accomplished that, you know? Now at last I'll have some peace—not *having* to look for that bastard son of his. Utterly perfect: that Custer's survivors are keeping me from putting my hands on Custer's half-breed son."

In a way the captain felt sorry for Fagen, a sad and pathetic man, driven and obsessed with the hunt—something that had driven him these past thirteen years. The quest had given his life purpose. Tripp truly felt sad, he finally admitted, knowing that he would likely never enjoy such passion, such grand dreaming, never find something that would so take hold of his life. Perhaps never to have Fagen's all-consuming lust for the hunt.

"Yes, Mr. Fagen," Tripp finally answered, gazing back down the slope at the valley where Big Foot had brought his Miniconjous to the camp of the Seventh Cavalry. "It will be a grand procession at that."

"Will General Miles really be there, Captain?"

"That's what I'm told."

"Splendid! I must see it, Tripp," Fagen pleaded. "You must do everything in your power to allow me to see that review—and Miles himself. Damn, won't that be something!"

Tripp tugged his collar up against the windward cheek. How it blasted a man's face, even with the new beard he had started growing in the last two weeks. Ever since leaving Sumner's Camp Cheyenne. His eyes misted in that wind as he watched the Seventh in the process of breaking their camp below, looking every bit like dark, bulky ants bundled against the cold, each man of them stark against the white of snow and canvas backdrop tents.

That review scheduled to parade at Pine Ridge before General Nelson A. Miles would be for many of those soldiers a most solemn affair. Not a company of the gallant Seventh stood at full strength. Some companies had but one officer left in command. What with their dead or the wounded already transported to the agency hospital, the regiment was but a shell of its former strength and glory.

Not only was it the deadly toll taken at what the newsmen were touting as the Battle of Wounded Knee, but the regiment had marched itself into a corner when the next day, December 30, Colonel Forsyth sent his troopers after the escaped Miniconjou warriors. Not that it was Forsyth's fault when he did not listen to his scouts who said the Miniconjou ranks were being bolstered by enraged Oglalla and Brule warriors who had either watched the bloody destruction of the village firsthand or had heard of it from some Sioux who had.

The Seventh took more casualties as they marched confidently on the hostile camp north of Wounded Knee in the White Clay Creek valley, ambushed near Drexel Mission by a good share of the eight hundred to a thousand vengeful Sioux warriors. Penned down and fighting for their existence, the soldiers somehow managed to get word out. It was the gaunt Colonel Guy V. Henry's Ninth Cavalry who galloped a hundred miles without a bite of food or a wink of sleep to pull the Seventh's fat from the fire. Those yelling, screaming buffalo soldiers rode like hellions through the stunned ranks of the angry Lakotas, then set about methodically clearing every ridge and hillock with a deadly, controlled volley fire.

Their self-effacing grace in that daring rescue had brought tears to the eyes of many of the grateful among the ranks of the Seventh. White and black soldier embraced in heady celebration on that valley battlefield once the Sioux had been driven off. Not one man had to say a thing about how Custer's old regiment needed rescue from the Sioux and annihilation this second time. Young soldiers who did not remember, and those old veterans of the '76 Campaign who could not forget, all joined in the tearful jubilation at their deliverance.

It had been the first, and he hoped the last, battle Preston Tripp would ever take part in—swept along as he had been with Henry's brunettes. Despite the bluff and bravado of those Seventh Cavalrymen, war was not glorious. To the captain who had watched his hair begin to gray during this long search at Sheridan's behest—war was a profession best left unpracticed. Only to the uninitiated soldier, or to the officer who cared not that he left the field littered with human refuse, could war be so glorious an occupation.

Yet, as Tripp had returned to the Seventh's camp at Wounded Knee, he felt he was finally understanding the final link in that complex personality that was Custer the man. Never one to think and brood on matters, Custer took control and charged ahead. With his particular brand of luck, the brash and youthful Custer landed again and again at the right place and at the right time, to become a war hero not by his skill but by his wit and courage.

His repeated successes in that bloody four-year conflict had forged a Custer that simply could not retreat. But those successes and the grand assault on Black Kettle's Washita village only served to bring him eventual ruin at the Little Bighorn.

Fourteen years later that Custer bravado almost spelled disaster for his men of the Seventh Cavalry, attempting to live up to the Custer code.

That same day, the thirtieth, the first blizzard of the season swept down upon them, as if to punish the land and man as well. The following day, New Year's Eve, the sun had finally broken through as the clouds retreated, revealing the many humped mounds that dotted both the battle site and village. Many more of the snow-covered corpses lay clustered in the council area where the warriors had gathered. Beyond the open battleground stood the blackened spires of lodgepole and burnt canvas clinging to the lodge skeletons, flapping in the insistent wind over the silent carnage.

And that afternoon Captain Tripp had brought Harley Fagen with him to the council ground where it had all started two days before. He stopped the prisoner and guards by some blackened ruins and a frozen corpse.

"Some of the Miniconjou survivors tell me that's the body of the man they called Yellow Bird," Preston said, studying the detective's face for reaction.

For a long time Fagen stared at the burned and puffed body lying amid the black-and-white remains of the snow-crusted tent where the Minconjou medicine man and Ghost Dance shaman had made his last stand.

"You think that's Yellow Bird, do you?"

"The Miniconjou tell me it is," Tripp glanced quickly at the ghastly figure, contorted in an agonizing death. "Said yourself the other night, he was supposed to be among the Miniconjou. So there he is, Fagen. Yellow Bird was a shaman for them for some reason. He led them in their Ghost Dance."

"That's all news to me, Captain."

"You're the detective, Fagen. I brought you here to confirm it."

"I can't."

"You won't."

"I said I can't, Captain," and he broke off laughing with that hysterical cackle that raised the hairs on the back of Tripp's neck.

Below them now as they were leaving the valley, Paddy Starr's band of civilian laborers were beginning to dig the trench atop the hill that had two days before held the deadly Hotchkiss guns. Starr had been awarded the contract for burying the Miniconjou dead at two dollars a body. Tripp was glad he was leaving for Pine Ridge at last, relieved he would not be here to watch the civilians toss the frozen, contorted corpses into the mass grave.

His trip from the agency to Fort Robinson with his twenty-man escort and Harley Fagen would be the last of it, he prayed. After all these years he would be able to put this matter to rest for General Sheridan, if not for himself.

He had mixed emotions on releasing the escort to return to their regular duty here in the west where today there was a little less tension concerning the chances of the Lakota rising up in revolt. The army had seen to that. What began up at Standing Rock, when Agent McLaughlin's Indian police killed Sitting Bull, continued with the tragedy at Wounded Knee and would soon be brought to an end by General Miles when he had coaxed the hostiles out of their stronghold up near the badlands.

The Sioux nation was no more.

Yet it troubled Captain Preston Tripp to look back at the surrounding hilltops, watching those silent, sullen Oglalla and Brule warriors who sat on their worn-out, condemned army horses, staring down at the burial detail going about their grisly business. He wondered what went through the minds of those Sioux now, weighing the odds of riding off to help their brothers in The Stronghold, or staying here, frozen in time against that clear blue sky, watching the white civilians bury the Sioux nation in a mass grave at Wounded Knee.

General Sheridan would be satisfied, he knew, to learn that Yellow Bird had been shot and his body burned during fighting. For the little Irishman it would be the tidy end to a very untidy affair. Time and again in the last few days, Tripp had tried out some of the words he would use in composing the telegram informing Sheridan of the death of Yellow Bird.

Why he found it so damned difficult, what with this nagging doubt he was unable to shake—the impression that he had not brought the matter to a tidy conclusion but had instead only run into a very thick stone wall?

Why for the past two nights had he awakened in the cold of his tent, watching his blue breath smoke before his face, feeling that he would never know the truth, feeling that the truth was as fleeting as that warm vapor disappearing in the freezing tent?

Sheridan was back there in his mahogany and leather, horsehair and cigar-tainted office in the east, untouched by the west any longer. There were days, Tripp had learned, those days when Sheridan himself had been a man of the west. Someone like Custer.

No one could be like Custer again. Time was catching up with the west. The survivors were all becoming like Sheridan.

The old Indian fighters were getting a little soft around the middle, a little paunchy, perhaps a little tired. And all too ready to put an end to things.

Yes, Tripp decided atop that hill. He would not tell Sheridan of his doubts that he had for certain looked down on the body of Yellow Bird. Despite the claims of the Miniconjou. No other choice but to let the old soldier believe everything about his old friend Custer was finally put to rest.

"You coming, Captain?"

He looked at the lieutenant, who had his escort column halted, waiting, each man hunched against the wind in their buffalo coats, the clouds of cold vapor like a tent of gauzy muslin over the entire column of man and horse. Harley Fagen sat hatless, staring at him with that crazed look of the

madman he had become—looking for a half-breed an
finally willing to accept the death of any in return. Perhap
willing now to accept his own death at the end of
rope . . .

The scent Captain Preston Tripp had followed for s
long had suddenly gone the way of fire smoke carried awa
on a brutal scut of winter wind knifing off that blood
battlefield below him.

"You coming, Captain Tripp?" Fagen mimicked th
young lieutenant, his face wild. "Might as well—no sens
in tarrying here no longer. You're never gonna find tha
bastard son of General George Armstrong Custer now!"

Tripp sighed, refusing to look any more at the prisone
"Very well, Lieutenant. Let's get these men moving."

He waited at the side of the snowy road as the soldie
rode by in column-of-twos, the cold jingle of bit chains ar
the squeak of protesting leather accompanying the esco
down the slope, staying with the road that would take the
to Pine Ridge.

As Captain Tripp nudged his horse behind the last pa
of troopers, the cold wind brought him Harley Fagen's wil
off-key song—for twenty-four years now the martial air f
Custer's Seventh.

> Instead of Spa we'll drink brown ale,
> And pay the reckoning on the nail,
> No man for debt shall go to jail
> From GarryOwen in glory!
>
> Our hearts, so stout, have got us fame,
> For soon 'tis known from whence we came;
> Where'er we go they dread the name
> Of GarryOwen in Glory!